JACOB ROSS

TELL NO-ONE ABOUT THIS

COLLECTED SHORT STORIES
1975-2017

PEEPAL TREE

First published in Great Britain in 2017
Peepal Tree Press Ltd
17 King's Avenue
Leeds LS6 1QS
England

ISBN13: 9781845233525

Supported using public funding by
ARTS COUNCIL
ENGLAND

CONTENTS

I: DARK

DARK IS THE HOUR

The boy raised his head when the door scraped open. His heart leapt with a relief that surprised him, then he closed his eyes and sank back on the floor.

'Gertrude?' His father's voice was gruff.

The boy didn't answer. He peeped under his arm at the man's dark shape leaning against the door. He held a bundle in his right hand; in his left he balanced his machete. The boy watched his father's shape double as he dropped the bundle and the cutlass in the corner near the door.

'Gerty!'

The boy pressed his face into the bedding until the floor was hard against his cheek. He felt the weight of his father's boots sinking in the floorboards as he stepped over the little girl, then the younger boy and finally himself.

The room darkened further as the man's shadow fell on him. His father reached for the tiny kerosene lamp on the table and turned it up.

The boy knew that the man was staring at the bed against the wall. He waited, fearing the wrath that would follow when he saw that the bed was rumpled and empty.

His father's silence was unbearable, his breathing low and deep.

The boy's body bunched when the man's hand dropped on his back and he went through the motions of someone just awakened.

'Stanford! Fordy, wake up, boy. Stan boy! Where you' modder? Tell me, where your modder is?'

When the boy sat up and raised his eyes, he stared directly into his father's. He shifted his gaze to the paper-pasted board walls across the room. From outside came the drone of jeeps, and louder, sharper sounds. He knew that beyond the flimsy house the darkness threatened.

'I talking to you, boy!' This time his father shook him.

'Sh... Sh... She gone!' the boy said, and the pain of the day and the night began to show on his face. His father's eyes followed the trickle down his cheeks. The man raised his hand and the boy shrank back. His father brushed away the tears with a knuckle.

'Hush!' he said. 'When she gone? She say where she going? She leave any message? Who... What she went wid? She leave any message?'

The little girl woke up crying. The boy turned to her and began patting her back, cooing softly in the child's ear. He felt his father's eyes on him.

The man straightened up, the lamp held a little way above his head. He replaced it on the table, stretched himself out on the floor and pushed an arm under the bed. A basin rattled against something hard. He kept on feeling for a while. Then he stood up. In the yellow lamplight, his face glistened with sweat.

'She gone,' he said. 'De grip, she take dat too. You' modder gone for good.'

Now the little girl was crying in loud, sharp spurts. The boy lifted her onto his lap. He began to rock her.

'*Hush Po' Po' hush, Mammy gone to town...*'

His father stopped him. 'When last you feed her?'

'Dis evenin. I make sweet-water fuh she. Milk done yestiday.'

The boy pointed at the empty beer bottle on the table with a rubber nipple over the mouth.

'And you, y'all eat?'

'Steve was crying from hungry. I boil de last green fig dat was there. I save some for you.'

The little girl had fallen asleep again. The boy turned his head toward the door, his face twitching.

'Mammy, she leave since morning, just after you... you...' His voice trailed off. He was shaking when he spoke again, 'She send me by Nen-Nen... to borrow salt, an' when I come back, she gone.'

His father left him, began to stray around the room. He was passing his hands over the walls, the table. He stopped and stared down at the bed.

'Didn't even make it up,' he said. 'Not even de bed.'

Words began to flow from him. 'Is how I mus feel? Not cold I mus feel? Is me who cause crisis? Me who en't want to give wuk? Is not cold I mus' feel? Is nothing I could do. She know is nothing I could do. Is the same drown I drowning that everybody on dis islan drowning. Now she leave y'all in me hand – for what? What I mus do? Is not cold I mus feel?'

He trailed around the room and stopped at the doorway. He lifted the bundle that he'd dropped there, removed the cutlass and opened it.

'Look!' he told the boy. 'I bring somet'ing. I *get* somet'ing; I wasn idling. I *get* somet'ing.'

He laid a jumble of items on the floor – what looked like yams and sweet potatoes.

'Look, these ripe,' his father said. 'Full yuh belly.' He handed him two ripe bananas. The boy took them. They were wet and he wiped them on his nightie. He dropped them when he saw the blood.

'Is all right,' his father said. 'Blood come from the fowl.' He pointed at two heaps on the floor. 'Is better when dey dead, easier to carry, no noise.'

He took up the bananas, wiped them on his own shirt and gave them to the boy. The boy took them, turning his eyes to the sleeping children.

'Let dem sleep. It have more,' his father said.

The man turned away and settled himself in the doorway. The boy ate quietly behind him.

'She didn have to go, no reason to go and leave me with de chil'ren. Okay we been fighting, but she didn have to leave me. Me didn believe her when she tell me she going go. Look the food I bring tonight. She could've cook something nice. Give y'all a good feed.'

He raised his head and stared out over the sleeping houses down below. It'd been almost two months since all the lights went out. The night was pressing close. He heard the growl of police jeeps in St. George's Town below, the far-off howl of dogs, gunshots, and the wind snoring through the bamboo clump that hung over the little house.

The boy yawned. The man stirred; turned towards him. The last banana skin, licked clean, was dangling between his fingers. The man watched him, remembering the way he put his sister to sleep, the little maternal ministrations of his son. He was small – too small for his eleven years.

The boy was watching him too and swaying on his feet.

'Come. Look, more fig. You wan more ripe-fig?'

The boy shook his head.

'No? You wan' sleep den?' The man tapped his thigh. 'Come, doh-doh, on me.'

The boy shuffled closer, the lamplight exposing his naked front.

'Res' yuhself. Lemme put you to sleep.' He lifted the boy, and settled him in his lap.

The boy turned searching eyes on the man's face. His little body relaxed into a shy smile before his eyes drooped and closed.

COLD HOLE

Somebody was chopping wood on the other side of the valley. Sunlight dripped through the holes of the old board house and settled on his stomach. From the yard outside, there came the smells of wood-smoke and early morning breakfast.

The boy's feet propelled him from the floor through the open door and into the yard.

He was thirteen today and nobody remembered, not even his mother. But the sun and the wind and the trees knew it because they had given him a special Sunday. A day for the river.

The house was too quiet. He did not trust the silence. His mother was not singing.

If she caught him running off this early, when there were the rabbits to feed, the goat to tie out, well… water more than flour.

Still, nothing was going to stop him going fishing today, still burning as he was with a week-old memory that hadn't left him, even in his sleep – that afternoon after school when his two cousins and his little brother, Ken, were admiring him as he told them his latest river story.

'Cold Hole was deep! I dive in. I dive down, down, deep-deep down, and guess what I see? A guaje! De biggest crayfish in de world… I spend one whole hour underwater, tryin to catch it, so when…'

'You lie!' Two voices had boomed behind him: Ashton and Mandy. They smelt like men, walked and talked like men. Even the teachers stepped out of their way.

Ashton, a big grin spread across his slab of a face, was standing over him. Mandy the taller of the two, his hands pushed down his pockets, was throwing him a nasty sideways glare.

He felt his mouth go dry. 'Who say I lie?'

Ken, flimsy and defiant, stood at his side, 'Is true. My brodder never lie.'

The young men laughed and the child flinched at their loudness.

'Who 'fraid of Cold Hole more than yuh chupid brother here? Me an Mandy tired lift him up to cross deep water or climb river bank.'

'I not 'fraid now!' he'd shot back.

'Since when?'

He'd rested his hand on his brother's shoulder, balancing on the balls of his feet. Everything had become still. Vehicles droned in the far-off distance. Leaves fell and made clicking sounds on the road.

'Since I know I'z me and not nobody shadow,' he said.

Ashton stuck two fingers in the air. 'Talk sense, likkle boy!'

Swallowing on the shame, he'd stood on the grass verge and stared at their shifting shoulders until they disappeared.

He ducked beneath the house, gathered his line, the bait, a rusted piece of machete and – still doubled at the waist – tiptoed toward the stool of bananas fringing the house. The trick was to disappear when no one was looking.

'Hold it, Mister Man!' His mother carried her heavy body easily over the stony yard, her hands stripping a whip from the bowlie tree that hung over the house.

A couple of months ago, she caught him trying to chop down that bowlie tree with a blunt machete. She'd complimented him on his efforts, assuring him that the smaller branches would all be kept for warming him up. He would, of course, have to dig a coalpit, and make bags of charcoal with the rest of the wood.

'What day today is?' Her voice was almost caressing.

He searched his head for a way out, 'You see, Ma, today is my birthday. You – everybody – forget.' He sensed her hesitation. 'And I thought that, well… I goin go an fish for my birthday.'

'Come!' She drew him out into the yard.

The windows of the surrounding houses swung open and spilled the upper halves of full-breasted women.

The other children were quiet. Even the fowls in the yard ceased scratching.

'Is a naaasty habit you have! Every Sunday so, you leaving tea behind, tying the goat any old place to starve, and you gone and dreeve-way whole day in the river. Suppose you drown? Suppose you drop down an' dead!'

She was piling up his sins – her war dance.

'Last Sunday, I hear that Gordon cow nearly butt you and break yuh likkle arse. You so farse. You been jookin the man cow wid stick.'

The yard shook with laughter.

'And yesterday, you been voonging stone at Ayhie mango tree. You nearly bus' the old lady head in she own garden.' She shook him violently when he denied this.

'The other-day, you tell me you goin and help Nen pick peas. You end up quite in the sea with Ashton and Mandy. Which part of the sea you does pick peas eh? And where you learn all them bad-words that you could cuss Missa Joe-Joe, who worth yuh gran'faddah, and tell im how he born 'n where he come from? You get too damn mannish now!'

The whip curled around his shoulders. Pain snaked down his back. He twisted like a mad worm. Subdued, the children counted. Fifteen.

It was then that Dada's voice cut in. 'Stop! You want to spoil the blasted child skin, or what!' It checked his mother, as though a hand had pulled her back.

Pain-crazy, he ripped himself loose and bolted through the bushes beyond the house.

He sat there for a long time and fought his tears while his mother regained her voice. It rose and fell in the near distance, then broke into song.

Ken came fumbling through the black sage and borbook, trouserless as usual. 'I bring yuh fishin rod an' t'ing for you.'

His brother handed him a rumpled paper-bag. It contained

home-made bread with a spread of guava jam. It was his great-
aunt's way of saying that she felt for him.

He gathered his rod and bait and began marching down the
hill.

'I want come wit you,' Ken called.

'Nuh!'

'I carry the bait and crayfish for you.'

'Nuh!'

'I cominnn!'

He looked back at his brother. 'You not wearin no pants. Ants
go bite yuh ki-kiss. Today, I goin all de way down to Cold Hole.
It have a mermaid down there that like nice-lookin boys wid
pretty face like you. I bring a mango, piece-a-cane and a red-tail
crayfish for you, okay?'

''Kay.'

He took the mud track for the river, said 'G'morning' to some of
the elders he passed, ignoring those who brought complaints to
his mother. He met Elaine, tall and big-breasted, balancing a
basin of river-washed clothes on her head. She was grinning
wickedly. 'It damn good yuh modder cut yuh arse!'

Elaine's laughter bounced down the hill behind him and did
not stop until he reached the river.

His hook was a needle he'd held over a burning candle, then bent
and attached to a fine string which he tied to a slender stick. Baited
with earthworm, it became a living thing in his hand. He flipped
beating crayfish out of the water and skewered them on the spine
of a coconut leaf as he moved steadily downriver.

He would have to go past Concrete Basin where the mullets
were. They liked the smoky-blue pools surrounded by tall, black
rocks. It took a quick hook and rapid hand to catch them. Then
Dragon Place where the water-grass and crestles made a pale
green carpet, and the stones surfaced like heads from the water.
River crabs and zandomeh lived in Long Water and Young Sea. A
couple of miles further down he would come to Cold Hole.

From there the river deepened and darkened, its banks reduced to slippery humps riddled with crab-holes. Branches drooped and brushed the earth, hiding my-bone nests and serpents. Dada said there were other kinds of water creatures in the darkness of Cold Hole. Come nighttime, she added, Dealer-men met on its banks to barter the souls of children with the devil. And it was true that sometimes he thought he heard them joining the chorus of crickets and bullfrogs that sang all night to the moon. Besides, the old woman had told him, Cold Hole was waiting to swallow any boychile who left his work at home and went off fishing.

Halfway there, four coconut flexes bristled with crayfish in his hands. Boys working their way up-river whistled at his catch. He'd passed men kneeling over pools with machetes, slashing at mullets as they ghosted past. A mad man's game, Ashton always said, because a cutlass swung through water became a crazy thing that flashed back at its owner's legs. Others, pushing their bare hands under rocks, dragged out river crabs, water snakes and bull frogs. If they chanced to pull out a ling, its claws crunched down on their fingers, and he would watch them dance the shuddering dance of agony.

He tossed some of the sun-yellow guavas and water-lemons he'd gathered to some women labouring over multicoloured mounds of clothes. A mango or two, if he knew them well. He'd hidden the sapodillas and sugar-apples in his shirt. The gru-grus were for sale in school tomorrow. His mouth was white, his stomach tight from chewing sugar cane.

The sun was melting over the Kalivini hills when he arrived. From where he stood, he could not see Cold Hole, roofed as it was by the interlocked branches of kakoli trees and thick-hanging lianas. But already he felt the chill. He halted outside the wall of vegetation, took a breath, parted the weave of vines and entered the smell of fermenting leaves, heard the hollow hum of the river further down, the shift and groan of branches overhead.

The pool glinted like a giant reptilian eye. A wall of moss-covered rock buried its feet in the darkness of the basin.

He rested his things on the bank beside an overturned calabash. There was a toss of rice around it. Saraka-people came here,
too, to offer saltless food to Oshun.

He stripped and wrapped his crayfishes with his clothes so that
lizards could not get at them. He walked to the edge of the pool
and stood above it until his eyes adjusted to the gloom.

Somewhere beneath these silent waters there was a hole in the
rock where Ashton never failed to catch the king of all crayfishes
– a guaje. A great lobster-sized creature, so ancient, a hardened
crust of silt covered it from head to tail. Its saw-toothed pincers
could cut through any line.

He packed his lungs and plunged. The cold closed around his
nakedness and shocked his senses. He surfaced, snorting, and
struck out for the dripping rock wall. There, gripped in the vice
of the freezing water, he allowed his body to sink and began a
sidewise groping along the rock. Moss and mud gave way between his fingers. Now, he felt the heavy drift of the water
nudging him toward where the river flowed out and carried on.

Starved of air, he heaved himself to the surface. The water
churned around him and something slippery slid across his chest.
He threw himself backward and began thrashing for the bank. He
scrambled onto it and remained there, stooped, teeth chattering.
He realised it was a river-eel, a zangri. An image of the fish swam
inside his head: flat and silver like the blade of a new machete,
with the teeth of a barracuda.

It was a while before the shivering stopped.

At the dripping rock face, he raised his eyes. Flecks of sky
winked at him through the canopy. He thought of the eel, then
turned his mind to home. It would be easy to gather his fruits and
crayfish and walk away. All that food would put his mother in a
good mood. She would sit beside him on the step while they ate,
sidle a glance at him, nudge him with an elbow, then offer him a
smile. But this vision was muddied by the memory of Ashton and
Mandy sneering down at him.

He rose, shuffled to the edge, tensed and plunged, this time
angling his body the way he'd seen Ashton do, heading for an area

of darkness at the base of the rock. Once there, he allowed himself to sink.

The hole was much further down than he'd expected. Its jaggedness surprised him. He felt around its edges for a while, relaxed his arm and eased it in, following the upward angle of the opening until his shoulder was flush with it. Something stirred against his fingers. He withdrew rapidly, surfaced, took in air and went down again.

He blanked his mind and sent in his arm. Something erupted against his palm. A jolt of pain flashed down his arm, stiffened his spine and convulsed his legs. It was as if he'd been driven through with nails. Bracing himself, he closed his fist around the armoured head and pulled. It was like ripping away a piece of rock, but inch by inch the creature came, and it came out fighting.

He heaved to the surface and struck for the bank, levering his body up the slippery incline with his elbows. There, he half-lay, half-knelt among the stones and grass and watched the enormous creature clinging to his hand. A lacework of blood trickled down his wrist and forearm. The guaje swivelled its crablike eyes at him – the tail splayed and thrashing the air with heavy strokes. He forced open its pincers and dropped it on the ground.

He lay there cradling his injured hand, the pain pulsing through his arm and pooling at his shoulder. He turned his eyes on the creature. It had raised its pincers, its tail curved inward under its belly.

'So is fight you want,' he hissed.

He stood up and nudged it with a foot, passed a provocative toe along the coarseness of its carapace. It convulsed, then lay still. He prodded it again, tensed his legs and raised his heel above the creature's head. For a moment he hung there in a dreamy paralysis, seeing himself walking up Old Hope Road with the guaje wrapped in cocoa leaves, strung from his shoulder with strips of vine. He pictured the unbelieving eyes gathered along the roadside, the amazed utterances of his name. But the vision stirred nothing in him, no anticipation of his mother's pleasure, or what Ashton's and Mandy's words might be when they saw him with the giant crayfish. In that dreamy pause he felt the creature's whiplike feelers stroke his toes then come to rest there, and its gentleness surprised him.

With a scooping movement of his foot he flipped it in the air. The pool received it with a gurgle and a sigh. Then came the churn of disturbed water followed by the quiet.

He pulled on his clothes, gathered his things, halted at the vine-door to look over his shoulder. And with a voice that pulsed from his throat and shocked him, he shouted down the long river-corridor.

He listened for his echo. Heard none. Spun on his heels and headed home.

ACQUAINTING

Thomas came back from school to find a man sitting in his mother's yard. He had deep wide eyes, and the lashes of a woman. His hair fell about his face like the petals of some dark mysterious plant.

The boy dropped his books on the step and walked around the stranger slowly, never looking directly at the man's face, never responding to his smile.

He shifted his eyes towards his mother in the doorway, then back to the man. He was thin as a whip, but not frail; the skin of his arms and legs were cocoa-dark. A quiet, watching man whose long dark fingers remained still in his lap. Thomas noticed that his toes – peeping from the busted front of his canvas shoes – were almost as long as his fingers.

Thomas felt his mother's eyes on him. Her gaze was underhand and secretive, and however quickly he turned his head he was never fast enough to catch her eyes. She kept wiping her hands on her dress and twisting the little plaits of hair at the nape of her neck.

He didn't like that look on her face when she handed him his dinner. She was smiling at him too much. Didn't even tell him to change his school clothes before he ate. He raised a hand and pointed a finger at the doorway.

'Mammy, what kind o man he is?'

He saw the irritation in his mother's face as she turned to him. But he really wanted to know and Mammy must have seen this because she clasped both hands in front of her and made a small step back, as if she were holding a bat to protect herself from the googly he might bowl.

It wasn no googly he had in mind. Was a coupla bouncers. He

goin remind her that, after all five of his uncles came to their yard last year and dragged Missa Ashton out of the house and sent him away for good, she promised she would never bring a fella to their house again, unless he, Thomas, tell her that he liked the man. And if she bring a fella, he had to be a gentleman. An' even if he was a gentleman, she would test him for a couple weeks to see if he was any good; and even if he was any good she go give him a coupla months before she moved him in; and if she moved him in, she had her five brothers as backative to drag him out soon as he start behaving like bad-john.

'You never see a Indian man before?' she said.

He shook his head, 'Nuh, I never see a man like he. Where he from?'

The smile left her face. 'How you mean where he from? He from the same place everybody come from.'

'And where that is?

'Somewhere,' she said – as if somewhere was a place that he should know. 'Everybody come from somewhere. Talk to him, he won't bite you.'

'He could talk?'

'He not yooman? He ain got a tongue?' Now she seemed aggrieved. 'A gen'leman come to a pusson yard, a gen'leman come to stay with us and people not saying boo to him. Look how you was walkin round the Mister like if he's a maypole. Is a miracle you didn get giddy an fall down. Is so people does make acquaintance? Eh?'

Thomas turned his head and looked out. The stranger hadn't moved. He did not have the barrel chests of his uncles. His muscles snaked along the bones of his arms like rope. It crossed his mind that if this new fella had been a plant he would be bamboo.

Thomas pushed his plate aside. A little knot had tightened in his throat. He didn't feel hungry anymore.

He wanted to tell Mammy that he didn want no father, 'specially since he never meet the one they said was his. He thought about the fella she brought home the year before and asked him to make 'acquaintance'. She said *he* was a gentleman – not so? And mebbe he was – until he lost his job and started beating up the boss through her.

His mother was standing in front of him, her eyes large and moist. Thomas saw the tension in her body. All of a sudden he wanted to take her hand and press his head against her side. He stared out the window at the stranger, lifted his face to hers and mumbled, 'He awright, Ma? Not so? I hopin and supposin he different.'

His mother smiled. She blinked at him and turned her gaze towards the window.

'Go way,' she told him softly. 'You come here to upset me?'

THE CANEBREAKERS

Evenings, I used to watch the women coming home from work, wading through the orange light, their frocks fluttering like wings. I would stand on the only boulder in our yard and peer down, searching amongst that line for my sister.

I struggled to pick her out, not by her face but by that long stride of hers and the curious way she angled her body forward, as though she was pushing against winds felt only by herself. But these women were no more than shapes against the white feeder road that stretched behind them till the distance narrowed it to a needlepoint.

'Sis,' I asked her once. 'Why I could never make you out from mongst all dem wimmen comin home from work?'

'Coz we'z de same, Ah s'pose.' Then she looked me straight in the eyes: 'Yep, we de same. Besides, y'all men never choose de right light to look at us in.'

I didn't know what she meant by that, what my sister meant by most of the answers she gave to my questions. She hardly ever talked straight. Most people thought she never talked at all.

I used to think it was the canes that made her like that. Any person would feel small and confused and lost in those lil spider-legged houses of ours, standing at the very edges of a tossing ocean of sugar cane.

Dry Season, she became even more firm-lipped. It was not a sudden change of mood, but a sort of deepening inside that grew with the shooting canes, their blossoming and their ripening.

I sometimes looked at her and found myself wondering about my mother. I couldn't recall what she looked like, though people said my sister was her spitting image. I dreamt of this woman of indistinguishable features who had left for Trinidad.

I never met my stepfather, a brother and a little sister whom I only heard about.

Rumour had it that my mother gave Sis the chance to live with her. That was the year after she abandoned us. I was four, my sister, eighteen.

The boat ticket arrived and my sister's departure date was fixed. She left me with my aunt with the promise that I would come soon after. The evening before she left, Old Hope threw a lot of farewell kisses and speeches at my sister.

She took them all in; left the following morning dressed for Trinidad, carrying a brown cardboard suitcase.

Imagine the confusion when the workers on the estate saw her return in the taxi she left in, borrow a machete and set to work – still in her best dress – as if leaving for Trinidad and returning a short while later was the most natural thing in the world. She said one of those puzzling things that I had grown accustomed to.

'You have *to break* cane, not *escape* cane. Besides, it have cane in Trinidad too.'

She took me back from my aunt to live with her in the house my mother fled.

Sis got up every foreday morning, waking me with her. It was so quiet out there, you could hear the cane leaves rubbing against each other, and get the smell of molasses and rum from the sugar factory miles away. She told me where to tie the goats for the day, and while I was out she prepared our lunch – mainly steamed vegetables, salt-fish and a drink of black sage or lemongrass tea, which we also had for breakfast.

She tied her head, wrapped a band of cloth around her waist and strode out into the morning, the little machete in one hand, the old fire-blackened tin marked DANO MILK, which contained her lunch, balanced in the other.

She never said goodbye. But I didn't mind.

Later I left for school balancing my books with the same care that my sister held her machete. I carried my lunch in an identical can in the other hand.

I never discussed school with Sis. She never asked. I told her what I wanted and she got it. I would hand her the slip of paper folded exactly as the teacher gave it, with the name of the book he'd scribbled there. Sis would take it between her fingers, as though she was afraid of hurting it and without a glance, she would place the note where she kept her money – in the cleft of her bosom.

One night, I woke up and caught her staring at the note I had brought from school. She did not know I was awake. I'll never forget that picture of her, sitting on the edge of the little bed, squinting at the paper, her lips forming letters, words – or perhaps a wish? I dunno.

That very Saturday she got up early, put on what folks had come to call her 'Trinidad dress' and left for St. George's on foot.

She returned in the afternoon with the new book and, like all the times before, asked me to open it while she sat in the corner near the window, staring at me with such a strange expression I felt nervous and proud and foolish at the same time.

I used to take these things for granted – I mean, getting up on mornings, tying out the goats, watching the people leave their homes and head like a long column of worker ants for the stretches of estate cane that fed the factory in the south.

Cane was always there and we expected to live and burn out our lives in the fields – less abruptly, perhaps, than my father who had passed away after being hit by a tractor carrying cane. My mother? Well, she gave up.

I was always home before Sis. Having brought the goats in, I did my homework sitting on the doorstep, hastening to finish it before the rest of the daylight faded. Then I climbed the boulder and watched the old cane road for her.

Arriving, she would lower herself on the steps and I'd hand her the big, white enamel cup. She drank with a satisfaction I envied, because she seemed to get such pleasure from a cup of water.

If working for the estate made water taste so good, then that, for me, was reason enough to want to spend my life there too.

★

'Your sister don' want you to work on no estate,' Tin Tin told me once.

Tin Tin was my best friend – somebody I talked to and daydreamed with. We were the same age and shared so much of our spare time together, I often forgot she was a girl who was not supposed to throw stones, climb trees, pick fights and steal sugarcane. To be honest, she could do all of that better than I. Worse yet, I couldn't beat her in a fight and was often obliged to retreat into silence whenever our quarrels became too heated.

'My sis didn say she don' want me to work on no estate.'

'She don' have ter, chupidy. She send you to school. Give you eddication, not so?'

'Your modder sen' you to school too.'

'Yes, but she don expect me to – well, she not workin she soul-case out for me. My modder different, see! Is you an your sister alone; my modder have eight o' we. Besides, my fadder pass away.'

'My fadder pass away too.'

'Yes, but not in no sugar factory. Is a lil ole tractor dat bounce off yours. Mine is a whole factory.'

'Factory don' bounce off people,' I said.

'I didn say dat.' Tin Tin was getting annoyed.

'Nuh, but you implied that. If you assert…'

'Ass-hurt,' she echoed scornfully. 'Big wud! You start showin off!'

'The word jus slip,' I apologised.

'Slip what. You showin off coz your sister buy you big book an' you done scholarship exams. You know damwelly if…'

I knew what she was going to say. She was brighter than I. We used to be in the same class until The Accident; she would have been doing the exams, too, had not her mother said it made no sense. The two eldest boys would have to work in the fields alongside her and she – Tin Tin – was not going back to school 'coz she couldn' afford no school-expense and there wuz two lil children to take care of durin de day.

★

'Sis, how come Tin Tin can't go back to school?'

'Ask 'er.'

'She tell me arready.'

'So why you askin me?'

'Tin-Tin bright,' I said.

'I know dat.'

'Nearly as bright as me.'

Sis raised her brows at me. This was one of the times when I felt she didn't like me at all.

She ignored me for the rest of the evening.

The season deepened. What had once been growing cane became a brown expanse of parched straw as they were chopped down and the trucks took them away.

The overseers walked up and down in their wide straw hats – potbellied men with thick books from which they looked up and thundered orders to the men who chopped and to the women who heaped the cane together and loaded them onto the waiting trucks.

Sis was one of the few women who chopped cane. She did it because choppers were paid fifty cents more than loaders. It was hard work but she had grown accustomed to it.

'Your sister is a chopper coz…'

'Coz what?'

'Coz she in favour.'

'Ah don't unnerstan.'

'Chupid boy. She have two overseer boyfren.'

'Don't say dat about my sister, Tin. I goin' tell 'er.'

'Favour for favour, my modder say.'

'Don say dat 'bout my sister.' I was close to tears and no longer afraid of her.

'Well, is what I hear say.'

'She work harder dan your modder an' fadder put togedder.' I couldn't stop pounding my knee. 'Is not only man should chop cane for money.'

'Okay, Baldie, awright. I didn mean it. I sorry.'

'I goin tell 'er, you hear. I goin' tell 'er.'

'Sorry, Baldie, sorry.'

'Don' talk to me.'

We didn't speak for weeks. Tin Tin tried to make up several times and finally gave up, which disappointed me since I had planned to soften a bit the next time she came round.

I tied out the goats, waited for Sis with her cup of water and studied her with greater care. I asked her no more questions. In fact, we barely spoke.

I really missed Tin-Tin when the nights of the chill, bright moons arrived. We should have been sitting with the rest of the village children on the mounds of cut cane, sucking away and talking about anything that came to mind.

We talked about the things we had heard and read about – strange inventions, planes that flew backwards, machines that talked, wondering how our little world fitted into all of that. Our dreams for ourselves never went beyond the tallest cane.

Nothing compared with the pleasure we got from invading the fields. You would hear the dull *poks* as we broke the canes, the swish of the leaves as we hauled the plant, root and all, into the road.

There was a watchman somewhere in the night out there, but we didn't care. He never caught anyone. Besides, it didn't feel like stealing. Thinking back, there was something vengeful in those nighttime raids. We called it breaking cane.

I passed my exams, had done well enough to go to the secondary school of my choice. My name was even in the papers.

The following week, Tin Tin brought me a sapodilla. It smelled so good, I almost fainted. It would be my first for the season. The first fruit was always the best. You got more than just its taste; you got the promise of a whole season of ripeness ahead. We often did this with our first fruit, yunno – come together and argue over the first bite.

I forgot our quarrel and all the weeks of not speaking to her.

'I wan' de firs' bite.'

'Nuh,' she said.

'Gimme de firs bite, nuh.'

'You say, 'nuh'. Dat mean you don' want it.'

'Yeh, man, gimme de sappo, nuh.'

'You jus' say 'nuh' again.'

'Jus' one bite.'

'Okay, come for de bite.' I was blind to everything but the fruit. I came forward. She bit me hard on my arm. Tin Tin couldn't stop laughing. Then she offered me the whole fruit. I ate half and handed her the rest. She shook her head. I had never seen her so serious before.

'Tek it, Baldie, I bring it for you.'

She was lying and knew I knew it.

'What you want for it?' I asked.

'Nuffing. Let's go break cane.'

In a week or two the season would be over. We had a spot where we used to sit and chew our cane and argue. It was the steps of a broken-down plantation house.

'You find place like dis all over de country, in all dem islands, always on de highest hill,' I said to Sis, pointing at a picture in my history book. 'I wonder why nobody never bother to pull dem down or p'raps build dem back?'

'Lots o' things remain besides dem old house,' she muttered. 'If I have my way, I pull everyting down, dig up de foundation an' start clean – from scratch.'

'Talk to me, Baldie,' Tin Tin said.

'Bout what?'

'Anyfing. Like we uses, erm, like we 'custom.'

'Bout when we get big, you mean?'

'Yup.'

'Okay, like I tell you; we goin build a house wid – lemme see – nine room an…'

'No, ten – you say ten is a balance number, remember?'

'Oh, yes – ten.' I looked at her. 'And after?'

'Don' ask me. *You* tell me.' She was angry. 'You forget arready? You don' even start Secondry an' you ferget arready. Go ahead.'

'An mebbe, mebbe we married, s'long as you don beat me up when I make you vex.'

'You never say 'mebbe' before.'

'Well…'

'Wish I was a boy an didn have no lil brother an sister to care for. Then I would ha show you.'

'Is not my fault.'

'Is mine?' she snapped. She lowered her head at me, 'What you wan to become?'

'Lawyer mebbe; p'raps doctor – make a lotta money.'

'You don' want to drive cane-truck no more?'

'Don fink so. Why you ask me all dem questions, Tin?'

'Cuz is not fair.'

'Is not my fault'

'You say dat again, I hit you.'

'Well is…' I stopped short. I was struggling to clear the tightness in my chest and throat. 'I hate cane,' I said.

She, too, was close to tears. We rose and, together, picked our way over the stones of the same road that I watched the women walking on every evening after work.

'Baldie,' she said. Her voice was clear and strong again. 'I hate cane too. Cane not always sweet. It have some dat salt, some dat coarse. It spoil yuh teeth, an if you not careful, you cut your mout' wit de peelin. Take my fadder; take your fadder. See what happen? Dat's why I don' like no sugar in my tea. I 'fraid I might be drinkin 'im.'

She was talking like my sister. Did they all talk like that when things upset them?

'I startin Secondary on Monday, Tin.' I felt I had to tell her.

'I know.'

We were almost home. Tin Tin was looking into my face. 'Luck, Baldie.' I saw that she meant it.

'I see you tomorrow?' I said.

'Dunno, Baldie.'

'We goin break cane togedder, right?'

'I don fink so, Baldie.' She dropped my hand and sprinted off home.

'Sis?'

'Eh?'

'Why Tin Tin tell me good luck as if I done dead o' something? As if she never goin' see me again? She don' even want to talk to me no more. She say if everybody can't get eddicated, den nobody should.'

'Coz she unnerstan.'

'Unnerstan what?'

Sis looked at me. She began speaking so softly her lips barely moved. 'Coz dem offerin you a ticket so you could up an leave – like your modder – alone – and never come back. Leave everybody else behind. Tin Tin should've gone before you – you know dat?'

Her eyes seemed to have gathered all the lamplight, and were holding it in.

She was no longer my sister when she became like that. She was somehow stronger and stranger than anyone I had ever known or dreamed of – staring past me, through the walls, beyond the night.

'What you want to become?' She had pushed the new uniform on the table in front of me, as though I had only to put it on to become whatever I wanted.

'Tin Tin ask me de same question.'

'An you tell 'er?'

'Yep – doctor mebbe, o' lawyer.'

'Nuh.'

I looked up, surprised.

'We don' need no lawyers now, and we been gettin' along fine widdout doctors. We want teachers and a school firs'.'

'But we talkin 'bout *me*; not no teacher an' no school. Who it have to teach round here…'

'We,' she hissed. 'We! Teach, Baldie, coz secandry ain't no real escape. Long as we tie down, you tie down too. Learnin to escape cane not enough. How to break it – break out ov it, is what you have to learn. You unnerstan?'

I shook my head.

'Tin Tin unnerstan: *Sheez* de real canebreaker.'

'I could break cane too.' I was hating them for making me feel so useless.

'Den teach. When de time come, build a school; stay right here an teach de children so'z it don't have no more Tin Tin; so'z it don't have no more *me*. Canebreakers come *befo* lawyers, y'unnerstan?'

I wished she hadn't thrown that weight on me. For the first time I saw the lines of fatigue on her face. I was wishing I could still experience the pleasure of handing her a cup of water and watching her drink.

WALKING FOR MY MOTHER

Old Hope turned out their children to watch Nella go. It was wonderful and frightening because the quiet in the air was all for her. All for her, the gifts, the utterances of pleasure, the sideways glances and sweat-rimmed smiles. Like they were seeing her properly for the first time.

Ken had gone into the bushes and brought back two glistening guavas. White and rare, they smelled of the last days of the Dry Season. Even the wrapping was unusual – a dasheen leaf, shaped like a heart and patterned with a web of purple veins. Her uncle placed the guavas on the table beside the bread they'd baked specially for her.

Aunt Gigelle had brought her a boiled egg. She came swaying down the hill, balancing one in each palm as if they were the globes of life.

'Pretty peee-ople!' she sang, bending low and curving her very, very long fingers around her face and Liam's. 'One from Bucky and one from me. One for Liam and one for you.' Then, preciously, she placed them on the flowered tablecloth.

Uncle Ian had polished the new black patent leather shoes till they shone like pools of water in the morning light, while Gran Lil moved around her strangely. Her grandmother had taken off her headwrap and allowed her white hair to uncoil and settle like a halo round her face.

Even her twin brother seemed amazed. Liam had promptly offered her the other egg. Every now and again, he examined the brilliant white polyester shirt, passed the back of his hand against the dark-blue skirt and lifted the tip of the gold-striped, carmine tie.

They'd already begun preparing her. Aunty May had bathed her with the Cussons Imperial Leather soap they'd bought for the occasion. A new toothbrush that matched the ochre wrapping of the soap exactly and a little packet of Colgate toothpaste waited on the table while she ate in brand new socks and underwear. Occasionally, her mother glanced at her and then at Liam, furtively.

Breakfast over, her mother dressed her. Her hands were trembling slightly.

Over the weeks she'd seen her mother take complete command of everything. Her moment had arrived and she'd slipped into it like a garment cut especially for her. She'd become strange and secretive and oddly compelling, for her Mammy now ruled the yard with worry.

Mammy had worried for a month about the money she didn't have, might never have, but had to have in order to buy the books and uniform. And gradually the yard began to worry too. She fretted for another week – her voice low, complaining, and very mildly accusing – till one Sunday, moody and fed up, Aunty May sent her, Nella, off to take the good news to a friend of hers in some place named La Tante.

She had returned home with fifteen dollars, which Mammy promptly took off her.

Gran Lil had also had enough, and spent an entire day rummaging her memory for names of distant cousins, nephews, nieces and great aunts up north. She then sent the good news off through friends, by bus. Soon, crumpled packets began to arrive with pairs of socks and underwear; and bags with beautiful, obscure books – whose only purpose had been to sit on shelves near Bibles because they looked important. Sometimes they came wrapped on top of sacks of provision or between a couple of live chickens.

That was good, but not enough, her mother fretted. What the chile needed most was money. 'Mooneeey.' Her voice drifted with the word, reluctant to let it go.

So over the evening meal, they helped each other recall ancient favours to old-time friends and once they'd settled on some names, they sent her off again, on her own. It was always on her own. Never, they warned, to mention money, or to remind them of the favours, just to pass the good news on.

Then one Sunday morning, with a long, momentous sigh, Mammy sat down on the steps, plunged her hand down her bosom and pulled out a handful of notes. She kept dipping and dropping fistfuls at her feet while they looked on fascinated.

'T'ree hundred dollars an...' She paused abruptly, her face rigid with anxiety. She beat a frantic tattoo on her chest, thrashed her skirt, stomped and heaved herself, before bringing her nose down to the stones in the yard. Finally, fingers poised as if to pick up a needle, her mother retrieved something, grinned a large democratic grin, and muttered fervently, victoriously, '...an one cent!' which raised a wave of laughter.

Then she left the money there for anyone to examine it, as if to say that her figure was, well, just that – hers! – a mere probability – and they, after counting it themselves, might just as easily come up with a different but equally legitimate sum.

Some stared at the notes, others prodded them with their fingers, or nudged them with a marvelling toe, or, not uncommonly, brought their noses down to them. For nothing on earth smelled as satisfying as three hundred EC dollars, and one cent.

With that money, her mother had bought her everything, including the breakfast of bacon, the bowl of steaming Quaker oats, and the Milo drink she hated but felt obliged to drink because it was what eddicated children was s'posed ter have on their first day at any secondary school, anywhere in the world.

Now that she was about to set out, something tight and warm had settled in her stomach. A hush had settled over the valley. The neighbours had brought their children to the side of the road and placed the younger ones directly in front, holding them there with hands firmly on their shoulders.

The new bag of books dangling from her shoulders, and a few dollars stuffed down her pocket, she made her way down the track to the road. Aunty Paula had set off in front, clearing the path of leaves and stones and whatever else she thought might make her trip and bruise her dignity.

'Yuh modder don't want you to take de bus from here,' Aunty May whispered.

She nodded – she would have nodded to anything. Aunty May also told her that Mammy, at the last minute, had decided not to come with her. 'She ain got nothin to put on,' her aunt explained. 'Never mind, she going ter be watching you. Everybody goin be watchin you.' Then she'd paused a while. 'An I not comin eider, so don't bodder look at me.'

'People gettin on as if I not comin back!'

'You intend to?' Aunty May grinned cheerlessly at her.

'Is just a secondary school I going to, dat's all.'

The woman stopped wiping her face with her hand. 'You de first dis side of Old Hope Valley; in fact de first dis side of anywhere as far as I know to go to school in town. Once dem lil ones dere see dat you kin get to secandry, dey know dat dey kin get dere too, by de hook or by de crook. Dem tinkin mongst demself dat if Hannah girl-chile kin do it, deir own chile kin do it too. Jealousy,' she chuckled loudly. 'Dat kind o jealousy is good.'

'People talk as if I deadin o someting.'

'Hush you mouth, you always complainin. Deadin me tail! I hope you not going ter talk like dat when you reach inside dem people hifalutin, low-fartin school. You got to speak proper. Deadinggg – pronounce your G proper, hear? You got your handkerchief? 'Kay! Hold orrrn, Hannah! Stop frettin at me! You can't see I fixin 'er?' She gasped and laughed and stepped away. 'Gwone chile, we give you broughtupsy, now go and get de eddication.'

'And Liam? I want Liam to walk wit me, I want…'

'Never mind Liam. Liam goin to be awright. Liam always goin to be awright. Liam is a boy!'

Aunty May moved up close. She did a strange thing. She licked a finger and made a circle on Nella's forehead. She then kissed the spot she'd marked.

'When you reach Cross Gap, you stop an wave, okay? Cos all o we goin be watchin over you.'

She knew straight away where they would be standing. Glory Cedar Hill was the only spot from which the whole snaking thread of asphalt could be seen all the way to Cross-Gap Junction.

'Walk, Nella. Walk tall an proudful like you never walk befo. Gwone gyul! Start walkin for your modder.'

She lifted a querying face at her aunt, 'Walkin fo my…?' Then she understood.

Aunty May turned and hurried back up the hill.

Miss Ticksy broke away from the crowd lining the roadside, wiped her hand on her dress and handed her a dollar bill. The woman stepped back and wiped her hand again. 'Hannah is me friend,' she explained. 'An Nella is she daughter.' And she laughed a laugh that was loud enough for all of them.

She heard Missa Ram's dry voice. 'You break away, gyul! Look at my crosses! De lil gyul break away!' It was one of the rare times she had seen the old man off his donkey.

She took her time, feeling lost and not a little awkward. The new unfamiliar leather shoe made walking appropriately difficult. Shereen called her softly from the verge. She smiled back, shyly, uncomfortably, from the distance that her friend was placing her. Their faces were open and friendly, but they were not reaching out to her. They seemed to be taking her in with a new interest.

Half an hour later, still dazed, still drifting, she arrived at Cross-Gap Junction. Turning, she squinted up at Glory Cedar Hill.

Shapes they were, just shapes: her granny, Mammy and Aunty Paula and Aunty May and Shereen and Miss Ticksie and the rest of them. Shapes, dancing against the morning sky.

She thought she heard them singing. Or perhaps they were shouting something down to her. It all sounded like music anyway.

She waved back, walking as she waved, sensing with a sobering, abrupt sadness that she was also walking away from something else.

THE UNDERSTANDING

Something is wrong with you. They keep telling you that because you burn to break through the iron door and go flying across the gravel-yard, over the wire fence into the sun.

What will they say if you tell them that this month the rainbirds sing their last songs and the yam-shoots will come snaking from the earth, redder than blood from a fresh-cut finger?

If they would only listen, they will hear the garden-people chopping in the deep bush, the sound, like heartbeats, coming, going, coming over the cane-fields, up and beyond the river-valley. Like you, they wouldn't need to close their eyes to imagine that the trees, the grass, the vines are living things that talk among themselves of this, the rich time of warm soil and new leaves.

The river will be bright with sunshine. The stone on which you like to sit and watch the girls come on Fridays to laugh and tease and do their washing is cool.

The girls make fun of you – the boys too, who gather like blackbirds on the bank to stare at Ela, Jenny, Sara, Pansy, standing wet and almost bare in the pools, pounding clothes on the stones.

Then the bigger boys come racing through the sigin and wild calaloo. They chase the blackbirds off. But they leave you alone as they wrestle on the bank among the water-grass and shout in men's voices.

In the pools, they splash white water and fish among the stones – their trick to draw close to the girls and fondle them.

'Behave!' the girls used to scream. Now they no longer laugh like girls; they plant their hands on their hips and leave their washing floating on the water.

Ela leaves the water and follows Carl. She is laughing as he tugs her along. They go through the guavas, past the tall breadnut tree, up where the kakoli tie their branches together and make leafy caves. Ela's woman-laugh comes loud and clean above the bush. Then silence – except for the cee-cee birds, the johnnyheads and the pikayos cheeping among the foliage.

Jenny follows Masso; Sara, Sam, until they are all gone, leaving ugly Polo standing on the bank, his miserable eyes on Pansy who never looks up from her washing.

You used to wonder: what made the girls go? What happened there in the quiet where the vines hang down from the cutlet trees like a bright green waterfall?

It was Pansy who made you know. One day, when no one else was present, she woman-laughed and began teasing you. Why, she asked, did you always sit on the same ole riverstone, dumb like makookoo, and just watch the world run away? She said it nice and friendly, so you answered her. And she, pretty with her smile, was surprised.

You told her that the world never ran away if a person held tightly onto it; it just took them along. She laughed, which made you brave enough to go to her and take her hand.

You were both afraid: Pansy, because she had never gone up the bank before, through the guavas, past the breadnut tree and into the silence of the vinefall; you, because you had always gone up there alone.

Nothing more should be said about this. It was not like in the book Steve lent you. You did not feel to boast. Your voice did not deepen and you did not grow taller. Was that why Pansy couldn't look at you, or you, her? Was that why you've never spoken to each other since?

Still, you like the river and your stone – so different from this hateful place that smells of ink, paper and old furniture. This scratch-scratch-scratching of chalk on board, pen on paper; the endless hive of whispering, tittering voices you cannot shut out, even in your dreams.

But you cannot leave here. Mammy always finds out.

Each day she comes from work, sets her tray down and asks, 'You went to school today, boy?'

'Yes, Ma.'

'Show me what you done, then.'

She squints at the notebook. Ma does not read or write but she knows that a red X means you got it wrong and a tick across the page is what you ought to have there.

No fresh writing means you did not go to school. So she takes out the whip and, while thrashing you, complains that she is killing herself for a pittance on the gov'ment road. She has to swallow the abuse of schoolchildren who call her 'travaux'. And what for? – one useless boychile who prefer to dreeveway rather than put some learnin in iz head. A child, too-besides, who 'fadder' was a nastiness that left her heavy with him and run off with some jamette who dunno how to wash she own face.

Your father, who is he? You cannot make a picture in your mind, though in the evenings, after work, Mammy sits describing him in detailed cursings. She stares at the roof as if he lives up there and abuses him until she falls asleep in the chair. You do not miss him. You have many fathers – all the tall, nice-looking men you see on your way to school. You give them a voice, dress them as it pleases you and they are your father whenever you wish, for however long you want.

Mr. Celestine could never be your father. He never smiles, is happy only when his leather strap is crashing down on some poor pupil's behind. Besides, he can't have children because he has only one seed. That might not be true, though. The boys who say so do not like any teacher who could make them shut up with a glance.

But there must be a reason why he is so full of rage. Always. He brings it with him in the morning, spills it out on the class and at lunchtime, goes back home to refill. He is hungry-thin – no one ever sees him eat – and he shuts himself up in his office for long hours after school.

He hates you. Else, why does he look at you as though you're a fly sitting on the edge of his ruler?

You still remember the morning he read an English comprehension passage to the class. In the story, Tarvy and Jane had cereal with milk, toast with butter and eggs for breakfast. Mr. Celestine spent half the morning talking about balanced diets.

'What did any of you have?' he asked the class.

Most of them had bread and eggs and milk. Most of them were lying. Then he came to you. 'Anthony Skinner. Skinner! Yes, you! Wake up, boy! I asked you what you had for breakfast?'

'Ham and egg and bacon, Sir. And wholemeal bread.'

Mr. Celestine looked into your face and smiled, as though he could see the two green bananas boiled in salted water, and the plain black sage tea you consumed that morning. But he silenced the class savagely when they started laughing.

Now you really want to escape because soon the bell will ring and Mr. Celestine will collect the test he has asked the class to do.

You have not done the test. The papers lie untouched before you. Instead, you've chosen to do yesterday's assignment – the composition he had belted you for not doing because you were in a mood for reading Geography. He will not want yesterday's work. In fact, he will murder you when he finds that you have not done the Maths test. For some strange reason, you felt compelled to write the composition.

'Honesty,' Mr. Celestine had said, 'is the hallmark of good writing, so, keeping in mind the Queen's English, I want you people to write about anything you like. Just be honest about it.'

Now, yesterday's assignment lies almost complete. The test untouched.

Mr. Celestine has begun to collect the test. He must not see what you have written about Pansy, Ela, Jenny… about the river calling, your mother staring at your father in the ceiling, about Mr. Celestine himself. So you put the three pages of the composition together and begin to tear.

'Hold it there, Skinner!' Mr. Celestine's voice cuts through your head like a whip. 'Why you tearing up the test. You mad?' His eyes are hard. He is striding toward you. You have to get rid of the composition.

'I said hold it, Skinner! What you doing there?'

'Nothing, Sir.'

'Nothing! You call tearing up your Maths Promotion Test nothing?'

But he'd never said it was a Promotion Test!

'Come, come, come! Let me see what you're not satisfied with. Pass those pages.'

Mr. Celestine snatches the torn pages, looks at them a long time and becomes very, very confused. 'Something is wrong with you,' he reads. 'They keep telling you that...'

The bell rings. He stops. Looks up. 'Okay, class. You heard the bell. Stop looking at me as if it's the end of the world – though it might well be for you, Mr. Skinner! The rest of you leave your work on my desk and file out, you hear me? In an orderly fashion. I don't want anybody hanging around my office. You will proceed there, Sir Anthony Skinner and wait till I come. I advise you to pray for your personal deliverance while you wait. Now move!'

'Sir...'

'I say moove!'

The office is quiet, white, small. A single desk stacked with paper. It smells of books and Bristol board. On the far wall, a single picture of a small boy clutching a bunch of dried flowers.

Mr. Celestine is sitting at the desk. The strap is in his right hand. 'Skinner, what is the problem?'

'No problem, Sir.'

'You call playing the arse in class "no problem"?'

'Nuh, Sir.'

'Well what is the problem then!'

'No problem, Sir.'

'You realise you spoil your chances for promotion to scholarship class?'

'You didn't say it was a promotion-test, Sir.'

'I don't have to say so.' Mr. Celestine's right hand convulses near the strap.

'I suppose you expect me to write the answers on the black-board for you too?'

'Nuh, Sir.'

'Well then, what's happening to you, man! Like you gone stupid or something. You do everything wrongside: you walk wrongside, you think wrongside, you even look wrongside! Sit up and button up your shirt. Look at those fingernails! Jeeeez! Your hair comb?'

'Yessir.'

'I have a good mind to spend this hour lacing you. But licks don't make no difference to you. You Missa Tarzan himself. Like your skin harder than this strap, right?'

'Nuh, Sir.'

Jeeez! You miss that by a nook.

'I don't know why the hell I so concerned about you...'

'Me, Sir?'

'Shut up!' Mr. Celestine gets up, walks a few feet from his desk and stands glaring at the closed door. His anger fills the room. He reseats himself and levels a finger at my face. 'If you were stupid I wouldn't mind. I wouldn't even look at you twice. I know what the problem is: you're ashamed! That's what. Don't think I don't know. You watch the children with shoes on, then look at your own bare feet and feel the world owing you a pair. Since when a new pair of shoes becomes equal to how well you perform in class?'

'I didn't say so, Sir.'

'Shut up! You refuse to come first in class – like is a responsi-bility you 'fraid of. Don't look at me like that! You damwelly know you wasting yourself, letting those shoes in class frighten you into playing the jackass. You think they don't know it! Ask yourself why they keep flashing them in front of you. Look at me! You think I was all that different from you?' Mr. Celestine dawdles with the strap. He does not speak for a long while, then:

'So the class don't like me?' He speaks as though he couldn't care less.

'Well, Sir... uhm... You see, I won' really say so. They jus' a lil' bit afraid of you.'

Mr. Celestine smiles. He plays with the strap and looks up at the picture of the boy with the dried flowers.

'Amazing,' he tells the picture. 'Where did you learn to write like that?'

The picture doesn't answer.

'I ask you a question, Skinner.'

'Sorry, Sir. You mean the composition? Dunno. It just come. I write and it just come.'

'"I" – no – "you" – second person singular. "You told her that the world never runs away if a person held tightly onto it. It just takes him along." You believe that?'

'Yessir.'

'I had faith like that once.' Mr. Celestine speaks to the picture on the wall. 'But now, I don't know. I jus dunno. Listen, Skinner, don't repeat this, but your crazy composition that you should've done yesterday was more useful to me than the whole damn Maths test. And to think I was beginning to dislike you. You know that?'

'Nuh.'

'You hungry?'

It is less embarrassing to leave the question unanswered. Mr. Celestine takes a plastic container from his bag. He pauses a long moment, then with a strange smile, he opens it. Inside, there is saltfish and green bananas steamed in coconut juice.

'Here, Skinner!' He holds out the container and grins. 'Have some of my ham and eggs and bacon with wholemeal bread.'

The food is good; the odour sweet.

'Listen, Skinny,' Mr. Celestine chuckles and licks his fingers. He looks happy to have someone licking fingers with him. 'Hear this. Next year I will be teaching scholarship-class. It means I have you fools for two years straight. When I finish, y'all will be as sharp as cutlass on grinding stone. You will pass, even if I have to kill you to make you do it. Because I want the island scholarship, and you, mister-man, will get it for me. Then it will be my chance for Teacher's College, and after that, university. They can't refuse my application if I get the best results. Five years in this place is enough. A man must move on. I want to go. Go! That is why I don't want no children – and not for any other reason, y'understand?' Mr. Celestine's eyes are black and reproachful.

'Yes, Sir.'

'So no more jumping around on riverstones and playing bush-car with little Miss Fancy or whatever-her-name-is. You catch me? From now on is books, books, books and more books. Agreed? Now, come shake hands, because this is an understanding between us – a contract if you like. You get the Island Schol and I get what I want.'

The food was nice. A pity there wasn't more. There should have been more. His hands are warm, firm – like a father's should be.

'Take this envelope. Give it to your mother. Don't open it. Tell her to buy a good pair of shoes, a real shirt and a pair of long pants. Some underwear too. I don't want to see all your spare parts sticking out at everyone anymore. Now get out of my office before I do something crazy with this strap. By the way, if the class ask what happened, tell them I near tear the skin off your backside. Stop grinning at me, Skinner.'

'Yes sir.'

'And do me a favour, man. When you get outside, go to the standpipe and wash the mud off your feet, seeing as school really begin for you on Monday.'

'Yes, Mr. Celestine.'

'Now… er, before you go, tell me, little man, why doesn't the class like me?'

'Well, Sir, they don't know you like I know you now.'

'Who! You? You know me?'

'Nuh-nuh, Sir, I don' know you. I don' know you at all.'

'Good. Go on – and close the door behind you. Erm, Skinner?'

'Sir?'

'Don't let nobody fool you; nothing wrong with you, y'unnerstand?'

Mr. Celestine does not seem to hear the door closing. He is glaring at the picture on the wall.

GIRLCHILE
For Navice

It shamed her, just the thought of telling her mother the things
the men said each evening as she walked past them. But since the
stranger arrived and joined the idlers on the root of the white
cedar tree that faced the road, they stopped doing those nasty
things with their hands and mouths, and no longer loud-
whispered dutty words to her.

Now the weight of their gaze felt much worse than their
teasing as they sat – all eight of them – just like the stranger, with
their elbows on their outspread knees watching her approach.

Just before she reached them, she drew breath, her arms
tightening around the schoolbooks pressed against her shirt
while the muscles of her legs grew heavy as if she were wading
through a pool of mud. In that shaky passage before the nine pairs
of staring eyes – not that they would ever see her shaking – she
smelled the stale rum on their breaths and heard the wheezing of
the thin man with the big voice they called Stinkweed who sat
swizzling a piece of stick between his teeth.

A couple of weeks ago, she'd almost lost her temper. She was
so concentrated on holding it in she bit down on her lower lip
until it bled.

She barely noticed the others now – just the new man: his big
rum-yellowed eyes dropping to her white school shoes, travelling
up the rest of her and settling on her face, watching her in a way
that made the skin of her back feel prickly.

Over the weeks she'd tried to make herself not hear them by
whispering:

Shoo fly doh bodder me

Me an you not no company…

but sometimes Stinkweed's rumble broke through her recitation. Today, he was saying something about de way the girlchile growin… pretty likkle face… skin nice-an-smooth an deliket… s'matter ov fact… leavin aside de fact dat… girlchile still in school… she's a ooman now… and a man had a right to…

'Watch y'arse, Stinkweed!' The voice of the new man was rough and sharp, and despite herself, she looked at him, met the staring eyes, took in the thin brown face, the veins that ran down his neck like cords, the imprint of his shoulder blades against his shirt. Then she swung her head away. She wished she had someone to walk along with, like her mother's boyfriend, Missa Byron, because Byron didn make no joke with nobody.

Long after she went past Missa Elton's shop and home was just around the corner, Stinkweed's thundering trailed after her. She was too far off to make out his words but they raised a wash of laughter from the others and it made her wish there was some other way to get home after school.

The next day the stranger wasn't there. A fine drizzle was insinuating its way into her starched white shirt. A downpour would spoil her books and drawings, soak her clothes and mess up her hair. Her mother had passed a hot comb through it just this morning.

'Come shelter from the rain,' Stinkweed called. He raised a hand at the darkening hills. 'Look it almos reach. And is a big, long one that comin.'

The men laughed, while the little man eased himself along the root and patted it.

She concentrated on her recitation.

'Cuttin style!' he called. 'Yuh think yuh nice; not so? Well you could ha been nicer if you didn have yuh fadder k-foot.'

His words almost stopped her, and he must have seen this because he nudged the friend beside him and they high-fived.

★

Then it was Friday and she didn give a damn who lookin at her. They could watch until their eyes dropped out becuz she had the whole weekend ahead and, come Monday, her mother and Missa Byron goin give them what they asking for.

The new man was back, standing with his shoulders against the tree. Stinkweed's stick hung at the corner of his mouth. The others sat with their hands propping up their chins. They were not looking at her. The change in them felt strange.

From the corner of her eye she saw the new man push himself away from the tree and step onto the road beside her.

Her mother had told her what to say to boys who brought their forwardness to her, but she'd never given her words for no long-neck, dry-up ole man, with gru-gru hair and hammer-foot.

Her mother had also warned her about her temper. Every morning. With her breath on her neck as she fixed her hair and tied her ribbons, her mother warned her, over and over, to walk careful. 'Don' give nobody no back-chat. Don' bring no more embarrassment on me again. Y'unnerstan? Watch yuh temper.'

She told her mother the same thing every time. Is not deliberate. I can't help it. The temper does take me by surprise. When the vexness come, what a pusson s'pose to do?

'Pray,' her mother said, 'pray for the sonuvabitch dat cross you. You didn get dat temper from me. Is from dat no-good jailbird…' At which point her mother's voice retreated down her throat.

Pray, her mother said! Well, right now she praying dat dis ole bull didn bring his freshness to her. Becuz…

'Eh heh!' Stinkweed boomed. The man brushed his ears as if he were shaking off a bumbo fly.

'Jackass,' he said, and threw a sideways glance at her. 'Sorry about de fellas.'

She sucked her teeth and glared at him. 'What de arse y'all want wiv me. Cuz I not havin no ole bull watchin me all de time and followin me down de road. I goin tell my mother about y'all, and if she bring Missa Byron with her, is ten planass you goin get in y'arse. Is like all ov all-you want to dead.'

A rustle of a chuckle escaped him. 'Thought you couldn talk.'

He shoved his fingers down his shirt pocket and pulled out a packet of cigarettes. He turned a shoulder against the wind, struck a match and cupped his hands around the flame, then he slid another glance at her.

'You dunno who I is. Not so?'

She kept her silence.

He rolled his eyes at the sky and chuckled. 'And she not even curious. You not curious?'

The girl shifted the books and frowned. 'Nuh.'

They were at the junction between Cross Gap and Top Road. He slowed, then stopped.

She lengthened her stride.

'Tell yuh modder, Gideon say hello,' he shouted. She heard the drag of his rubber sandals as he headed back up the road.

Her mother was at the stove when she got home. She was dressed the way Byron liked – a loose flowered dress, high at the hem with thin straps that left her legs and shoulders bare.

'Who's Gideon, Mammy?'

Her mother stiffened, dropped back the lid on the steaming pot and swung around to face her. 'Where you get that name from? Who give it to you? Eh?' Her mother made a step towards her. 'Where you been to get it? Yuh bizness is school, not no shit-talk. Go change your clothes. I don' have the strength…'

The girl retreated to her room, sat on the bed and examined her feet.

I don have the strength… is what her mother says when the letters arrive from school or when Missa Byron smashes the plates, or like that last time when he kicked the new colour television and broke the screen. Her mother would sit on the steps, massaging her shoulders, staring at the day and saying it.

Now, her mother's words had replaced her recitation whenever she saw the waiting man. She repeated them, not out loud as her mother did, but to herself – though yesterday the words came out of her mouth, jusso, when she sat in front of the headmistress. Didn' even realise her own lips were moving until she heard herself. *I don have the strength.* And she wasn't sure what she meant by the words, but what her mother had been feeling all this time became, somehow, a little clearer.

Every evening, just when they got to Cross Gap Junction, she would wait for the slap of his rubber sandals to slow down and then to falter, and as the distance grew between them, the man who called himself Gideon would throw words at her retreating back – sometimes meant for her, most times for her mother.

'Word reach me that she christen you, Agatha. She name you after my modder. Tell she I feel good 'bout dat.'

The next day: 'I not makin no claim, but yuh have to know, two river run inside yuh. Half is from yuh modder; the other half belong to me.'

Sometimes he hung behind as if held back by the goading of his men-friends, but always, when they arrived at the junction, his gravel voice addressed her.

'People say you doin well in school? I hear de other ones I got doin alright too. But you the one who got my brain. You should study for doctor. How old you say you is right now?'

This time she turned around to face him. She was calm – and glad for it. There was no rush of heat in her head, no tightening in her chest that shortened her breath and made her want to break things, like this morning when the new teacher bent over the back of her chair for the third time, pressed his chest against her shoulder and leaned into her. She'd caught his arm with her pencil rather than the eye that she was aiming for.

This was different: the mix of reluctance and curiosity she felt – the repulsion and the pull of him as he rose from the group and placed himself beside her, or behind her. Nothing in her mother's coaching was useful now. But at least she could be honest – follow her feelings like her English teacher said.

'You don' even know my age?' She paused to right the little thing inside her head that his words had just misplaced. 'And –

and – and you say that you my…' She couldn't say the word; it had never been said between her and her mother. And despite all his talk, he had never said it once.

She was almost as tall as him. When she looked at him, she had an impression of bones – the print of his collarbones against his shirt, the knobs of his knuckles always working because his hands were never still, the trousers that fell straight down from his waist, held up by a thin belt too narrow for the large loops. She'd only seen eyelashes like his on coolie men, and on women.

'Wait,' he said, 'if I think back a lil bit, I could figure it out easy. By the look ov you, I would say you thirteen?' He lifted his head and rubbed his chin. 'Nuh – you fourteen, or thereabouts!'

'Yeh!' she said, 'I fourteen, and in all this time – where you been? Where you been all this time?'

'Nowhere far. Was, yunno…'

'Nowhere far is still too damn far. I askin you again.' She adjusted her books and openly appraised him. 'Where you been all dis time?'

'Sometimes, yunno, life take over. Sometimes…'

'I didn ask you that. You a jailbird like my – erm – like people say?'

He threw a quick glance at her face. 'Things happen… Is like anodder country up there, yunno. A fella…'

'What you do?'

He licked his lips, seemed about to say something, then changed his mind.

'What you do?'

'Ask yuh modder.'

'I askin you.'

For all the staring he'd been doing during the past few weeks, he would not look at her now. He lifted his shoulders and dropped them. 'Someting I shouldn ha done.'

'Uh-huh?'

'Uh-huh!'

'And what's the somefing?'

'Tell yuh modder I say I sorry.'

'Fuh what? Is someting yuh do my modder?'

He moistened his lips again. 'In a way,' he said. 'Tell er I say…' His words trailed off in a mumble. 'Anodder time.' He waved a hand at her and turned back.

She watched him go, in a fever to chase after him, but just as suddenly something cool and shadowy draped itself around her.

'That's why she hate y'arse.' The words erupted from her throat louder than she expected – almost a scream that halted him mid-stride and turned the heads of a group of strolling women a little way ahead of him.

He wasn't there the next day, and she was smiling because it was the August break – three whole months of not walking this road, of being away from the chafing of her teachers, and the growing attrition with Patricia who used to be her best friend.

The space beneath the tree was empty. Abandoned beer bottles and a broken dice board lay in a heap at the far edge of the clearing. A dizzy of feeding flies blackened the rolled-back lids of scooped-out corned beef tins.

Someone had nailed a rusting square of corrugated iron against the tree, with freshly painted words in red.

The devil does fine wuk for idel hans to do
All mancrab mus fine they hole from now on.
By order of the propitor.

She began stepping to the rhythm of her ring-game rhyme, making a medley of it.

Shoo fly doh bodder me
Me an you not no company
Sly Mongoose
Dog know yuh way
Yuh come inside ah me modder kitchen
Yuh tief she shoe and you eat she chicken.
Sly mongoose…

Then she saw him. He was sitting on the wall above the culvert facing Missa Elton's shop, a cigarette drooping from his mouth.

It stopped the bounce in her walk and drained away her words. He came quickly to his feet, dropped the cigarette butt and crushed it with his foot.

'Y'awright?'

He was swaying slightly, looking at her with a chupid half-smile on his face. She smelled rum on his breath.

'Where you think you goin?' she grated. She'd read his intention in his manner and it made her mouth go dry.

'I walk wiv you a lil' way. No trouble. I promise.'

'You not following me,' she said. The walls of their house was a shimmer of red and blue between the shifting leaves of the yellow poui trees that hung over the road.

'Why not?' he said. He hadn't raised his voice, but something in his tone reminded her of the time he shut up Stinkweed. It brought her back to the men sitting on the root chipping away at her every time she passed.

She took in his hair – roughed-up and uncombable – his parched lips, the rubber sandals with their broken straps and the faded yellow shirt with its signs of clumsy ironing.

Missa Byron would want to know who he was. He would force it out of her mother. And when she told him he would never let them forget it.

Suddenly she was hating him for the embarrassment he was about to cause them, the trouble and the shame to come. The urgency to drive him away broke out in sweat on her face.

She held his eyes and spoke in a semi-whisper, words she'd been rehearsing these past few weeks, except that now they felt not spiteful as she had planned, but sorrowful and hurting.

'My modder don't want to see you,' she said. 'In my mother head, you dead. A long time now. She never even tol' me yuh name. And I never ask. An – me – I wish I never see you becuz it too late. I fourteen now an it too damn late for everyting. Y'unnerstan? I don want to know you. S'far as I concern, I don' have no father.'

He stood before her, quiet and unblinking, as if he were absorbing her words with his eyes. He grunted something, reached into his back pocket and pulled out a handkerchief – white and pristine – folded as if it had just come from the store.

He held it out to her.

'Wipe yuh eye,' he said. 'You cryin.'

She did not take it.

He rested the square of cloth in the gap between her school shirt and her books, turned around and headed back up the road.

She pressed herself against the bank of the road so that if he turned he would not see her watching him – the way he leaned his body forwards, the slight outward swing of his right foot as he walked. She stayed there until the shadow of the yellow poui trees that arched over the road swallowed him.

Her mother was on the steps observing her come up the path. The girl greeted her, then pointed at her head. 'Headache,' she said and hurried up the steps.

In her bedroom, she unlaced her shoes, dragged her chair against the old wardrobe and stood on it. She was up there for a while rifling through old school books and notepads.

She dropped the notepads on the bed, climbed down and began sorting them, pausing over every drawing – from the little stick-men of her infancy to the delicate pencil etchings of her primary school years that her friends and teachers used to marvel at. All of them efforts to conjure up the body of a man her mother would not put a face or name to whenever she'd asked.

The latest ones, in the sketchpad that she walked to school with every day, were less detailed, the charcoal strokes much fainter. None of them looked anything like him, except the eyes, heavy-lashed and very dark, like hers, with wide wing-strokes for brows, and the long, long scoop of his neck and throat. She'd never bothered to colour them in.

Hearing her mother's footsteps on the floorboards, she tossed the sketchpad at her feet and lay back on the pillow. Her mother tapped the door frame and walked in. She cleared a space on the bed and sat beside her, resting a hand in the curve of the girl's neck and fingering the tiny earring on her lobe.

'Y'awright?' her mother said.

She smelled of the soap she'd been washing Byron's shirts with.

'Uh-huh,' she said, pressing her chin against the hand. 'I awright, Mam. I feel a little better now.'

A GAME OF MARBLES

Last night he dreamt of new marbles, each staring up at him with foliated irises of purple, red and blue. He also dreamed of birds with shiny eyes of steel circling the ring of marbles.

In the road below, a jeep snarls past. All through the night they have been bolting up and down the road. He wonders if the soldiers ever slept.

His granny won't have slept. The old woman will talk all day about the gunshots she'd heard during the night, the jeeps tearing through the dark, and all those terrifying things she says she is too old to understand. Later, she will ask him when the strike will end and people can walk the road again to find food.

He'll shake his head and say nothing because he is not sure he understands either. Marbles he understands. Playing makes him forget food and his grandmother's upsetting questions.

There are no more wild yams in the bushes where he used to search them out. He is not the only one who hunts the hills for food.

He's sick of the green bananas his granny boils, steams, stews, fries or roasts for him every day. Green bananas and wild yams are not enough. His granny needs meat.

His body begs for it too. Even saltfish will do, but the shops are closed, their doors padlocked. The whole island has stopped.

The day before, he went into the bushes to cut himself a Y-shaped branch. He stripped it, pared it down to size and shaped the handle of the slingshot to his liking. He covered it with strips of rubber that he'd razored from a car's old inner tube. At each tip of the forked stick, he tied two straps of red rubber cut from the thicker tube of a truck. He joined the rubber straps by a single leather-tongue taken from an old shoe. The straps became a loop; the tongue, the place where he would fit the stones to shoot.

Then he goes into the bushes. His craving pushes him to the upper reaches of Mount Airy. There, he sends a pikayo careering earthward in a cloud of grey and white feathers. Finds that it is not the same bird which, a moment before, was perched on the branches of the tall silk-cotton tree. On the carpet of rotting leaves, it is just a heap of feathers still warm with the life of its unfinished song.

He buries it beneath the same tree with an apology and a prayer. His granny has told him to leave the birds alone. Birds were lucky, she said. They could fly away from problems.

The road is dangerous. Every twenty minutes or so, a jeep comes roaring round the bend. He plunges, with the other boys, headfirst into the roadside bushes. They lie still till the soldiers pass in a cloud of scattered pebbles.

The boys emerge, wary of the sounds that come on the wind. But the game must go on. The ring in which they've placed their marbles is more important than the fear of soldiers on the road. Only winning matters. They want to start the game before the jeeps return and scatter them again. But Sip is taking his time.

The boy stands loose-mouthed, counting his marbles. He shows them off like some men would their money.

'I have four new ironies.' The steel marbles shine in his palm like droplets of solid light.

'How much veinies you got, Sip?' he wants to know.

Sip says five. A *veiny* equals two marbles.

Sip holds up an extra large marble to the light. 'I have one big *tor*. One jack's eye. Plus six ordnary ones, not counting the ironies.'

He wants Sip's marbles badly. He is worried that the soldiers might return too soon.

'We playin' till one of us go bust,' he says. 'No raafing – nobody grabbin' up dem marble like crazy when them soljer pass. We play till somebody bust.'

Sip looks worried, so he adds quickly, 'If I win, I give back some.'

He sends his marble crashing into the ring, collects the four that he's knocked out, kneels and pitches. He misses the one remaining in the ring. Sip knocks it out and is encouraged to play on.

He is thinking while he plays. In the evening, when the road becomes too hot to walk on with his naked feet, he will take the dirt-track through the bushes and the sugar cane of Old Hope to visit Mrs. Ducan.

Mrs. Ducan has a big concrete house, a pretty lawn, two cars and a tall barbed-wire fence that goes all the way round their lot. She also has a generator – a Delco – in a shed behind the house which gives light at night when all the other houses are in darkness. Mebbe if his granny had a fridge to store things in and a Delco to keep it going, he wouldn't have wanted Sip's iron marbles so badly. And he wouldn't be going to the Ducan's house this evening.

He will stand at the gate and call. Bo, the massive Alsatian, will come tearing across the lawn at him, showing his teeth behind the iron bars of the gate. Mrs. Ducan will slide open her big glass door, push out her head and shout at the dog. She will throw him a bone or something and with her nice voice say, 'Stop it, Bo.' The dog will follow her into the house and the lady will lock him in.

He will enter the gate only when Mrs. Ducan tells him to. Little Robby, her son, will be standing just in front of the big glass door, watching him come up the driveway.

Missa Ducan might not be in. He works for the government and drives on the road anytime he likes. The soldiers never stop him or shoot at him.

Missa Ducan's wife will hand him a small knife and he will go behind the house, walk into the small swamp there and begin cutting calaloo leaves for her. He will cut until he has a bunch bigger than himself. The turkeys in the yard will crowd around and gobble, shaking their long pink jowls at him.

Missa Ducan loves the turkeys. He has given each one a name. He rears bantam chickens too and has got the boy to clean their coops for him many times. The turkeys have no coops; they guard the yard like dogs. Mrs. Ducan says her turkeys never sleep.

That was true because, before the curfew started, he used to see them strutting beneath the floodlight on the lawn.

'You bringsing.' Sip snaps at him.

He draws his hand a few inches back to appease the angry boy. The others are losing all their marbles to him too, but they do not seem to mind.

Mrs. Ducan will pay him twenty-five cents for cutting the calaloo and, if he is lucky, some food wrapped in a piece of foil. She is doing him a favour. Mrs. Ducan always tells him that, just when he begins eating. Little Robby's voice would chime in: 'That was my food; I ate that today.'

His mother will fondle Robby, ask him to be quiet, but he will go on: 'See where I bit that piece? There. There is where I bit.' He will smile because Robby is just three, plump, and very cute to play with. Missa Ducan though, never looks pleased when he tries to cuddle Robby. He'd even slapped his son once when he boasted: 'My daddy has a gun – a big, big one; everybody knows he has a gun.'

'Last game,' Sip growls.

''Kay,' he says.

A blast of horns shatters the mid-morning calm. A Land Rover has come quietly coasting down the road. The boys have just enough time to fling themselves into the bushes and go pelting down the hill. The soldiers' laughter rises in the air and dies with the passing of the vehicle.

He halts with his friends in the shade of a large mango tree. He gives each of the boys a quarter of the marbles they have lost to him. Twenty remain in his pocket. Sip is not satisfied.

'Tha'z all?' Sip says.

'I could give you back all of yours,' he says. 'Or more.'

'Gimme then.'

'Nuh.'

'You *say* you was goin' to gimme back all.'

'I never say so. And who the hell you bawlin at. You can't fight me like you fight Tomo an' dem, yunno.'

'Because you got dat slingshot,' Sip says.

'Soljers have gun; I have slingshot. Lissen, Sippo, we could make a bargin. You gimme them four ironies, I give you all your marbles back.'

'Naw.'

'I give you fifteen – seven veinies, one extra.'

Sip shakes his head.

'Eighteen,' he says. 'Take it or leave it, I don care.'

Sip is working his mouth like a fish.

'Twenty. No more. Ten vainies for four ole ironies. What you say?'

Sip surrenders with a nod.

'What you want all dem ironies for, Kenno?'

'C'mon,' he says. 'I think I hear the old lady callin me. Mebbe she want water o' something.'

There is a low moon over Hope Vale – yellow like an over-ripe paw-paw. It hangs on the crest of Mont Airy as if it were about to roll down its slopes and burst at the bottom.

He would have preferred if there were no moon, no soldiers patrolling the night, no sound to listen out for except the pit-pat-pattering of his feet on the mud-path through the fields of sugarcane.

The night is chill. The sugarcanes glitter silver in the moon-light. On the road above him, jeeps growl past, their headlights cutting a white path through the canes.

His granny does not know where he is. He told her he was going to the latrine a few yards from the house; that he could be some time since his gripe was very bad. She would be calling him now, wondering why he was taking so long, sitting in the dark listening for his footsteps. His granny never complains. Tonight though, she spoke of food like something remembered, and it made his heart feel heavy.

Earlier this evening, he visited Mrs. Ducan who asked him to sweep the yard. The driveway was packed with big, bright cars.

Men in jackets and women in long, pretty dresses were laughing in the verandah. They drank from very slim glasses and poured their frothing drinks from pink bottles with slender necks. Mrs. Ducan told him she was busy so he must leave as soon as he finished sweeping. She looked pretty in her long blue dress and the chain of beads around her throat.

Bo barked at him from where he was chained beneath the house. The turkeys crowded around his legs and gobbled among themselves, polite and genteel, like the people on the verandah – only they didn't have glasses to drink from – mebbe because they didn't have no hands to hold them with.

Mrs. Ducan must have said something about him because two of the pretty-looking ladies looked at him. The one in red muttered something nice – he could tell that by the way her lips moved and her smile. But Mrs. Ducan gave him nothing. She was too busy with her friends.

Emerging from the canes, he finds himself at the foot of the hill on top of which sits the Ducan's house. A cool wind comes up the valley from the Kalivini swamps, bringing the scent of crabs, frogs and rotting cane.

The boy pauses in the shade of a french-cashew tree; takes out his slingshot; tenses the red rubber straps. He pulls the bird he's shot this evening from under his shirt and wonders if one lil ground-dove is enough to keep Bo busy. If Bo doesn't get him, Missa Ducan's gun might.

First, he must get through the barbed-wire fence, crawl along the ground on his stomach – the way Sip said the soldiers did in wars. He flattens himself on the grass and inches beneath the lowest rung of wire. His lips are chafed with dirt, his stomach bruised with pebbles but he clears the fence. The Delco is putt-putting away. The Alsatian is standing near the steps, its nose pointing towards the fence. He thinks he hears the dog's deep-throated growl.

The fence would shred him if he tries to throw himself back out.

He is sure now that the dog's body has gone rigid. Its ears upright, its nose directed at the fence.

The boy eases himself off the ground, swings his right arm high. The bird's small carcass sails over the grass and drops with a *plap!*

just behind the dog. Bo growls once, turns to sniff the object on the ground. The dog lifts his head, sniffs again and, still growling, takes the bird between his jaws and retreats beneath the house.

He slips along the grass and stops just outside the rim of light. The turkeys seem to sense his presence. They are in the centre of the lawn. They lift their heads with jerky movements, chuckling among themselves as they scan the perimeter of the fence. The tall gate is a little way to his right. He checks for the dog.

He strains against the rubber, aims at the biggest bird and releases.

He's shot the turkey exactly where he aimed – just behind the jowls. But it does not lie still; it begins thrashing on the grass, raising a noisy, chuckling protest that brings the dog leaping from beneath the house.

He knows he cannot run; besides, he does not want to. He edges backward until the barbs of the wire begin to nip his skin. The dog leaps at his face; he throws himself aside. The growl becomes a yelp as it crashes against the fence, and gets tangled there. That is when he shoots him with the second marble. Bo scrambles to his feet and, still yelping, bolts for the shelter of the house.

There is a stirring in the big house: chairs falling, a man's deep voice, lights switched on in the rooms, a woman's voice pitched high. He remembers Missa Ducan's gun but does not move. He takes his third marble, aims at the blazing bulb and fires. The light explodes in a shower of sparks and tinkling glass. Only the moon shines now; its light is soft on the grass.

The turkey is a dark heap where it has come to a stop against the gate. Sprinting across the lawn, he lifts it, opens the gate, just managing to throw himself flat as the man comes out on the verandah.

Missa Ducan is a giant shape against the half-opened doorway. The gun is in his hand. The man is shouting and looking into the night. The boy lifts his slingshot. It is his last marble. He narrows his eyes, aims and fires. The night explodes with the shattering of the glass door. Missa Ducan ducks and with flailing arms throws himself backward into the house.

The turkeys are a huddle on the lawn. Bo is somewhere behind the house, gone silent. He slings his load onto his shoulders and is soon bouncing with quick, cautious steps along the mud track through the cane fields – his ears tuned for the sound of the soldiers' jeeps.

THE ROOM INSIDE

The doctor wouldn't come. Said he was tired. Didn't they know that doctors needed sleep too?

Yes-yes! Of course they'd told him that the nurse wasn't there, that the Medical Station was locked because a man had half-killed his wife in Roebuck and Nurse Finchley had gone there to look after the woman.

They'd thought the doctor might've changed his mind, but his wife came to the doorway and reminded him that he'd just finished having the car fixed and it had only enough petrol to take her to the wedding the following day.

Yes! That was what she said. She had to do the flowers o' somethin. She complained 'bout the weather too. Impossible, she said. All this rain and thunder made the road bad for cars. Besides, a doctor could break his leg climbing that slippery hill. Old Hope was a bad place anyway – yes, that's what she said, a bad place, even in the best weather.

She even blamed the doctor. Hadn't she often warned him about spoiling *those* people with kindness? It didn't pay to be so nice to them.

Yes, they *did* tell Dr. Raeburn that Elaine was a sickly girl and the child was coming early; they couldn't get her to the hospital in time. He became really angry then; said nobody couldn blackmail him; no two so-and-sos could open his gate, walk into his yard and stand there in his verandah, trying to make him do what he didn't have to do.

He was a doctor, not a midwife. That's what he said.

They were in the yard – a tight circle of men, women and children, the rain beating down on them in hard white sheets.

The two youths who had run the five miles to St. Paul's and back, fidgeted and dug their naked toes into the wet earth.

The three women drilled them until they learned the details of the boys' trek through the storm, to the Medical Station, the doctor's house and their even hastier return. Only Ray and Mike had returned. Jim had taken the road for St. Georges, to the hospital. He'd done so after he'd called at two houses with telephones. The lines, it seemed, had been broken by the storm. Cars were hard to come by, their owners even harder to persuade to venture down the road.

St. Georges was ten miles away.

Nana lifted her eyes to the sky. The pelting rain hit her in the face. She did not shift her gaze until she appeared to find what she was looking for. Patsy, Elaine's mother, was quiet, her eyes dull as the pools of water settled at her feet. Aya, Nana's older sister stood slightly apart from them, making and unmaking bead-loops with the chaplet around her neck.

Gigi knew something was wrong. She thought Cecil, Elaine's boyfriend, was weeping, but it could have been rain washing down his face. Why was everyone standing here in her mother's yard talking about Elaine when the girl was, according to them, close to dying in the little house further up the hill?

She realised that she was standing exactly as the adults were: arms making handles on her hips, feet buried in the mud.

'Okay,' Nana said. 'No choice! We have to bring Elaine here.' She rested big dark eyes on the women's faces. 'De only person I know who could do something now is my modder. But first, I want Patsy to agree, 'cause I dunno what might happen. We could leave Elaine up there to dead or we could do something.'

She turned to Miss Patsy, 'You agree for my modder to try to deliver the child?'

Patsy shifted her feet, looked down at the stones. She raised her head and nodded.

Nana turned to Aya. 'Go talk to the old woman. Tell er – tell er Elaine baby comin early and we ain got nobody qualify help. Tell er you know is years she stop deliverin – since that blasted nurse report her, sayin' she ain't qualify. Careful how you say dat, 'cause it still does hurt her. And mos' important, let her know dat Patsy agree to have her deliver the baby. If she refuse, tell her I say she must do it. Dis is stickin-togedder-time. Gwone!'

Aya looked at Nana's face and, still fondling her chaplet, drifted into the house.

Nana raised a finger at the boys. 'The men – where the men? Go to every house on dis hill and tell the men I want them. If anybody drunk or sleepin, leave dem 'cause I don' want no more problems. I want four strong men. Tell dem to meet me at Patsy house and bring the stronges', cleanes' sheet they got in deir house. Y'all still there? Gwone!'

The boys scattered, shouting commands at each other.

Nana glared at the children. 'Go home!' she snapped. 'Y'all want to ketch cold? Y'all modder know where y'all is? Break that stick for me, Gigi – Gigi what you doin' there, child? What the…!'

Nana lunged at them. The children bolted off. Gigi had no-where to go. Nana didn't have to tell her that once the men brought down Elaine, her mother's house would be out of bounds.

She sought shelter beneath the ant-blighted grapefruit tree beside the little house. Her teeth were chattering, her dress dripping.

Cecil stood beside her. His eyes were swollen, his thin hands fluttering at his side. Water was streaming down the dark-leaved tree. Cecil took the dripping onslaught while Gigi strove to dodge the heavy drops. At another time it would have been a game.

'Missa Cecil?'

The young man did not look at her. He was rubbing his small growth of beard as though it was bothering him.

'Miss Elaine sick bad?'

He did not answer.

'She deadin – she goin dead?'

'What de hell you askin' me, gyul!'

'Nana say she makin' a baby.'

'Dat don' mean she goin dead.' Gigi heard the tremor in his voice. She raised her face at him.

'You know what I been thinkin, Missa Cecil?'

She tried to hold his gaze but he would not look at her. 'I been thinkin dat y'all could tell Papa God to take back de baby; not so? He don' bung-an-compel to send it now if it make Miss Elaine sick. Y'all could ask 'im to keep it for you till she get better; not so?'

She couldn't understand why he was smiling. She was trying to help de stupid fella and he was makin joke ov her advice.

Something else was bothering her. 'Missa Cecil – how come Elaine sick and you not sick? Is only cry you cryin', but you ask to be de baby fadder; not so? So, you should be deadin too…'

'Shut up! You don' know what you talkin 'bout. What likkle gyul like you want to know 'bout dat anyway? Move, before I clout you.'

'You touch me, I tell my modder – she break you' head wit' one cuff!'

Cecil turned his back to her, brushing the water from his hair.

'Next month,' Gigi informed him, I goin' ask Papa God for *four* baby. But I don' want 'im to make me fat like Elaine. Besides, I want only girls – dolly-girls. What Elaine ask for – a boy?'

Cecil didn't answer her. Aya was at the doorway calling: 'Gigelle, come in from de rain – look at the child clothes, Lord! Cecil, why you don't shelter below de house? Don't worry, son. Elaine goin be awright.'

Aya's voice was always soft – as if forever on the verge of song.

'Come here, Gi!'

Gigi ran into the house.

The woman set about stripping her and drying her with an old towel. Her grandmother's mumbling came from the little room next door. Hers was a never-ending conversation with herself, broken only when she was eating or speaking to someone else.

Aya dressed the child in her best dress, stepped back, eyed her and said, 'Dunno if you modder goin like this, Gi. Nana have she ways and I have mine. But we goin need you. I don' think de lesson too big for you either! Light the coalpot – yuh granmodder goin' need hot water, plenty of it. Make sure your hand cleaner dan a whistle when you boil that water.'

Moments later, the fire was going and the largest pot in the house sat on it. Other pots were filled and waiting. She worked with the sense that she was fighting to stave off something terrible.

There came a babble of voices above the sound of wind and rain. She beat Aya to the door.

They brought Elaine down in a sheet. Each of the four men held a knotted corner of the large white square of linen. Uncle Arthur, the giant, and Mr. Joe were at the front. Mano, the mute, was straining beside Nathan at the back. The swaying sheet ballooned inwards with the weight of the girl.

During dry weather, the narrow dirt-track led all the way to the top of the hill. Now, there was only slipping mud and running water. Sometimes the men sat down on the wet ground, holding the makeshift hammock above their heads, and slid down on their behinds till they reached a lower, more secure level.

Every now and then a sharp cry came from the depths of the swaying sheet and Nana's voice became insistent, urging the men forward.

When they were in the yard, Cecil hung over the sheet like a condemned man. The men brought Elaine inside, then returned to the yard – their breathing low, their eyes avoiding each other.

Nana stopped Cecil at the door, turned and faced the men.

'Dunno what we'd ha done widdout y'all. But I don't want nobody hangin around here while this bizness goin on. Go home. I not sayin' so twice.'

There was something cold, almost insulting in the way she addressed them.

'And pray for us,' Aya added, 'if de spirit move y'all.'

'Right!' Nana cut in. She nudged Aya aside. 'You – Cecil – I know how you feelin, but you got to find yourself somewhere else. I don't want no man 'round here; this is woman bizness! Gigi…'

'She boiling the water. We need her.' Aya's tone was firm.

The old lady's voice came through, demanding their presence. Gigi retreated with her mother, Aya and Miss Patsy. Nana closed the bedroom door.

Gigi kept the fire burning low. The smoke stung her eyes and helped to keep her awake, but at one point she must have dozed off, because her mother was shaking her.

'Water,' she said.

The girl stirred and filled the outstretched basin. Nana rushed into the room. There was no end to it, filling and refilling the basin, placing the other pots on the fire to boil, responding to her mother's demands for water.

Elaine must want she baby really bad, she thought. To be groanin and cryin so much for it. Papa God was long in handing it to her. Mebbe h'was still searching the sky for the right one. Miss Elaine too impatient though! A pusson should learn to wait and not to suffer demself like that. Besides, it wasn fair; Cecil should share some of the suffering too.

Gigi reconsidered her decision to ask Papa God for four babies. Four might be too much and p'raps she should wait until she was as big as Nana.

The storm was over but the house was still cool from the wind. Behind the closed door, the women had been whispering. Now there came a flurry of activity, followed by her mother's command:

'Now.'

'Hold on love,' crooned Aya. 'Make an effort. Come on.'

'What you relaxin' for?' her mother snapped. 'I cyah do it for you. Come on, child!'

Then Miss Patsy's voice, 'I holdin' you, Elaine.'

The old woman told them to shut up.

The little girl shut her eyes, absorbing the drama in the room. Nana laughed and the suddenness, the strangeness of the sound shook her. Elaine was now silent. Patsy came for more water. The old lady muttered something. Her mother chuckled.

'At least the girl goin' be awright,' said Nana.

'But the child…' Aya sounded unable to say the rest.

Aya's face was strange when she came out.

'Come, Gi. You want to see?'

The child got up, not sure about her mother's reaction to her presence in the bedroom. Aya took her by the shoulder and led her in.

Elaine lay on the bed, covered and asleep. Beside her was a small doll-like thing, all pink and curled up and perfect. Nana had seen her come in but did not appear to mind. The old woman was mumbling to herself about doctors who didn't allow her to do her calling and didn't come when a pusson really need dem. Now this – the failure of her life right there in front of her – to haunt her for the rest of her days.

Gigi couldn't figure out their problem. She edged toward the bedside and touched Elaine's baby – the toes, the hands. She found herself liking their softness. They were smooth – more smooth than warm.

'Is not my fault de baby didn live,' the old woman said.

Her mother reached down and lifted it off the sheet. She wrapped it in an old towel, brought it to the hall and placed it on the *atama* near the fire. She stood over the small bundle for a long time, said something under her breath and went back in.

The little girl stooped and nudged the bundle, hoping that by touch, she could better understand what the old lady had just said. Nana always told her that a person must never beg. It was better to do without. Elaine must have begged too hard.

The women were discussing what they should do. They would need the men to dig a place for it. Funny! if they had to send it back, it should be sent up – back to where it came from, not down. There was no sense in that. But…

'Naana!'

'Yesss!' Her mother's voice came low and irritable.

'Nana, it movin.'

The four women seemed to shoot out from the room together.

'What you sayin?'

Gigi rested a finger on the bundle. 'Watch, it belly movin.'

Miss Patsy took the bundle in her massive arms. They hustled back into the room. A sharp slap from Nana and it wailed a long, piercing baby-wail.

It must have been morning when Gigi walked out onto the

step, closed the door and pressed her back against it. Cee-cee
birds were quarrelling in the grapefruit tree. Laughter came from
the bedroom. She saw Cecil hurrying up the hill.

'She awright?'

'Who? Elaine?'

The young man nodded.

'Yep, I fink so.'

'An' – An'…'

'An what?'

'Lemme pass. I goin in.'

'You sleep?'

'Lil bit.'

'I didn' sleep!'

'Lemme pass. I want to see my woman.'

'You don want to know about de baby?'

'Lemme pass, nah, lil girl! Step aside before I…'

'You can't go in.'

'Is my girl.'

'Is a lil' girl.'

'I want to see my 'ooman. Move!'

'Nuh!'

'Why not?'

'Dunno – is – is ooman bizness.' She opened the door a crack
and quickly squeezed through it, shutting it in Cecil's face. She
crouched before the glowing coalpot listening to the voices in the
room, and Aya's song, softly sung, that always made her think of
sunlight.

SONG FOR SIMONE
For Peck Edwards

Every morning the soft bleating of a clarinet and the tinkling of a piano woke the town. At quarter to five for the past fifty years the music came wafting down from the hill above St. George's. It would pass like bubbles on the wind so that the silence became part of the melody.

It was always the same: the melody, then the silence that was music too.

As soon as it died, the cathedral clock on Church Street struck the hour.

Simone stirred on the fifth and final stroke and stretched her legs over the arm of the settee in the hall where her mother had relegated her – *You'z a big girl now. The bedroom too small for two.*

The girl opened her eyes and listened. Sure enough, there came the rumble of Togo's cart, trundling down her street – Togo, the funny ole fella who foraged among the bins before the trucks arrived to take the refuse away. The thunder of his wheels was fading when the trucks arrived with their usual bang and clatter.

Soon there would be cars going past, doors banging, feet shuffling in the rooms next door. On the Carenage below, the watchman's whistle would rise like a stricken bird, releasing the stevedores from their night shift.

Nita, her mother, came out and switched on the naked light-bulb that shared its light with the two rooms. Still heavy with sleep, she stretched and yawned, shaking herself as though angry at the lethargy of her limbs. There was a stirring in the bedroom, a grunt, the bedsprings protesting, then the scrape of feet on the concrete floor.

The girl did not like her mother's new man-friend. She'd decided that the moment he crossed the threshold the night before. But then, she'd never liked any of them – though she said she did when Nita asked.

'Come on, Sim! Get up, girl.'

With a deft movement, the girl was on her feet. She was as tall as Nita, slim as a whip and still growing.

Nothing disturbed Nita more than her daughter's height and what she called her 'strong complexion'. She couldn't account for it, she said, since she was not-so-dark and Sim's father was a regular-size, light-skin fella. *Must've been de weather o something.*

Simone busied herself with the small gas stove on the table near the settee, hearing, but not listening to Nita's girlish voice – a tone she'd learned to associate with the presence of a man-friend.

The girl worked swiftly, kneading the flour, breaking and rolling the dough into small balls, then flattening each before placing it in the pan of sizzling oil.

'No eggs dis mornin,' she grumbled. 'So, is de usual dry bakes an' milk. Good enough for de man. Not so good for me and me mother.'

The church clock boomed the half hour. Nita came out dressed for work, the man trailing behind. He avoided her gaze. She had that effect on people. She remembered her mother telling her once that her friend – it was Peter then – used to complain that Sim made him uneasy with those big dark eyes looking right into his head. Well, they *were* looking into his head. He proved to be a scamp after all – a married one, to-besides.

Only once did this man look at her – a frank, curious stare. The girl knew how fiercely her mother would attack him if she suspected the slightest hint of an advance in that look.

Her mother's fears grew even as Sim grew, warning her always of the same thing. First, it was to stay clear of boys; now it was men she had to beware of. Her mother no longer introduced her men-friends either. They came, stayed a while – some longer than others – then disappeared.

A frowning, serious fella, this one. He chewed the food as though he was thinking with his jaw. At least the others used to try to smile.

'You know anything 'bout music?' Simone asked, staring directly at him. She'd promised Nita she was never going to ask that question to any more of her men-friends. But there it was, a pusson couldn help it; it just popped out.

Nita was smiling.

The man took a long time swallowing. He swilled his tongue around his mouth, passed his hand across his lips and raised his brows at her. 'You call steelpan-music, music?'

'Well... erm – why not?'

'No-no-no! I want a straight answer. Yes or no.' He placed the rest of his breakfast on the table and rested both elbows on the surface. He'd clasped the fingers of each hand together.

'Yes,' the girl said, irritable now. 'S'far as I see, is music, oui.'

'Then,' the man said, pushing aside his plate. 'I'z a boss musician. I know all about it.'

Before plunging into the noise of rushing cars and work-hurrying feet in the street below, Nita turned and fixed the girl.

'James leave some change on de bedroom table. Buy some foodstuff when you come from school. Five dollars is yours for lunch. An' make sure none ov dem likkle boys or nobody interfere wid you or follow you from school. Don' cook nothing. I goin see what I scrape up by de ole birds. C'mon James.' And with that, they were gone.

Scrape up... Her mother always said that and she hated it. She scraped to make a living, to pay the rent and to send Sim to the Anglican school on Church Street. She bowed and scraped to keep her job as a domestic with Mr. and Mrs. McWiggin – the old couple who lived in the big cream house on the hill above them. It was from their house that the music came each morning to insert itself into the town's half-sleep.

To escape the rush and squabble of the tenants from the neighbouring rooms, the girl hastened to the shower outside – a long stem of pipe standing in a small enclosure of corrugated iron sheets. She stripped herself quickly and let the cold water fall on her, scrubbing herself with long luxurious strokes, wary of the eyes that might be fixed on her from the windows of the small dwellings crowding the alleyway.

There were so many things Nita didn't know about her. Her mother wanted to be told everything that happened at school. Wherever she wanted to go, Nita made it her duty to accompany her; else, she would have to remain home. The month before, she'd told her about the arrival of her periods. Nita did not react the way the girls at school said *their* mothers did. Nuuh… the blaastid woman come close to tears, an' she start talkin funny.

'Don't want you to do like me, Sim. Do me anything and I goin' take it, s'long as you give yuhself nuff time to become woman. Sometimes I wish you never grow up. Be glad to take care o' you for the rest of me life. When I was fourteen I had you. I don't regret, but it spoil me chances. If you was a boy I wouldn't mind so much.'

Then Nita kissed her and she was sad with her mother's sadness.

If she was a boy! How many effin times Nita goin tell her that? Eh?

Simone hummed while she washed. She knew every note, every nuance of the morning melody. Something was missing in that music. Every day for the past year she'd struggled to put her finger on it. T'was like sal'fish without salt; like dumplin that knead too soft and didn go *chic* when a pusson bite it.

Last year, during the Carnival, it was terrible. The clarinet and piano played all day, clashing with the chants on the streets below because the people on the hill had put it on loudspeakers. She barely slept that night, and when she did, she dreamt of clarinets and pianos lined upon on Market Hill in an all-out war with the calypsos and steel drums down below.

'Nita!' she'd begged, 'Ask dem people you work for, what is de name ov dat music they play every mornin.'

She knew now that it was called Minuet in G, made up by some ole fella who lived a long-long time before she and she mother born.

'High class music,' Nita said, as if working in the kitchen of Mister and Mrs. McWiggin made her high class too. 'Is real music. Classic music o' something. Dem ole birds been playin it for the past sempty years. Dem fadder an' gran'fadder used to play it. Dem uses to be gentry once – own a lot o' land and servants. Now dem have only dat big house and what their son send dem every month from Englan – jus' enough to keep their nose pointin up. De ole lady always talk about ole times as if she regret it ever change. She say she from pure Irish stock. But somewhere along the line a little nigger-blood creep in. You can't tell she that though. She'll drop down dead. De only blood she want to hear about is Irish. Like is a diffrent colour o somethin. Irish is de place where all dem white potato come from, you know.'

'I don' like no Irish potato,' Simone muttered.

'Is why you eat it so greedy,' Nita laughed.

Fortnights, Nita cursed the meagre sum the McWiggins paid her for washing them, feeding them and cleaning the big ole house. Occasionally, she blessed them for the food they allowed her to take home. She'd begun to worry because the old man was going blind – and dotish too, she suspected – and the old lady's legs were failing her. 'Dunno how I goin manage if I lose dem.'

Simone had never seen the old couple. Yet she felt she knew their faces, wrinkled like white raisins, their nagging voices calling – always calling Nita to lift them, lead them, clean them…

There was a name for it – if only she could remember the word. It had the same ring of the bell-tower on Church Street. On her way to school, it arrived jusso and perched in her mind: *Decline.*

Nita warmed the bowl of chicken, rice and mixed vegetables she'd brought from work. One of the usual power failures had thrown the town in darkness, giving the night outside a closeness that Simone liked. People talked. Cars passed. The night breathed.

The dirty light of the sputtering stove threw fat shadows across the room. Simone unwound her length till her legs jutted over the settee and waited.

'You like 'im?' Nita asked, without turning to look at her.

'Who?' The girl knew, but thought that she would ask.

'Him, erm, James.'

'Nuh. Don' think so.'

Nita turned. 'You never say that before with…'

'Them others?'

'Yes! You always like dem.'

'Dey was diffrent.'

'How?' Nita frowned at her.

'Dunno.'

'You goin like 'im, Sim. He really, really nice. I know 'im long time. I jus didn have no time for him, yunno. He serious; dat's all. Used to be a school teacher, and you know what school teacher face look like.'

'What work he doin now?'

'Gov'ment work.'

'Doin what?'

'Uhm.' Nita's face was a mixture of anxiety and confusion.

'You not tellin' me?'

'Is music he teachin.'

Her mother would have left it at that, but the girl went on, 'Pan-music, not so?'

'Something so.'

'So why you 'fraid to say it?'

'You say you don' like 'im.'

'It don' have nothin to do with that.'

'He comin' later.' Nita's eyes were pleading.

'Let 'im come then.'

They ate in silence. Nita sulked over the food. Simone chewed with pleasure.

She extended her arm and traced long, loving fingers down her mother's face, pausing briefly at her chin. 'Is nice food,' she purred.

Nita smiled back, a child's smile. 'Wash the wares,' she yawned, and went in.

Mr. James visited regularly. The McWiggins declined slowly. Nita worried increasingly.

Sometimes, the girl listened to her mother and the man talking long into the night. They laughed a lot. Their laughter even woke her on mornings, just before the minuet came sneaking down the hill to play on her mind for the rest of the day.

Early one morning, Mr. James got up to work on something he called his 'new arrangement'. He sat on the only chair in the hall. Through lidded eyes, Simone observed him mumbling over a jumble of lines and scratches on a sheet of paper. Occasionally he hummed, scratched the paper with his pencil, tapped his feet, then mumbled and scratched again. She recognised the tune. It was a calypso called 'Busy Body'.

The man stopped when the minuet started, cocking his head at the notes that came raining down on them.

'Ludwig Van Beethoven,' he breathed. 'Minuet in G. "G" as in Jeezan Christ. You travel damn far, man. Not bad. Not bad at all. It have some conviction there. But it come from de head. Not de heart.'

Simone sat up abruptly. 'You notice too?'

Mr. James dropped his pencil on the table, then swivelled on the chair to face her. 'What missin'?'

'Dunno.' The girl shook her head and dropped back on the sofa. 'Dunno. Just a feelin, dat's all.'

'Explain it, then.'

She threw him a suspicious look. But she saw he was not smiling. A long face, pleated forehead, a moustache that sat like a little black caterpillar under his nostrils.

'Well,' she said finally. 'To me is like food – nice food. You eat and eat as much as you want, but it never full you up solid-like. In the end you still left empty. It got the sauce but the dumplin missin, kind of.'

Mr. James grinned. 'Nice way ov puttin' it.'

'You know what missin, then?'

'Is not for me to say, Miss. Is for you to find out. You want to find out?'

'How?' she asked, her voice sullen, eyes bright with hostility.

Nita was standing at the bedroom's entrance, regarding them.

'Well, perhaps if you learn to play music – pan, I mean – you'll understand what buggin you. You talk like a person who have music in them. You ever hear about Calinagoes? Is my band; I arrange the music.'

He hesitated, threw a quick glance at Nita. 'The band-leader don't like girl-players, though. I could try to bust through his ignorance.' He took up his sheet of paper, folded it and rose. 'All I saying is, you couldn say what you just said if you didn have music in you.'

'You think so?'

'No,' Nita said.

'No what?' Mr. James cocked his chin at her.

'I don' want her mixin with all dem ramgoat who does play steel band.'

'That make me a ramgoat too, because I does play steel band. Not so?'

'I didn' say dat.'

'So you one ov dem too. I could find a lotta name for people who call us ramgoat. Why you don't let she decide for sheself?'

'I say, no! And it goin stay no.' Nita had raised her voice.

Nuff to wake up every dog in de place, Simone thought.

Mr. James didn't answer. He folded the sheet of paper, slipped it into his shirt pocket and strode out the door.

Simone soon realised that the man's temper could be just as scalding as her mother's, but he preferred to battle with Nita outside of her presence. His voice never rose above the confines of the tiny bedroom, though she could hear his rumble rising and falling like the waves on the Carenage during bad weather.

She followed the arguments by her mother's responses to the man's remarks. What did he mean by giving the girl a chance to find sheself? Afraid of what? It was easy for him to say she wasn helpin she daughter by tyin she down because *he* didn have no girl-chile to worry about. He had no right to ask her if she knew what Sim might be feelin 'bout all this. What? By limitin the girl she was limitin herself too? What de arse did he know? – sonova...

Nita must have hit him because Simone heard the thwack of flesh on flesh, then prolonged scuffling that ended abruptly in silence.

Her mother threw him out the next day, then became miserable in a way Simone had never seen before. She ate little, went to bed early and no longer complained about the ole birds on the hill. There were no new men-friends either.

Simone counted seven weeks before she decided she could no longer stand the gloom.

'Nita, he goin come back?'

'You want im to come back?' her mother said.

'Is up to you.'

'No-no-no, is not up to me! You think I should...'

'Sort of... Is up to you, Nita.'

'Is not up to me!' Her mother's nostrils flared. She was shifting her eyes from side to side. 'Is not up to me, y'unnerstan? You – I want *you* to tell me to talk to 'im.'

'Well, talk to 'im, then.'

Nita smiled. 'I never see a person selfish like you,' she said. 'Leavin everything up to me. No mercy! Dat's what! You talk like big woman who dunno how to advise people. No heart! I goin' sorry for yuh husband.'

Husband! Simone soured her face. Didn't want no husband. Not if they make a pusson so soft-an-chupid an crazy at the same time. Spoilin a pusson appetite for everything – like this Missa James gone an done to her mother. Mebbe that was the point of growin' up? To become all softee and weaky and cry-cry. She couldn't see the sense in it.

'He say he goin come back on one condition. I have to give you likkle more freedom – you should play pan if you want to, and explo' the world. Crazy talk if you ask me, because I never hold you back from explorin de worl', does I?'

'So you *does* see 'im?'

'Not really. I call 'im once-or-twice on de ole bird phone. Most time he not in office. He never does call back.' Nita sounded aggrieved.

'You done ask 'im to come back, not so?'

'What chupidness you askin me? I never answer no chupid-girl question.'

Simone raised a brow and stared at the light-bulb.

Mr. James returned and the two were laughing and arguing as though nothing had happened between them.

The man did not take Simone to join his band. He wanted to teach her the 'basics' first, he said. Nita should sit with them while he told them how and why steeldrums were made. At the end of his talk, the girl's head was buzzing with images of fire, gang wars, police, steel and blood.

'In other words,' he said, 'when you hear the sweet notes from a steelpan, you hearin love and violence turn music. The violence ain't finish yet, or the love.'

He tried everything to get girls into his band, but Moose, the bandleader, would not have it. They were recruiting new players for the Carnival just three months away. He'd proposed Simone.

'Problem is,' he scratched his nose and fixed his eyes on some spot above their heads, 'to get Moose interested I tell 'im a half-lie.'

'What you tell 'im?' Nita asked.

James lifted his shoulders and dropped them. He winked at Nita and smiled. 'I tell him that the girl in question not just a good player but the best tenor panist this side of St. Georges. She could even teach them a thing or two. I offer to bring she with me in six weeks.'

Nita cursed him until she was out of breath. He waited until she'd burnt herself out. Then he turned to Simone. 'Your mother got a temper. One day it goin' fly up to she head and kill she. Pay attention, girl, because I have just six weeks to make you the best tenor panist this side of St. George's.'

From then she recited chords: majors, minors, sharps, flats, sevenths and ninths. The man spoke of melody and phrase, of tempo, timing and attack till her head became a hive of jumbled words.

The girl had never felt so pushed in her life but at the end of the second week, beats took their places within bars, notes within phrases, phrases within melody – until she could listen to the minuet from the hill, dismantle it and toss it aside until the following day.

'Now take a look at this.' James placed a sheet of Bristol-board in front of her. He'd drawn a lifesize tenor pan on it. Had even coated the sides in silver paint, and like the real thing, the face of the instrument seemed to belly inward with the notes tapering down to the bottom. The man handed her two rubber-tipped sticks and ordered her to strike the notes. Nita giggled and Simone became numb with embarrassment.

'Shut up!' It was the first time he'd raised his voice at her mother. Nita muttered something nasty and sulked back into herself.

'Is a waste o' time,' Simone said, injecting as much sting as she could in her voice.

'Gimme!' James snatched the sticks from her and began tapping the drawing, humming the notes as he struck the paper.

The girl giggled. Nita's burst of laughter joined Simone's. Mr. James looked up, creased his forehead and began laughing too. He rested the sticks on the table, told them he was hungry and stepped out to the shop across the street. He returned with three tins of corned beef, condensed milk and a large loaf of bread. They feasted until sleep dragged them off to bed.

Each evening Simone returned early from school, tapped and hummed the notes. She learned to string together melodies and, to stretch herself, she wrestled with Beethoven's Minuet.

Mr. James taught her portions of 'Busy Body' and showed her

how to make runs and extemporise on themes. From time to time her mother would butt in when she thought something didn't 'sound right'. By then Simone could close her eyes and locate any note she wanted.

The six weeks passed. 'She not ready yet,' James said.

Nita told him to get off his magga-bone arse and take them to meet that Calinago Moose fella.

Calinagoes was a wide, open tin shed with two gas-lamps hanging from the rafters. It stood at the edge of Tanteen playing field. Inside was packed with steelpans of all sizes. Most were hung on stands of metal piping. At the back, the cymbals and high hats of a drum set glowed like full moons. Near the corners stood two sets of full-sized steel drums, six to each set, ranged in such a way that a narrow passage ran between them. Pans of intermediate sizes queued in neat lines in the centre of the structure. At the front were the shallowest instruments of glittering chrome.

Several young men were hanging out at the front of the shed with sticks in their hands. Their voices dropped to whispers when they arrived. Four girls were sitting with their heads together, on the grass at one side of the shed.

Mr. James left and returned with a sour-faced young man. He wore a sleeveless T-shirt, a red cap turned back to front. A gold tooth glimmered from his slightly parted lips. 'She the one?' he pointed at Nita.

'So what if is me?' Nita said.

'Is this young lady here.' James nodded at Simone.

'And you say she could play?'

'Boss, man.' James didn't sound sure of himself.

'You could play?' The young man rested deep brown eyes on Simone.

'She could play.' Nita said.

'I not custom to no girls in my…'

'We went through that already,' James cut in.

'I givin you a test,' Moose told her.

Simone followed the man on shaky feet. He led her to the big drums at the back.

Sensing the drama, the girls on the grass stopped their chattering, stood up and drew closer.

'Run something on this.' Moose pointed at a rusting tenor pan. Simone looked at the man, then at the pan. The light was weak in that corner of the shed. She bent over the instrument.

'Can't see the notes,' she said feebly.

'You need to see the notes?' Moose grumbled.

'Nuh... Not, not really.'

'Play then.'

She selected a note and touched it gently, humming as she was used to. She tapped each one, pulling her brows together when a couple refused to yield the expected sound.

Moose's voice blasted her ears. 'I thought you could play.'

The girl straightened up, the sticks pressed against her chest.

Mr. James rushed over. 'You can't see the pan not tuned? Is a condemned pan you give she.' He shook a finger at the row of shiny instruments up front, took Simone by the elbow and placed her before one of them.

'C'mon,' he whispered. 'Just relax and blast those buggers to pieces. O God, girl! You can't fail me now.'

Again she explored the surface of the pan. The notes rang true.

Tentatively, she began stringing the notes of a melody together. It trickled out of the instrument at first, became an easy stream, swelled and spattered in torrents around her.

She heard Nita's shriek of delight, looked up to see Mr. James, his body thrust forward in that way only Nita and herself would understand. He was telling her to attack. Now she felt strong and spiteful. She began teasing from the instrument notes that were bright and round and clean. Then with a flick of her wrists, she launched into 'Busy Body', holding down the rhythm with her tapping feet, and smiling.

One of the boys made his way to the congas at the back of the shed. The rhythm came in gently on her, then grew into a pulsing tempo that never rose above the tune.

She stopped abruptly and left the music hanging.

'We want her!' the drummer shouted.

Moose threw him an irritated look. 'Not bad,' he said.

'Not bad! She good!' One of the girls threw back.

'I take you for a couple months – on probation and if…'

Mr. James raised his head at Moose and squared his shoulders. 'Lissen, man. I can't tell you how to run your band. But if you decide to put this girl on probation, I finish with you, and I take my arrangement with me.'

'I like your arrangement, man.'

'That is not the issue now.'

'Okay, I decide to take she.'

'No conditions?'

'No conditions. Now all them little 'ooman going pressure me to join.'

'Is about time.' James turned his back on him.

The young drummer – he called himself Steve – followed Simone around the shed naming the different pans for her. 'You play in band before and you dunno the difference between cello, double-tenor, bass…'

'Me – I was too busy playin to learn all them names.'

James threw his arms around Simone's and her mother's shoulders and jigged them all the way home.

From then, the man talked only of Carnival and winning the Panorama competition with his 'Busy Body' arrangement.

They went to practice everyday except weekends. Occasionally, Nita tagged along, in worsening mood each time they returned home after midnight.

More and more, Simone found herself explaining combinations to her companions. But she could never please Moose. He accused her of adding her own colour to the tunes and lost his temper when the others said they preferred it.

They polished pans, welded new stands and added wheels to the floats that would carry the instruments along the road. She went often to the back of the shed to watch Steve on the six bass drums. The youth played every instrument in the band. On the bass drum he would throw his arms back and forth, drawing heavy, healthy music with two extra-large sticks tipped with rubber balls. It seemed impossible that a single person could play six drums at the same time, but the boy did it with joy.

'You like that boy,' Nita said.

'Which boy!'

'De ugly likkle kobo-face one who play dem drum back dere.'

'I tell you I like 'im?'

'Don't give me no rudeness!'

'I like to *see* 'im play, that's all.'

'You have yours to play, not so?'

'Tenor and bass different: them *look* different; them *sound* different!'

Mr. James stepped between them. She couldn't stop Simone now. That was what she was about to tell her mother. She couldn't. There would be trouble if she tried. And that was all.

'Something not right with you,' Mr. James said later that night. 'I feel it. You bring out dem notes with conviction and everything, but you not happy. When dem fellas play is like the water of life they bend over to wash dem soul in. They play as if pan is the world. But you – you find out what missin from the minuet? No? Well, I think I know the problem. We goin see.'

Mr. James put her on the bass drums on Wednesdays – the day Moose stayed home and left the band to him. The big six-pan bass fought her and drained her but she couldn't wait to return to them the following week.

Moose dropped in one Wednesday and caught her. He stood with his hands on his hips, his mouth half-open. He spent the rest of the night teaching Simone to keep up with a calypso version of Beethoven's Minuet in G.

'Busy Body' had finally become the band's own. They had given it shape and colour. The runs were glorious, shooting in bright cascades into the night, drawing crowds that would later become supporters of the Calinagoes tribe.

★

They were halfway through practising the road march when Moose shot a hand in the air and cut the music. He shouldered past the cluster of girls who came everyday now to watch her play. The bandleader stood over her, staring into her face. 'All dese people here think you playin great. Even you think so. Well I tellin you right now, you not. Bass is not dem six oil drum you beatin up. Anybody could do dat. Bass is what come outta you.'

He looked as if he was waiting for a retort from her. She said nothing.

'I see how yuh mother siddown on you an tie you up. I watch how she does fret you. All de things you want to say to she; everything you want to tell yuh teachers when dem downpress you...' He jabbed a finger at the drums. 'Dat is where you say it.'

He turned and went back to his pan. Simone laid her sticks on the drum and told Mr. James she wanted to go home.

He looked surprised. 'You tired? Pan don' make people tired... Not if they... Gimme a coupla minutes.'

She shook her head and left.

At home, she stretched out on the settee, closed her eyes and replayed in her head what Moose had said to her. They felt like the truest words she'd ever heard.

The following day she stayed home, laid back on the settee and stared at the ceiling. On the third day she returned to the band.

From that evening, the crowds began gathering at the back of the shed to watch her play.

'That whip-ov-a-girl – who happen to be my creation,' Mr. James said grinning at Nita, 'See how she makin big-people fight for space just to watch she kick-up-an-stir murder with she bass-line – how you feel 'bout that?'

Her mother, who'd come along with them, said nothing for a while and Simone sensed the hurricane beneath the quiet. She didn't want her daughter to play on no govment road with a whole heap ov jumping ramgoats round her, she said at last. Panorama

– the steelband championship – was alright with her. But not the
street jump-up.

Simone observed the sidelong look Mr. James threw at her –
the way his eyes narrowed and his mouth clamped down. He too
kept his silence.

Panorama came. Eight bands were lined up for the vast, floodlit
island that was the stage. Calinagoes was fifth in line. Somewhere
in the crowd Mr. James and Nita sat. The rivalry between the
bands was there in the smiles and the sheen of sweating faces.
Most bands had girl-players. Like her, they were dressed in the
colours of their band. Simone eyed them; they eyed her back.
Calinagoes had been losers for the past five years; they were
expected to lose again.

Before they wheeled on stage, Moose had gazed into their
faces. His eyes were red; he barely shifted his lips when he spoke.

'People,' he said. 'Don think about winning nothing. Just play
– for all them nights ov shapin and polishin James' arrangement.
All James' ole talk 'bout fire, steel an love – put that in de music.
Remember all de cuss I cuss y'all arse to do tings right and put dat
in the music too. And if y'all can't manage it, den play for de sake
ov pan, for what it done to y'all – for what it still doing. Jus play.'

Calinagoes played to win.

Calinagoes won.

It mattered little to Simone that the days after their victory was a
happy time for Moose and the others. Nights, she stared into the
darkness, fretting over the minuet like a dog with a plastic bone.

J'Ouvert morning, while the amplified music poured down on
the town, Mr. James walked the short distance to Market Hill with
her and Nita. Herds of revellers were pouring into St. George's.
Jab-jabs, coated in oil and charcoal, stomped and intimidated
throngs of sidewalk limers. The air shimmered and throbbed with
the colour and chant of Vécoup, Powder Mas and Wild Indians.
Ole Mass shuffled along with placards and props, scandalising
politicians and priests, ministers and neighbours while the ampli-

fied strains of Beethoven's Minuet wafted over everything, stopping only when the town withdrew to rest.

'The violence ain't finish yet,' Mr. James had said. 'Or the love…'

She'd wondered what he meant by that. The love was making sense; she understood that part. But the violence? She thought it was the bloodshed – the killing laws that had sought to abort the birth of pan music. Then she remembered Moose's resistance to her joining his band and her struggle for his acceptance. That was violence too, not so? And dat music from de hill – what de hell was that?

Carnival day, another row. Mr. James was shouting down her mother, and all the adjoining rooms had gone silent. As soon as he drew breath, Simone cut in, 'None o' you can't stop me!'

Mr. James stopped short and swivelled his head at her.

'Y'all don't leave me alone, I walk outta dis house and never come back.'

A shadow passed across her mother's face. She opened her mouth a couple of times, then turned her palms up at the girl. 'But Sim…'

'What kind o' modder you say you is – always tryin' to tie me down. Eh?'

Nita licked her lips and stared down at her feet.

'Okay,' James said, 'Is enough. We…'

'Gimme a chance. You always butting in when I talkin with Nita. Is the last day o' carnival and nobody goin' stop me joinin Nagoes. Why you always tryin' to stop me, Neets?'

Her eyes rested on her mother's face and she felt a rush of softness for her. But there were things she would no longer accept from her, or anyone else for that matter.

The girl turned and strode through the doorway. She heard Mr. James' quick footsteps behind her. She lengthened her stride.

The afternoon sun was hot on their necks when they prepared to roll. Busloads of masqueraders in glittering costumes passed along the Tanteen road.

It seemed as if the whole island was gathering its energy for the toss and tumble of late evening.

'Arrrigght!' Moose shouted. 'Remember we is a people's band – anybody could join us. Lissen to de strategy: we goin into the City silent. I don't want to hear a note from nobody till I say, go. And when I say, go, we hittin dem hard. We de-vas-ta-tin them, and is non-stop we playin till midnight.'

Moose turned to the crowd. 'Those of you who pushin the floats, remember: no fightin. De only war Nagoes makin today is with music. Any questions?'

'Yeh.'

'What happen now, Sim?'

'I wan't to make a request.'

'Make it, den.'

'On Lucas Street I want us to switch to Minuet.'

'Mornin music? You crazy.'

'We play it soca style!' she said.

'This is Carnival, yunno; is not…'

'Soca-style,' the girl insisted.

'Well.' A ghost of a smile crept across Moose's face. 'If erm, if de fellas – fellas, y'all want to play mornin music the last day o' carnival?'

The band nodded, grinning.

They chose a quiet corner of St. Georges to dry out after the hot haul across the Carenage.

Moose slung words at them in salvos till they were snapping to break loose on the town. The church clock boomed; Moose gave the order. The pushers dug their heels into the asphalt and the floats began to roll.

Crowds poured in behind them, became a shuffling, gyrating whirlpool that spilled onto the sidewalks and sucked in bystanders.

This madness that swelled her hands, demanding and receiving thunder from the six oil drums; this surge of blood and rage felt like a response to every question she'd ever wanted an answer for. Now ,Simone thought she understood Mr. James's word, *Pan never make you tired…*

Street lights came on, spilling a wash of yellow on the streets.

They'd been seven hours on the road, her body slicked with sweat, when they rolled onto Lucas Street. Above the heartbeat of the masquerading town, there came the amplified strains of the music on the hill.

Mr. James, his face glistening, looked up at her and nodded.

'Awwwrright,' he shouted. 'The song – the song for Simone.'

Moose relayed the call, the others took it up and passed it on; and for a moment a lull descended on the players. The eyes of the band were on her.

Moose saw her hesitation; his voice cut in. 'In this order, people: frontline first, then midrange; engine room follow; background come in last.'

Moose raised his cap and fanned his face. The gold tooth glimmered briefly. 'Okay, Simmy-girl, we got de instruments and de muscle, is for you to give de mood. Ready when yuh ready.' He turned back to his pan.

The girl took a breath, clenched her face, and beat a rapid tattoo with her sticks.

The steel-rims erupted; the kata-drums reacted; double tenors muscled in; then the rest piled on a dazzling succession of sounds.

Simone waited for the four-note bass and when it sounded, she gritted her teeth and rumbled in.

She began pounding out the rhythm in short, hot flushes; felt the faltering – a ragged wave of discordance – until Moose bellowed something and Calinagoes shifted gear. All hell broke loose in the crowd behind, and Simone stoked the pandemonium. The guitar pans were screaming, the steel-rims and the congas throbbing with a stammering outrage. Her six-bass and Steve's four-bass, belching thunder, Simone played with a tight-lipped, joyful abandon till the churchbell sounded the passing of carnival.

When they came to a halt in Market Square, she was surprised to see her mother with her arms around Mr. James' waist.

Moose came over, dropped a hand on her shoulder and made a show of fanning himself with the other. She soured her face at him, then grinned.

'*That's* what I mean,' he said. He drained his beer bottle, dropped it in the gutter and strolled off.

Togo's cart came and went; after him, the bin truck banged and grated until the sound of its engine faded. The church-tower struck the hour.

For the first time in her waking life the minuet did not come.

'They tired,' Mr. James said.

'Don' think so,' Simone said.

'You make for bass,' the man said. 'Moose say you de best. Bar none.'

Simone smiled and drew her knees up to her chin.

Nita left the house in a rush. It was mid-afternoon when she hurried through the doorway. She couldn't understand it, she wailed. She had prepared everything for them people to pass the holidays on deir own. Had to call de hospital, who didn even wan to send nobody becuz dem was recoverin from carnival. The old man was just there, sitting on the floor, crying and soiling himself, same as any child. He done gone right off his head. Didn't know where he was. And de ole lady…'

'I tink I know what missin from that music, Missa James.'

'Yeh?'

'I talkin!' Nita screamed.

'Me too,' James said. 'You was sayin, Sim?'

The girl stretched, yawned, 'De drum, yunno… blow down the flippin' erm… de flippin' erm, yunno…' Simone sighed. Her eyes drooped and stayed closed.

'What dis little woman sayin?' Nita asked.

James rubbed his face, stood up and yawned. 'Dunno about you, woman. But I wan to catch some sleep.'

2: DUST

LOOK WHO TALKIN

Nuh. Is a lie; is not so it happen.

The trouble didn start with Ambo and the boat. The trouble start with y'all – long before Ridley boy-child, Nimrod, come back from San Andrews and say what happen to his father.

He tell y'all that he walk the twenty miles to the prison on Edmond Hill. He say he climb the high stone wall, hang on to one of them iron pole that anchor the barb-wire fence on top of it and watch a man walkin his father to a post that bury in the ground. He talk about the cloth that they put over his father' face, he say he hear his father cussin an protestin when the hangman hand reach out and drop the rope around his neck.

And then Nimrod stop talkin. He was lookin up at y'all face and gulpin like a fish. And all the words that Ridley boy-child know, leave him, jusso. Words lef him for good, and to this day that same expression stay on Nimrod face. No way y'all could forget that. And if is forget y'all forget for true, is time that y'all remember.

A bright wet mornin it was. The night before it had a full moon – a blood-runnin moon because it red no arse, like a pusson eye that bust, and people almos stiflin from the smoke comin down from them burnin charcoal-pit on them hills up there.

Miss Evie was the one who talk to Nimrod. True, she was a tight-face ole machete of a woman. Sh'was short and hard like a wood-knot, but that mornin she show she had a soft heart, even if the softness give birth to terrible words.

She stoop down in front of lil' Nimrod, hold his face is her hands and look straight in his eye. 'Your fadder gone,' she say. 'He not comin back. Forget you ever know him, becuz rememberin will spoil your life. Rememberin goin blight you. Make yourself forget your fadder.'

She shake him hard, like if she want to empty his head of all them tings he just done see. Nimrod body was floppin soft and loose in Miss Evie hands as if he got no bones. Then Miss Evie clear she throat, wipe she eye and went back to she washin by the river.

Lookin at the boy standin dere amongst y'all, it didn have a pusson here who didn know that the child in Nimrod was dead. It got kill by what he see. And the thing that replace it was so strange and frightenin, it follow y'all to bed and take over all-yuh dreamin. It wake y'all up next mornin in a sweat, becuz it didn make no sense how, chupid-so, Ridley dead; how a man could be so tall-walkin and alive one minute, and swingin from a rope the next.

Funny how you fellas here don' want to talk about Ridley, and your wimmen refuse to forget him. Yuh see, wimmen round here quick to recognise a scarce ting when they see it. They realise straightaway that the world not full of man like Ridley.

He tall. He easygoin. He got beyootiful, rovin eyes and a smile that come generous and quick. Y'all wimmen use to love to watch him walk – with the promise of good lovin in every shift of his hips and shoulders. Uh-huh! Ridley was the kind of fella that make god-fearing, Christian wimmen sin demself jus by lookin at him step.

You fellas couldn figure him out. The only thing y'all know about Ridley is what y'all see. Was like if he got no history past the fact that he come from the north with his one boy-child, no woman trailin after him. He rent a lil place by the beach, go snorkelin along the shoreline every mornin and bring back just enough fish to feed himself and his son. When a pusson ask him where he from, he point up past them hills and shake his finger. He never pick no argument with nobody, and he always with his boy-child. They laugh a lot; they hold hands when they walkin. Sunday evenins, when they comin back from catchin crayfish up the river, every woman raise she head and drop what she doin, just to watch Ridley returnin home, strollin in the middle of the road, whistlin some lovely tune, with Nimrod curl up fast asleep in his arms. As y'all know, the sight of a fella motherin his son so shameless and tender is a wundaful ting to wimmen in these parts, and a fuckin embarrassment to fellas like y'all.

Y'all couldn' take it. That's the truth. Nothing in y'all life prepare you for a man like Ridley who, jus by bein himself, make y'all feel worthless. It happen before and it goin' happen again that a beyootiful man, who find himself 'mongst other men, is a provocation. Is a big insult to the ordinariness of y'all self, even if that fella arrive holdin the hand of his one boy-child, build his house with his own two hand, and never pass a glance at all them wimmen who throw him sweet-eye while they goin about their business. Leasways, Ridley ignore dem, in the daytime for sure – since a pusson can't vouch for what might happen nighttime. But like ole people say, if you didn see it happen, then it never happen. If everybody live accordin to that one commandment, they never goin have no problem in life.

But no! Not Ambo. Everybody know that Ridley neighbour, Ambo, never like him. School-chilren used to say Ambo so damn ugly, even ugliness embarrass to associate with him. Accordin to them chilren, his forehead take up most of his face and god plant his eye too near his temple. But yunno school-chilren! They see somebody they don' like and they multiply everything they notice by ten.

To make a long story shorter, Ambo see the way Ridley draw the warmth out of his woman, how the sight of him make 'er drop she voice soft-soft. He hate the fuss she make over Nimrod and couldn stand the brazenness in she laugh whenever Ridley pass by.

Mek it sufficient to remind y'all that eleven months later, Ambo woman make baby and Ambo say the colour of the infant not his. He say the shape of the baby foot not his either, and the hair too soft to belong to him.

Is after all that come to pass that we kin talk about Ambo and the boat, becuz, regardless of all the hate that Ambo hatin Ridley, and the furrin-lookin baby that he tell his woman is not his – all that might've pass as nothing if Ridley didn build himself a boat.

Remember the boat? It didn have no name. A beyootiful thing.

A red-an-green twenty-footer, with a blue storm-bird on the prow where the name should be. Deep keel, yunno! A high bow and a new five-horsepower Seagull engine to push it ahead of him.

What refuse to cross y'all mind when Ridley start fishin was that some people got a gift for it; they got a natral intimacy with these waters. It go deeper than all the learnin-an-experience in the world. Was true that when Ridley rest his right hand on his tiller, it behave like it got a mind of it own. Some of y'all say was obeah. Ole people, who smarter than y'all, believe was Yemanja – the woman of the livin waters sheself – who watch that smooth-skin, sugarcane of a man and favour him. She guide him to the most unlikely places in the sea. First time, y'all laugh at him until Ridley beach his boat with more fish than a sensible fella could wish for.

Remember them days y'all come back empty and, couple hours later, y'all see Ridley returnin low in the water, laden with whatever the sea decide to offer him?

And is what the sea used to offer Ridley: yellow-fin tuna and mahi-mahi thicker than a man' waist; grouper almos the size of his boat. More coevally, big jacks and bonito than he know what to do with. What he couldn sell, he give away. He never forget the ole people that y'all neglect or dem half-starve chilren who parents too damn proud to beg. Used to fill-up y'all woman cocoa-basket to the brim with coevally and flyin-fish.

But yunno, sometimes givin is insultin. It stiffen pride. It make a fella feel small in the eyes of his woman and his chilren when the man next door – who doin better – offer him someting. And is jusso that envy does turn round and murder gratitude.

And Ambo – the fella might be ugly, but he not chupid. Give him that. Ambo know eggzackly what goin on inside y'all heart, becuz he feelin it too and he feelin it worse.

In the evenins, in the rumshop, when the catch was magga and the drinkin make y'all head giddy, Ambo raise his voice. He want to know what make Ridley Bowen different from everybody else. What make him feel he better than the rest of you? What make him think he is Christ – givin away fish like he lookin for disciple? How come Ridley is the only one to bring back a full boat every

time? That normal? That natural? Eh? Specially since everybody
know that fishin is a gamblin game an' God always have the upper
hand. Weather is God mood, not so? And nobody kin change God
mood unless that pusson got dealins with the devil.

Ambo take y'all mind back to the week Ridley launch his
boat. That was when Miss Ellie pass away. True, the woman was
ole when she dead – a pusson couldn deny that – but Ambo want
to know how come she pass 'way on the very same day that
Ridley launch his boat. He ask if y'all sure is not her soul that
Ridley sell to the devil, so he could empty the sea of fish.

He sit down there, chippin away at y'all feelins of wutlessness,
sharpenin y'all suspicion of a stranger who come from somewhere else.

But to give credit, you fellas was harder to budge than Ambo
expect. Why so? Becuz every one of you worried about what you
might be knockin out of place if y'all lay hands on Ridley. Becuz
the sight of him walkin with his sleepin boy-child on Sundays
give him anchorage in the heart of every woman in this place. And
like y'all learn later, ain' got nothing in the world more frightenin
than a bunch of hurtin women.

In the end, of course, Ambo didn need y'all because a touris-
fella give him what he want. The touris-man was headin for
Suhtyez along this road in a lil open jeep wiv a camera sling
around his neck and restin on his big fat belly, like his belly was
a shelf. Nobody didn pay him no mind when he stop on top of
High Rise to point his camera at someting out there on the water:
a boat p'rhaps, one of them lil islands out west, or just the blue of
the sea on a ordinary day. Touris-man didn notice the drop to the
water coupla inches from his flip-flop slippers, cuz all dem bush
and vine and high grass rise up to the edge of the cliff and hide the
danger.

Ridley see the touris-man slip and fall over. He was comin in
at the time, laden as usual with fish. He turn his boat and head for
the rough water at the foot of the cliff. He drag the man out and
call for help.

Like y'all know, it was on the news next morning. Opposition

politician blame the govament for makin the roads a deathtrap and
mashin up the island' only source of income. Govament turn round
and blame y'all for not puttin up no sign explainin the danger.

And Ambo – Missa Ambo point his finger at Ridley.

When dem policeman reach here with notebook and walkie-
talkie, Ambo swear the white-fella was alive an happy and talkin
when Ridley bring him to the beach. It was the way Ridley drop
the fat fella on the sand that break his neck.

Y'all stand up there and watch them arrest Ridley and take him
away. Nobody say a word. Nobody open their mouth to say, boo!
Not one ov y'all say, No officer, is not so it happm. Make it worse,
y'all shut up your wimmen and chilren, sayin if they draw a single
breath to talk, is cut-arse and bust-mouth they goin get from you.
Why so? Becuz some of you stupid enough to believe that when
Ridley gone, all the big-fish in the sea goin turn round and start
jumpin inside y'all boat.

So right now, ask y'all self this question – is who kill Ridley? Eh?

What y'all didn realise at the time was that truth got teeth. It
does rise up and bite yuh on y'arse real hard when you least
expectin it. Is eggzackly what happen between y'all and Ambo.

After Ridley gone, y'all still acceptin Ambo offer of a drink or
two. Yuh even ask him for the details of his testimony in court; the
big words them lawyers use to trap-an-condemn Ridley Bowen;
the look on the face of the judge and jury when the hammer fall.
Yuh even tell him thanks.

How long it take before Ambo make his move on Ridley boat?
Coupla weeks? A month? None of y'all remember?

Well, was three weeks and three days eggzackly. Is true to say
that none of yuh here go near the boat. It sit on the water of the
foreshore, clean and new-lookin as the first day Ridley launch it.

But Ambo – hm! – every mornin he come out, he glance at the
craft before liftin his face at the horizon. Every day he take one
step nearer. He busyin himself with twine or the bamboo frame
of his fish-pot. He layin out his fishin rods on the sand and
inspectin dem. Little by little, he find himself at the edge of the
water. And all the time he talkin to himself, but loud enough for

people to hear him. Is a cryin shame, he say, that a decent boat like that jus lyin dere on the water, wastin.

He get no answer, not even when he drop his tackle on the deckin of the bow and lef it there. Next few days, his bait-hold and two empty kerosene can on the seat. Coupla days later his canvas bag and a can of petrol lyin in the belly of the boat.

Nimrod, Ridley son, watchin him with his two dead eyes.

People laying down in bed one night when they hear the engine chuckle. It run for seven minutes and three seconds and then cut off.

'Just checkin tings,' Ambo say next day in the rum-shop. He order a bottle, take a handful of glasses and pour each of y'all a drink.

'I'll take her out tomorrow,' he say. 'Just to see how good she workin. I hate to see a good boat goin to waste.'

Then you, Squingy, your voice come across the room. 'What about the lil boy?' you say. 'What bout Ridley boy-child?'

That make Ambo rest his glass on Barry counter and turn around to face you.

'What about him?' he say. Ambo voice full up the whole shop, and a pusson wouldn be surprise if it travel right across the beachfront. He lookin at them rum glass in y'all hand as if he want to snatch them back.

'Lil fella useless,' he say. 'Soft as shit. Ridley make a girl of him! And besides, I work for that boat. I save y'all from Ridley. Is me who give witness in court. Squingy, you sayin I didn earn that boat?'

And you, Squingy, you raise yuh head and say, 'Naah, man, Is agree that I agreein wiv you. I jus sayin what you say yuhself, Ambo. You work damn hard for the boat.'

Ambo blow his nose; he show y'all his teeth and buy another bottle. All the time he talkin fast-fast-fast. 'Is not as if I got a hard heart. Squingy, you right, the lil boy didn do me nothing. Ridley was the criminal, not he. Even if the Bible say when you don't like the fadder, you mustn' like the son, I got nothing against the lil boy. I goin take care of he.'

S'far as Ambo concern, takin care of Nimrod mean restin a lil fish near his foot at the end of every trip.

Ridley boy-child didn refuse the fish. He didn take it either. Instead, he bring his face down towards the dead mud-mullet, take one of dem flat nail that lil boys round here does carry, and he run the sharpen tip from the gills right down to the tail. He stoop over it for hours like if the lil fella searchin for some kind of answer in the insides of the creature.

Was the sight of that lil boy stoopin over a stinkin mullet that make y'all women see blood. S'matter of fact, that's not true! From the time y'all lock up their mouth with the threat of a good cut-arse, them gone underground. They start runnin conference over them basin of clothes they washin in the river; they makin conversation with their hand and eye and waist – with their mouth push out long-long-long and stiff like cocoa-rod. Uh-huh! They holdin plenary in the fish-market without a single word passin between dem. Is dangerous when forty woman bring their head together over a single basket of jacks, drop their voice soft and start slidin the whites of their eyes at each other, fas'-fas'-fas' like fish.

And once them reach consensus, the pressure start on y'all arse. Was a mystery how dem get so forgetful overnight, not so? Dem wash y'all clothes, but never remember to use soap or to hang them out. No salt in y'all food, or food too salt. No seasonin in fish. No sugar in tea cuz dem didn remember to buy none. A whole pot of oil-down gone sour soon as it done cook. Make it worse, all of dem start sufferin from cripplin headache, specially when nighttime come. And they could only find ease from the pain by sleepin on the floor. By demself!

Men think they smarter than women? Joke! Watch how women does use their brain – and learn! Cuz y'all couldn take it. Two weeks wasn up and y'all surrender. You fellas give up long before y'all even realise it was a fight. Because if y'all have a choice between God and y'all nighttime comfort, God lose every time, far less ugly Ambo.

As for Ambo, it take a while before he notice the hardenin around him. Women buy fish from him only when the others couldn supply, and they get vex when he offer extra. No more slap on his shoulder from the fellas. Ole-talk stop soon as he enter the doormouth of Barry rumshop, and all man full up their glass before Ambo could offer them a drink. Then the chilren stop hearin him when he greet them. One evenin, the woman he livin with say she takin the baby to see she mother, and he never see the woman and the baby again.

Like a jumbie umbrella that spring up on a heap of manure overnight, it come to Ambo mind, sudden so, that no matter how loud the world is, a whole heap of silence surroundin him. He didn want to believe it, but the feelin stay. That feelin stick-an-settle quiet-quiet like the barb of a hook that sink so secret in the flesh, a pusson hardly know it there until, jusso, it start to hurt.

And y'all remember how Ambo try to fill that silence with his voice? He keep remindin y'all of the murderer that Ridley was; the disgrace that sonuvabitch from wherever-he-come-from bring down 'pon dis lil fishin village halfway up the coast. It was even on the news, he say, not so?

Nobody say nothing. No matter what he say, nobody answer him.

As the weeks unroll, Ambo take his talkin to the steps of every house, his voice gone dry and high and cry-cry. And still nobody answer him. People went about their bizness as if Ambo wasn there.

Is a hard ting that: when you exist in your own skin and you always know that, but then you find out nobody else kin see you. It start makin you wonder if you real, and you'll do anyting to prove it.

Mebbe that was what push Ambo onto the public road, in a fever of words, takin his story to strangers first, then to anyting that move.

Now look at him! Look at him across there! Gone thin and hard like Dry-Season; stand-up on the edge of the same precipice the whitefella fall off.

Talkin – always talkin. Like he can't stop himself. Makin a whole heap of ruction on that hill.

Arguin his arse off with the wind.

DE LAUGHIN TREE

When the white man tell Granny she stupid, she didn give im back no forward answer. She didn even cuss im afterwards an call im no sand fly, no beke, no big guts, half bake so-and-so from Englan. No red-arse, no lobsterface, no bleachout nothing. I tell meself it wasn fair, cos if was me dat even raise mih eyelash too fast at she, she would ha grab de palette by de door, and right after, I would ha been rubbing mih skin an bawling.

I tell meself dat mebbe she tired becos this quarrel with Missa Coleridge start off long time. Long before my mother leave me with Granny an say how she goin to Trinidad to make a livin, and she goin send money and after a little time she goin send for me. I still waitin, like I waitin for Granny to put some words in Missa Coleridge tail. Nobody never talk to my Granny like dat an get away, jusso. People always comin an askin if we want to buy someting: provision, fish, sweetie, even costlymetics from de Avon lady, and once a man come offerin to sell a little donkey and Granny ask him what she want with a little jackass – ain't he think it have nuff jackass round here arready? De man ask if she talkin bout sheself. I sure he still regret it, becos she tell im a couple tings dat make im look like he wish he never born.

Now I never fraid to put some serious wud in Missa Coleridge tail meself, specially when my granny wasn goin to do it. People always tellin de ole lady how I rude, but if is one time I feel glad for mih rudeness was when dat white man tell my granmother how she stupid. BIG PEOPLE does get away with too much freshness, jus' because dey feel dey BIG. In fact, if it wasn for Granny palette, and de fact dat BIG PEOPLE does tell she all de tings I does say back to dem, and dat I got too much mouth, it have a lot o time I does feel to put some serious wuds in BIG PEOPLE tail. I does want to ask if dem have myopia, if dem arthritis reach up in dem eye an dem cyah see dat is a little mouth I have. Cos I like to put wuds, specially for people who talk to me as if I is deir child, as if I don't have no mother, just because she gone away an never send for me – though sometimes, when Granny vexin over my mother never writing, I does feel to put some wuds to my mother, too – only in my head, cos Granny wouldn like it.

I 'member de first time Missa Coleridge come he was grinnin all over he face. He tell she how everybody done sell out deir little piece over de sea – as if she didn notice – and seein dat all she friends gone to a nicer place down by de Chichiree, near de swamp, didn she think dat was a good idea to go an live wid dem?

Granny kinda smile an tell im no, she didn think so. Missa Coleridge get red. Although h'was red arready, he get even redder like cook crayfish. He didn say nothing more. He just pull off he white canvas hat an start to fan he face real fast. Den he walk off.

Now de same way I does look at a sky an know when rain makin up to fall, I know was trouble coming. Granny know dat too cos even if she didn batten up de window an look up at de roof to make sure dem hole up deh plug good, she mouth gone tight and she eye turn flat an dark, as if all de battening happenin inside o she.

'Ku-Kus,' she say (is how she does call me, an I not suppose to tell nobody why), 'Ku-Kus, go bring de grip, come, gimme!'

I go. I put it on de floor.

'Open it.'

I try. 'I can't open it, Granny. It tight.'

'Rudeness is all you good for,' she say in a frettin kind o way. I notice how she hand tremble. Was a shakin dat start from she shoulder and work itself all de way down to she finger. Dat worry me. She not de kinda o pusson you kin make tremble easy.

She straighten up as much as she back allow, and look at me an say, 'Feather,' (dat's another name she does call me, an I not goin to tell nobody why), 'Feather, don't ferget about yuh mother, jus because she ferget about we. But yuh have to tell yourself dat she never goin write we, an she never goin send for you.'

Was sad I feel, not for meself but for Granny. An I put some wuds to meself an say, 'Ku-Kus, Granny damn right to bring dat palette to y'arse sometimes, even when you think you don't deserve it, cos you does ferget how hard she try with you. Ent she does send you to school? Ent she does give you a piece o meat same size as she when she cook an sharin food? Ent she does sew up dem hole in yuh clothes, even if she finger tremblin an she could hardly see? Ent? So, Ku-Kus, why you does give er so much trouble, EH?'

I was puttin dem wuds to meself while Granny was lookin at me in a serious kind o way. Same time de grip open, an it let go de nicest smell I ever smell. Ain't got no nicer smell in de world dan cinnamon an sandalwood an camphor, an a whole heap of ole time smell mix-up. Dat's how Granny grip did smell.

'Feather,' she say, real serious, 'it have a lot o different way to fight. When I had strength in mih body, I was strong as any man. Ask yuh granfadder, who try to hit me once. He could never use dat hand de same way after. Trouble was, after dat, I had to do all de hard work. Ask im.'

Was a lot o tings to ask my granfadder. Trouble was he done gone an dead long before I born. De first time she ask me to ask im something, I take she serious and start looking about de house, even under de bed to see if he was hidin there o something. Dat was de first time I make she laugh so much. 'Chile, how you chupid so?'

'Open dis,' Granny say. She hand me a yellow piece o paper dat fold-up small, like nobody was never intend to open it. When I open it, it had a drawin on de left-hand side on top, an a pretty piece of string dat stick to a red round ting on de paper, like a big drop o blood dat mix up with candle wax an harden. I never see a piece o paper dat look so serious. If paper was priest, then this would ha' been de Pope. Not even Granny big leather Bible did look so serious.

'What dat is?' I ask she.

'Read it,' she tell me. Now Teacher always tell me how I is a boss reader, an is mosly because I interested in puttin wuds to people who fret me up. Dat is de only way dat I could answer back BIG

PEOPLE an don't get a taste o Granny palette for mih rudeness. Like when Missa Jojo shout at me for bathin naked below de standpipe by de road, an call me a shameless little so-an-so. 'Nutting obnox- ious o anonymous, o even obstreperous about havin de benedic- tion of water on meself, Missa Jojo, sah,' I say, an I went on bathin, like if he wasn dere.

He open he mouth, but he didn have no tongue to give me back high quality, bigtime wuds. I smile because I did put de benedic- tion in deliberate, just in case he tell Granny, because was a word dat Pastor does use all de time in church, an everybody know dat it mean niceness, o someting close to dat.

But! Dat paper was different. It write like how Moses in de Bible would ha write. Anyway I start to read:

In the name of God Amen.

I, John Munchford, in the Parish of St. Albans on the 30th day of October 1904, Anno Domini, being weak of body but of sound and perfect disposing mind and memory, praised be God, bequeath unto Ursula Auguste Jameson a plot of land measuring half a hectare squared, the which begins at Hill Cray Rise and proceeds northwards towards the adjoining estate of Carl Strong, said land having no agricultural merit and ceded by myself in lieu of and in recognition of thirty years service as maidservant in the employment of the Munchford household.

It is also hereby deemed that the Inheritor of the aforementioned property becomes henceforth sole proprietor of said and shall have the powers vested in herself by law to bequeath or dispose of said property as she deems fit.

John Munchford.

When I done read, I look at Granny an say, 'And den it have some big-time scrawl, like if somebody wrap up a piece o wire, drop it in a bottla ink an den press it on de paper.'

'What it say?'

'Is a signicha. It not s'pose to say nutting.' Same time I tell meself dat I must practise to write me name just like dat.

'Nuh. De paper what it say?'

'I jus done read it for you,' I tell she. An I start scratchin mih ears, which I does always do when I little bit embarrass, cos I could see dat Granny wasn satisfy at-all. An I wasn neider. I damn vex dat people could be so boldface as to write down a whole heap o wuds on serious paper an I couldn understand dem. As if dey want to make a fool o me in front my granmother.

'It say someting bout land,' I tell she, 'land an property.'

Well… I figure it have to say someting serious and it could only be dat she own de place. Besides, nobody didn have no doubt dat *was* she place – till Missa Coleridge come an say she have to sell, an ask she iffen she really own it.

'I sure it say so, Granny. We definitely own dis property an land. Perhaps.'

Now de time dat man tell Granny dat she stupid wasn de first time he come. De first time he was smilin. Wasn a pretty smile. I notice de yellow teeth an how dem thin little lips pull back over dem, but he speak polite and proper. He touch de brim o de white sailor cap he wearin an say, 'Evening Maam,' an Granny say, 'Evenin, suh.' He say, 'How're you today?' Granny say, 'I awright thank you. De little ramatism does bother me sometimes, but I survivin by de grace o de Almighty.'

De man smile an brush he shortsleeve white shirt. I vex becos I feel dat Granny coulda find some prettier wuds to answer with. She coulda tell he dat she not complacent an she aint got no botheration, dat she was of a salubrious constitution an feelin damn well good with it. But no, she tell im bout she ramatism!

'Nothing grows here, I see,' de man say. 'Not good for gardening, is it?'

An yunno, someting happen when he say dat; I look round me an was like it was de first time I see de place; dat de only ting dat grow was mint grass dat was brown an parch like asham, and a whole heap o cochineel dat nobody could use for nothing except to wash dey hair. I see dat de hill we livin on was dry an white like flour. We was plant between de big wide sea in front and de Chichiree swamp behind, an de only ting dat conneck we with de outside world was one little dust road dat go right down to de pretty pink beach below.

'Is de will o de Lord,' Granny answer. Dat fret me, but I didn say nutting.

Missa Coleridge didn smile dis time. He jus walk back to he car.

Next time he come he look a lot more serious. By dat time everybody know dat he want to buy up de place, an everybody was preparing to sell real quick, cos was a lot o money he payin.

But Granny tell im no, De Lord was takin care of her well enough, thank yuh. Missa Coleridge look at she as if she mad. Dem turkey wrinkle dat hang down below he neck get kind o purple and even more wrinkle-up, an he hand agitate. He look at she an den he look at me, cos I was in de yard pretendin dat I was sweepin. Den he look at she again an say, 'D'you expect me to accept that? Everybody's sold up. They were glad to have the money. Your government even undertook to move your houses for free! What reason have you got for not moving with your people?'

Granny didn answer. I look at de man under me eye and it occur to me he had a point. Since he change de way dat place look for me, I didn like it no more. All my friends done move. Dem mother and fadder had money dat Missa Coleridge give dem. Some o dem was even buildin concrete house. So how come Granny gettin on so foolish?

'Maybe the child has something to say about this?'

Now, ever since dat man start comin, he never once see me. Now he want me to say someting an make contrary with my Granny.

I look up quick. De man smile at me. I look at Granny. She didn look as if she was payin me no mind. In fact, I feel as if she was encouragin me. So I put down de broom an I wipe mih mouth an say: 'Granny doesn got de dispositioning to concur wid nobody proposition.' De man look at me as if I hit im. Wuds, I tell you! Dem is wunderful! I thought de man was goin to fall, but he push up he chest an say, 'My Gawd!'

Well dat make im leave de yard very quick, and I thought dat dem wuds o mine goin make us see de last of im. But a coupla weeks after, he come back and call my granny stupid. Like I say arready, something tell me dat it wasn goin to end up easy. I could see dat Granny know dat too becos dat same night, after she put back de serious paper, she didn sleep at all. Or if she sleep it was like dem boat I use to watch fightin to cross de bad water near Goat Point. In all my time wid she, my granny never toss and groan so.

Dat night I wonder bout everyting. What my mother was doin in Trinidad? Mebbe she had a husban now and I had brothers an sisters I didn know. Mebbe she did never like me and did decide from de start dat she wasn goin send for me.

Granny get quiet close to mornin. I suppose she must ha fall asleep. But not me. All dat thinkin wouldn leave me alone. An when I get tired thinkin, I find meself lissenin to, well, de worl. De night was like a pusson out dere rubbin 'imself against de house. I could hear de sea, too, like a million ole people quarrellin mongst demself. An de wind dat pass across de galvanise was a gadderin of ghosts dat makin church above we head. But it didn' frighten me, cos I had Granny close, and nothing never frighten me when me an Granny lay down close.

Before I fall asleep, I member de las ting dat she say to me. 'Feather,' she say. 'Is tired dese ole bones tired. Dem see too much in dis life arready. All dem wan to do is rest. Feather,' she say. I didn answer but I lissen. 'You tink dis lan useless for true?'

She always tell me dat I mus never lie for she, an if I have to lie it must be only to protect meself. So I didn lie. 'Yes, Granny,' I say.

'Why?' she say.

'Cos everybody sell dem own an gone to live cross by de swamp, an Paula fadder goin to buy a Lan Rover, an Grace say she mother goin sen she to Englan to study history when she get big; an Teereez say she gettin a big big dolly for Chrismas and she goin travel round de islan an write everyting down dat people say, an Jacob say is only we dat stupid an'...'

'Ku-Kus?'

'Uh?'

'You say teacher say you bright?'

'Yes, Granny, cos I know big wuds.'

'Well answer dis: if dis property so wutless, how come de Mister want it so bad, an nobody didn know it wutless till he start to tell dem so?'

Yunno, I never thought o dat! Dat never cross mih mind.

'Ku-Kus?'

'Gran?'

'S'pose I say dat it have a whole heap o tings big wuds can't teach you.'

'What about dat paper? Is dat paper dat make Missa Coleridge can't touch we; an is dem big wuds self dat make it so.'

'Is not de big wuds, is what de big wuds mean. All it mean is dat dis piece o land belong to me fair an proper. An look how easy dat is to say. De people who write dat paper jus too damn show off an pretenshus.' An she laugh kinda dry an funny. I didn like dat laugh at all, specially becos she was lookin at me as she was talkin. Den she face get serious. 'I hardly got de time to see de endin o dis fight. Is ole yuh Granny gettin ole.'

I tell she dat I know how to fight, and if was stone she want me to stone dat man, next time he come is stone I glad to stone im.

'Nuh,' she say. 'If yuh stone im, den we lose. With people like dat is a different kind o fight yuh have to fight. Not like we does fight, an not like how dem does fight.'

'How den?'

'You mix dem, Feather. You mix dem an make a different way.'

'I don unnerstan.'

'Patience, chile.'

An yunno, is a long, long time after dat I realise dat she did give me de answer right deh.

Is when Missa Coleridge come back and she ask me to show im de paper, but don let im touch it, dat tings really turn sour. Granny tell me afterwards dat nutting in Missa Coleridge worl make him prepare for people like we to refuse him anyting. It have people who tink dem own everyting, like if dey entitle to it long before dem even born. Dem teach deir chilren to believe someting is deirs even before dem know what ownin mean. Dat for people like we to tell dem no is worse dan steppin on dem big toe, o spittin in dem eye.

Is a belief dat dem born inside of – same way dat a fish o tadpole does born surround by water.

Mebbe dat was why Missa Coleridge get on like dat when I point de paper in he face an show im de stamp an de candleblood.

De man blow like a lambi shell, tellin we how we silly, how we is ignoramus (I write dat down); how Granny cantankerous (I write dat down too); how we obstructin progress; how de govment give im rights an we humbuggin dem rights; how he wish we little chicken coop of a house fall down an kill we (yes he say dat!); an how it ain got nobody who goin help we when we dead, jus wait an see. An if we tink dat we goin spoil he plans, we go soanso see!

I get so vex I nearly put some wuds on he, but I member what Granny tell me, an it sort o throw cold water on mih tongue, so I constraint mihself.

Nex day Granny send me to call Missa Jojo.

'Joseph,' she say, 'I want you to get me a laughin tree.'

Missa Jojo laugh. But me, I wasn laughin, becos I hear bout all kinda tings dat trees does do, but I never hear bout no tree dat does laugh. Missa Jojo laugh again an tell she, yes.

When he leave, Granny rub she chin an say to me dat she sorry she insult de man who try to sell she de little donkey, dat she shoulda buy de creature, cos she goin be needin a lotta manure.

I didn know what I did expect Missa Jojo to bring for Granny, but it definitely wasn what he pull out from he jola bag an pass over to she so secret secret. A stick. A little piece o nothing. I was well disappointed and I make sure I show it. To mek tings worse, Granny walk round de house and den de boundary o de land for a whole day before she jook it in de ground an leave it dere. Den she have de boldface to call me an tell me dat is my responsibility to water it an manure it, an whatever happen to she afterwards, I mus never root it up, an never let nobody touch it. An even if she dead an gone, she goin be watchin me to make sure I care dat stick. I don tink I ever see my Granny look so serious before.

A lotta tings begin to happen straight afterwards. Dat question dat Granny ask me bout why Coleridge want de lan so bad sort o answer itself for me. First ting, a whole heap o truck arrive with sand an gravel an drums o tar. An den a bulldozer wit caterpillar wheel come. After dat a stone leveller arrive to keep it company an mek a whole heap of noise in people head.

An yunno! De same people who uses to be we friends, who Coleridge send off to live in de swamp, dem same people come out with shovel an tray an start widenin de dust road an pouring tar an gravel, an cookin, an eatin lunch by de road. An soon de road wasn a dust road no more.

Missa Coleridge used to stan up in de selfsame road mongst all dem people an point he quail-up red finger at my granmother an say tings, an dem people who used to be we friend, who used to borrow a pinch o we salt, an a cup o we sugar, dem selfsame people used to laugh with im.

Mornins after waterin de tree, I goin to school wit me little hanbag an mih lunch in me Dano pan and dem lookin at me an shooshooin mongst demself an laughin. Grace fadder always askin me how is de ole lady, but I never answer he cos he have a kinda grin in he eye, which I didn like at all. But I have to say de road was easier to walk on, pretty an shiny like a ribbon you buy in de shop an iron till it smooth.

I feel foolish wit me Dano pan o lunch, cos everybody mother buy dem three an four-storey foodcarrier to bring deir lunch to school in. An it wasn no steam fig an breadfruit without no meat eider, cos dem mother an fadder wuckin for Missa Coleridge and dem have payday every week. So imagine de vex I vex when I reach home an Granny still say she not sellin no land to nobody.

After de road, more truck come with cement an lumber an all sort o ting. For a whole year de worl start changin before me eye.

Dat hotel tek five years to build. I count dem. Granny count dem too. A lotta pretty concrete house, brown an white with a swimmin pool, dat was bright in de sun like a white man eye, shoot up over de sea.

'Cottages,' Jacob fadder say. 'Cottages wit lectric light an runnin water, an bath an everyting. Is progress. Yuh can't beat white man for brains.'

I couldn find no wuds for dat. But Granny had a few.

'Ask im if *he* allow to go an bathe dere, or get a bucket o water in Coleridge pipe to drink. Ask im if all de work he work for Coleridge, iffen dat mek him have electric too.'

So I ask im. An he get vex an call me a rude mout' soanso who didn have no mother, with one ole shegoat for a granmother, so who de hell I tink I is?

I cry.

I didn tell Granny, cos it hit me dat it didn have nothing dat she could do, an even if it hurt me, was true what Jacob fadder say.

But Missa Jojo must ha tell she, becos dat night she was extra nice to me. She fry plantain and give me, seein as I like fry plantain so much. An she call me, 'Darlin'. Now, when Granny call me darlin is like she givin me someting nicer dan a sweetie. Is a wud dat don come from she mouth too easy.

'Darlin,' she say, 'don let none o dem upset you. How much chilren it had in class today?' Was a question she always ask, ever since de trouble start an I could never figure out why. Sometimes she even ask de name o dem who didn come to school. Is how I come to tell she eggzackly who an who stay home an what dem sick with – cold o fever.

'Half-class,' I mumble. She didn ask me no more question. She was lookin at me kinda sorry.

'Ku-Kus,' she say, 'You notice how dem chilren sickin all de time?'

'Uh huh.'

'You notice how you never sick?'

I coulda tell she dat it have sick an *sick*, but she would say I rude.

'You not sickin cos you not livin by de swamp. Is all dat bad water an mosquito cross dere.'

I still didn say nothin.

'Feather, I wan to show you someting.' She was speakin in dat ole lady voice o hers dat frighten me, cos was like a ole mango dat dry up in de sun. She didn use to have dat voice befo Missa Coleridge start on we.

Dese days de only time I see she happy was when she waterin dat

tree. First coupla months dat piece o stick didn shift. I tell she dat
it dead an she tell me no, it was jus gatherin strength. But I could
see it worry she, cos in de middle o de night she uses to get up an
tek de lamp to go an look at it. Mornin time she water it an feed it
wit a little manure dat Missa Jojo bring for she. She even used to talk
to it. Den one mornin I hear she crow – was de way she use to laugh
– and when I run out I see she tremblin with excitableness.

'Look,' she say. 'It takin off. It takin off!'

I watch dat stick, I watch Granny, an I ask mihself, 'Ku-Kus
wha you goin do? Who goin tek care o you till you get big an get
a work, cos yuh mother ain goin send for you, an now yuh granny
jus gone dotish.'

But she was right, cos sudden so, dat piece o stick was full o leaf
an in a coupla months you'd ha tink it been growin dere all de time.

So, a week later, when she tell me she wan to show me
someting, I think mebbe was another coupla leaf dat tree sprout.
But no, she didn take me outside. She take me to de window.
Now, all de botheration mek me ferget to tell y'all dat Missa
Coleridge was buildin a highrise someting right in front o we. It
didn finish yet, but it had four concrete pillar an a whole heap o
iron dat push up to de sky. Jacob fadder say was a skyscraper an
Joan fadder say he lie, is a big-time water tank for dem tourist
when we have Dry Season, cos even if dem touris not too fussy
about bathin, dem does really suffer when dem thirsty.

In truth, nobody never get to know what that tank was for, cos
Granny see to dat for good.

Was evenin and I was fed-up an fuss-up bout everyting, so I
didn wan to watch no laughin tree dat didn laugh or count how
much new leaf it have.

'Yes Gran,' I say, 'it growin.'

'Ferget de tree, chile. Jus watch cross dere by de side o where
de sun is.'

So I lif up mih head a little bit. An yunno, I custom to seein de
sun an de sea an de sky mosly from de corner o me eye. I custom
to seein all o dat when I doin someting else. De sea was de sea an
de sun was de sun, an dat was dat. Is so I always tink till Granny

make me stop an watch what happen to de world come evenin time.

Now I tell y'all dis: it ain got no wuds in no book dat could tell you what happen cross dat sea water when de sun goin down. It ain got no dream in de world dat could dream dem light an colour.

You watch dat sea turn wine, turn blood, turn fire an smoke an you feel little an big, an sure 'bout everyting – same time as you thinkin dat you dunno where you goin, o who you is, o why you is what you is in de first case.

Like it had a voice inside o me dat was sleepin, an is only dat sight dat wake it up. It tell me dat nutting can't belong to nobody. Dat dem fish down dere an Granny laughin tree got de same rights as you an me an Missa Coleridge. It make you don't want to dead, but same time you don feel fraid to dead no more. An yunno, on top of everyting, it mek me glad dat I have Granny for mih granmother, an jus sorry for mih mother.

'Praise de Lord,' Granny say, really soft so I nearly didn hear she. But I hear, an it make a lot o sense cos dis sky was bigger, prettier, brighter dan de nicest church window in de world. I was sure o dat, even if de onliest church window I ever see was de big Catlic one in St. George's.

Dat was when Granny look me straight in mih eye. 'Dat, Ku-Kus is what Missa Coleridge wan to take from we. Is what he want for hisself an hi friends alone. Not even to let we have a little piece.'

We stay deh till night come up like smoke from down behin de sea an wipe out everyting. Dat mek me sad an want to cry. But Granny rub mih head an tell me to don't ferget dat de same sun was comin back tomorrow. Dat's life, she say. Missa Coleridge was chupid, she tell me, cos he was too blind to see dat. He behave as if de sky belong to im and he friends alone.

I think bout it a lot. We didn have no road no more to go down to de beach cos Coleridge block it off an make a pretty little set o steps dat go only from he swimmin pool straight down to de sand. And it had a big wall round everyting with a gate. He pay Jacob fadder forty dollars every month to wear a blue shirt an khaki pants to prevent all o we from usin it. An he pay Grace fadder fifty

dollars every month to wear a khaki shirt an khaki pants to prevent
we from bathin on de part o de beach dat had nice pink sand, cos
dem touris complainin all de time dat we, *de natives*, comin too
close to dem an dey don want us to tief deir tings. Even Jacob fadder
an Grace fadder didn like dat name. Dat was why dey was strict with
trespassers only when Missa Coleridge was around. Still, nobody
complain, cos dey fraid dat Missa Coleridge goin stop dem sellin
straw basket, an little steel pan, an coconut hat, an seashell, an all
dem tings dat nobody didn have no use for – except touris.

'Is why you mus promise me, Ku-Kus, dat when I gone you
never goin get rid o de property. An dat tree, treat it like you chile,
treat it like I try my best to treat you, like you mother never treat
you. Be good to de property an de tree.'

Now I tired ask she what so special bout dat tree, an all she say
is dat I askin too much question. De property. Dat was how she
start to call it now. Before Missa Coleridge come it was jus 'de
little piece o lan' or 'de groun behin de house', but now it get
promote to property.

Dese days, too, she keep talkin bout when she gone, as if she
was goin somewhere. But I never see she so content, specially
when she watch dat laughin tree dat didn laugh at all.

But truth was, Granny didn have to tell me to tek care o she
property, becos dat voice dat wake up in me when I watch de sun
go down, tell me dat it ain got no way I goin pass Granny property
to nobody, long as I live, even if I have to make meself a legalisin
lawyer o someting like dat to fight dem back.

Time pass an I get kind o proliferate wit wuds, which was just as
well cos dat fight between she an Missa Coleridge never stop. Was
like de whole govment come to we little yard to force we to move
out. A man from de Ministry of Touris come an tell we how we
mus give up de land, cos we standin in de way of evolution.

Granny uses to leave me to handle dem people, so I tell de fella
dat evolution is a Darwin phenomenon dat have impertinence, an
application to sheep an goat an bacterias, so I did want to know
iffen he is extenuatin dat we is some kind o ectoplasm o what. Dat

confuse he an he left straight away. Den Public Works arrive in overalls an hard hat, an I didn bother to put no heavy wuds to dem seein as dem is not s'pose to be eddicated like me. I didn wan to throw no pulse to swine, so is straight bad wud I cuss dem, which I will desist from quotin here.

I tell Ministry of Education dat dem is irrelevant, cos I soon to leave school anyway.

Foreign Affairs was a nice young girl dat run back to de road soon as she see me. I s'pose was becos she see me with Granny cutlass in mih hand cos I was cleanin dem weed round de laughin tree. But I stop she wit a few big wuds and den I cuss she up an down, an den back up again, an dat was dat.

Agriculture nearly get me. I never see a fella nice so. Black an smooth an long like a garfish, wid nice nice eye. He look at de tree, den he look at me an den he look at Granny and I sure a flash o someting pass between dem two. He turn round an look at Coleridge hotel below. Den he flash dem pretty teeth at we. An even iffen I feel a little self-conscious to say so, dem moonlight teeth mek me feel same like when Granny show me de sky dat evenin long time back. Except de feelin was a little more localise.

'Arbores Sinistres,' he say. 'It start to... er?'

'Happen soon,' Granny tell im. Mih tongue was too block up for me to ask im what it was dat tree didn start to do yet.

Well, a month after, I learn. It start with a cackle. One bright evenin I hear cacklin an I run out. Was Granny under de tree an she was holdin open she hand like if she was beggin it for something, an she was cacklin like mad.

'Come an see dis, chile. It start laughin.' An she grab mih hand an hold it up same way like she hold up hers. Well was only a little bit o water drippin from dem leaf an branch. I tell she I didn know why she fussin over a little bit o dew.

She cackle again an tell me how I dunno how to use mih brain. 'What time o day it is, Ku-Kus?'

'Evenin.'

'Dew does fall in de evenin? An when last rain fall round here?'

Dat was when it hit me. Dat tree was drippin water in de middle o Dry Season. How come, I wan to know. 'Now I could rest in peace,' was all she say.

Well God grant she satisfaction to see de first part: how Coleridge big white wall jus begin to split apart, startin with a little crack an den growin, growin, growin till was like a mouth dat somebody bust open with a cuff. It happen over four months an every time Granny look out, she smile. Was a happy smile but, like I say arready, tired.

She prepare me, little bit by little bit, for what was comin to pass with she. She tell me dat it was no different from de sun goin down an I shouldn worry cos she was arready risin, like dat selfsame sun, in me.

I does still cry when I think of it, but soon after I 'member de fight dat Missa Coleridge fight to keep all dat concrete standin. Jacob fadder tell we how de floor of de dancin hall jus split apart so slow you barely notice it. An den it was a snorin, gapin hole like de sea dat Moses part with he own little piece o laughin stick. Dat take a coupla years. An den it was de bungalow he call de King Room dat crack up like biscuit an start crumblin. An den everyting else start fallin down.

Grace fadder say dat he was by de swimmin pool when de water start to leak. He was de one dat empty de pool, which was empty from ever since, cos no more touris was comin dere. Jacob fadder say Grace fadder lie. Was he who see Missa Coleridge eye turn glass an his face go red like if de finger o God was on he throat an chokin he, when he see de root of dat laughin tree peepin out de bottom o he swimmin pool. I tell meself dat really was Granny hand. Coleridge look up at we little maggabone house on top de hill and was as if he see de tree for de first time.

Jacob fadder say dat he was standin by where de gate used to be when he catch sight o Coleridge runnin up de hill 'at a vory, vory forst rate.' (He start practisin to speak like Coleridge from de time he turn watchman.) 'But was onforchnate for Coleridge because soon as he foot hit de road is attack he heart attack im.'

Well, it had a whole heap o confusion an confabulation after dat. An talk didn finish till long time after govment deport Coleridge body back to he famly in Englan.

But quiet come and a whole heap o realisin follow after dat.

Now I is many tings, but one ting I definitely not is agriculturally botanical in my knowledge. But Cyril (which is dat pretty fella name) siddown on de chair dat Granny uses to sit on, an he explain everyting to me.

He say de laughin tree is a collokyalizam for a tree from de mountain where my Granny come from when she was young. An dat tree grow down more dan it grow up. It does push down root like if it tryin to reach de navel o de earth. It don' have no respect for rock an stone eider. Dat tree jus keep pushin till it hit a table full o water (I didn ask im to explain dat, cos I didn want him to tink I ignorant) which he say, is always dere below de ground, even in dese dry parts where we live. Once dat root reach, it start drinkin like Coleridge tourist used to drink deir funny-lookin drink from straw. It drink so much dat it start to fatten up an spread an sweat through every leaf an branch. De sweatin is de laughin. An I have it from good autorities – my Cyril imself – dat is so tree does laugh.

My Cyril say dat de trouble does start when dem root on de side o de laughin tree start to spread out an run. Is a tree dat curious an a little bit aggressive (he look at me an smile). It just mash through anyting dat in it way, which is what Missa Coleridge find out jus before he heart attack im.

An yunno what de best part was? Well, my Cyril say dat soon as dat centre root siddown at dat table o water down dere to drink, a laughin tree don care what happenin on top. You chop it an you burn it, you kick it an you cuss it – it jus cyahn dead. Dat's what my Cyril say.

Well, it upset me little bit when he mention chop an burn.

'Whats the matter, girl?' he say.

I had to ask im: 'Cyril, why de hell I goin to want to chop-an-burn a tree dat my granny bury under?'

FIRST FRUIT

Fellas say was the woman who start the trouble; woman answer back and say is man who carry the trouble inside himself and he use woman to bring it out.

Anyway, is bush that really know what come to pass, becuz bush got eyes and ears. Bush know everything. This is how bush say it happen.

One scorching afternoon this woman, name Gracy, come to George place to buy provision. Is what people used to do, yunno. Most of them never hear him talk, so they believe he dumb. They pay him the money, take the provision and go.

P'rhaps was the heat that stir George blood or mebbe was one of them feelings that hit a fella sometimes when he realise he ain't got nobody in the world except himself.

He watch them marks on the woman' arms and legs, and the girlchild by she side; then he look she in she face and say, 'The man finish with you?'

'I livin with me mother,' she say.

'I didn ask you where you livin, I ask if the man finish with you.'

The woman tell him, yes.

'How long since?' he ask.

'Last week make two months,' she tell him.

'He never touch you since?'

The woman say, no.

George look down at the girl, then at the woman. 'I have three room. I not including kitchen and veranda. I got electric light and pipe water. I never hit no woman and I tired eating my own food.'

'I got a daughter,' she say – like she not sure he see the lil girl by she side.

'Leave she with your mother for a coupla weeks; see if this suit you first.'

George look straight at she again. 'You leave the man or he throw you out?'

The woman sour she face. 'Why you want to know?'

'If you lef him he goin come to my yard looking for you and I don't want no trouble. If he throw you out and then come to play bad-john in my place, I kill im.'

George drop a whole heap of provision at the woman feet. He point a finger at the house. 'Is y'all place if you come. When y'all break something, tell me and I fix it. One thing I askin, though. Never lie to me.'

'Me! Me?' And sudden so, Gracy get blastid vex. 'I'z a practisin Catholic, y'unnerstan?'

'Eh-heh,' George say.

'You didn ask me name,' she say.

'Tell me when you come next time. I got them animals to feed.'

They live nice, yunno. Nobody never hear them quarrel. Not even when Elton come one day drunk as hell, claiming the lil girlchild was his seed and he want some kinda, uhm, reparation. George didn kill the fella, he just break his arm. And while Elton on the ground bawling, George ask him a lil common-sense question: 'If you fling-way corn in a fella garden; the fella manure it and water it; corn-seed grow, make corn – who you going say the corn belong to?'

Elton couldn't answer that; he was in too much pain.

Girlchild really like George, though. P'raps she see that he's the kinda man will bust she wutless father arse for she, and besides, he treat she like his own. And for children, it ain't got no feeling more secure than that.

It happen that it had a priest name Father Ambrose in that big stone church up there. Ambrose was a tall ole fella – white as cane flower. Had a pretty voice – like Irish people got – with a lotta music in it. But he was thin and hard as bone. Ambrose used to visit George woman all the time. That priest always talking about sacrifice to she. A true child of Christ, he say, offer the first of everything to Him. First fruit belong by rights to the church, like in the time of Moses. Is the only way of saying thanks and calling down more blessings.

George never pay no mind to what the woman say the priest tell she. His religion was his garden and his animals. The woman take Ambrose serious, though. She didn't realise she could buy she way to heaven so easy until Father Ambrose tell she so. And now she know that, she like a tick in George backside. First, she tell him they have to married because they living in sin, and she not going to sin no more until they married. So is married they married.

Well, like everybody know, woman got a way of turning rock-stone to putty if she put she mind to it. Soon as they married, the first and best of everything from George lil farm went up to that church. Add to that, every coupla days after vespers, the woman send she daughter with a basket full of flowers for the altar table.

Was a flourishing girlchild, polite and pretty as hell. On them flower-visits, the mother dress she in patent-leather shoes, flow-ered cotton dress, frill-top socks turn down just so, with two red puffer ball dancing around the lil girlchild ankles. Hair comb-up neat-an-nice too.

It continue, it continue, it continue for a year till one evening in the church, in the sacristy on the cold stone floor, under the alabaster gaze of the Lady of Fatima and Saint Christopher, 'mongst a scattering of canna lily, bougainvillea and crush-up lantana, Father Ambrose lay he hands on the lil girl. Left she so full of shame, and so frighten with all he tell she about hell-fire and damnation, *if* she tell, that the girlchild almost lose she senses.

Back home, the mother didn't notice nothing different about she daughter that Friday. George didn't either, but come Saturday, in the kitchen, at the table in front of their plate of stew-chicken and rice-an-peas, George raise he eyes at the girl face and kep' them there. 'What wrong?' he say – like he didn have no doubt about it.

Girchile wouldn't look at him.

'Talk,' he say.

She never lie to him – was the only understanding between them. Still, it take a long time to squeeze it outta she. George wait like he had all the time in the world. He wait till he got the details outta she. The mother start crying.

'What make him do that?' George say.

Girlchild didn't know how to answer that, so she start crying too. That was enough for George. Like he find the answer in the water dripping down she face.

He get up, breathing like he got a whole forest inside him, with a high wind running over it. He turn to the mother. 'Tomorrow Sunday, not so?'

The woman drop she head and say, yes.

'Priest gettin them flowers same way,' George say. 'I going bring them to him meself.'

The woman look at him quick, but she can't read George face. She could *never* read George face. But them words is not what she expect.

'What you going to do?'

'What you want me to do?' George ask, like if he waiting for she to pass the order.

'I don' want no trouble,' she say.

'You already got it,' he say. 'But I not going to touch him if that is what you 'fraid.'

He push he hand behind he back and pull out he garden knife. Was a wicked looking thing – half the length of a fella arm. The steel bright-an-shining like it make outta glass, and so sharp a pusson could split a hair longways with it. They only see it when he butchering animals. George rest the big knife on the table in front of Gracy. 'Hold this if you want to rest your mind. But come tomorrow, is I takin them flowers to the church.'

And that was that; George done talk.

Sunday come, the wife stand-up by the window looking down the hill at George in the flower garden that he help she make – a whole half acre – pretty with alamanda, bird of paradise, all kinda calla lily, heliconia, mimosa, russelia… Name it and she got it – all for the church.

She watch George collect a whole heap of crimson rose, a handful of hibiscus, the tongue of a banana flower. Then he move among them lilies and bring the kitchen knife to a row of white anthuriums.

Gracy stand-up on the step and watch him leave, the bunch cradle across he chest. She watch them white lily circling all that red and, sudden so, it bring to mind a bandage round a wound.

The priest was by the altar when George reach. The ole-fella head was bow, he two hand busy. Ole Miss Mona was on one side of the church, following a broom around them pews. Father Ambrose didn't hear George walk in. Heavy fella like George – he could move like he got no weight when he had a mind to.

First thing Father Ambrose see was them white lily, then a big black hand pushing them out to him. Then he see the red. He swing round to see George, his shoulder so broad like it block out half the light from the big church door, and them cave eyes of his so dark it was as if they got no light reaching them. The ole priest jump back, fling up he hand like he fighting off Lucifer himself. The ciborium he was wiping hit the ole stone floor and raise a noise like a bell striking the hour.

'I frighten you?' George say. 'Word reach me dat you have a weak heart?' He even crack a smile. 'Careful,' he add. 'Work like yours need a real strong one.'

A lil while pass before Father Ambrose find he voice. 'Yes, my son. This mortal coil… It happens to us all…'

Imagine George listening to that sing-song voice – smooth and pretty as if Father Ambrose soften it with sweet oil. A pusson close them eyes and they'll think it was a youngfella talking.

Priest face different though. Them eyebrows of his like two line of ashes. Watery eyes – some colour between grey and blue, like weather that can't make up it mind.

Father Ambrose bring he palms together and George look at the fat gold ring on the second finger of he left hand, then at the

sleeve of he robe that look so much like gaulin wings. George
raise he head at them pretty church window and the organ at the
back of the nave that rise up to the dark, dark roof.

'What happen to all ov us?' he ask the priest.

Ambrose look confuse.

'You say it happen to all of us…'

'Did I? Ah well – a manner of speaking, son. A manner of
speaking, so to, er, speak.'

George point at them cherubim, left side of the chancel. 'Ah
notice you surround yourself with children.' Then he lift he chin
at Jesus of the bleeding heart, and turn to face the priest. 'Was de
people de fella trust do that to him, not so? But you know what
I say? I say a man must know de people he move among. A pusson
could even say that fella on de cross up there ask for it. Too damn
busy talking to take notice of what they had in mind for 'im.'

'We are in His House!' Priest raise he voice so high it full-up
the church, and them white eyebrows start trembling. 'To speak
like that in His House is blasphemy. I must ask you –'

'What I sayin, is that Fella was a big man. He could've save
'imself, is what I sayin. Now if he was a child – that different.
Becuz to spill de blood ov a child – yunno – that's…'

George swing round, drop them flowers on the altar and walk
out of the church.

George not stupid. It must've cross he mind that this wasn't
the first time Father Ambrose been suffering poor-people children to come to him, and shaming them into silence afterwards.

One thing for sure, Father Ambrose didn't visit George house
after that.

Make it sufficient to say that six weeks later, the mother say she
worried she daughter not sheself no more. The young-girl whole
body upset. George didn't answer, but Gracy get hopeful when he
leave the house and go down to the garden, because George know
plants; he understand the secrets of their sap.

But the woman heart drop when all he come back with was
provisions and conversation: The heifer going to the bull next

week. The white ram in the paddock useless – five weeks gone and none of them ewes get catch with lamb.

'What about she?' Gracy roll she eyes at the girl. 'She still in school an…'

George lift a hand to stop she. 'You Catholic, not so? You tired tell me is de one thing you not givin up or changin for nobody. You say you rather dead. So why you want to change that now?'

And that was that. Talk finish.

When the girl begin to show, they pack she off to Gracy family in the north. Maybe it was to spare the woman the shame; maybe it was something else. Dunno.

Meantime, First Fruit never change. A basin of full of mango every second Friday in June and July; sweet potatoes, eddoes and pum-pum yams in Dry Season. Dry corn for Easter, pidgin peas in January. Pumpkin, watermelon and guava whenever they bear fruit. A coupla heads of lettuce and cabbage any time of year. Flowers for the altar every Friday and Sunday…

George even turn artist with them flowers: purple yam shoot that he lace around them roses and lilies like blood vessels; potato vines with streaks of blue and crimson. A coupla wax apple and French cashew 'mongst the yellow of them flowers.

The woman didn't trust it. She begin to feel that the man take over the church-duties of the daughter to mock them. Particularly becoz this silent, heavy fella never ask after she health, never mention she name or how she getting on, all the time the girl away. And yunno, in them months that pass, the woman start to hate George. In them quiet ways that woman does hate, holding it close to she chest like it was a secret. She walk softer in the house, she two eye sliding away from George face whenever he talk to she. She never use to notice the size of him before – yunno, how heavy he weigh on she; how he breath on she face oppress she.

Maybe Gracy didn't know what to look for. Maybe she so full up of embarrassment and worry for she daughter, she miss them sign. Like that Friday after vespers when George bring a bag of coconut to the church, pull out that knife of his and slice off the top of each one with a clean swing. He line them up on the steps, look in Father Ambrose face and say, 'First fruit.'

Was a special High Mass the Sunday of that same week – must've been a couple weeks before the girl come back home. Candle on the altar burning; congregation head turn down; light coming through them pretty stain-glass-window and falling on them head. That light brighten up everything inside the church, especially the fella with the bleeding heart, who looking down kinda poor-me-one on all them head.

When Mass finish, congregation walk out to a nice-an-quiet afternoon and Ambrose come out on the step to pass last-words to he flock. One of the wimmen turn she head and sudden-so she face twist-up. All eyes follow she finger.

Was George she pointing at, walking up the road, trailing a white ram on a piece of rope.

When he reach them, he tie the four foot of the animal and throw it on its back.

To this day, nobody know where the blade come from; all they see was the flash of the steel. He butcher the sheep right in the doormouth of the church.

And while George working on the beast, words coming outta he mouth like a sermon. Fresh words, yunno, because people can't remember ever hearing him talk, far less make speech.

'Sheep stupid,' he say. 'They see the knife coming and they bow their head and tek it. They dead without a sound. A chicken know better. Yuh cut off chicken head and it beat round the yard like the life don't want to leave it. That make sense. Chicken got no interest in heaven o hell o purgatry. Chicken don't give a shit about where it go after it dead. Chicken want to hold onto what it got right now. Chicken got sense. Is why people should never eat chicken.'

George pass he hand across he face, then he look up at the priest and say, 'Sheep get what it deserve.'

A flick of George wrist, a twist of he hand and he slide he arm beneath the ribcage of the beast. And then... and then... he pull out he hand and raise it in the air. 'First fruit,' he say. That voice come from he belly, thick like molasses.

He hold out the dripping heart to Father Ambrose like it was a mango. Priest face go white. Priest shake he head like Eve shoulda done when Satan offer she the apple. He grab he chest and back-back fast inside the church with a coupla acolytes running after him.

People make their own lil congregation around George. And yunno, Ole-Man Joe-Joe was the one who take the bleeding heart because he say he got a weak back and it got many uses he could put that lovely piece of flesh to.

George offer a piece o the rest to everybody. That was enough to pull them outta the shock and have commonsense take over. Because, yunno, if folks round here have a choice between pleasing God and a nice lamb stew, them choose the lamb stew every time – them damn well know they could always pray for absolution next Sunday.

Make it sufficient to say that after that it didn have a time when Father Ambrose didn't raise he head in the middle of he sermons, to watch the entrance of the church.

The girl was a mother when she come back. Sh'was a little more plump and a lot more serious-face. She look like she mother.

Giving birth – that kind of pain – does teach acceptance, or p'rhaps it force acceptance on a woman. Dunno.

Right now, the young-girl not thinking how the ole priest spoil she future; she not remembering the terrible thing he done to she. S'far as she concern, what done happen, happen and done. She look at the infant in she arms – the little hand and eye and foot so perfect, the tiny mouth searching for the sustenance sheself give – and that is all that concern she now.

She come home in the dark, so the dark could shelter she from people eyes, give she a lil bit of time before they start bad-talking and twisting the story to suit themselves.

George and the mother see the change in she, of course. But George and the mother see different things. All George notice is the colour of the baby against the young-girl skin. It yellow like a ripe paw-paw with hair somewhere between white and brown.

The mother see the way the girl flesh out and them small pleat-line across she forehead that wasn't there before. So, when Gracy reach out and touch she daughter, was like if the distance between them shorten. Both of them was mother now. Both of them carry a seed that take root in them, and bring it into light. It ain't got no fella in the world could understand that feeling.

'Yellow chile,' was all George say.

The girl look up at him as if she hear some kinda rustling in the bush, but she not sure whether is good or bad. Gracy watching George too. She alert like a dog. But they follow him into the house.

A pusson could suppose that in George mind the child is evidence. Round here, where people colour run from sapodilla-brown to starapple-black, that baby stand out like a ripe banana in a basket full of pum-pum yam.

Still, in the days that pass, the mother and the girl relax, because when the infant cry is George self who get up whatever hour in the night and feed it. Is he that rock it back to sleep. Is George that carry it most times on he shoulder.

Is he decide on the Christening.

Sunday, three weeks after the girl reach home, the mother dress-up in a pretty cotton frock with a pattern of black hibiscus print all over it. The girl in a light-blue, long-sleeve dress. She wearing white sandals that buckle round she ankle. She pull back she hair so the morning sun fall on she face.

Is so them walk up the road to the church, the girl holding the baby, the mother by she side, and George one half-step ahead. He walk stiff in he new press-up khaki shirt and clean black trousers. He wearing a new pair of water-boots. The sound of the rubber on the road drown out the few lil words that exchange between the mother and she daughter.

People was shock. That young girl carrying the baby in she arms didn't make no sense to them. They never see no youngfella dogging round George house or courting she in secret. Bush does talk, an, bush wouldha' find out and report back. So how come nobody never know?

Nobody had to tell them the baby belong to the girl. The way she carrying the child alone make that plain. Besides, the yellow of the infant tell them it didn't belong to the girl mother and George, because nutmeg don't bear mango and snake don't make short children.

The surprise send the gossip hurrying ahead of them. People start to line the road. By the time George and the two wimmen reach the church it was a proper procession.

The three of them walking in a heavy silence now, with only the sound of George water-boots on the road. The mother holding she head straight, she mouth tight like a twis'-up purse.

They reach the steps, begin to climb them – the young-girl lifting she foot careful with the child, she face calm as one of them Mary statues inside the church.

Was when they reach the door, George turn round and lift the baby from the girl. The mother grab George arm. The girl push out she hands to take back the child. George look at she, and whatever the young-girl see in George face must've been stronger than the pull of motherhood, because she drop she hands and stagger back. Then she gather herself and begin to hurry along beside him, she whole body push forward, she two hand reaching up to the infant that George was holding high above he head. And is like that George march up the aisle, the child in the air, like Abraham holding up lil Isaac.

Church was pack. Congregation in the middle of some hymn with the morning sun running across the old stone floor all the way up to the altar, where Father Ambrose sprinkling a baby forehead while the parents looking on.

Was the sound of George boots that kill the hymn and raise people head. Or maybe was the bellow that come from him, or perhaps it was the sight of the upraise child, or the vision of that wall of darkness bearing down on the priest. Dunno! Make it sufficient to say that Ambrose see George right hand dip inside he shirt. He see that same hand rising with the knife. And sudden-so church turn Babel with the bawling of the young-girl and Gracy and the terror that rise up from the benches. Plus them words that come from George mouth. Words that make sense only to he and the priest, because Father Ambrose shake he head and stagger back; he bring up one arm to cover he face, while the other hand start tearing at he chest. As if he just catch sight of the God that left him all them years ago.

Whatever it was, it knock him down so hard on the old stone floor, it shut up the congregation.

Father Ambrose never get up.

Look at George now! Watch what them years in jail cut him down to. See how he in two mind about that place? A pusson can't blame him. Bad weather beat down the cattle shed. Rainy Season wash away the pig pen, and them banana and peas grow so crazy they start strangling one another. A stranger would never know it used to be a farm that lay out neat-an-nice, as if George know geometry.

People don't remember if they ever see the woman and the girl after George got taken away. Now and then, them window-blind does shift, but that could be the wind. When nighttime come, a pusson *think* they hear a bucket knock across that valley there, or the soft laugh of a woman, and a younger laugh that follow it. But who know for sure?

If them two woman still in there, what keep them waiting all these years? It couldn't be love – that's for sure. People say it didn't make no sense for them to run away because wherever them go, George sure to find them.

Commonsense say is what happen when woman lose religion; when God tumble off he throne and become ordinary in she eyes.

ROSES FOR MISTER THORNE
For the fallen (June, 1980)

Anni pushed a reluctant hand toward her little plastic radio and cut off the outraged voice of Mister Thorne. She would have liked to listen to his whole speech but she had work to do. Her yams were strangling the sweet potatoes, and today she was going to tame them.

Out in the garden, though, her head was full of Missa Thorne: his talk of Bloody Thursday, the bomb-blast that was meant to kill him, and the retribution he'd let loose on the *Counters* who'd placed the device beneath the stage on which he stood.

His words brought back pictures of the three girl-children they'd made posters of, and spread throughout the island, their destroyed bodies splayed on the grass like gutted fish.

She felt again the quiet that had fallen on the island, and the loveliness of that afternoon eighteen months ago: a clean blue day; the air over Old Hope sweet and humming because, during all that week, the mangoes had been throwing out their blossoms,

He was returning to The Park next week, Missa Thorne reminded them. He'd been reminding them for months. He was going to stand on that very same stage and speak, so that all the Counters on the island knew-and-understood that the Revo was not afraid of them, and if they tried it again, *the people* will give them *heavy, heavy manners.*

Voices broke through her thoughts. On the road below, Slim, the young, fast-talking militiaman, stood among a buzz of young people. He was fingering his red beret with one hand, the elbow of the other making jerky movements above the pistol on his hip.

They'd already cut away the overhanging trees, fed the leaves and branches to a snapping roadside fire. The girls had tied back their hair with the flag of the Revo – a white square of cloth with a blood-red circle in the middle. Small outbreaks of laughter rose above the slap of machetes and the grate of spades.

She was wondering what the hell *them* find so funny this time-a-mornin' when Slim pulled back his shoulders and raised a long brown arm at her. 'Crazy-Anni, how you this morning?'

Even from this distance she could see the broad spread of the young man's teeth.

She muttered something nasty and turned toward her rosebush.

It stood on its own mound in the half shade of her cocoa tree, its roots covered with a layer of sea kelp, compost and manure. She'd protected it from the spite of wind and rain, and direct sunlight with a ring of coconut fronds.

And to think that once this perfect rosebush had almost died – *that* July morning of heavy dew that had caught her unawares and blighted the leaves with black spot. She'd taken the bus to Saint George's to see the man in the Agroshop who knew everything.

'Cut it back,' he said. 'Hard! You'll be hurting it to save it.'

He'd handed her a tiny bag of Epsom salts. 'Tonic. Magnesium. And don't forget a few spoonfuls of gypsum and a sprinkling of sulphur.'

Now here it was, bristling with thorns, its leaves dark and glossed with health; the petals, furled tight like an infant's fist, straining against the sepals that held them in. She'd taken cuttings from it. The best was for Missa Thorne. She would take it to him next week because he'd asked for it.

He'd come to Old Hope the month before the bomb. She was bending over the vermillion tendrils of her pum-pum yams when the thundering of engines straightened her and pulled her gaze down to the road. The grate of wheels on gravel. Men's voices.

Something in her quickened when she saw the soldiers stepping out of two green jeeps, and between them, a long black car, so brightly polished it looked silver in the hot light.

A brown man in a blue suit stepped out of it. Another in a white waistcoat stood at his side. Their eyes were on the path that led past her place to the new co-operative farm further up her hill.

She'd straightened her headwrap and turned her face down to her yams again, pulling at weeds that weren't there while the hum of voices drew nearer.

The thud of footsteps stopped. A voice reached across to her from the narrow feeder road across the small ravine below her house. 'Greetings, Gran!'

She'd gathered the tail-ends of her dress around her knees and straightened up, wiping the soil from her hands onto her clothing.

She looked over at the smiling man and nodded. The whole village had come up the hill behind him.

Slim had pulled away from the crowd. The youngfella's eyes were wide, his hands agitating at his side. 'Craz... erm, Miss Anni, is the Chief self saying hello to you, y'unnerstan? Is Missa Thorne greeting you. Is is...'

'Uh-huh,' she said, and raised her eyes at Mister Thorne. 'That's you for true?'

A chuckle rumbled out of him. 'I'm afraid so, Granny.'

She'd imagined a darker fella – grim-faced, with the barrel chest that the bass of his voice suggested on the radio. Missa Thorne was slim and brown. He slipped a cigarette between his lips, pushed his fingers into the pocket of his blue shirt-jac and pulled out a lighter. She watched him bring the flame to the cigarette. The smile was still there, even through the cloud of smoke.

The tall youngfella beside him in the white waistcoat, with a wire in his ear, wouldn't take his eyes off her. Those eyes of his and the little jerky movements of his head reminded her of birds. The Birdman made her nervous. Missa Thorne took in her patch of corn, her pigeon peas and sweet potatoes. His eyes paused on her bed of roses.

'Nice,' he said. 'Really nice.'

'They my children,' she said, angling a sideways glance at his face. 'They grow happy when I touch them.'

He nodded as if he couldn't agree more. For a moment, she

was conscious of her little two-roomed house, leant up against the calabash tree.

She didn't know what came over her. She hurried over to her roses, brought her knife to her best plant, cleared the thorns and cut the fattest flower. She walked back and held it out to Mister Thorne.

The Birdman chuckled. She caught herself and chuckled too because she'd forgotten the small ravine between them.

Missa Thorne's face pleated in a wide smile. 'Roses for the Revo, right? Thank you all the same, Comrade.'

He lit another cigarette and said something to the Birdman; then he pointed at the garden. 'Grow one for me, Granny. Maybe next time?'

She'd nodded, said she would and watched the crowd move off; kept her eyes on Missa Thorne's blue shirt until he turned into the co-operative. He'd stopped at the high steel gate, raised a hand above his head and waved. He hadn't looked back, but she knew that wave was meant for her.

She might have forgotten all about that promise, if eight weeks later, there hadn't been the bomb that almost killed him. Something new had settled on the island. She sensed it straightaway, like the arrival of bad weather – a darkening that a pusson could not put a name to but felt all the same. She saw it in the gun that Slim began wearing on his hip, in the children sneaking off at night with him in those green jeeps, and returning in the small hours of the morning. Their faces were grim, and they talked only of blood and *heavy manners*.

The young children had changed their ring-game songs, their chants now full of little cruelties.

Ole Miss Anni
She went crazy
Cuz she belly
Kill all she baby

What would she say to Missa Thorne? She wasn't going to prepare no words becuz the truth need no rehearsin'.

She might tell him – *if* he had the time – about the year it had taken to bring this cutting to what it was now. Of how in growing this gift for him, there was also cruelty: the destruction of the stunted and malformed, the burning and uprooting. She might make him aware that she paid for her cruelty with blood. Becuz this rosebush wore a fortress of thorns that did not spare her hands.

But it was worth the trouble, not so? Was enough to know that its flowers would fill his office with their lovely scent, to be replaced with new flowers even as the cut ones died.

The morning of the rally, she dressed in her white canvas shoes, the blue cotton dress and soft straw hat that she took out only for funerals and church. She visited the rosebush with her fork, a small milk tin of kerosene, her cutlass and a knife. She prepared two small parcels – one with the rooted cutting, the other with freshly cut flowers – both of which she nestled in a larger bag.

Slim was down there, urging the village into two government buses on the road. He saw her coming and stopped his words. The militiaman looked her up and down, then at the thick brown paper bag in her hand. 'Crazy Anni, where you going?'

'Town,' she said and headed for the open door of the vehicle.

'Town close down,' he said. 'Is to the rally people going today.'

'Me too,' she said.

His eyes wandered to the bag. 'Is your lunch you got in there?'

'You could say so,' she said.

'Pickup time to come back is seven o'clock. By the big green bridge. Make sure…'

She didn't hear the rest of what he said. She'd already stepped into the smell of old leather, perfumed bodies and the abrupt silence of the packed bus. She ignored their eyes. The row of girls on the backseat brought their heads together. A burst of stifled chuckles shook their shoulders. *Ole Miss Anni…*

Linda, who sold sweets and groundnuts by the roadside, roared at them and shut them up.

An hour later, she was looking down on the bright-red galvanized roofs of St. Georges.

The big bus bucked and shuddered as it swung onto the Western Main. Then a slow crawl along the Esplanade through a river of bodies with fluttering banners – all heading for The Park.

Slim dropped them off at the beginning of the curving road that ended in The Park.

'Seven o'clock,' he shouted, directing a rigid finger at the old iron bridge that spanned the dirty river where it met the sea. 'And I not waiting for nobody.'

She stepped out into a sizzling sun, a dizzying swirl of flags and the heavy press of bodies. Voices throbbed the air around her while she stood at the edge of the curving road, the bag dangling from her hand. *So much blastid people…*

In her mind this journey had always been a straight line from her doorstep to the receiving hands of Missa Thorne. *Chupid me!*

She walked along the edge of the forward-creeping crowd, and when she could no longer get past them, eased herself into the press. Bodies carried her forward. From time to time, a meaty shoulder floundered into her and she tightened her grip on the bag.

She lost track of time, was mindful only of the shuffle forward. At some point, a loudspeaker crackled and a voice washed over them. It shouted names, paused for a long moment, then called out Mister Thorne's. At the sound of it, a clamouring seemed to rise out of the earth. Comrade Thorne, the loudspeaker said, would be the last to address them. That, she knew, was not going to be anytime soon.

She lifted her eyes above the vast procession of heads, over the awning of the high stage, shivering with red and white flags. The Grand Etang Hills were blue-brown in the distance, against a bleached out sky. Her mind drifted to her garden – no rain for a month; no promise of it. The island was crisp as a biscuit, and these young people – so full of sweat and sap – did not give a damn.

It was evening and she'd almost reached the stage. Further back, she'd lost her left shoe. One moment there was a surge, next the grass was prickling her foot. Even if she'd seen it, it would've been impossible to retrieve it.

She could see them on the platform now; she could match their voices to their faces. She'd already heard the short man with the head of piki-piki hair talk about better roads and drainage; the thin youngfella with the pointy beard explaining why the island needed newer, bigger guns. And that grinning yellow woman in the loose brown dress who told them what women of the island wanted and weren't getting – her quick mistrust of *that* one startled her.

Not like the woman who sat to the right of Missa Thorne, with big bright eyes, hair cropped close to her skull like a boy's. A young-girl face, but broad at the hips like a full-grown woman. That one talked of schools and books and learning, all the while with a cigarette in her hand. She lit it when she returned to her chair beside Missa Thorne's and blew a fan of smoke toward the crowd. She never looked at Missa Thorne, sat cross-legged, her eyes sweeping the faces in the crowd – exactly like the Birdmen in their heavy-looking waistcoats with coiled wires sprouting from their ears.

For the first time Anni was touched by doubt. The paper bag felt much heavier than it had this morning. *Chupid me* – to think that offering it to Missa Thorne, him taking it and thanking her, was going to be worth all them early-morning trips down to Old Hope river, just to load a wicker basket full of loam and rotting leaves.

The movement of the crowd had taken her to the side of the platform. A young man with a wide stance and clean-shaven head was all that stood between her and the stage.

The man in the soldier's cap was almost finished speaking and the hum of the crowd was shuddering the air. Yet she felt a quiet underneath that noise. A new electricity.

Now there he was, Missa Thorne, rising to his feet, lifted by the roar of the thousands that he'd called before him. For a moment, she was distracted by the face of the woman who sat and smoked beside him. She'd turned up her face to him, and was smiling for the first time.

Missa Thorne raised an arm and drew a sky-roar that went on and on, and got bounced back by the encircling hills. Then silence, because he was nodding at a sway of braceleted arms on the grass below. A pair of arms untangled themselves from the others. A woman called his name, and then her body began to rise, lifted on the tide of bodies under her. She teetered on the lip of the platform, held there by a forest of hands. Then she righted herself and was on the stage.

Heavily pregnant, the woman opened her arms to Missa Thorne. Already five Birdmen had gathered around her, their hands busy on her body. The tallest embraced her from behind, grinning and whispering in her ear as if she were the bearer of his child. He traced the roundness of her stomach with his palms; stopped only when decency would not allow his fingers to go further. Then he patted her shoulders, spread his fingers wide, and all the other Birdmen stepped away.

The woman delivered herself to Missa Thorne. He embraced her as if, all his life, he had been waiting for this woman so that he could press his beard into her hair and rock her with the slow care of a lover. And then he released her to the Birdmen who guided her off the stage.

Now Missa Thorne was speaking. He was saying the same things that those who had come before him said, and yet it sounded different. He was gathering all their words and putting his life-breath into them. Like the children in this park, Anni, too, felt the lift – of being carried on a voice that needed no choir to support it and no big black book to give it weight.

She saw how all this giving of himself had aged him. Even from that last time when he'd come to Old Hope, the lines had deepened on his forehead, the beard was now salted with white. Mebbe it was from remembering the bomb that killed the girls. Mebbe it was because it made him turn to killing in return.

Yet, he did not pause in the middle of a speech to look behind him; he did not throw quick glances to the mid-distance, or seem to be listening for something in the air beyond the hearing of this crowd…

She must have been lost for a while, her attention drifting, because Missa Thorne was lifting his head in that concluding way of his, before the stroke of thunder that always came from him at the end of every speech: 'Forward ever, backward never…'

She didn't know what she said, or if she said anything, but the young man in front of her turned round blinking, as if she'd pulled him out of a dream. He dropped his eyes to the bag she opened up to show him. He stepped aside and let her through.

She'd almost gone past the Birdmen when a hand closed on her elbow and the world around her dimmed. A body bounced her backward. She felt herself falling but hands closed around her armpits and kept her on her feet.

On the stage, Birdmen had made a circle around Missa Thorne, their backs to him. A big fist closed around the hand that held the bag. Fiery threads of pain ran up her arm and pooled around her shoulder, as the thorns of the rose sank into her.

They were hustling her backwards when a voice cut through. She recognised it as the woman's – the one who sat by Missa Thorne. A Birdman pushed out an arm in front of her. The woman raised her chin at him and they locked eyes. He stepped aside and let her through.

She found herself walled in by the Birdmen's heavy flesh with the woman in front of her. Those bright dark eyes were on her face. Close up, she looked much older.

Anni followed the woman's downward gaze, saw the vine-trails of her own blood on the paperbag. 'Is the rose,' she said. 'The rose for Missa Thorne. He ask for it.'

The woman was gentle when she took the bag, opened it and peered inside. Her eyes were softer when she raised her head. She slipped in a hand and eased out the flowers. She raised herself on the balls of her feet and hoisted the bunch above the Birdmen's heads.

'Thank you, Comrade Sister,' the woman said. She stripped away the leaves, dug a thumbnail into the base of each thorn and plucked it off. She curled steady fingers around the stem of each flower and broke it short.

'Thank you,' she said again.

The Birdmen followed the woman to the other side of the stage. The crowds were spilling out onto the road, their voices raised in song. The last of the sunlight haloed their shapes against the darkness of the old iron bridge.

The woman joined Missa Thorne, the five roses pressed against her breasts. He placed a hand in the small of her back as she held up the flowers to his face. He said something to her and smiled. She jerked a thumb over her shoulder.

Missa Thorne took the flowers and brought his face down to smell the bunch. At the open door of the long black car, he handed them to her. The bright-eyed woman took the gift with cupped hands, her face turned up to his. Then they lowered their heads and shoulders and disappeared into the vehicle.

The park had emptied quickly. Just the darkening expanse of grass, pockmarked by discarded cans and paper flags. She looked down at the remaining bag, spilled from the larger one, torn in places, the imprint of a boot on it, and stooped to pick up the crushed cutting, its tiny wormlike roots still smeared with the mud.

She headed for the old green bridge. Ahead of her, gulls were squabbling above the shallow waters of the dirty bay. She sat on the low wall beside the bridge facing the sea. She was still staring at the shifting waters when a vehicle pulled up behind her. She heard her name, turned to see Slim stepping out of a small green van.

'Crazy Anni, where the hell you been? I was looking for you.'

'Bus gone?' she said.

'Long time,' he said. 'I tell y'all seven! Where you went! And where's your other shoe?'

'The left got lost,' she said, and let his irritation wash over her.

The young man peered into her face, leaned closer, then dropped an arm across her shoulders. 'Okay, no sweat. Come, I take you home. You enjoy the rally?'

'They take only de flower,' she muttered, holding up the broken cutting. 'They didn take the part that grow.'

RUM AN COKE

Norma Browne got up early, cried a bit, stared at her hand and muttered to herself with bitter conviction. 'What a waste. A waste!'

Nobody heard her except perhaps the boy, but even if he had, he would not remember much, come daylight.

Come daylight, he would lurch out of the house, hungry, ill and angry, his body starved of something that neither she nor any food on earth could satisfy. He would be away a couple of hours or maybe the whole day, and then he would return to lie below the house, the turbulence gone except in the working of his eyes. He would not be able to look at her, not until the shivering started again, very late in the evening, and he began, once more, to hit her.

She got up early because a thought had nudged her out of sleep, an idea which, with the coming daylight, became a resolve.

She waited until he left, then put on the light blue dress that she'd bought for his christening and which, ten years later, she also wore to take him to that scholarship school in St. George's.

He was a beautiful boy then, clear-eyed and quick, his little body full of purpose. 'Remarkably intelligent' was what the teachers said; and to prove they were not lying, they'd written it on a pretty piece of parchment paper, framed it and handed it to her.

Not like now. Not like now at all. What she used to feel then went way past pride. If, in those days, she felt embarrassed or even terrified, it was only because she could hardly believe that some-one like her could be so blessed.

With awkward haste, she knelt and reached beneath the iron bed. She dragged out a pillow and emptied its contents on the floor. Several objects rolled out, things she would never use, but kept 'just in case': a couple of heavy silver bracelets, a ring of pure Guyana gold, an old passport with a photo of a man who looked exactly like her son and a small blue book on which 'The Co-operative Bank' was printed in large letters.

She took the little book, stuffed it down her bosom and went to the main road to wait for the only bus that travelled the twenty miles, twice a day, to and from St. George's.

It was evening when she returned. The migrating birds that spent the November and December months in the swamp half a mile away were already dropping like black rain out of an in-flamed sky and settling on the mangroves.

She went to the bedroom to replace the book and leave a small but heavy parcel beneath the bed. Then she began to look for things to do. She would have gone to the garden at the top of the hill above the village, but she'd already sown more corn and peas than she had ever sown before; she'd weeded the sweet potatoes, reinforced the mud rows with wattle and bamboo, trimmed the bananas and cleared the stones which, every year, appeared miraculously in the soil. She'd put new campeche pillars under the house, added a kitchen and re-laid the yard with stones that she'd gathered from the roadside – anything that hard work could possibly achieve to ease her days. If she could have undone it all and started again, she would have. Hard work saved her from remembering – though that was not the same as forgetting. Not remembering was holding back the shame, or redirecting it – the way the drains she dug during the rainy season turned excess water away from her garden.

She saw him coming and studied his face, his walk, the set of his mouth. Such clues determined how her day went, although when he first returned he was never violent. He would have gone over to Teestone's house next door, or to some friend of his, and pumped his veins with a needleful of that milky stuff that did such dreadful things to him.

The milky stuff, she did not understand. She thought she had already seen or imagined every awful thing there was, but nothing had prepared her for what they called *de niceness* – niceness, because of the way it made them feel, they said;

niceness that had sucked the life out of her child and replaced it with a deadness that had reduced her to nothing in his eyes.

Before the deadness was the hunger. He was hungry all the time, but the more she fed him the thinner he seemed to grow. He'd become secretive and had lost the even temper he was born with. When the shivering started and there was nothing she could do for him, he would scream and hit her.

She wondered which was worse: his torment or her own shame before the village. Once she caught him doing it to himself, panic-ridden and slobbering, until he'd fed the beast inside his veins.

For this – for this especially – she did not blame him because he was her child and she had known him as a different person. True, she'd seen him do things that did violence to her sense of decency – like the time she caught him with his cousin, younger than him by two years, on her bed. She'd almost killed him – but Daniel was still her boy.

She would never know how it started, or what she had done or had not done that made him need 'de niceness'. But now she knew who gave it to her boy and that was partly why she went to town. Nobody had told her; they'd only confirmed the truth for her.

It was that gold chain she'd bought him as a present that made her know. He'd asked for it before he did the exams, told her that if he got an 'A' for all of them, she should buy him a gold chain with his name written on it. And of course she'd sent her macmere, Grace, to St. George's to get it straight away. Then she hid it in her pillowcase and waited. When he came home one day and told her that he'd got all his 'A's, she went straight to the bedroom and brought it out. That amazed him, not the chain but the fact that she believed he would get the 'A's, just because he said so.

So when she saw that gold chain around Teestone's neck, it suddenly made sense. Everything made sense: the house Teestone was improving, the way the children flocked to him, the girls warring amongst themselves for his attention.

Over the months she'd studied him. Teddy Stonewall – that boy! That boy who'd never seen a classroom in his life, who'd never lifted a finger for his mother, who'd grown up by the roadside near the rumshop watching the world slip past; that boy who, having worked for nothing, wanted everything. Now it was all coming to him: the pretty clothes, the new, red Suzuki bike, other people's children. Then the large cars with darkened windows began to arrive from St. George's.

She would watch them come and go till well past midnight, or till the beast awakened in Daniel's veins and she had to attend to him.

At first her interest in Teestone was no more than curiosity about the goings-on of the young. That was in the early days when she knew nothing of the powder. She had seen Daniel suck it up his nostrils a couple of times and believed him when he told her it was no different from a sweet, a new something to tantalise the young; and she thought that it would pass like those little obsessions her boy had developed from time to time, and then relinquished for his books. It didn't seem to make him ill, and he hadn't begun to hit her.

Why she hadn't thought of going to see Teestone sooner amazed her. Now, she couldn't wait to meet the young man whom a powder had made so powerful.

The rest of the day burnt itself out rapidly. When her boy began to stir in sleep, she straightened her dress, left her house and crossed over to Teestone's yard.

He came out when she called, his body blocking the doorway. She had to look up to examine his face against the darkness of the door mouth. This she did quickly before bringing her head back down. Now she watched him with her eyes upturned.

'What you want, Miss Lady.'

'I want to come in,' she said.

'Come in where!' He glared down at her. 'Come inside o my house! What you want in my house?'

'Is someting,' she lowered her voice and her eyes, afraid that he would not let her in. 'Is someting I want to buy. I kin pay,' she added hastily.

'I tell you I sellin anyting? What you waan to buy!' He was still fuming, but his voice, like hers, was lowered.

'I waan some niceness,' she said flatly, and lifted her eyes at him. He paused a moment, shifted his body and she slipped under his arm. Teestone pulled the door behind him.

Now that the door was closed, he was transformed, almost another person. Relaxed, smiling, he drew a wooden stool from under the mahogany table in the middle of the room and placed it before her. Carefully, she lowered herself.

Teestone grinned. 'Miss Norma, what you say you want?'

'I jus waan some, some of dat ting dat make my son, make my son so happy.' She halted on the last word, made it sound like the most frightful thing on earth. But she managed a smile and that put Teestone at ease. He seated himself a few feet in front of her. He smiled wider and she noticed the gold tooth. She did not remember him having a gold tooth. He'd had bad teeth, the sort that prised his lips apart.

His shirt, she also noticed, was of a soft material that hung on him as if it were liquid, made, no doubt, from one of those fabulous materials she had seen in pictures in Grace's magazines, and in the large stores through whose wide glass windows you feasted your eyes but never entered.

'What you offerin?' he whispered. For a moment she did not understand him. 'What you have?' he repeated.

She allowed her eyes to wander around the room before easing her fingers down her bosom and pulling out an old handkerchief. It was rolled into a knot. The curl of her fingers holding it accentuated their frailty. There was a scar at the back of her left hand, as if she had been burnt there. She unknotted the bit of cloth to reveal a ball of crumpled notes.

'A thousand dollars,' she said, and dropped it on the table. It was all she had. The gesture said so, that and her trembling hands. She was never likely to have that much again, for it had taken a lot to get it. One thousand dollars that would have gone to her boy, along with the house and the piece of land that had been in the family for as long as anyone could remember.

Teestone did not reach for the money. He looked at her with a sudden probing suspicion, as if he were seeing her for the first time, . She was an old woman, in trouble and confused because her son was in trouble and confused. The stupid kind. The kind he despised most: those women who would do anything to please their sons, who never saw the sky because all their lives they were too busy looking down, digging and scratching the earth. It always puzzled him how people like that ever came by money. A thousand dollars? It had always been his! If she had not given it to him herself, her son would have, bit by bit. They were all coming now, these old women. When their children could no longer get to him on their own, they were the ones who came and begged for them. Norma Browne was not the first, and she would not be the last. These days he did not have to do a thing. These days, money made its way to him.

'Hold on,' he told her, opening the door behind him and disappearing into his bedroom.

Slowly, her eyes travelled around the room.

In the centre of a tiny table in the corner there was a framed picture of Teestone, his mother, and the man his mother had lived with, but who, she knew without a doubt, wasn't his father – although she'd made the man believe he was. To the right of that there was another photo of a child.

She examined the picture of the baby sitting on a straw mat, staring out at the camera with a wide-eyed, open-mouthed, bewilderment. He hadn't grown out of that wide, wet mouth, nor indeed those eyes that seemed smaller than they really were, because of the heaviness of the lids. She replaced the picture, cautiously.

He was rebuilding the house his mother had left him, or rather he was replacing the wood with concrete, which meant erecting blocks against the board walls outside. When they were set in cement he would knock the planks out one by one from inside. Now, even before he'd done that, the wet concrete was seeping through the boards, leaving a pale sediment that left an ugly trace of powder and tiny bits of wood on her fingers. Electrical wires ran everywhere – along the floorboards, the ceiling and the walls. The rumours she'd heard were true. Teestone was bringing electricity to his house. Or he was having that man who came in the long, black car on Fridays – the man they called The Blade – make the government do it for him. A couple of large, soft chairs lay upturned in a corner, completely covered with transparent plastic, and to the left of her there was a gaping hole through which she could see the earth below the house. Perhaps they had opened it up to replace the wooden pillars too. The smell of concrete was everywhere.

She was still contemplating this scene of devastation when Teestone came out with a small brown bag, the type the shop sold sugar by the half pound in. He did not place it in her hand but on the mahogany table in front of them. She took it up, and for a moment she felt confident, self-possessed.

She opened the bag carefully and dragged out the small plastic sac that was folded inside it.

'S'not a lot,' she said, shocked. 'Not a lot for all my money.'

Teestone laughed till the fat vein at the side of his neck stood out. She watched it throb and pulse. 'S'what you expect? Dis, dis worth more dan it weight in gold, y'know dat? More-dan-it-weight-in-gold.' He spoke the last few words as though he'd rehearsed them till they sounded rhythmic and convincing. 'Ask anybody.'

'Didn know,' she apologised, and then she brought it to her nose. She froze, fixing very dark, very steady eyes on him. 'It s'pose to smell like dat? Like, uh, baby powder?'

Her question had taken him by surprise. The slight narrowing of his eyes and the way he tried to close his mouth without really managing it, confirmed her suspicion.

'It not s'pose to smell o baby powder,' she told him quietly, a new hardness in her voice.

Is so it smell, he was about to tell her, and ask her what de hell she know 'bout niceness anyway, but her directness stopped him. He snatched the packet off the table and went back inside the bedroom. This time he returned sooner, dropped a different packet on the table and sat back heavily.

Norma took it up and passed it under her nose. She could see by his expression that he wanted her to leave. He was tired, or perhaps, now that his business with her was over, he just wanted to be rid of her. But she was not finished with him yet.

She wanted to know how she should prepare the stuff and he showed her. Her hands shook when she took the needle to examine the thin, evil thread of metal that slipped so easily into flesh. The first time she saw her boy use it, it had made her sick. He had taken it standing and had fallen straight back against the floorboards, his body rigid, like a tree deprived of its roots, doing nothing to break the fall. He'd cut his head badly and did not even know it, just laid there with that smile, that awful inner peace, while she turned him over and tended to his wound.

In her hand, the metal shone like an amber thread of light against the lamp.

'All of it is for de boy?' asked Teestone, showing her his tooth.

Some was for her son, she answered, and well, she was goin to use de rest. Was de niceness nicer if she used all of it in one go?

No, he told her, and the gold tooth glimmered in the light. If she used more than he just showed her – at that he pulled out a pack of razor blades, extracted one, opened the packet he'd handed her and separated a small portion, working it with the same care that she used to mix medicine for her boy's illness when he was a child. If she ever used more than *that* – he pointed at the tiny heap he'd separated – it would kill her.

'Too much niceness does kill. Y'unnerstan?' He laughed at his joke, lit a cigarette and leaned back against the chair. That too was new, the long cigarettes with the bit of silver at the end. In fact everything about Teestone seemed new. There was not the redness in the eyes, the dreadful tiredness that went deeper than age, the loosening of something precious and essential in the face, the damp surrender of the skin – once smooth and dark and beautiful with youth – to that terrible hunger that made her son strike out at her. Teestone looked fresh and happy and as alert as a cat. Money had made him handsome.

'Could be a nice house,' she said, looking around the room,

smiling the smallest of smiles, happier now than she had been for the past twelve months.

It was perhaps out of that odd sense of abeyance that she reached out suddenly and fixed Teestone's collar – or she might have been prodded by a desire to get an idea of what that shiny material really felt like. Her fingers brushed the side of his neck, touching the laughing vein. The young man recoiled with a violence she thought entirely undue.

She pretended not to notice his outrage, got up slowly and shuffled towards the door. There, she stopped and turned back.

'He lef school last year,' she told him with a quiet, neutral look. 'My Dan jus come an tell me dat he leavin school, and I say, "You can't. You can't, because you always tell me dat you want to see de world, dat you'll make me proud and build a nicer house for us when you become someting. You say you know how hard it is for me. How much I does do for you and how much I'll always do for you." An he laugh, like he was laughing at someting he know inside he head. He say he don't need to go nowhere no more to see de world, because he could see it from right dere where he lie down whole day on his back below my house. He tell me what he see sometimes and I can't make no sense of it. Cos I can't see inside mih boy head. I can't make no sense o people walkin over precipice an dem not dyin, o animal dat talk an laugh with you inside your head. I can't. But he say he see them and it make im happy.

'But is when de niceness get bad,' she added softly, apologetically, 'and I can't do nothing and I just hear im bawl an bawl an bawl, an he start hittin me, dat I does – well I does jus tek it.

'Y'know sometimes he hit me – my son? Hit me like he father used to?' Her voice had dropped to a whisper, thick and dark and gentle. 'I let him. I let him till he get tired an fall asleep. He don' sleep no more like he used ter. Is like someting in he sleep, in he dreamin, beatin him up same like he do with me. All de time. Dat's why – dat's why I does…'

Teestone got up. 'You get what you want, Miss Lady. Go!'

He'd already pushed open the door for her.

She walked out into a close, choked night. There were some

girls outside, one or two not more than fourteen years old. Their precocious eyes fell on her incredulously, before turning back to the doorway with that still and hungry gaze she'd seen so often in her son during the quiet times when the shivering stopped and she'd force-fed him, or tried to. She knew all of them. Some she'd even delivered before her hand went funny. As children, she'd kept them for their mothers when they went off to St. George's for medicine or some necessary thing that their hillside gardens or the sea could not provide.

At their age, life was supposed to be kinder than it would ever be again – a time of an enormous promise that never lasted long, but was part of growing up. It belonged to that age. Was part of what kept you going for the rest of your life.

She decided not to go home. Her boy would be there now beneath the house, laid out on his back. He would remain there until she came and brought him in. If she did not feel like it, she would leave him there until some time close to morning when he would beat on her door until she let him in. Tonight he would not touch her because she had what it took to quiet him.

And that was another thing: he would not beg anymore, or offer Teestone anything for the relief of a needle. Once she saw him beg and it had shamed her. Saw him do it yesterday and it had shamed her even more because Teestone's refusal had brought him raging to her yard.

She took the track that ran off from the main road, which used to take him to the school in St. George's.

It was a long, hard walk because the rains from the weeks before had made a drain of the mud track and she was forced to steady her progress by grabbing at the bushes at the side. Ordinarily, she would have taken a torch, but she had not planned this visit; tonight, it had suddenly seemed like common sense that she should visit Grace. It was Grace who first told her about how, when he left for school, Daniel got off the bus a mile away, and doubled back to feed his veins on Teestone's powder. It was Grace who, without moving from her house, had found out where it came

from and the nickname of the government man who visited
Teestone every Friday night.

Grace was the only one to whom she spoke these days. Grace
who'd had the gentlest of husbands; whose five daughters had all
gone away and sent her money every month, from England,
America and Canada; who'd offered to buy her son's uniform as
a little present for winning the scholarship.

The back of her hand was itching – a deep, insistent itch that she
could not reach because it was beneath the skin. It was the white
scar where the skin had been cut away and then healed very badly.
Many people thought she had been born that way, but she hadn't.

Grace's place was neat and small and full of colour. There were
large blood-red hibiscus on her curtains and the enamelled
bowls, cups, and the glasses in the cabinet had bouquets of
flowers patterned all over them. Even her dress was a flower
garden. God had given her eyes that shone like bits of coloured
glass which, in some moods, were exactly like a cat's. Three
kerosene lamps burned in her room. Their combined brightness
gave a stark, shadowless quality to the room.

Grace settled her down and retreated to the kitchen. She
returned with a bowl of soup and handed it to Norma.

'Eat!' she grunted.

'I done eat already.'

'Then eat again. When trouble eating people, people have to
eat back! So take de food an eat!'

The sweet smell of stewed peas and provision and salt meat
almost made her faint. She hadn't eaten and Grace knew that she
was lying. She'd lost her appetite for everything.

She placed the packet on the table and took up the bowl. Grace
looked at the brown bag frankly, a question in her eyes.

'How's de boy?' she mumbled, still staring at the paper bag.

'Cost me everything. All that was left – a thousand dollars.'

'What cost what?' asked Grace.

'That.' Norma nudged the bag with the handle of the spoon.

Grace reached for it and opened it. The powder was on her
fingers when she withdrew her hand. It could have been the effect

of the candlelight on her silver bracelets, but her hand seemed to tremble. Her face went dead. 'A thousand dollars! Fo' that?'

'What money I had left, I draw it out today.'

'Jeezas Christ, you buy dat poison for your boy! You mad!'

'You think so?' The unconcern in her voice left a chill in Grace's stomach.

'Where he is?' Grace asked.

'Below the house. Sleepin. He tired.'

'Still – erm hittin you?'

Norma stopped short, the bit of meat held between her thumb and index finger. She nodded.

'First the father and den the son. God bless me I don't have no boychild. But I wish, I wish I had a boy to raise his hand and touch me! Jeezan bread, I wish that if…' she stopped breathless, eyes flaming in the lamplight. 'God forgive me, but I'd make dat sonuvabitch wish he never born.'

Norma smiled, 'Dat's de problem. You don't see? If he's a sonuvabitch, dat mean I'z the bitch dat make dis son. I don't wish he never born, but sometimes, sometimes I wish he don't live no more. To ease him up a bit.' She looked up apologetically.

Grace grunted irritably. 'You – you not goin to let him continue!'

'Nuh.' Norma licked her fingers. 'Nuh, I goin stop him. Tonight.'

The certitude in her voice made Grace lean closer. 'You goin ter… Jeezas, girl. Jeezas!'

'I not goin to, y'know… But like I say, I think of it sometimes – sometimes, all the time – I think of it. If y'all hear im bawlin, not to bother. Tell everybody not to bother.' Something in her tone turned Grace's eyes to Norma's hand, the one that lay curled up like a bird's claw in her lap.

That hand alone was reason enough for everyone to bother. What kind of woman would place her hand between the cogs of a machine so that she could get the insurance to send her boy off to a high-class school in St. George's? Inside a canemill, besides! And if she could do that to herself for him, what on God's earth wouldn't she do to make her sacrifice worthwhile?

'Go easy,' muttered Grace, taking up the bowl of unfinished food and heading for the kitchen. It was both a warning and a farewell and sensing this, Norma got up.

'If you hear him,' she started.

'Uh-huh,' Grace answered without turning round. 'Rum-an-coke is what they call it – mix with something else.' She called out from the kitchen. 'They take dat ting and drink down rum right after. Dat's what make dem mad an beat up deir own flesh-an-blood so bad.'

'Ah know.' Norma curled her hand around the packet. All of a sudden the room felt too bright. She lifted her bad hand above her eyes as if to shade them from the sun. She paused briefly at the doorway, made as if to say something, then changed her mind before slipping out into the night.

Back home, she helped the boy from under the house and led him to the bedroom. He was quiet and aware of her but she knew that soon he would be shivering. She lit the lamp, undressed him and bathed him, like she used to. The way she thought she'd forgotten. And then she went back to the kitchen.

There, she carved out a portion of the stuff exactly as she'd seen Teestone do. She knew where he kept his needle, knew what she had to do.

She went in. Laid the small bag down beside the door. He'd already begun to shiver.

'C'mon Bumpsy, take this for Mammy,' she said, and he seemed, from somewhere deep inside, to recognise that tone; began curling his shirt ends between his fingers like he used to when he was a child, while he looked at her with a tired, helpless uncertainty.

'Is for you. Tek it from Mammy,' she urged, her voice soft and angry at the same time.

He took the needle and she watched him unflinching, while he served himself, so hungry for the ease it offered he was almost sobbing. Then, while he recovered and began floating away from her, she reached below the bed, opened the bag and took out the length of chain and the padlocks she had bought in St. George's.

Still cooing her mummy-talk, she fastened her son against the bed.

If you hear him bawlin, she'd told Grace – who would, come morning, pass the message on to everyone – if you hear him bawlin, tell everybody not to bother. She knew the bawling would begin soon, or some time in the morning, or perhaps the next day, and it would go on for a long, long time.

Back in the kitchen she mixed most of what remained of the powder in the paper bag. Finished, she leaned out of her window and observed the precocious girls, the motorbikes, the occupants of the occasional car sneaking back and forth between the road and Teestone's house.

Soon the traffic would subside, the lamps go out and the whole world come to a pause while Teestone slept.

It is a warm, tense night and the great, starless emptiness above her makes her think of futile distances, of the vastness of the world, her own smallness, and the place she feels she no longer has in it. Because a time does come, she thinks, when a woman can only hope for what comes after her – her children and the children that will come from them, that would pass on and on, if not her name, then her blood and perhaps a memory of her – an acknowledgment that they were alive only because she once existed, and that was what does mek life worth someting.

Her hand is itching again. Perhaps it will rain. Her hand always itches before rain. A low wind stirs the air, shakes the trees above the houses and leaves a smell of cinnamon, swamp and charcoal over the village. As if this is a signal, she straightens up, steps out into the night. Full height, she is much taller than most people have seen her, and she has lost her shuffle as she walks across the yard.

She remembers the hole in Teestone's living room and avoids it. In her head, she carries a very clear picture of the house and everything in it.

The lamp is lit in his bedroom and he is asleep, rolled over on one side and snoring softly. He is naked. One of the girls lies curled up in front of him, also naked, the young hips turned inwards, giving her a curious air of innocence. Sleep has stripped away what remains of the womanishness she wears by day and made of her a child again.

She kneels beside Teestone and he stirs, perhaps sensing her presence.

The jab wakes him. He erupts out of sleep, his hand clutching that laughing vein at the side of his neck, but she is strong and she keeps him and the needle there until she empties it of her thousand dollars worth of niceness. Eyes wide, Teestone stares at her. His fist closes on her wrist. It is the bad hand that he is crushing and it hurts. But she offers him a smile – beautiful and alluring – something wonderful to take with him.

He eases back on the pillow, releasing her, and sighs the longest, most restful of all sighs, his face still incredulous, still profoundly outraged.

The girl has not stirred from sleep, and for that Norma Browne is grateful.

She walks out of the house, turns and spits carelessly at the dark before crossing to her yard.

Before she goes in, she pauses, turns her face up at the sky and sniffs. She could smell the morning. But it is still dark. And the world and the birds down there are very, very quiet.

AND THERE WERE NO FIREFLIES

The girl saw the shape of the older woman against the window. She slipped off the bike and in a flush of pique reached over, wrapped her arms around the boy and kissed him long and deep. Her aunt would get a good view of her tight behind and more, she hoped, since she had not bothered to arrange her skirt.

Joseph muttered something in her ear about tonight and the beach, and though he often said that, or something of the kind, when he dropped her off, she still laughed out loud, so that the woman could hear her, think that it was meant for her, and be suitably appalled.

The bike leapt away in a faked rage – so like the way Joseph was with her, especially when he made her follow him to the beach. The sound bounced off the walls of the sleeping houses – the Kawasaki's red brake-lights a glowing scar against the dark. She patted her hair, smoothed her butt, high-stepped beneath the single street light and blew a final kiss.

When Mariana turned to face the door, her aunt was no longer at the window. She knew what to expect, and the smile that came so easily with her friends was replaced by a grimness in the eyes, ready for the reproach she knew was coming from her aunt.

The woman irritated her in ways no other person could. Over the past eight months she had concluded, with the disgust of someone who had uncovered something nasty in her food, that her aunt shamed her. This was why she always asked Joseph to wait for her across the street; why she never asked him in; why she visited the houses of friends after school, but never invited them home; why, always, after the throbbing darkness of the nightclub in the south, the hip-whipping wind-downs and smoochy oozes on the dance floor, she would succumb to Joseph's demands and linger on the beach with him.

Martha – *what kind of name was that?* – was waiting for her in the cluttered living room, her thin arms hanging down her sides. The thumb of the left hand made little convulsions against the index finger, but those trembling hands were a threat that would never materialise. They had never struck her, not even as a child. Many times she'd heard Martha explain to the group of country women, who passed on Saturdays to beg for a cupful of iced water, that her sister's – 'God-rest-er-soul' – offspring was not, and never would be, hers to punish.

The girl thought of the women's laughter and the stridency of their speech as they drew attention to their basketfuls of fish or fruit above the thundering traffic of the town. Since her immersion in Joseph's world of parties, cars and light-skinned girls, that rawness had become painful. At times, she wished her aunt, with her high cheekbones and taut, dark skin, framed always by an old headwrap, never spoke at all.

'What time you call dis, Marie?'

'Don't know, don't care and my name is not Marie.'

'Where you been with dat boy?'

'My business.'

The hands convulsed and the girl flashed her eyes at them, then at the woman's face. She'd already trampled on every taboo in this house, but this, to stare down her aunt, was the best of all her victories.

Martha shifted her lips. 'Dat boy.'

'Like I say, is my effin business!'

'He fadder's a big-time lawyer. Same people like dat fadder ov yours who…'

'So what!'

'He don't wan de likes o you. Dat boy usin you. All o dem – they usin you. Your mother…'

'My mother dead.'

'Marie…'

'My name is not Marie.'

The hands convulsed. 'Mariana, you sempteen. You got your studies to study. You got all your life in front o you. An besides, you still a girl.'

Those last words – the one thing that Martha had not allowed herself to be bullied out of – had been the last hold her aunt had on her. On the beach with Joseph, she'd worked out her answer.

'I got everything a woman got.'

If Martha was shaken by those words, she showed it only in the sudden rearranging of her head-tie. 'Still don make you one,' she said. 'This red-boy goin leave you with de selfsame trouble dat dese people boy-chilren does always leave poor-people girlchile with.'

She stilled her hands. 'I not strong enough for you. Was not easy to admit that to meself. I didn prepare meself for de pusson you become. You change and I been prayin to God dat you not spoil for good. Is all dat love... It weaken me. But I got a cure for you. Yuh aunt Dalene will have to come.'

The girl laughed prettily. 'Don't know her; she don't know me.' That was how Sandra, Joseph's sister, would have said it. Making words dribble with contempt was one of Sandra's talents – along with her pride of bearing, her slim-fingered finickiness with food, with clothes, even with the colours she painted on her nails – all talents Mariana emulated, though not without adding her own refinements. For these Joseph seemed to appreciate her all the more, not least with the way she now spoke. This had come easily since she'd learnt to imagine each word as something soft to chew slowly.

'You more like her dan you fink,' Martha told her grimly. 'You'll see!' She slammed shut her bedroom door.

The girl was not used to having their arguments end this way. The last word had always been hers. She was the one who closed her door and killed the quarrels mid-shout.

She noticed straightaway that Martha had been in her room. The towel she'd left lying on the floor had been folded and hung up against the louvres to dry. The dresses she had flung on the bed in fits of indecisiveness were folded and stacked neatly on the pillow. Scattered strap-back shoes were now paired and laid like rows of multicoloured fishes against the wall. She lowered herself quickly to reach beneath the wardrobe until her fingers rested on the softness of the packet she had placed there a few months ago.

She straightened up, threw her clothes off and turned to the mirror to examine the person there: the face smooth and oval, the dimples of her cheeks that Joseph liked so much. People said her eyes were catlike in the way they curved, large and lake-like in their darkness.

Beauty was the name that people gave the way she looked. Until recently it had felt like something she did not own, until she found a way to measure it in the brazen glances of the men who passed her on the streets; in the way a pair of eyes would pick her out amongst a crowd of girls and stay focused on her face; in the way her passage through a group of boys stopped their conversation. And, of course, in the value Joseph set on it, how he'd made her careful of her skin, because any blemish there would upset him.

She felt so utterly unlike Martha, and that other crazy aunt of hers. And she didn't give a damn about what they said about her mother. What she knew about *that* woman did not amount to much: an assistant to a head nurse in the hospital, who'd fallen pregnant for the husband of the very same woman she was assisting and who, one year after having her, decided to die from something.

If anything, it was her father who explained her. She had his hair, not quite as straight, but with an off-black bushiness whose tendency to curl she repulsed with generous swipes of Afro-Glo and Miss Unkurl. At least, mercifully, it was not at all like her aunt's recalcitrant pepper-seed.

She stared at her nakedness in the mirror, at the high backside, curved like a question mark, the long legs and hips that flared beneath a waist so narrow she had to take in every skirt she bought. Her eyes paused, with an anxious, questioning reluctance, at the slight rise of her stomach – the part of her that held so many numbing possibilities. She was still curious at what she saw – this body that had recently acquired, almost of its own accord, such power over Joseph and the men who, just two years ago, would not have known that she existed. Still naked, she dropped herself on the bed, reached beneath her pillow for the notepad and HB pencil and began to sketch with the same intensity she had regarded herself in the mirror.

Sketching was something she just did. The impulse had always been there from as far back as she could remember. A few lateral flashes of the wrist, a swift smudged arc capped by half a curlicue, and there was Joseph crouched above her on the sand. Because no one could have seen her, she was no more than a slight line – the jaggedness of a sensation, the bare suggestion of a presence so faint, it was hardly there – and even less substantial than her aunt whose shape against the window she now scrubbed onto the paleness of the page with rapid, vengeful movements of the heel of her left hand.

She worked until sweat beaded her hairline and ridged her nose. Its passage down her face onto the page did not distract her. Her wrist was tiring, but there was one last thing she had to do. She drew on what remained of the night's rancour to imagine a form for the aunt Martha had threatened her with. This was the woman – who had never actually cared enough to show her face – she referred to privately as Magdalene the Mad – a strange and wilful sister who had fled the Kalivini lowlands to live on some godforsaken hill named Morne Riposte.

Aunt Dalene, Martha had told her as a child, could make herself heard through storms from way up on the hillside where she lived, all the way down to Lower Old Hope, *clean and clear as if she speaking directly in a pusson ear*. Dalene was nourished by the violence of wind, rain and thunder, Martha boasted. She lit her fire with the lightning from the sky. But why, Mariana wanted to know, would any woman – even if she could talk across valleys and play god with lightning – choose to plant her house way up on the fringes of the forest ,above a wilderness of canes?

She examined the damp paper, saw that she'd made the woman tall, her hair rolling from her head like rope. Barely a face. All mouth. The limbs all angles.

Then, reminded of something, she fumbled beneath the

pillow for another pencil and just below the place where she had drawn Joseph and herself, she made a final stroke. Red and strong and certain, because tonight Joseph Mayors had hurt her.

She glared at her drawing of the demon aunt, tore the page away and crushed it in her fist. When she raised her head, the room was flushed with daylight. The town was waking up. She considered briefly pulling the curtains close then decided against it. She drew the sheet up to her chin, shut her eyes and slept.

Voices pulled her out of sleep, but when she raised her head, the house was filled with silence. Even the traffic of the town had settled down to a sullen deep-throated hum in the midday heat.

Her eyes travelled around the room and took in the things she had collected and pasted on the walls: the covers of two LPs, one by Third World – a Noah's Ark of rainbow-coloured creatures in a forest too perfect to be real, the other of a gleaming, long-necked girl standing on blue lettering that simply stated, 'Bacharach'. There was also a jagged-edged strip of colour snatched in a moment of reckless desire from an encyclopedia in the public library, which reproduced part of an early painting by Cezanne.

Leaves too. She had collected and pinned an almond's for the improbability of its redness; an angel leaf for its lacelike delicacy and a periwinkle whose blackened head was like an awkward full stop beneath the rows of sketches she had done.

She felt a sensation of heat, and the raising of the hairs on her skin. She realised that there was a presence in the room, a woman by the door.

She snatched the flimsy cotton sheet over her nakedness and pulled herself upright, a small cry escaping her.

'Dalene.' The voice arrived, it seemed, from a long way off.

'Dalene,' the woman said again, raising her voice as if she was not sure the girl had heard her. Eyes travelled the length of the bed and settled on her face.

'Wha – what you doin in my room?' The girl's shout was loud enough to fill the house.

Martha entered running. She closed the door behind her, and leaned her weight against it. 'Is yuh aunt,' she said, as if that explained everything. 'What all dis bawlin for?'

It might have been the way the light from the louvres fell on Martha's face, but the set of her jaw seemed firmer, and there was a clarity in her voice that hadn't been there before. Martha also held her stare. 'Dalene here, like I promise,' she said.

Dalene had not taken her eyes off her. *She* wasn't much to look at. Another country woman with the same dark, unsettling muscularity, especially in the arms. Mariana noticed, too, the curious concentration of life they all seemed to have in their fingers – as if forever testing the texture of some invisible bit of soil.

She was slightly taller than Martha. If there was anything that made her different, it was her carelessness with clothes: a faded, flowered cotton dress, a pair of rubber slippers – the nearest anyone could come to being barefoot, without being barefoot; and the inevitable pair of heavy silver bracelets passed down from God knows how many generations. No wonder she had fled from people into the hills.

Dalene had once occupied her child's story-world of trees that sang and lions that quarrelled with spiders. But there were no forests here in town. No sweet-talking, fast-thinking spider that tricked a murdering lion; no half-born or aborted child forever lost to the dark, searching for some woman's womb to grow in. This aunt had long been relegated to a place of dreams and lies.

The two seemed to be waiting for her to speak. The stranger's stare made her shift on the bed with rising annoyance.

'I want to put on my clothes.'

Neither seemed to hear her.

If their silence was meant to unnerve her, they were mistaken. She didn't know what Martha might have told her sister, but she could guess at the list of 'sins' she had spread out for her gaze. For them, 'family' meant everything. It gave them the right to poke and stare at everybody else's business – even this aunt here, badly dressed and awkward as a stone.

'Get out!' she snapped. 'You two, you –'

'Shut up! Get up! Go an bathe!' The woman's voice sliced across her words like the swing of a machete. It was as if somebody had struck her on the ear.

The woman stepped out of the darkness of the corner, and now that the window-light was on her, Mariana saw the shape of her face, how impossibly like Martha's it was, how dark the lips – and just how much rage a face could contain.

'Who-who de hell is you to tell me?'

Again the voice lashed out and lopped off her words. 'Y'hear me!'

'I not…' But something in the woman's demeanour dried her up.

'You!' she snarled, balling her fist against her waist. 'You call yuhself a Safara?'

The outrage with which she said the name was surprising. This aunt did not invoke her 'sins' against her mother's memory the way Martha did. Her anger seemed to feed on one thing: that Mariana carried a name that she also had a claim to.

'She goin be takin you with her,' Martha cut in.

'I'm not going anywhere with that!'

She would never figure out how anyone could move across a room so fast, or how the flat of a palm could hold the power of a thunder clap. Joseph had slapped her once in front of his friends to prove that he could do it. That was like one of those pecks on the cheek that Sandra practised on her friends compared to the explosive, dizzying darkness that now flushed her head.

'Go and bathe,' the face above her said.

She had barely recovered – the woman still hanging above her – when something soft was thrust against her cheek.

'Three months pass an you don't use none o dese tings once. How come!' Martha said.

Finding her fire again, the girl raised her head, but was checked by Dalene's sudden movement, pushing her face close to hers. The girl could smell her hair, the musk of coconut and nutmeg oil. The woman's thumb shot out and brushed against her throat. It was a feather of a gesture, but it seemed to bring a new grimness to Dalene's face. 'Done happen,' Dalene said, and straightened up.

Martha's eyes had gone dull and deep and sorrowful. Her hand reached up and brushed the head wrap, adjusted it and remained up there.

'What you tink you hidin, chile? How long you tink you kin hide a ting like dat?' Dalene said.

Unable to hold the woman's gaze, the girl fixed her eyes on the dried-out periwinkle on the wall.

'Go an bathe; I takin you with me.' This time the woman's voice was softer.

Mariana began to cry.

That was how she found herself heading for some place named Morne Riposte, her suitcase packed with books, a couple of jeans, two large, ill-fitting dresses – *becos it ain' got no partyin up dere* – and the little things she could not bear to leave behind: a ring fashioned from the shell of a gru-gru palm nut, three pebbles, a bit of pink glass she'd picked up from the beach, and the only thing that Joseph had ever given her – a small bottle of gold-flecked paint for her fingernails – which she'd later learnt had been his sister's.

On their way through the hills and quarries, past the tired-looking houses that leaned away from the road, through the smells of fermenting fruit and leeching soil and the dark, cloying rankness of vegetation, she discovered she'd forgotten her comb – and this felt like the most damning confirmation of her helplessness.

The journey was more potholes than road. It imposed a silence on the bus, packed with women laden with dry goods. After the raucousness of the early part of the journey, they'd come to rest their eyes on thoughts she could not guess at. This was a side to them she had not seen before: people who handled silence with the same ease with which they made conversation.

She noticed, too, the way they responded to her aunt. They rarely looked Dalene in the eyes and it galled Mariana to realise that she, too, had come to fear that gaze.

The driver was a thin young man with skin the colour of nutmeg. Throughout the journey he threw glances at her from the rear-view mirror and seemed indifferent to her hostility when she caught him staring. When he stopped the bus to let them off, he pretended she was not there.

Dalene pulled a small sac from somewhere down her bosom and handed it to him. 'For your mother,' she said. The young man took it like someone receiving a secret. He laid it carefully against the dashboard and thanked her.

'Your fourth cousin,' Dalene said to him. He nodded, his eyes glancing at Mariana, then quickly sliding off her face.

In a fit of nervousness her hand crept up to her throat and stayed there. What was it there that had exposed her and drawn the woman's wrath? Dalene's fingers had paused there briefly and had confirmed the one thing that for more than seven weeks her mind had shut itself against. *It done happen.* Those words had made her a frightened child again. How could a finger passed against the skin reveal so much?

'Is only Dalene could prevent de shame,' Martha told her.

This knowledge had suddenly made school important again, confirmed for her that she wanted all the things education had promised her.

With a mixture of belligerence and contrition, Martha had tried to prepare her for the journey. She had talked in the language of parables.

'She will take you up de ole stone road. De one dat climb over Old Hope Valley. Glory cedar trees – you can't miss dem cos dem rise up wid de road – and long before you come to dem you kin smell dem like a greetin. You kin smell de wind too, an de salt-an-freshness from de sea. An cane…' Her eyes had darkened and that darkness seemed to seep into her voice. 'It ain got no smell like cane, Marie. Ain't got no feelin like de feelin dat cane cause you. Is a man smell. A sad smell. De kind o smell dat is sadder dan de saddest times you ever live. Ain't got no other smell kin full you up an frighten you without you hardly knowin why. Just keep you eye on Dalene when you follow she up dat road.'

At their parting, especially in Martha's kiss, she had felt something that went beyond forgiveness. Love, her aunt had confessed, had weakened her, and when Martha rested her lips on her forehead, Mariana had a sense of what she meant.

As they made their way through the woods, there was a humming that clung to the ears like damp cloth. If Martha had prepared her for the climb, she had not told her what came before it – the stepping into greenness, into trees that seemed to have laid eternal claim to the earth; the immersion in a world of wetness, stones and mud; wading in air that flowed around her body like cold water.

The demon aunt was no more than a shape ahead of her, a shifting darkness that moved amongst the trees. Just once Dalene stopped to dip beneath a bush and emerge with a machete in her hand. Then she stepped back onto what could barely be called a path, hardly pausing to pick a leaf here, to chip at a bit of bark there, to rummage at the foot of some tiny growing plant before uprooting it. These she stuffed in a small plastic bag that had suddenly appeared around her wrist. They crossed a ravine and while she struggled behind – a rising anger gathering in her chest – the girl slipped and the bag of clothes spilt its guts out in the mud. Her aunt stopped but did not look back, seemed in some uncanny way to know exactly when to take off again. Just when she was about to shout her defiance, to say that she was tired, couldn't *people* see that she was doing her best to keep up, they stepped out into day, and the brightness struck her face like a sharp, unwelcoming slap.

'You dirty yuhself,' Dalene said, glancing at the mud-soaked canvas shoes and the scar of mud that ran down the front of her dress. Mariana clamped her lips and glared hatefully at the back that was abruptly turned on her.

The climb was an eternity. Dalene had begun to gather bits of dried wood which, after close inspection, she trimmed with a brisk flick of her machete and added to the ever-growing bundle on her head. The girl wondered if there was a limit to the size of the load this woman could carry.

She waded through the scents of flowering glory cedar like a drunk, her footsteps fuelled by a hate that killed the tiredness and kept her climbing with a focused, tight-lipped determination. She was only dimly aware of the rising chill, the land receding below, the total absence of anything human but themselves. In this landscape, all the things Martha said about this woman who never tired, who walked as if no one else was there, seemed all too believable. It occurred to her that in this landscape she could be made to disappear without raising a whisper. She did not put it past this woman.

She almost missed the house, a tiny wooden thing with a narrow tin gutter running the length of the eaves and draining into a large yellow oil drum perched on a nest of stones. It squatted on very short thick concrete pillars a foot or so high. From a distance, the house had appeared legless because the lower part was hidden by a flourishing fence of dasheen plants.

The bundle of wood rolled off Dalene's head and crashed onto the earth. She turned to the large drum, lifted a calabash which must have been floating on the water. She filled it and began to wash her arms from the shoulders down. Finished, she turned to her feet, rubbing them vigorously on one of the nearby stones. Straightening up, she took the bag of clothes from the girl, handed her the calabash and muttered softly, 'Bathe.'

She was too tired to retort that she would have done that anyway, that she was not like *people* who only washed their arms and feet after a sweaty half-day journey. Instead, her hand on her throat, she sat on a stone and stared at this new world.

Night was already hemming the tops of the hills. Below, the canes were a darkening green. The smell of glory cedars reached her even here. A mile or so further down the valley, a huddle of hillside buildings sat amongst the green, like an untidy pile of dried leaves.

She would spend the night outside. It would be her declaration of war with this demon woman. Her life was hers; nobody could own her, and that was that.

★

Dalene came out, her headwrap gone. She'd thrown a loose shapeless dress over her shoulders. She picked up the calabash at the feet of the girl and walked over to the drum.

Mariana watched from under hooded lids as Dalene undressed. It was the darkest body she had ever seen, impossibly young, muscled and curved; too strong, too straight, too assured of itself to be a girl's, and clearly a thing that light loved. What remained of it from the dying day settled on the woman's skin like dust.

She was throwing water on herself with careless, fluid movements of the arm, dipping over and over again with the same rapid, flowing gesture that seemed more like dance. The girl wanted to reach for the paper and pencil that were not there. The realisation of their absence left her feeling deeply deprived.

Mariana bathed with an odd sense of privacy out there in the yard. Night had fallen when she finished. That and the sudden chill that gripped the air had killed her desire to stay outside. She realised that in the town she had never really seen night, not without the amber haze that always gave some shape to things. Here, the valley below had been swallowed by a dark and depthless void.

She entered a room suffused with candlelight. Dalene was a moving darkness at the corner of her vision, rummaging inside the plastic bag she had carried on her wrist earlier on. Mariana halted, her eyes darting beyond her aunt to the darkness outside for some steadying thing to brace against, because for a terrifying moment, she'd lost a sense of where she was.

Dalene's small room was another world. An odd world of trees and rocks and skies and, above all, in the middle of everything and directly before her, a road. It took a while before her heart quietened, before she realised it was a picture. A collage. The kind she used to do before she turned her hand to drawing.

She stared at the road, the light and shadows there, the lines converging to a needlepoint in the distance. It had, for a brief, terrifying moment, seemed so real. Then she turned her eyes on the woman.

'You, you did that?'

Dalene paused to look her briefly in the face. She was less than three feet away and still she seemed to be peering from a distance. She did not answer.

Mariana retreated inwardly, troubled that her first attempt to say something to Dalene without being asked meant nothing to the woman. She might have gone on and told her it was good – though 'good' was not the word for it. 'Good' could not account for the piles of magazines and newspapers that Dalene must have gone through to create this beautifully haphazard yet coherent world, with photographs stripped of their skies and made to meld with the skies of other worlds. Trees that shot out of stones, and strips of empty air and grass sprouting flowers as heavy as hibiscus.

Her eyes returned to the road and lingered there – wide and dark and inviting where it began at the join between the floorboards and the wall, heading, beneath a jagged sky, to God-knows-where.

In smaller ways the rest of the room was like that – lots of colour, shine and patterns: a white hand-knitted cloth covering the centre-table that was frilled with pink paper roses that looked almost real; two chairs made of bamboo; nine gold-rimmed teacups that sat on a large matching tray on the top of a small mahogany table. Underneath the table was a nest of speckled snails' shells gathered in a pretty heap, and beside it what appeared to be the tail of an animal – a donkey's perhaps – patterned with tiny white shells that sheened quietly in the soft light.

Her aunt had pasted pictures all around the walls. Hundreds of them: unfamiliar reaches of rock and mountains; storms and deserts; wild and wrathful seas – not so much objects as sensations, like the sudden flush of light through leaves, or drops of water making chains around a cobweb. Her eyes paused on a tree rooted amongst black rock, so tortured by the wind it crouched low to the earth.

She could not help stealing glances at the woman, bent now over the coal-pot on a dresser built into the window.

'You, erm, you don't like people?' In Dalene's landscapes there was nothing that moved or lived.

Dalene reached for a pot, placed it on the fire and poured in several cups of water.

'Yer have to decide tonight, cos what we eat from now depend on what you want.'

Dalene retrieved the plastic bag of herbs and roots. The girl stared at her, as the woman's meaning slowly settled in her head.

'De-decide?' What decision could there be other than what had already been decided? From the moment she had left Martha, from the time Dalene had confirmed the thing she did not want to know, the decision had been made. That, surely, was what Martha meant by ridding themselves of the shame? You did not choose an illness. An illness happened and you simply did whatever was required to get better.

Dalene's statement, so flat, so void of feeling, had raised a possibility that had not existed for her before and she felt as if a block of ice had settled in her stomach.

Dalene placed bits of plants on the table in two formations: one nearer the girl, the other to her right. Long-fingered, dark and sure, her aunt's hands teased them into neat heaps.

Then, with the same casualness with which she'd reached out and brushed her throat, Dalene slipped her hand into the bag and brought out what looked like several onions, only they were smaller and a glistening bluish cream in the lamplight. She laid all eight of them on the table.

'These,' she gestured at the heap before the girl, 'kin make you strong an prepare you. Those,' she nodded at the small pile on her right, 'will kill it by tomorrow.'

'Will?' The girl stared at the arrangement.

Dalene sighed, drew up one of the bamboo chairs to the table.

Mariana licked her lips and tried to hold the woman's gaze. 'Kill... I... I don't like de way you put it,' she said.

'How else I mus put it?' Her aunt spoke as if she was really prepared to learn something.

'Is not a life. Not – not yet.'

Dalene reached beneath the table, her eyes still on Mariana. Her hand emerged with a bit of broken mirror. The girl realised that she must have placed it there just for this purpose. Dalene shifted the candle and held the mirror up to the Mariana's face.

Then, with the other hand, she took one of the girl's fingers and placed it gently against the hollow of her throat.

'Dat not what it tellin us,' she said. 'Look dere. De pulse, dat's de baby tellin you it dere.' Dalene shifted her weight on the chair, and although it was a gentle movement, it seemed as if the whole house quaked.

'I dunno nothin 'bout dese tings. Besides, my school… I'm, I'm still a, still a…' She turned away, biting back the tears.

'I not tellin you to keep it,' Dalene said. 'I tellin you what I told your mother when she come to me with you. You was a pulse on her neck dat time, too. I tell er a pusson never get rid of tings like dat. Either way, it stay wit you. An your mother was a big woman at de time, a Safara.'

'I'm a Safara too,' the girl snapped. 'I didn't ask for the name.'

The wine-dark lips sketched a smile. It suddenly struck the girl that Dalene had tricked her into owning something she'd taught herself to be ashamed of.

'I don't want it,' she said.

'P'raps it don't want you either. A child does born knowin that you didn want it, and it carry dat knowledge in de blood. Vex till it want to burst. All de time. Without hardly knowin why. Ain got nobody in de whole wide world more full of vexation dan a child who come like dat.'

Dalene fixed considering eyes on her. 'I tell you what is true though. Ain't nobody kin love you more dan Martha gone and done, an certainly not no little red-mouth, long-arse, pissin-tail boy who mek imself believe he is man by ridin poor-people girl-chile. Ain't got no amount of ungratefulness goin change dat. Martha love you like a curse. An a pusson got to be more full o spite than dog to turn and spit on dat.'

Her eyes were still on the girl, even though her mind seemed somewhere else. From time to time she glanced at the pot of boiling water.

Mariana felt alone. She stared at her hands, then lifted her face. There was a smell in the air, perhaps from the smouldering fire or the herbs on the table. The odour brought a heavy choking sensation that pressed against her chest and with it, the memory of a bright Saturday morning when, carefully dressed, she'd walked into a government building on the Carenage. She'd passed through several rooms until she reached the office where she'd learned her father worked. The man she stood before did not get up from his desk to greet her. The office was exactly as she had imagined: large black desk, filing cabinets, two telephones. What hadn't been part of it was a photograph of that man beside a grey-eyed, light-skinned woman and three children smiling out at the world.

She'd stood before him and said, 'I'm Mariana. Crissy – Christina Safara's daughter, and you are my, erm…' She'd stopped then, hearing her words as if they were issuing from another throat. She could not say the word. The man was not helping her. There was no welcoming smile from this tall, tight-lipped, staring stranger. Hostility or hate would have been better, for they were things she would have recognised, not this flat-eyed, battened down indifference.

She'd run out of his office into a day that had gone dull and oppressive. She had wandered home and wept. The periwinkle she had uprooted from between one of the cracks of the old colonial stone building had been pulped and sappy in her hand.

'That smell,' she muttered tearfully, as if it were the source of all her hurt.

'De canes,' Dalene told her. She sounded almost sad. 'De cold does make dem sweat.' Almost as an afterthought she added, 'Is de time o de fireflies. Martha say you never seen a firefly…' Dalene got up, unwound a string from around a nail and flung open the window that faced the valley.

Mariana dragged herself off the chair. The smell hit her in the face, and she clamped down her jaws on the sickness that welled up in her chest.

And there it was just as Martha had told her – a glowing, shifting, twinkling mist of light stippling the void below them. For the first time in that day her face softened. She turned to her aunt, childish and amazed.

'Fireflies? I, I would like to catch one.'

'Ketch one?' Dalene's voice came back surprised. 'Fo what?'

'Fo me.'

'Never worth de trouble.' Dalene's chuckle was a soft cough. 'You ketch one an it die. An when it die, de light does die. Besides…'

'Besides?'

For the first time the girl detected a reluctance in her tone.

'You sure you wan to hear?'

Mariana nodded.

Dalene's hand fluttered above her head – another of Martha's gestures. 'People dis part o de world believe dat firefly is not jus little tings dat fly 'bout here come night time. Is de spirit o all de unborn dat visit us, to ketch a glimpse of dis world dem never get to see.'

The girl shifted her weight against the window.

There was a new depth to Dalene's voice. It seemed to match the awful smell that came up to oppress them. 'You see, Mariana Safara, dat's why they carry dat light, so as to see jus a little bit of dis worl. Just enough to mek dem decide whether to try to come again, or not. Used to be a time amongst dem cane down dere when a woman might decide she didn want no chile ov hers to inherit dat abomination. It had Safaras amongst dem too. What trouble me sometimes is if all o dem did decide to do de same, me an you wouldn be standin here. We'd ha been two firefly, too. Besides…'

'I don' want to hear no more.'

'You ask me,' Dalene said, and returned to the pot.

Joseph would laugh that derisive laugh of his if he could see her now with an aunt she'd barely admitted to herself, far less to him. Joseph of the rough-gentle ways, who rarely listened long enough to really hear what people said, whom she sometimes irritated with the little things she showed him, like the colours on a hillside, the patterns on a seashell, the curve of a road. She wondered where he was now. Perhaps on a beach somewhere with his friends, not staring at the sea, not listening to its cough and thunder, but trying to shut it out with the music of Credence Clear Water Revival or Joe Cocker and his Mad Dogs.

'I believe he spite me,' she said suddenly, drawing from a well of resentment that rushed up and surprised her. And with that statement, it was as if something had been unplugged in her: the flood of little humiliations; the tiny, teasing resentments; the accepting without wanting. All the things he'd said and did not say, did and did not do, which she hadn't really registered before. The fact that her presence here with Dalene was because of what Martha called her 'foolishness' took nothing away from the bitterness she felt now, the sense of having been betrayed.

It was a bitterness that Dalene echoed softly, preoccupied now with laying out two plates of fried fish. 'Man is a hoe,' she said, gently placing the plate before the girl. 'He always leave a mark. Eat and sleep. We'll both be surer in de mornin.'

FIVE LEAVES AND A STRANGER

The stranger told us that he came from one of those green mysterious valleys inland, beneath the buckled ridge of mountains that rose above our heads. Up there, he said, they woke to soggy mornings and everything dripped with mist.

It took some time to get that out of him, because his history left his lips in fragments. It was only the few among us with the memory and the mind for fitting things together that could make a story of his mutterings.

They were the last of a breed of people, he said, who believed themselves to be pure and wanted to remain so; but there weren't enough of them and their inbreeding had begun to show up in their offspring.

Their children lacked the strength to run. They were born as frail as kite flexes and prone to the chills and illnesses that a normal baby's body took for granted. Nowadays, many of their babies did not live for long.

Blood, he said, was a river, and the river in them was dying. It needed another stream to make it strong again. Their women knew this. They would receive a man, but refuse to have his children. That was why their childbearing women ran away. Most left at night to escape the machetes of their men. The brave ones, preferring a quick death to a slow one, took their chances any time of day. It was life fighting to save itself.

He had climbed out of that dripping valley one morning, not knowing where his feet were taking him, not sure of anything except the rejection of the women and a stirring in his guts. It was not his loins aching for relief. It was the same thing their women knew long before he did.

His feet had taken him all the way down the eastern coast of the island with its straight-legged, snake-hipped women. They looked on at his passing as if he were a ghost. He'd travelled through villages full of silent men who stood erect like palisades along the roadside, their very silence a threat.

Maybe they sensed what had put him on the road, and so they'd moved him on past the rocks and black sands of the coast, from where he'd once again turned inland, being more at ease in the shadow of the mountains.

He knew mountains. This one at whose feet we lived was the darkest he'd ever seen. The trees that covered its slopes were different from the ones that clothed theirs. Its peak led him to our place of wilted vines and scorched rocks.

We don't like strangers. We don't like drifting men who trace the shape of our women with their eyes. The few who pass through walk quickly and keep their gazes on the road.

But this stranger came as secretive as water. We were not aware of it until we saw him with Minerva. He saved himself that way, because which one of us would ever want Minerva? Who remembered she existed? A hard, flat wedge of a woman who, after her day in the quarries, returned home a ghost, white with the dust of the stones she worked in. Minerva the Stonebreaker, thin as drought, who walked with the stiffness of the boulders that she fought with every day. We let him have her.

Minerva must have told him the kind of people that we were. She must have suggested ways to keep us interested, so that we would not want to make him leave. He brought little marvels into our children's lives, like that strange flower he said he found among the granite and the mosses of the foothills. In the fading evening, he sat them down, made them watch the petals spread until the flower was a living flame. We were there; we saw it too. It was like witnessing the passage of a lifetime in this blooming of a plant that did not pause for jubilation, that did not stop to boast its beauty, but started dying as soon as it had given the best of itself. We watched it sink into itself, become a papery mess of ashen petals.

We can speak of many more such things: the morning he woke us up to watch a fat worm as it broke the prison of its skin and turned into a butterfly; the fish we never ate because of the poison in its bones. We saw how, in his hands, over a fire of herbs and sweating plantain leaves, it became the tastiest thing we'd ever eaten from the sea.

Of all the enchantments we witnessed, Minerva was the one true marvel. To this day we do not understand it: how the spirit of a woman could be so watered by the attentions of a man; the way the planes and angles of her body rounded and then softened with his presence; the bright new clarity of her eyes.

She preferred this man's language to our own – this stranger's way of not saying; his glances and nods and finger-flutterings; the tilting of an eyebrow that would draw a smile; the quivering of lips that caused a small convulsion in her shoulders. We envied the richness of their silence.

Then the baby came – a little girl born on the cusp of the Dry Season. We heard that the stranger delivered the child himself, and that he held the infant to his chest and wept. We were not there to confirm this, but from then on we noted the stranger's gratefulness in everything he did.

As the dryness of the year gave way to cooler air and soft rains, we watched the way he loved his child, and it is true to say that it was from him we learned the joy to be had in our own children.

It lasted eight months. Then the baby fell ill.

It was no ordinary sickness. Rumour said it had been brought to the island by the child of a foreign woman on a boat. The illness left the body of that child and came ashore. It took the children to bed and fed on them; it left their bodies and moved on after five days, almost always taking their lives with it.

We did not know that it had reached our valley until Minerva's baby began crying at the sight of food. Then came the fevers and the wasting. On the second day the doctor came, jittery from lack of sleep, or perhaps at the sight of us, and told us what it was.

With the fading of his child the stranger began to fade too. Nights, we heard him pacing the stones of Minerva's yard and when morning came we found him sitting on her step, his hardwood body rocking to the rhythm of his torment.

With Minerva, we couldn't tell which was worse – her pain at the grief of this man who had come to her from nowhere, or the slipping away of their child. Sometimes we saw her leaning out of her window, staring at him, her eyes so red it was as if she were crying without tears.

Word reached us on the fourth day that there was a cure, but it was no more than a rumour that had been travelling across the island like a slow wind. We learned of the remedy from the mouth of a woman in one of the deep blue valleys further west. She'd seen this before, she said. They'd been visited by that same illness in '35. To send it back to where it came from, we must boil the leaves of three plants together and force the infusion down the child.

We knew chado beni and colic weed. We scattered our children across the valley and up the foothills with instructions and a mouthful of threats. They rushed back in a swarm with half a forest between them. There was enough to cure the island if we only knew what the third plant was. But we were not given its name or told what it looked like; we'd only heard about what it did. And what it did sounded like a wish. We'd lived through every illness this plant was meant to cure. We'd suffered fevers and constipation; yaws and gonorrhoea; the stomach troubles of our children; the difficulties of childbirth. But no single plant we knew could fight them all on its own.

We sat in Minerva's yard that evening and ploughed our memories for clues, for some little thing that might have been said by our people who came before us. We talked until our mouths grew numb with tiredness. At the end of it, the stranger rose swaying to his feet, his eyes inflamed with the fever of his grief. He told us he would go out there and find the plant, even if the effort killed him. We looked at him and nodded. It has always been our way to let hope die a natural death; it is criminal to crush it.

Night had already gathered its skirts around our valley when he left, heading west, up and over the spine of the Mardi Gras

mountains. There are forests up there, high winds and entangle-
ments of every kind. We could not imagine him emerging on the
other side.

And us? We sat on the stones, watched a July half-moon break
the hills and make its way across the sky, until the first early-
morning wind came off the sea, crept up the valley and under our
clothing. We were not sure what we were waiting for. We did not
pray because we had no faith in Faith.

The humming of the women in Minerva's house had stopped.
The one among us who heard everything said the child inside was
still breathing. Someone began to hum. It sounded like a dirge.
We shut them up.

After a very long time of silence and many shiftings of our
bodies, the one among us who heard everything, cleared his
throat. He told us that beneath the sigh of trees and drip of water
he thought he heard something. We asked him what that something was. He was not sure.

We were preparing to call out words of sorrow to Minerva and
leave her yard, when the one among us who heard everything
detected the drag of footsteps on the asphalt. Not long after, we
saw an unsteady shape in the grey light.

We were never much given to strong feelings, but something
moved in us. We hurried down the hill and lifted the stranger off
the road. We brought him to Minerva's yard and set him down.
Minerva rushed out, lowered herself beside him and brought her
face down to his neck. He sighed something in her ear. She slid
a hand into his half-opened shirt, drew out a twig with five glossy
leaves the size of coins.

The mutterings among us were deafening. We knew the plant.
Even in the dimness of the morning we could see it down there,
in the lap of our valley, tall as god, its great water-seeking roots
straddling the stream.

Hog Plum, we shouted. In our relief and outrage we forgot to
be grateful. We cursed the fools who did not say it was a tree. We
berated them until we remembered the ailing child and what little
time we had.

Fire. Water. Leaves. A little butter tin. The hands of our women brought them all together. We watched the rising smoke dissolve in air and refused to see it as an omen. Then it was done: a cooling cup of sap, plain as the water it was boiled in.

Minerva came out with the infant wrapped in an old white sheet. Many of us saw the baby close-up for the first time: a mahogany child, its skin gone lustreless with the creeping ash of death. The baby had her father's hair, straight like the fronds of a royal palm, and glossy black. We saw Minerva's lovely mouth and nose; it was a mystery that we'd never noticed the beauty in this woman of ours before.

The stranger lifted the child with shaking hands. He held it against his chest as a nursing mother would, took the cup and began tilting it against the baby's lips.

Minerva hovered around them, her arms thrust out as if to gather them both into herself. And because the stranger would not look at her, she pressed her face against his neck and muttered something in his hair. He shook his head, then turned to her. We do not have words for that look. We did not know that so much could be said with eyes. Whatever it was that passed between them softened Minerva's face, it loosened her arms and shoulders and made her step away from him.

She scanned our faces. We saw how thin she had become, how the bones pressed against her skin. In her shifting gaze we thought we saw defeat. A woman knows things about her child a father can't. It is her flesh. The child itself would tell her it's too late. We had learned this over time. It has happened to us many times before. So when Minerva begged, in a voice tight with trepidation, that we call her only when it was done, we thought her flesh had spoken. She left the yard and headed for the road, and the weight of the early morning pressed down heavier on our heads.

We tried to help: two fingers placed on the bud of the baby's lips; the careful prising; the slow drip, dripping of the fluid; the liquid disappearing. But no shifting of the baby's throat; no sudden catch of breath.

For a moment the man looked lost. We felt lost too. He rested the cup on the stones and plunged a hand inside his pocket. When he withdrew it, we saw a guava in his palm. The skin of the fruit was pale. It glistened like a small moon in the early light. He burst it open, scooped out the soft pink flesh with his thumb and pressed it against his daughter's lips. And she among us who saw everything was the first to claim the child's lips twitched; swore there was the quick flick of a tiny tongue, the smallest tremor of its throat.

And while the stranger drip-fed his child he spoke. Words we'd never heard before. They rolled off his breath like a song; and yes, they seemed at last, to reach beneath the stillness of his little girl, because she stirred, ruffled the sheet, twisted her face and cried.

Our utterances of relief must have frightened her because she kept on crying for a while and then fell silent. And we told ourselves that it was a good thing – a very good thing indeed to make Minerva's baby cry some more.

The stranger left the yard with us hurrying after him.

Minerva was a crouched shape in the middle of the road. She must have heard our footsteps, or perhaps the wordless calling of her man had roused her, because she rose to face us, a terrible question in her eyes. The man held out the bundle smiling. She stumbled forward, flung out her arms to steady herself. But in that swift and effortless way of his, he was already beside her, making a prop of his body.

We left them there leant into each other in a frenzy of mutterings and kisses.

We looked back just once when she among us who had a view on everything, said we must, from this time onward, greet the stranger by his name.

3: OCEANS

A WAY TO CATCH THE DUST

For Bineta Gaye

Something the sea says in my night of blood

For the past five days, Mantos has been feeling the eyes of the young man on his back. From the moment he begins the slow climb up the stony track, past the white graveyard of lambi shells to the clearing above the precipice, that boy's been following him. Sometimes he does not spot the white shirt, the lean and angular shape against the black sand of the bay, but he knows the youth is somewhere down there among the decaying boats.

This morning, he climbs to taste the wind. It is not a normal wind. It does not have the grittiness of hurricanes, followed always by the stillness a day or two before it strikes. He knows the taste and texture of a hurricane, would warn the village a week before they hit. 'Storm coming. Watch y'all arse, brace y'all self.'

The men would drag their boats further up the sand and chain them against anything they hoped would hold. They replaced old pillars and caulked the crevices of their homes. They'd long learnt that he was not called the wind taster for nothing.

It is this certainty the young man wants from him: how to taste the wind and *know*. To hell with that boy! This wind disquiets him. It has no taste. What it carries is an odour and a colour.

In his mind it is a wide, yellow wind. In the first few days it will nibble at the land with a steady, intent grazing; in its final days, it will begin to shed the dust – fine as air, the colour of ground corn. It will release it on the mangroves that darken the southern fringes of the bay. The dust will settle in the cracked bark of the aged sea grape trees, the grooves of their wooden houses. A barely visible corn-yellow shroud.

The dust stirs memories: a storm, a rising curling wave, a naked girl – dark as the sand on their beach. A voice so soft, so throaty, as if it came from somewhere else.

The bay has assumed the greyness of the water. Perhaps sensing something, the boats have come in early. The men and their scrawny families are ragged bits of windswept colour on the beach. Every now and then they shift their heads his way. In the past few days they have seen him climb this hill too often and stay up there too long.

The sky is a wound when Mantos leaves the hill.

'Make me know de weather, ole fella. I want to be like you.' From behind him, on the beach, the voice rasps against his ear. He did not hear the boy approaching.

'Can't be like nobody except yuhself.' Mantos turns to face him. 'And I suttinly don't want to be like you.'

'I kin be anything I want to be.'

Mantos looks into a hard, dark face. Might've been a fine young man if not for the too-tight forehead, the too-small, too-dark eyes magnified behind those glasses, the thinness that he carries like an illness, the way he stands inside his body like he does not own it.

'Teach me to read the wind.'

'You don read de wind – you taste it.'

'Den teach me how to taste it.'

'You got a tongue, not so?' Mantos spits at the sea, turns and walks away. He could feel the boy's smile on his back.

'I know what you trying to catch up there.' That coarse sandpaper voice again. 'You tryin to catch a cold.'

Mantos swings around to face him. 'You got a heap o jumbie in yuh head, an you not goin get rid of dem on me. You is a fucken crazy youngfella.'

That wipes the smile off the young man's face. He disappears inside the mangroves.

Ocean birds – those with the great unmoving wings as wide as sails – are coming in. Birds that hate the land are gathering on the branches of the mangroves and sea-grapes. Amongst the assembling flock, he spots a couple that he hoped would not be there: white everywhere except the tops of their night-black wings, edged with bright white feathers, like chalk-marks on a stone.

'Brace y'all self,' he mutters. This time he will keep his warning to himself. If, afterwards, they ask him why, he will remind them of a girl and what they did to her.

There are signs they ought to see and hear themselves. There, past the white hillocks of lambi shells, past the swamp, just beyond the Point of Shadows, is the rock they used to call The Sound – a jagged chunk of granite that rears out of the water and straddles the air like a horned beast. Its great twisted mouth is turned up at an angle to the sky in a scream that remains silent, even in the storms which sweep in from the north and west. It is the east-storms that give The Sound a voice. The night before, it began to hum.

There is also the beach. For days the ocean has been emptying its stomach in the bay. The black beach is strewn with piles of wood, algae and canvas bags that are weighted around the sides with chunks of lead. In days past they would gather the bags and burn them when the weather eased, or one of the young men would go past a few horizons and return them to the sea where the waves would reclaim what had once been clothing for white men's corpses. Once, they would have seen all this, known what it meant, and begun to brace themselves.

A hard wind comes off the water and slaps him in the face. It leaves an aftertaste of salt and bitterness. Mantos pulls his shirt closer and readies himself to climb down the hill.

He is about to turn when he feels something like the limbs of a crab against his neck. Then the voice – the soft chuckle at the back of it. 'I catch you, ole fella.'

Mantos becomes aware of the fall below, the waiting rocks, the writhing mouth of the sea. He shudders, feels as if the cliff has shifted beneath his feet. He tries to step back, but the hand of the boy is strong.

Mantos closes his eyes. He hears the birds across the bay, their sudden agitation. Then, like a quick release of wings, the fear lifts that's been haunting him all these months. And he's glad for it because this boy, like a mangue-fly that feeds on blood and poison, would have grown strong on it.

'Well,' he breathes. 'You *catch* me for true.'

The weight of the hand has grown on his neck. All he hears now is the boy's breathing. If only he could turn around, see the youngfella's eyes, face him, he... but the thought of falling backwards is much worse.

They are alone in the remnants of a day that has begun to trickle down the sky and stain the water red. The birds have settled again in a huddle amongst the trees. *Brace yuhself,* he thinks, cringing at the new meaning they have suddenly assumed for him.

'What you want to know, Sonny?'

'Everything!'

'Like... uh... Like how to catch de dust?'

'De?'

'Yes – is all around you – de dust. You let me go. I show you.'

He quickly licks a thumb and holds it to the wind. He counts from one to nine. Just as quickly and without turning, he pushes his hand behind him. 'Pass your hand across mi thumb.'

There is an increased pressure on his neck.

'Pass it!' he mutters thickly.

The pressure eases and he feels a hard, dry finger brush his thumb.

Mantos waits, hoping that the boy has the kind of fingers that could feel the film of dust. Not everyone can. The boy withdraws his hand abruptly and the old man flinches. He bows his head and waits. Then he sees the boy's arm thrust forth in front of him, the thumb glistening with spittle.

'No, too much,' he mumbles. 'Not *too* much! You turn the finger round like dat.' Cautiously, he takes the boy's wrist and turns it. The hand does not resist him. He glances round at the face, dark against an even darker sky. He realises the youth's eyes are closed, the narrow nostrils flared as though prised wider by the wind. This is his moment. There will never be a better time. He feels strong enough to spin the boy around and throw him down.

The thought must have communicated itself. The youth opens his eyes, as if startled out of sleep. Mantos sees the curiosity in his face, the dare that is also a desire and he realises that if he has lost his moment, the boy's threat to kill him has also passed.

'Come!' He lifts his eyes to the first flush of lightning down the edges of the sky. 'Lemme show you how to do it.'

It has taken him more than four times the years this boy has lived to learn to catch the dust, first to know that it was there at all, and then to find a way to retrieve it. Now, here he is, on a precipice above the sea, trying to teach an insane boy – in minutes.

Just the right amount of moisture on the thumb.

No – not too long, the finger will dry and the wind will take it back.

Don't make the thumb too flat, the dust will never settle.

He demonstrates with a quiet, focused urgency. He can feel the coming storm like the breath of a beast against his ear. Now, there is the distant smell of rot. Soon the rain will come and there will be no difference between earth and air.

The boy can feel the dust at last. It shows on his face – the satisfaction of finding what, before, had not been there and grasping it. But it is not enough.

Mantos senses his dissatisfaction. How can he begin to make him understand that these little grains in the air are doorways to a time and a woman with a soft and throaty voice? That it proves to him that she once existed?

Up here, with a storm over their shoulders, the boy is just a frail face, propped up by an even frailer frame – a human who has every limb in place but, somehow, still appears malformed.

'I used to think you ugly,' Mantos begins, cautiously.

If the boy is hearing him, he shows no sign.

'Right now, I don't tink so. If people think you no use to nobody, especially yourself, is because you believe you is no use.

What *make* you come like dat? You think I *like* dem? You think…
I'll tell you why this storm will come and dey wouldn believe *what*
hit dem. Why I prepare dem for every wind dat blow, every livin
drop o rain. Why I been preparin dem all dis time, so dat dey will
never be ready for dis one. I been waitin for dis storm, Sonny – all
my life.' His arms take in the sky, the wind, the sea. 'Dis storm is
de one dat bring de girl, last time.' A chuckle escapes him.

'De?'

'Y'hear me right – de girl. A hurricane is a sneeze. A lil' fit o
temper compare to what is about to come. Dis – dis one is a
stinkin, kickin rage.'

He gestures at the houses down below. 'I have more reason to
hate dem dan you could ever have.'

The boy's shirt rustles like the wings of a disturbed bird.

'I tell you a story,' Mantos mutters. 'I don expect you to believe
it. Sometimes it feel like a dream – like some creature dat settle
down inside my mind and make a little nest in dere, and now it
gone to sleep. It don't feel like it real no more. De only proof I got
is de dust.

'I'z eighty now – yunno dat? De last of what y'all call "de ole
ones" – me an Maisie Green. But I used to be young like you, and
empty-handed, but my head was full o dreams. It have a time in
a pusson life when dey don't believe dey'll ever die – all dat hope,
all dat life! I never had de chance to be like dat – young an strong
an feedin on de bread of hope. You – you should unnerstan dat.
Cos you was never young. Dem never give you o me a chance to
be.

'Yuh see, my mother got me from a man nobody never meet.
Or if dem ever meet him, she never tell dem it was he. Somewhere in dem hills above dere, 'mongst de mapou and de mist, she
lay down with a forest man – a man not from the sea.

'I dunno what it was dat make her keep her silence – shame, o
pride, o love, o perhaps all of dem mix up. I dunno. Anyway, he
fill her up, not just with me, but with dat selfsame silence dese
forest people carry all de time with dem. I born dat way – with all
dat silence in mih blood and something else – a sort of knowledge

of de world. De little things – de way a leaf does curl, the colour of de veins on dem, de shape of a bird wing, how a sea gull spread it toes. I could hear de crabs under de sand; the turning of de worms. Dat forest man carry all his learning in his seed, and he pass dat on to me.

'Once she tell me I was jus like him. Was de only time she mention him. It was a warning. She was tellin me dat in dis place if you different, den you good as dead.

'Now take a child dat could point a finger at de sea an say what kind o fish it have out dere. Or throw an eye at what de wave bring in de night and say what kind o weather dat goin mean tomorrow. Now dere ain't no reasonin for dat. An de ting dat nobody can explain is de work o de devil. So I become to dem a devil chile. Something dat possess my mother in de bush. Something dey had to get rid of. An worse, my mother had no place amongst dem. From de time she got me, she wasn human no more. A *thing* was what she was, de bait for any nasty man who decide to lay a claim to her. One man after another.

'I was fourteen when she went out for de last time. Dis time it wasn a man dat call her out. She just went an didn come back. I get up dat mornin, didn see her dere, and know she wasn't comin back.

'I s'pose dat what protect me was deir shame when, a coupla days after, dey lift her body off de tide. Dat an de fact dat she did prepare me for it. She tell me what I must and musn't do. Why I should abide my time. Why, to protect meself from dem, I must teach meself a kind o blindness: kill de smells dat nobody else could smell, shut down my hearing like you bolt a door. And wait.

'But ignorance is a beast with a stomach like de sea – it always hungry, and it feed on anyting. No matter how much my mother prepare me, no matter dat I grow up mongst dem, no matter how much like dem I did become, she didn prepare me for one thing: nobody would accept me to marry deir daughter.'

The boy lifts his chin to speak. Mantos stops him with a gesture.

'Yuh see, boy, I was de child o de woman dat lay down wit a demon in de mountains. Dat mean I carry his seed, and dey believe dat seed must die in me. Ain't got no loneliness worse dan dat! Ain't got no knowledge more bitter dan dat – dat yuh life stop with you, an you ain got nothing to show for it, dat de world end with you.

'But you can't strangle water; water always find a way. An life is like dat. Life always find a way, an it make a little room for me.

'It come in de form of a girl. And to dis day, I believe it was a storm like dis dat bring her. I see three in my whole life and I count meself cursed, or p'raps lucky, because some people live and never see one. De first one come when I was a child, and I don't remember much of it, except a smell, and a old woman name Androvy passing her tongue across my finger and holdin it up to de wind.

'De second time I recognise de coming by de smell – a smell dat was so small and far, you hardly know it there, de smell o sweat an dirt an breathin, like people livin in a tight, small place. It wake up all de tings I bury in mihself, de tings my mother encourage me to stifle. I feel it weeks before it reach, like a blind man feel somebody presence in a room. I warn dem. I dunno why. Perhaps was to show dem dat de gift I born with could serve some good. Dat if I was different, that difference have its use.

'Dem didn lissen at first – thought it was my madness. But about a week after, dey start seein de message dat de sea left on de sand. In my young days, people really know de sea. Dem know dat de ocean have three parts and every part is a world complete to itself. All we see is de part with all dat light, all dat blue. Dat's all we know. Past that, further out, you got another kind o deep. Is de place o shark and whale and big squid, and de fast fish: mackerel, tuna, marlin. And den past all dat, you have de bowels o de ocean.

'Is like a bad dream down dere. Ain't got no light. Hardly got no bottom. And what life it got is like nothing dat you ever see. Fish dat ain't got no eye. Creatures who whole body is a mouth. Creatures dat carry deir own light under deir skin, or hold it like a torch on top deir head. A kind o worm dat got root like grass, brown on top an white below. You smell it and it smell o sulphur. You burn it an it don't want to burn. How I know?

'Is what y'all ignorance been walkin over since last week on dat beach down dere. Is what I didn show nobody dis time. An lemme tell you someting else, boy, anyting dat kin reach dat deep to upset de stomach o de sea, can't be good for us.

'Besides,' he says softly, 'besides, Fatimi tell me. Dat was how I know was out o all dat darkness dat she come.'

He looks at the boy and blinks. 'No! Wasn't no mermaid. Unless de sea have black ones too with foot and hair like me. Was a real girl – flesh and blood and warm like you – an dat sea deliver her to me. Maisie Green will tell you. God blind her for de part she play in what happen afterwards.

'De night de storm reach, I walk out to de bay an meet it. Only it didn have no bay out dere no more. I went out to face it, cos mih life didn have no worth. So what difference if a east-storm tek it?

'I dunno how long I was out dere. What protect me was de way de wind was comin cross dis cliff – sort of bouncing off and missin us down below. I was thinkin dat p'raps dis was de end o de world, dat maybe was not fire dat would take us, but water!

'I was talkin to meself, cussin de wind, de rain, de whole damn world, an laughing. Yes was madness, but I welcome it, cos madness mek me happy for de first time.

'She come on de curl of a wave. Like you was sitting on de edge of a movin, rollin cliff that lift you up and rest you down right dere on de ground in front o me. I didn *see* her come. I figure dat out by de way she just appear. It had to be de only way.

'A girl – naked as de night, and just as dark. Standin dere in front o me, tremblin from de cold. She must ha' say someting, ask for help, tell me *something*. I dunno. I notice de voice straight away, soft like if it come from inside mih head. She didn speak like we speak and I couldn see her clear. Except dat she was slim an tall and she was in a bad way.

'Questions start poppin up straightaway. Mebbe she was one o dem foreigners in a boat out dere with other people, and de storm drag dat boat from under dem. But how she manage to swim across dat kind o sea? Well, miracle does happen, not so?

'My heart was goin like ah engine. I wasn frighten. I jus know I had to bring her in de house an dry her out. Which is what I do.'

Mantos lifts his head and stares at the boy. The young man is hugging himself against the wind.

'Don' think I didn tell meself I was mad or dreamin. Dat mebbe my distress fly up in my head an make a woman out of air. But if it was distress, I was damn well glad to stay distress de rest o me life.

'But she had weight, an voice an warmth. An when I carry her up de hill, de little light from de sky fall on her face and I see dat she was one ov us. I fix a bed on de floor for her. I do all dis in de dark, with de lightning dat come through de house from time to time. Don ask me why. It jus didn feel proper to light no light. And soon as I finish, before I could blink me eye, she gone to sleep.

'Dat night I sit down on de floor an watch her for a while, wonderin who she was, where she might've come from, and how *anybody* could come out of dat kind o sea alive. I fall asleep sittin on de floor wit my head full up.

'Next day de whole world look chastise – flat an mash up and turn upside down or wrongside out. Before I step out, I look on de floor to see if it was really dream I was dreamin. I was sort of hopin dat it was. Or at least, if I wasn dreamin, I was expectin dat whatever it was I meet out dere pass way wit de passin o de storm.

'She was still dere lyin on de floor. Still sleepin. Now I could see her better, I see how dark an smooth she was. Hardly any hair. Cut low on her head like a boy. Her face – I never see nobody so pretty – was long an slim an *quiet*. A face you couldn read. Everyting bout her was slim an long an smooth. It had three little mark right dere.' Mantos brushes his left cheek with his fingers. 'Just under de bone, like three little fish you lay down one on top de other. I never see a pusson so perfect. Is dat what make me fraid, not de strange way dat she come, nor even how I was goin to explain her to everybody else. Was de perfectness of dat girl.

'I think about it all day and I realise dat I had a problem. I couldn tell dem dat I bring her from somewhere else. I could hear dem wonderin, how come she didn speak no language dat nobody else round here know? How come dey didn see her de day before de storm? I think of hidin her, but it strike me dat I had to make her understand *why* first and I didn know how I was goin to do dat.

'I glad I never try to hide her, because I realise afterwards dat she didn like to be cover up by nothing. Dat was one of de two tings dat was really bad for her. De other ting – what dey use against us in de end – was, well… I'll tell you when I come to it.

'On top of all o dat she was different. A pusson could look de same like everybody else, but you know – and you dunno how you know – but you *know* if dem come from somewhere different.

'Anyway, she give me almos a week to think bout it, cos dat was how long she sleep – like she was sleepin off de toil o centuries, wakin up only for me to feed her, or jus openin her eye to say someting I didn unnerstan.

'I hardly go out meself – only a coupla times for dem to see dat I was alright. Nobody uses to come to my place anyway.

'People was out dere pulling deyself back together, but all I want was to sit right dere on de floor with my door bolt up and feed my eyes on her. Sometimes she catch me lookin and she look straight back – not offerin nothing, not askin nothing, jus lookin back at me.

'Love, Sonny, love come easy when you empty an you needin it; it come easier when you got to tek care o somebody an it's someting you been wanting bad and never expect to get. Love did come. And it was easy for both of us, cos some tings you don' need no language for. But with it, with it come de terror of de *outside*. Perhaps she realise it – long before me – dat I was afraid to take her out into de day. To let eyes fall on her. Mebbe dat was why she allow me to keep her in dere for so long, comin out with me only in de night and only for a little while. *Outside* – I realise dat I always been afraid of it. *Outside* was where my mother used to go. *Outside* was where she went one day an never come back. *Outside* was a place dat hurt.

'One mornin, must ha been a coupla weeks after she come, I decide to tek my boat, go out an catch some butterfish – she use to like butterfish. I tell er in my prettiest English, "Me, Mantos, going return soon."

'By then I know her name was Fatimi – leaseways dat was how I hear it. I went out, got my fish and hurry back, and what I see? She standin in de yard with my sheet wrap around her and she had a fire goin, a fireside same like we make, preparin for when I come home. I see her first, an den I see de crowd. Dem standin on de beach jus watchin an whisperin mongst demself, while she goin bout her business like if dey wasn dere. Watchin an whisperin like dem catch sight o something dat dey recognise but couldn't understand.

'I was so fraid, I could ha faint. Fraid without hardly knowin why, except it was de same feelin dat settle in my stomach when bad weather about to come. Dat same night I try to warn her, tell her dat I never want to see her near dem people, tell 'er what dey done to me.

'Dat day I see someting else. I see de mark on her right shoulder. Dunno how I miss it before, except perhaps was de first time I see all of her in proper daylight. A deep mark, like a burn in a pusson flesh. De way children would dig de letters o deir name on de bark of a livin tree. A mark dat had no place on pretty skin like hers. A big 'L' dat sort of tie up itself wit ah 'C' – LC.

'From dat time, dey had their eyes on us. Fellas come to my house de way dey used to come to my mother. Only dis time dey come with jokes, with rum, with a basketful o fish dey bring for Fatimi to cook for us. But dem eyes was always on every movement dat she make. You could see de cravin, no matter how much dey try to hide it wid deir grin. Men, Sonny, cravin what another man got, just because he got it. Dey ask me where a man could find a pretty woman so? It have more like her where she come from? How come she never talk? I always find some way to slip past de questions.

'De women had a different way. They make deir children come sometimes and try to talk to her, and all she do was smile. Sometimes she answer dem in dat funny, pretty voice of hers. But it was not words to dem, just sound dey didn unnerstan.

'It continue, it continue – till tings get quiet and I thought dat mebbe, mebbe dem decide to leave de two of us in peace.

'I was a happy man. Except dem nights when Fatimi tryin to say someting to me. I could hear de frighten in her voice, like it was de most important thing a pusson ought to know, but I jus couldn figure out what she was tryin to say. But I know dat it had something to do with de mark on her shoulder, dat almos everyting had to do with dat mark, includin why she couldn stand lyin down in the darkness o de house for long. Why she reach for me, sometimes, bawlin like de devil was in front ov her.

'Times like those I hold on to her all through de night. It always lef me with a sadness – a deep-down, rockin darkness in me chest. I know dat if I find out what dat mark is, I would know all about dat girl – who she was and where she come from, and why she come to me.

'De trouble start with Maisie Green. She was young at de time and I s'pose, till Fatimi come along, she was de pretties woman for miles around. Dem fellas didn have no eyes for her no more. An Mason Joe, de fella she hope to married, jus jump a boat one day and lef her with a full belly an a empty hand. Jealousy s'not enough to explain what happen. S'like de little stone dat slip and start de landslide rollin. She spread word dat dat girl was a mama malady – a demon-girl who come from nowhere. Proof was dat she couldn speak no language known to human. Besides, didn dey see de mark LC on her shoulder? It stand for Lucifer Cometh. And me bein a demon child meself, was only natral dat I should go out and bring me own kind here. She even blame her for chasin Mason Joe away. And when ole Miss Mertle Jones pass way dat same week, she spread word dat Fatimi tief she soul.

'Was de same ting when Rickman lose he boat on Trasher Reef – even if careless people been losin deir boat cross dere from ever since. And dat mark on her shoulder – she always went back to it – dat mark was suttingly de devil signature.

'And den come de strike of seventy-four when de islan stop sudden, like a man who catch a stroke, and money didn have no value cos it didn have nothing to eat except fish for breakfast, tea an dinner. Hard times does harden heart, Sonny, and children ain't no exception. It begin wit dem children throwin stones at her. I was never around when it happen. I was too busy huntin food. I tell meself dat it was a good ting, because I would ha tear all o dem little jookootoo rarse to pieces!

'She keep it quiet – never tell me nothing till one day I come home and see her in de yard, her face swell up an her forehead bleedin. I look at her and I understand what happen straight away.

'I went mad. I lose meself. Dis old rage dat been sleepin all dis while inside o me let loose and I couldn control it. I half-mash up a coupla houses, and start on dem boats on de beach, till something heavy knock me on my head an darkness fall on me.

'Was de beginnin of a war between us. A war without no words. Mornings, I would get up and see a big cross paint on my door. Or salt spread out on de doorstep. And Maisie Green was always dere down on de beach, keepin her eye on us.

We was in de yard one time, watchin dem watchin us. One o dem little chilren was playin with a tin pan, sort of knockin it on a stone and singing de way chilren who can't sing does sing. An every time she do dat, Fatimi jump. De chile, not knowing what he doing to her, continue knockin dat pan harder on dat stone till my ooman couldn take de noise no more and she begin to scream. Mortal frighten she was. Mortal! It bring a grin to Maisie face and brighten dem pretty eyes o hers.

'From den we didn have no rest, no day, no night. Everybody start knockin pan. Bucket too. Sometimes a piece o chain against a stone – like dat dey try to drive my ooman mad.

'I know she couldn take it for too much longer, dat it would kill her; and so I begin wishin for another storm to take she back. She got sick you see, wouldn eat no more, wouldn even talk to me.

'Was one o dem days o rain when you feel it never goin stop. I remember dat day so clear cos dat was when Maisie an some children decide to come with a big oil drum in front my door an beat it like dey gone crazy. I left Fatimi curl up on de floor, coverin she ears and shoutin. I should ha pay attention to dat shoutin, cos before she never use to shout, jus cry.

'But all I was paying mind to was de murder in my heart when I unlatch de door to meet Maisie an dem chilren in my yard. I didn realise it before, but over dem weeks, something did change in Maisie. All dat hate she had inside rise up to she skin an leave a ugliness dere. She was not a pretty woman any more. She was just a ragged, red-eye woman with a coupla teeth missin, an I was about to kill her.

'But I didn have no need to – a chip of de iron dat she been beatin dat drum so hard with just fly off and bury itself in her eye. I hear de scream and to dis day, I can't tell whether it come from Fatimi or her.

'Dem chilren fly down de hill and I watch dat woman holdin her eye and rolling on de ground till her father come and lift her up and tek her home.

'Fatimi was easy when I come in. Not smilin, jus staring at de roof as if something just done settle itself inside her. Mebbe she had something to do with it. I dunno. Mebbe.

'Was a little time afterwards she look at me an tell me – in de best English you ever hear, 'Man, return soon.' Exactly as I used to tell she when I leave to go outside. I figure dat she was trying to make me laugh, perhaps. So I laugh, and she repeat it, serious. 'Mon return soon, Yantos. No cry.' Which was another thing I used to tell her. 'Don't cry, Fatimi, don't cry.'

'She say de same ting later in de night. Late. Dat night she didn sleep – would raise she head from time to time as if she was lisenin out for something. Dere in front ov me was a different woman, no cry-cry girl dis time, but sure ov herself. Like what happen to Maisie make she realise something. I dunno.

'I was half asleep when she got up – sudden so – de sheet droppin off of her de way a snake drop off it skin, and before I know it, she was runnin out in de rain down towards de beach.

'Was a rising wind out dere and I could barely see. But between my shoutin and runnin like mad to catch up with her, I see de shadow bobbing and weavin ahead o me like something in de mind. I didn hear no water splash, no sound o wings, no nothing – jus my name soft, soft, like drizzle on a leaf.

'And she was gone. Like dat!' The old man's palms explode against each other like a clap of thunder. The noise seems to awaken the youth. Mantos wonders if he has been listening at all.

'I, I didn kill her, Missa Mantos.' The youth's voice is frightened and unsure.

Mantos draws his shirt around him. 'I know you didn kill er. You wasn even born!'

The youth steps back from him. He is angling his shoulders as if to protect his body from the force of the wind. Only there is no wind now, just a stillness.

They do not have much time up here. He knows this by the hollowness in his ears, as if the whole earth has sucked in its breath.

A murky twilight has descended on the land. Inland, where there were mountains before, there is only the darkness of descending clouds. 'We have to go down, Sonny. She goin strike us sooner dan I expect.'

The boy smiles.

'She'll come tonight,' the old man mutters. 'Sure as dat storm comin, Fatimi goin to come.' He lifts defeated eyes at the boy. 'An she wouldn change – not like me. Age got no meanin for de ones like her. De ones dat come with de dust. De ones dat got away.'

'You never tell me where she come from.'

'De rockin darkness. I don expect you to believe me, but since you ask, I goin tell you. *Mon return soon* was what she say. Well after a lot o thinkin, I take dem words to Kanvi. You know Kanvi people, dem got a knowledge dat we ain' got no more. A pussnal knowledge o de sea. De woman who show me de way to catch de dust was from dere. Had a fella dere name Winger who know everyting. Used to be a teacher there, who read till book knowledge drive im mad. I take dem words to him cos dey never leave mih head.

'Fatimi was vex, you see – vex in a way dat frighten me, like she gone to prepare sheself to come again. P'raps dat was what she was tryin to tell me all dat time. An dis time – *dis time!* – dey wouldn mek her leave so easy.

'*Man return soon* – Winger couldn believe me first time when I say dem words, specially when I tell im bout de mark pon she shoulder. He ask me for she name, de way she look, other words she say. I search mih head and I remember some: *Jerry jef – tooky – nub. Mon nub Mantos* – she always use to say dat.' Mantos sucked in air, steadied his voice. 'Winger tell me de language was a real one. *Jerry jef* – dat's thanks. *Mon nob Mantos* – I luv Mantos. And was not no 'man' she say but '*mon*'. Mon mean me, mean I. *Mon return soon.* I comin back soon.

'He tell me de only thing dat dis could mean, especially with dem three little fishbone on she face, was dat Fatimi was from de same place dat most of us here come from, on de other side o dese three ocean. And dat she come from dere *direct*.

'No storm didn blow her over – de mark on she shoulder tell him dat; if anyting it pull her up from down below. You see, dat mark was de mark of a Inglish man name Luke Collinwood. Captin of a ship dem call de *Zong*.

'Used to be a time when we wasn worth more dan de price of a cooking pot. Was like fish dem used to bring we here in de bottom of a boat across all dat water to sell. In a rockin darkness. Most ov dem never reach dis side.

'Dat Collinwood fella must've watch de water, think of all dem days an distance he mus travel, and he decide was too much trouble. So what he do? He drop everybody overboard – de whole shipload – den he turn round an claim insurance. Dat chile – dat girl was one of em.

'How come she reach here after all dis time?'

'I kin only tell you what dat madman Winger tell me. It got a road under de sea, he say, a road o bones dat join us to dat place cross dere where all de dust come from. An dat girl, mebbe she been walkin all dis time on de road o bones. It jus take her a coupla hundred years to reach.'

A sheet of rain sweeps in on them from the sea, douses them, then passes abruptly.

'C'mon young fella, we have to go. Right now!'

He allows gravity to take him down the track, hears the boy's feet behind him. A hard wind slams them against each other. They both fall over. Now they move in a rapid scuttle towards the houses. They cover most of the distance that way, pausing only to draw breath behind one of the larger rocks that stands between the houses and the sea.

Mantos turns his eyes up at the hill. The few trees that have stood around the clearing are no longer there.

'C'mon, youngfella, we almos home.'

'No!'

It's as if the boy has thrown a rope around his neck and dragged him backward.

'Now listen, Sonny, you…'

'I stay here.'

'You can't!'

'I stay, Missa Mantos. I wan to stay.' Despite the wind, the awful noise about them, Mantos could hear his breathing.

'You can't, Sonny. Ain't no place out here for nobody. Dat little wind is nothing. Dat wind is just a test. You come to my place I…'

'I stay.'

In the murkiness, the old man can easily imagine him there against the stone, like some wounded thing.

'Now, Son…'

Something explodes at the back of the rock and destroys the rest of his words. Mantos flinches.

'Somebody have to meet de girl.'

'She won't be de same dis time. I tol' you dat she change – not so? You could see it in dat wind. An – an perhaps she choose another place to land dis time.'

'Ain't got nothing you kin do to move me.'

The boy means it. He knows that now – and who could say he would not have done the same?

'Okay,' he grunts – scrambling up the slope. 'If you got any problem, shout.'

Mantos does not hear the boy's reply.

He does not wait for it.

DELIVERANCE
For Esau

Neither doctors nor the sap of herbs could cure him. Despite his daily dips in the sea and the layers of liniment he used to seal the wound below his ankle, he stank. The smell was as offensive to him as it was to the people who shunned him. He'd ignored the tiny abrasion made by the tip of his harpoon a year ago, expecting the sea to heal it, but salt and sun had not worked their miracle.

The sore had sapped his strength and made an old man of him. But last night's dream had revealed to him that the dolphin, the white one with the eyes like flames in her head, could heal him. Not only did she promise him a cure, she offered him a cleansing.

The other dolphins had not appeared with her in the dream and that made sense. Only the albino could cure the flesh of a foot gone bad. Only she could make him whole again.

These days, Skido was the only person prepared to listen to him talk about the dolphins. He never seemed to tire of hearing about the dream. Well, not until a couple of weeks ago.

'I see her, Missa Skid. White like god mek cloud. As if she was tellin me where to come to meet her so she kin cure this foot o mine.'

'Meet her where, Osun?'

'Past Dog Reef, Sir. Past…'

'Past Dog Reef is De Gate, Sonny, and De Gate is hell.'

'I know. Past all that. Even past Gull Island.'

'Past all that you find nothing. Only water and wind and storm. What de hell is de matter with you, anyway? Like that bad-foot make you crazy, o something?' The old man leaned very close to his face. 'Is like you trying to say something so – so, so fucken heavy, you kin only talk 'bout it in parables.'

'You can't call something nothing, Sir. Becos water, wind and storm is something. If that is where she want to tek me to cure me, then is there I gotta go.'

'You go searchin for any kind o white dolphin – especially white dolphin! Cross dat bad ocean water north o here, you never come back. Y'hear me? You die.'

'No I can't, becos she tell me…'

'You die, Osun! Nobody never go north o here, this time o year. And you know s'well as de rest of us dat is two weeks since the radio been predictin storm. You even think o trying, dat sea swallow you up and spit your little magga-bone arse out on some bird-shit island where nobody can't find you. S'only a dream! God never mek no dolphin white all over, not de kind o white you talk to me about. Dolphin is de colour o deep-water. I see blue ones, black ones, brown ones, even grey ones. But nobody never see no white dolphin dat shine like you say it shine, 'ceptin in de mind. Dat's not no dolphin, Sonny – dat's de devil calling you.'

'S'more dan dat, Sir.'

Skido had pushed himself off the sand, dusted the seat of his pants and walked off to the northern end of the bay. The old fella had avoided him since.

From the cot where he lay, Osun listened to the humming, buzzing voices in the room next door. They came in snatches – the high nasal tones of his niece and the chesty bass of her companion. These days they talked as if he were not there. He tried to blank his mind, but could not prevent his heart from thumping at their words, which came in fragments through the shaky, half-rotten walls of the house.

Edmund Hill. The Red House. Easier. The gov'ment…

She'd never talked like that before.

There was an edge of uncertainty in the woman's voice, a querulous seeking for assurance.

'Nothin to shame for, eh? Not as bad as before. Better now, not so?'

Osun allowed the words to sink into the deep pool that he imagined was his mind. Sometimes his body was a sea-snake on the floor of the ocean; in moments of depression he was all the old and sodden things the sea threw up on the beach.

A burden. That was what she said he was.

She had become more fretful since the man arrived. Lost her temper easily these days. Now his niece was too ready to remind of the effort it took to maintain him. Still, she looked happier than he could remember. But it was a happiness she reserved only for herself and the tall, sober-faced young man who had taken an instant dislike to him.

He lay quiet, but felt the tightening in his gut that used to flow through him just before he stepped into his boat and headed for the horizon. He was not going to rot his life away in a mad house or in a pauper's home on Edmund Hill. Everybody knew about the Red House: the stink, the decay, the dying and the dead. He would not allow Nesthia, or rather her new man, to force this on him.

He shifted his weight on the small bed, ignoring Nesthia's and whatever-his-name's noisy commotion. They go on like that, he thought sourly, they would get more than the child they were trying for.

He wriggled his toes, studied them. They were long and bony but still strong. The old muscles were weaker, but still there. His bones stood out against his skin now. It had to be tonight. All he had been waiting for was the moon.

A large spider hung from the ceiling on a thread so fine it seemed to be afloat on an ocean of air.

It had gone quiet in the room next door. Osun rolled off the bed. He'd already decided on the boat he was going to take. He had watched Chadoo prepare it for the trip out every morning at five o'clock exactly; watched him lay the heavy harpoon along the belly of the craft, the steel of its barbed end pointing towards the stern. Chadoo would lay the long oars beside the weapon before entering the craft. With tripping heart, Osun would watch Chadoo and his son fit the long white mast from which the single sail of pure black canvas would spread out against the early sky.

It had taken Chadoo three years to build that boat. Might have taken another man six months, but Chadoo was born with shortened forearms and hands turned out like flippers. No-one believed that he could do it. The little man had taught himself to hold a hammer with the crook of his arm and wield it. Even so, Osun thought, he might have finished his boat in a year, or at the most eighteen months, but this was the work of a man too obsessed with his own imperfection to build an ordinary craft. Three years later, when he stepped back to look at his work, Chadoo had fashioned something after the image and likeness of his own inside-self. The most perfect boat on earth. It was large enough for deep-sea fishing, but smaller than the twenty-footers in the bay; it was made to the measure of Chadoo's own stunted body, and balanced to perfection.

The craft was painted blue-grey, white and yellow, the colours of sky and clouds and sun and deep-water fish. Lean like a barracuda, it was easily the sleekest boat anyone had ever seen.

Osun felt he understood why Chadoo scrubbed its sides each evening after a hard day's work, patted the nodding prow and addressed it by the name he had given it as soon as it was finished. There was, for anyone who cared to see it, an understanding between *Deliverance* and her maker.

Lord ha' Mercy, what a name for a boat!

Evenings, Chadoo never brought her up on the sand. With a long, heavy rope he'd ring-bolted against the sternpost, he would tether the craft to the trunk of the largest sea grape tree on the beach.

He had forced himself to eat well, swallowing his pride and going down to the beach to beg for a handful of sprat or the odd fish head that he'd roasted on the sand or in his niece's coal-pot. If there was no offering of fish, he spent all evening combing the rocks on the southern end of the bay for whelks.

There was a small parcel of jack-fish and red snappers that he had salted, dried and then baked, hidden deep in the sand between the roots of the grape tree nearest their house.

Now he felt ready.

Half past six.

The sun was already a rusting coin at the back of the sky. The last of the buses from St. George's were screaming through the village, heading for the northernmost towns, Victoria and Sauteurs.

The boats were coming in, engines throbbing through the evening silence. He had once been part of the line of boats that pleated the water every evening, stretching all the way back towards the thundering edge of Dog Reef.

Recently, it had felt better not pottering about the nets, head bent under the humiliating scrutiny of hardier, healthier men; not fighting his own body as he added his feebleness to the hauling up of boats from the water's edge to the shelter of the grape trees. He had done this only because he needed the poor reward of fish, thanklessly given.

Chadoo walked past him, grunted a greeting. Osun nodded, his eyes on the gulls over the water. It made a fella want to weep just watching them plunge, beak first, into the water and then rise hard and fast as they shook the sea and sunlight off their wings.

Night rolled in quickly. Night and the tide.

'Osun!'

He ignored his niece's voice; he was watching red crabs hanging tensely over the gaping mouths of their holes.

'Ooo-sun!'

He did not answer.

'Osun!'

'Yaaar!'

'I callin you. You don't hear me callin you? How much time I mus stand up here callin you for food?'

'Awwright!' Despite himself his mouth watered. He looked up at the foothills, glimpsed the cold white eye of the moon just above the peaks of the Belvidere.

Night had fallen about him like a stone.

It must have been past midnight. Both feet drawn up, eyes wide, he concentrated on the quiet. Osun flicked his tongue across his lips, edged off the bed, careful not to hurt his foot.

He began to move the moment he heard the rustle of bed clothes and the heavy roll of bodies in the other room.

The bolt slid easily under his hand. The door grated; he froze, waited for the drawn-out sob-sighs of his niece, then stepped out into the night.

The moon hung full and low and heavy above the bay. And stars, numberless, Lordy! stretching beyond vision.

A low breeze tugged at his shirt. He glanced at the sleeping houses. He untethered Chadoo's boat, lifted the anchor and pushed the craft a few yards further out.

He had forgotten the food. Wouldn't survive without it. Knee-deep in water, he ignored the pain in his ankle and pushed himself back towards the shore.

He closed his ears against the racket he feared he was making, his hands quick and crablike in the sand beneath the tree. A grunt and he was hopping back towards the boat, terrified because where his room had been dark a while ago, there was now the flickering light of a lamp. He thought he heard the man's deep grumble.

He had not closed the door. The draught must have roused them.

He'd managed to get the mast up by the time he heard the woman shout his name. Frantic, he tied the sail against the tall, smooth mapou pole. The black sheet of canvas opened with an impatient flapping protest.

Osun thought he heard his name a second time, a man's heavy cough, footsteps on the sand. The sail had found the slight night-breeze. Cursing his feebleness, he guided the craft past the sleeping boats. A few hundred yards further out, the breeze picked up and the hull of the boat began its sibilant gossiping with the waves – a sound that never ceased to thrill him.

For a moment he lost his sense of himself and where he was. The gliding craft, the fluorescence of the water left him with a sensation of slipping away on light.

Osun turned his face up to the moon and grinned.

On the shore, the erratic flames of bottle torches bloomed in doorways. He didn't think they could see him. A black sail against a night sky was as good as not being there at all. Who would expect him to go out to sea at this time and in the heart of the hurricane season?

Already the boat was bucking like a thing alive.

Past Dog Reef, the sea was a frenzy of rolling water. His father had told him once that the sea had just one purpose: to reclaim the land and, long before Judgement Day, it would have its way.

Come morning, they would come after him with those new boats – those ugly, noisy things with big engines. Tonight, there was not a man who would leave the warmth of his woman for the open sea. Only Chadoo's oldest son, perhaps – the reckless one – but the little man would not allow him.

Already he was feeling the heavier tug of water as he rounded Short Horn.

Come morning, the whole island would be alerted. Afraid for him; marvel at his courage. His name would be on the radio, his picture in the papers. His real name, his long, full and proper name – Osunyin Ignatius Ezekiel Frazier – was going to be in people's mouths. The boats in the village would leave by first light. The police might join the search. He sent a glistening arc of spittle across the water.

The craft leaned hard right, shuddering with the force of a colder, harder wind that pounded his exposed chest. Osun threw his weight the other way and *Deliverance* steadied herself, the sail pregnant to the point of bursting.

Boiler Reef came up, a thunderous, frothing succession of breakers.

Too close! Girl, you taking me too close!

Boiler Reef was where the island made its last stand against the sea. Osun closed his eyes against the storm of spray, the better to feel the craft and struggle with it around the enormous suck and surge of waves.

Too fucken welly close.

He was soaked and slightly shaken when they emerged past the reef. Now all there was before him was the open ocean and tomorrow.

Tomorrow? What the hell he *mean* by that? Then it suddenly

made sense. Even if they caught him, brought him back and dumped him soaked and gulping on the beach, they – *all ov em* – would still be part of what he'd left behind. Tomorrow was wherever *Deliverance* was taking him.

Morning was first a feeling: the slight shift of wind in the sail, the changing tug of tide and the nature of the light down the edges of the sky. The wind had a sharper, fresher smell. A vague urgency had settled in his head. He had not slept properly for several nights. Perhaps he'd find some quiet water further on, let the boat drift and just, well – allow himself to doze a bit. Osun closed his eyes.

It was not until the craft juddered and yawed between two receding waves that he remembered The Gate. He threw all his weight against the tiller. The terrible concussive boom of breakers two hundred feet away hurt his eardrums and vibrated the craft. *Deliverance* slipped sideways down a mountain of a wave, her sails gone limp. An oar slipped and struck his foot. Osun screamed as he fought to right *Deliverance* on the long fall down. The craft was straining against the murderous drag, her mast so low, it was almost touching the water.

Another boat would have capsized and perished there with him in the clutch of a ripping headwind, where the currents of two oceans clashed. He'd heard stories of bigger vessels which went that way, ships spat up on some distant shore – Venezuela or some other country far beyond. But Chadoo's craft, running on its side, keel turned up almost to the sky, began the long and terrifying climb with him.

He thanked the boat. In a fever of fear and gratitude he tightened his hands around the tiller and stared back breathless at the heaving walls of grey. Even at this distance, *Deliverance* was still tossing and shuddering.

Some fool had named this hellhole Paradise. God!

Ole Man Tigga was the one who had renamed it The Gate. Now, Osun understood why. When he'd grown too frail to hold an oar, the old fella had taken his craft out here and never returned.

★

Paradise, The Gate – whichever it was – had long haunted him in dreams. Below those waters lay something dark and unapproachable. No ordinary reef or rock could take that pounding. Whatever lay down there had a nightmare hold on him. He'd tried to kill the fear by coming alone to the very edge of this fretful water, willing the glass-green hills to freeze so that he could see what lay beneath.

There'd been so many nights when his woman had to drive away the terror with her warmth, talking to him, rocking his wet head in her small hands. Loving him.

So hard to picture her now. Shuffling through the faces of the women in his life, rejecting them, shuffling again, barely conscious of the boat slipping up and down. Now there she was, her image sharp and clear before him, standing in his doorway, smiling that quiet, sweet-sad smile of hers. Clean and small like a bird.

The wind blew the breath of morning in his face, and her name, made warm and soft with feeling, came drifting back to him.

Lisa.

Gull Island came up in a grey haze. The cold light of the early day and a hard, insistent breeze had dragged him out of his dreaming. Hunger tightened in his stomach. The dried fish and water tasted raw. He should occupy himself. The big harpoon lay at his feet. He measured it with his eyes. He might not need it. It was the big fishing line – the king line – that mattered. It was lying in thick coils in the bow. The giant hook – the hidden fang to this great snake – was buried somewhere in the centre.

He wondered how Chadoo ever managed to use them, until he remembered that his son – the crazy one – worked the sea with him. Osun cursed his foot. Used to be a time when no man or woman on earth could run a line like him. Then, they called him King – King of the king line. He could haul anything out of the ocean: tunas, sharks, blue marlins that fought the hook like the gods they were. The great blue gods of salt and water that unfurled their fins like sails.

Sometimes it saddened him to bring them in.

The boat slid quietly into the small bay where heaps of rock edged down to the water. Through the morning haze, he saw the gulls wheeling in their thousands. The air vibrated with their cries.

Osun found the small line under the seat. He wanted bait for the king line. A bit of dried fish stuck at the end of the small hook was enough to attract the small black fish that lived off the mud on the sea-floor close to land. He caught one and it was easy afterwards. The flesh of the freshly caught fish, stripped and impaled on the hook, caught him as many as he wanted.

His anxiety had not left him. He kept glancing around at the rim of the sky. The Gate was way off in the distance, its roar faint on the wind. His heart began to race when he saw the boats. They were still distant; only the sun catching the sails made them visible. He used the oars to slip out of the bay, pausing to give *Deliverance* sail on the other side of the island.

Gull Island disappeared behind him, an arid place of giant cacti, mammoth stones and great rusting tanks once used to melt the fat of whales. The boats would not follow him beyond the island. But his fear grew as it slipped from view. It marked the boundary past which no fisherman would go. What lay beyond was more than ocean.

Then so be it, *Deliverance* would take him out there – to nowhere if need be – because that was where the dolphin said she wanted him.

Nothing around him now but sea. Now and then a frigate bird would speck the sky. The heavy king line trailed fathoms deep behind the boat, the other end secured against the keelson with Chadoo's own invention – a cross between a block and tackle and a rigging screw. Now and then he inspected it or watched schools of porpoises and corvally dash past the boat. He scoured the sky for gulls, wishing for their company and noisy laughter.

By the end of the month, they would all be gone, leaving Gull Island dead until their return, same time next year. At times like these, he thought he understood something of the vast unnameable threads that kept the world in equilibrium – the mysterious precision of the forces that synchronised the rise and fall of moon and tide; the times that birds and fishes spawned and died and spawned again.

He had learned to understand the sea. Old Man Tigga was his uncle, and there was his father too. It was in some place named Curaçao that the broken mast of the white man's yacht had fallen across his spine. Spent his last few years in hatred of his crippled self.

Then, of course, there was their son. They were laughing at a private joke when Skido brought the news. He cried openly. Lisa had reserved the pain and tears for the darkness of their bedroom. The boy was just eleven.

The humming of the king line woke him. He must have fallen deeply asleep, his back against the bow. He'd brought the sail down and secured the tiller at an angle so that while he dozed the boat would move around in a tight circle. *Deliverance* was rocking like a leaf on the water and the mast was describing crazy arcs above his head. The king line was spooling out so fast, the heat from the friction against the wood raised the scent of burning pine.

Osun pulled himself to his feet, noting that the sun had already gone down and the sky was grey. There was nothing to do but hold his breath and wait for the shuddering check of the line as it reached its end. When it came, it threw him on his back. Osun realised what a monster it must be. Whatever it was, it was running and *Deliverance* was at its mercy.

Bracing himself against the mast, he crouched low and waited for what he knew was about to come. The creature began to rise. Fast. From below.

This was the moment for which he had been saving his strength. He could imagine no greater glory than returning home, cured of his curse and with something the size of this monster. He could see the crowds on the beach, hear the voices, feel the eyes on him, the hands against his skin. He braced himself.

The ocean quaked.

A sudden swirl of water; the bare glimpse of a dark body. A

mighty mass of fin and flesh. A black back curving downwards. And then the flourish of tail-fins just above the water, a movement so incidental it seemed to contradict the enormity of the action, and its consequences. It created a storm that almost swamped the boat and stripped half of *Deliverance*'s spine away, taking with it the hook, the line and the anchor.

Then, it was gone.

Morning rose over dark water. The sun hung like a bruised eye above the eastern edge of the sea. He had arrived at the place he sought. He knew that by the nature of the water. It was opaque so that no sky was reflected there. Even the movement of the boat was different. The sea tossed like a sleeper trapped in dreams. Between moments of absolute stillness, the wind came in fitful bursts and spun the craft around. It was like that until afternoon.

He waited. At one point he caught sight of three birds that appeared from nowhere, a peculiarly joyous presence in the blank greyness. Yellow bills, perhaps, or white-tails with their beautiful, bright streamers trailing behind. Not terns for sure, or pelicans. They did not fly that beautifully. His heart leapt. They had turned, all three of them, in a slow circle high above his head and then just hung there motionless. Sky boats – flying frigates! Of all the creatures in the world, this was the one he would have most wished to be. Osun watched them slip away, spectre-like, on the wind.

His thoughts returned to the fish. What could it have been? His mind tried to span the dim reaches of the water below. Perhaps a tuna – he had seen how large they could become – over fourteen feet and several thousand pounds. Or perhaps a marlin. But a marlin would not have responded like that. It would have risen and hit the air in a fury of tail and fin and spray. With marlin, it would simply be a matter of time before it tired and he would send the harpoon through bone and flesh, into the small brain. Tunas were simpler; they ran until they drowned.

In the past, he could close his eyes and name a fish by the way it felt on the line. He was sure that he had not met anything like this creature. This – whatever it was – was a silent and sinister intelligence, all the more frightening because he never got to see it. That fish hadn't escaped him. It was he who had been saved.

He wondered whether even Skido would believe him if he told him about the fish. It did not matter. He felt at ease. Being lost out here wasn't all that bad. Not bad at all. Not like when Lisa left him. That was the day after he struck her.

With one blow he'd killed everything that had been precious between them, his hand rising and exploding against her face and her eyes wide and unbelieving, because it seemed so senseless, so uncalled for. He'd stood there watching the love drain out of her eyes. Even now, he did not understand why he'd done it.

Perhaps it was the death of the child. Or his guilt. For even if he had not been there when the boy was lifted limp out of the water and laid out on the sand, he believed he had something to do with it. The child had been keeping his secret, hadn't he? Something for which he'd been forever grateful, and which, he thought, had brought them closer. It was not something he could admit to openly. He'd done it out of a reckless pride to awe Jonah. He'd struck a dolphin, had gone against his own instincts and the knowledge instilled in every child long before they'd learned to bait a hook: that no-one ever struck a dolphin. A person looked into their eyes and knew why. Dolphins did not speak, but they could respond to everything a soul was feeling.

It was no more than an impulse in the presence of his son, a reflex as natural as the stirrings in the groin. The boy was eleven and as perfect a swimmer as anyone had seen – long-boned, lean and strong as a purple reed. Osun had taken him out a mile that Sunday to lift the fish-pots he had laid around the edges of Short Horn. A bright day, he remembered, so bright he had to narrow his eyes down to slits to see anything in the distance. It was the boy who had spotted the cloud of gulls first, a black smudge just above the horizon.

It took them an hour to get there. By then, the mass of migrating corvally that had attracted the gulls had moved further out. It was one of the biggest schools he'd ever seen, creating its own little whirlpool beneath the frenzied feeding of the gulls.

It was not as if he'd travelled this distance for any particular reason. In fact, even if he'd wanted to, he could not do anything but stand with his hand on the boy's shoulder and gape. He had not carried a net of any sort and the small line under the bow was useless without bait. There was the harpoon, of course, but using it would have been like using a cannon to shoot at mosquitoes. Again, it was the boy who noticed the turmoil in the middle of the moving mass of fish. Osun had to squint hard before he could spot them and when he did it was just the purple backs barely breaking surface, diving and rising in slick succession as they rounded up the fish.

It must have been the oddity of that white body amongst the others that shifted his hand from the boy's shoulder and turned it towards the harpoon, so that when the dolphins rose and hit the air in that magical, curving chain that was both dance and exultation, his arm was already drawn full back. They had swum close enough for him to see the sheen of the sun on their skins and that curious ridge that ran along their mouths that made them seem to be perpetually smiling.

The white had disengaged herself in what must have been a display just for himself and Jonah. With a twist of the powerful tail the creature scooped the water from the surface of the sea and fanned it out on the air in a spray so fine it created rainbows in the sun.

He might have paid attention to the shrilling of the child, but he thought it was just his excitement. On the fifth rising, the harpoon perfectly poised, Osun struck.

That cry!

Lord have mercy!

He didn't know to this day whether it was the dolphin or the boy. He'd turned around and found him crouched low in the boat, his hands grasping his sides as if it was he that had been wounded. Wounded, yes, because the dolphin had not died. And what happened afterwards, well, Jonah was there to prove that he had seen it: its companions did not leave that strangely pale and glistening creature there. They bore it away.

Osun couldn't tell how long he stood there with the boy staring at the slow procession till the waves and distance hid them.

Those eyes! Lord have mercy, those red eyes. The creature had come close enough for him to look into them. He would never forget those eyes.

It was those eyes he was remembering when, almost exactly one year later, he knelt on the sand and eased the wet head of his child off the piece of tarpaulin.

Lisa had decided to leave him the very day that he confessed about the dolphin and, unable to bear the betrayal in her eyes, he'd turned around and struck her.

Osun rested his eyes on the water and covered his face.

He sat under a stiffening sky. The piece of tarpaulin he'd dug out of the tiny hold took the brunt of the rain when the sky eventually opened up. He could smell the coming storm. The air was tense and crackling with the threat of it. *Deliverance* was tired. He hoped that she could take it.

He drank the last of his water, ate some dried fish and threw the rest away. Without water, the salted fish would only worsen his thirst. Food was not a worry. He could manage. Anyway, the dolphin should be coming soon.

It was with idle eyes that he watched the boat approaching through the rain. At first he thought it was the white crest of a large wave. Then *Deliverance* rose on a swell and he saw a yacht, sails trimmed, dipping and rising. Coming his way. They'd seen him. It came close. White faces stared down at him. Suddenly he remembered an old stone church, a tall cross and banks upon banks of pews and he, a small boy, standing before a robed figure, and hundreds of gleaming statues, staring back at him. Osun buried his face between his knees.

Some time after, he opened his eyes and wondered if he had been dreaming. But he looked up and around him and saw the boat disappearing, a white bird, through the mist of rain.

The air was dripping with the suspense of the storm.

Night had returned by the time the sky opened up, and when it did the whole world suddenly came tearing down on him. The images returned, stiffly robed and polished. Osun called them by their names, prayed to them like his mother had taught him, cursed them, and prayed to them again.

Deliverance fought back like a thing possessed. Sometimes he sensed her falling, falling endlessly downwards. Osun died many times, each dizzying fall a new death. He waited for the great engulfing wall of water. It never came. The craft recovered and brought him up again. It was on one of those upward surges that he was sure he heard his name, somebody calling:

Osunyin. Osunyin… Osunyin, Osunyin.

His first name. In full. Like his mother used to call him. Like Lisa always did.

Osunyin. Osunyin… Osunyin Osunyin – a quick succession of breakers dying on a dark reef.

'Lisa?' he called back.

Morning. Osun slept through most of the day. When he opened his eyes, the sun was a bright brass coin burning his skin. He heard gulls before he saw them. He'd woken up to a strange peace that was reflected by the calmness of the water on which *Deliverance* now floated. This thing inside him felt new and delicate. He felt afraid to move lest he should lose it.

How long had he been out here? Three days? Four? It felt like all his life. He hadn't eaten, but wasn't hungry. Just tired – tired like *Deliverance* and, like her, at ease. Nothing moved him now, not even Gull Island when it rose up out of the sea before him. He realised the storm had driven him back. He guided the craft towards the windward side of the island.

The beach curved like a wide grin before him, piled high with shells, mangled bits of clothing, and lengths of wood that were bleached bone-white.

At the last moment, he changed tack and guided *Deliverance* into the stony leeward harbour. Much quieter there.

Osun sat in the boat until the sun became a burning coal on the very edges of the ocean. The sky smouldered above him with a quiet rage. To die – and to die like this – was beautiful. Quietly, leaving all that beauty behind. For a while he sat there undecided, eyes fixed gratefully on the boat. *Deliverance* had been good to him.

Stiffly, he clambered over the side of the craft. The world spun. He was much weaker than he'd realised. The foot. He hadn't thought about the foot. It wasn't hurting anymore. Couldn't remember if it ever did these past few days. He climbed up the stone beach and chose one of the great flat boulders there. He wanted to rest. Just a while. Sleep the sleep he hadn't slept for so many months since he'd taken Lisa away. The stone was warm with the heat it had absorbed during the day, warm with the warmth of life.

Chest bared to the sky, Osun followed its domed curve with his eyes. Another realisation. Everything in life was a circle. Everything important: earth and moon and stars; his head, his heart, life itself. Once opened to make meaning of the world, the mouth became an 'O' of sorts. God expressed God's self in circles.

Some way off, the water was murmuring like a congregation deep in prayer. The stones, stretched out on either side of him, were giant pews. There was a soft humming in his head that drowned the psalming of the sea below. The boats from the shore that he'd escaped were coming, but he was travelling away from them. He was certain they could not catch him. Not now or ever. The Gate was before him, foaming high.

The waves, raising hell above him, were obliging him at last. They froze, and there below he saw it all, exactly as it had been brought to him in dreams. Except the whiteness. Stupid of him to think it was the dolphin. Lisa had been wearing white that last time. In white, that was how he'd dressed her before he'd brought her out here and put her to rest. After he'd struck her again, struggling with himself to stop. But his hand would not allow him. Was better that way, not so? Couldn' bear to see her leave. Had to make 'er stay, not so? Else, he would have lost his mind.

Smiling, Osun reached out beneath the waves, touched the whiteness and was covered.

Night came and settled over the island. A fish momentarily broke the surface and struck air before being reclaimed by the water.

A soft wind rocked the boat, cheeked the loose sail out and swung the bow of the craft towards the open sea. It hung there bobbing gently, battered now, but still very much alert with something of the spirit of the man who had so painstakingly created her. A firmer, harder wind took hold of her and glided *Deliverance* out towards the open water.

A DIFFERENT OCEAN

Sienna loved the play of light on the tiny whisky bottles, frosted by the waves, reshaped by salt and time. She collected them, along with coins and strips of green-caked copper that she scrubbed until they became as bright as the fire that shaped them.

Mornings, she sneaked down to the beach and those pretty things were there amongst the shells, the jellyfish and seaweeds.

The doll had been her greatest find. She'd come upon it one morning – a pale, outlandish flower sprawled against the blackness of the sand. It had half of everything: a single, sea-bleached leg which was cocked up at the sky in a most indecorous manner, one damaged eye that followed her movements whichever way she turned, and a portion of an arm. It had half a head of soft, corn-yellow hair.

She'd bathed it, dressed it and laid it on a straw bed as she would an ailing friend – as if expecting that it would become whole again.

She named the doll Lucille, thought of her as a sister. In time, she too would acquire sun-coloured hair that floated around her face, hair which she could squint through, comb and part with her fingers and shake in imaginary winds. She and Lucille would live in a blue room with pretty yellow curtains and windows that faced a flush of trees, laden with apples and pears and peaches, all growing on the same branch. Perhaps the tar would seep away from beneath her skin, leaving her as pink as the cheek of the one-eyed doll.

Tan Lin tossed Lucille into the fire the evening Sienna left her outside in the yard. She'd hurried down to the beach to watch the men haul in a giant octopus from the place they called The Mouth.

She bawled and railed while her cousin, Cedric, his face a mix of sympathy and pleasure, poked the sizzling lump of foul-smelling plastic from the fire and placed it at her feet.

'Chiiiile! Shut dat big black mout ov yours before I close it for good.' Sienna didn't wait for the rest of Tan Lin's words – words whose meaning she might not know exactly, but which would sting her like a splattering of hot oil. She was halfway down the hill and heading for the beach when they came: *'Petite jamette laide!'*

It was only when her feet hit the coolness of the sand and she saw the small crowd at the northern end of the bay that she stopped her bawling. They were standing on the part of the beach that strangers were warned against.

The sign that used to read, DANGER, SUDDEN DROP, in big red letters was still there, but the writing had long been chewed by rust. The sea hid the crater the government had dug there when it promised to build a yacht marina in The Silent. At the end of that election year, the excavating machines had climbed back onto the trucks and never returned. What they left was a patch of darker blue which reminded them of its presence in odd ways: a sudden flush of cold along the stomach of the person who dared to swim across it, or the way a boat or bit of wood would slowly drift towards it, in response to some secret pull. It had already swallowed the lives of two unsuspecting brothers. It was this readiness to suck in anything that possessed a will weaker than its own that made them call it, The Mouth.

Missa Jacko was in the middle of the group, his thin arms flailing the morning air above his head. Perhaps they had spotted another octopus down there?

'Some thief-an-criminal gone off and take mih fishpot and all the fish that was in it. I goin to murder the dog. I goin to search every house-an-garden. I goin to inspect every latrine in the area. I goin to scrutinise every fishpot in the sea and no matter how much paint dem paint to change it, I goin to find mih property. Is only a stinkin thief could thief de fishpot dat I buy de other day. It was full of fish, I sure o that, else why de hell dey thief it? Eh?

I want back all mih fish in mih fishpot. Who de hell dey tink dem is, eh? Who dem tink I is!'

Sienna's arrival turned the man's rum-reddened eyes on her. His hands froze in mid air, her presence presenting him with a new possibility.

'You! You know anyting about my fishpot?'

She stopped midstride, caught her breath and swallowed a sudden sting of tears. 'Me? Me! Me tief yuh fishpot? Me! Me? I goin tell my Tanty dat you say…'

Jacko fluttered his hands at her. 'Tell yuh Tanty! Tell yuh Tanty… Is only ask I ask, and I ask polite. I didn say…'

'I goin tell she! I goin tell she you say everybody in we family is thief an you goin search from de top o we house to below we bed, an even we latrine an…'

'Jeezas, spare me.' Jacko turned to the faces around him, his lips shaping an appeal. 'Anybody hear me say anyting like dat? As God is me witness, anybody hear dem wuds come from me?'

'Wasn't what you say,' Anna May cut in sourly, 'but who is to say is not what you mean? What make you tink is not dat foreign boat down dere dat cut your fishpot rope.'

Ten pairs of eyes turned towards 'down there'.

'Down there' was The Silent. It was a place that yachts liked. They started arriving in November like a flock of great white birds, so tall sometimes their sail-wings seemed to scrape the sky. They would remain there for a couple of days or sometimes for a week.

A beautiful skiff with a very tall mast was sitting in the middle of The Silent. It must have arrived late at night or in the small hours of that morning.

'So!' Anna May rolled bright, disdainful eyes at Jacko. 'What you goin tell me now? Dat Whiteman boat never does cut no fishpot rope?'

Everything happened quickly then. Martin, one of the younger fishermen, pulled his diving glass over his face and rushed into the water, heading for The Mouth. He began hovering around the edges like an insect at the lip of some carnivorous flower.

Then his voice rang out across the water. 'It down there! Kin hardly see it! Look like it full o fish too.'

Sienna hit the water in a rapid running dive. The momentum carried her right through to the blue lip of The Mouth. She sucked in hard and arced her body in a tight, downward curve.

The cold swallowed her whole and bruised her senses. She swam fast towards the dim shapes below, aware of the growing pressure in her chest and eardrums, even as she puzzled at the ease with which she was slipping down the throat of the hole. Her body was telling her what her mind already knew: water should resist. The sea never offered itself up to anyone that easily. But she kept kicking toward the bottom-darkness until she spotted the white blur that was the rope that secured the float to the fishpot. The wickerwork of the pot itself was no more than a patch of paleness somewhere further down. She focused on the rope, kicking harder as she reached for it, frustrated at the way it evaded her grasp by the circling dance it made. She milled her legs furiously, reached out and finally grasped it. Wrapping it around her wrist and ignoring the burning in her chest, she began the struggle upwards. Her efforts to fight the water's tug, and haul the weight up at the same time, forced her towards the other side and there, suddenly, the water opened its fist and released her.

Hands were waiting to lift her out and seat her at the back of Ragman's little boat. There was a dizzying din of voices on the beach.

They rowed her over and dropped her on the sand. Jacko was examining her like some creature the ocean had unexpectedly deposited in front of him. The morning had become a bright, featureless haze; she could not control her trembling.

'Cold down dere,' she chattered, gathering her clothes. 'Real cold.'

'One hundred and ninety,' Martin said. 'I count one hundred and ninety.'

Anna May sketched the sign of the cross across her chest and muttered something, while the rest stared at the fishpot at Jacko's feet.

'You could've dead,' Jacko muttered. Then after a pause, 'But nobody can't say is I who send you.' He seemed to be addressing the thrashing mass of parrotfish and snappers.

His words stirred something cold and bitter in Sienna. 'Dat's all y'have to say?'

Jacko shrugged. 'You didn drown.'

'De fish is mine,' she said.

'Like hell.'

Anna May chuckled, and something in that chuckle roused her son. Big and wordless as a boulder, Preeso stepped between the fishpot and the man.

'Not, not even a little one for me?'

'Not even,' Sienna told him.

Anna May did not accept the fish Sienna offered. She seemed more concerned to get off the beach, as if she'd sensed a change in the weather. Even Jacko, now that he had recovered his pot, had lost interest in the fish. Their sudden detachment had reduced her effort to nothing, and Sienna remained there facing the sea, hearing again Tan Lin's awful words.

That was how the two strangers met her: alone on the beach with a pile of dead fish at her feet, staring at the dark blue patch of water that had left a freezing place inside her. She had not heard them approaching. The first she knew of them was when a voice brushed against her ear. 'Nice catch.'

She looked up to see a woman in a sky-blue bikini smiling down on her. Her heart began to race. Perhaps it was because the woman was slim as the dolls Sienna had seen in the St. George's store that first and only Christmas Eve she'd been to town. Dolls with skin as pale and pure as manioc starch. The woman had their pink cheeks and Lucille's creamy-yellow hair, and her eyes were made from a patch of perfect sky. Those eyes matched exactly the little stone set in silver, fixed to a very fine chain around the woman's neck.

'I'm Sue – Sue Kramer. This is John Hedgcoe.'

'Hi,' the man said. His eyes were very different from

Sookramer's – a dark centre rimmed by a lighter colour, like the eyes of a bird, p'rhaps a seagull. He was barefooted like the woman, a bit taller and, like Miss Sookramer, everything about him was gold, even the hairs covering his limbs and stomach.

Miss Sookramer held out a hand. Sienna stared at it, then up at the woman's face. She could not hold those eyes so she fixed instead on the blue of the stone at her throat.

What was her name? The woman's voice was soft and musical. Sienna Miller? That was a nice name. Did they all have English names? In which of those houses on the hill did she live? Why did they build their homes on stilts? Did she know the names of the fish at her feet? Where did she learn to dive like that? A whole raft of questions, the answers to which generated even more questions.

The man, who'd never taken his eyes off her, spoke only when the woman paused for breath. Sienna could not decide whether he was talking to the woman, to himself or her. 'Nice teeth,' he said. That was when she was in the middle of responding to one of the woman's questions. In between another of her replies, he said, 'Good shoulders, deep ribs', and something else that wasn't clear at all.

Miss Sookramer excused herself and stooped to prise a shell from the sand. The man spoke directly to Sienna for the first time. Did she know why The Mouth behaved the way it did? Did she know that the whole ocean was like that, more or less?

'Warmer water rises to the top, colder water slides below; the way water boils.'

For some reason, he said, with a quiver of the little gold moustache, the effect was much stronger in The Mouth. Were there others, boys, who could dive like her?

'I'z the best,' she answered flatly. This made the man laugh and Sienna added, 'Everybody round here know dat.'

The man pointed at the small white craft in the lagoon. It was a blinding silver in the morning sun. 'That one – *Cincinnati Dreams* – is ours. Ever been on one before?'

Sienna shook her head.

'Wanna come over later? Susan thinks you're nice.'

'Tell us what time, we'll come in the dinghy and get you,' the woman offered.

'I kin swim,' she said, flashing a quick glance up at the houses.

The man was looking out to sea, his eyes so narrowed that all she saw there was a glint. She might have told him that it was Missa Mosan's little tray of a boat, coming in from his trip out to the reefs beyond Goat Point. She hadn't remembered Missa Mosan when they asked her if anyone could dive better than she did. But he could not be counted, because everybody knew he'd exchanged his wife's and children's souls to the devil for the secrets of the deep. He was not from The Silent anyway, but from that barren place, several hills beyond, that was known as The Waterhole. She also knew that he'd borrowed the eyes of gulls, which was why he saw things from great distances, before anyone else had an idea they were there.

'Well, we'd better be off,' the man said.

'See yah later,' Sookramer said.

They left behind a slight wind full of odours, which came off the sea and wrapped itself around her like a piece of cloth. She sniffed and grinned. She'd taught herself to pry beneath the first fresh layer of any seawind to get at the smells it always carried.

'Look like you conversatin wit de sea!' Missa Mosan was a little man with a big head and huge hands. He was smiling, as if he'd expected her to be waiting there for him.

'Is true you have a thousan chilren?' She'd asked this question hundreds of times before, but she knew that if he chose to answer her at all, it would be as if he'd heard it for the first time.

'How much twelve you got in a thousan, Miss?'

'A whole heap,' she muttered, frowning. 'Is true you use to have a hundred girlfriend?'

That was supposed to catch him unawares, but the man grinned toothlessly. 'What you fink?'

She shrugged, wondering how he would react if she told him that Tan Lin said she didn know what wimmen saw in this big-head little runt of a man.

He began tossing things from the boat onto the sand; first his machete, then the oars, followed by his fish-gun, then a crocus bag still writhing with his catch.

'They pretty?'

'They…?'

'Children. They pretty?'

He rested large and heavy eyes on her face. 'You know anybody who not?'

'No,' she answered quickly.

'Which make me ask meself what people who does never have one word to crack with us, what dem *want* with a little girl?'

She stared at him tight-lipped, but he did not seem to be in a hurry for an answer. He stepped back and reached beneath the stern of his craft, bringing out something large and heavy, wrapped in a piece of sacking. She watched as he reached into the bag and brought out a shell – the largest she had ever seen, caked with silt and seaweed. But its mouth, now that he'd turned it toward her, snatched her breath away. She had seen a queen shell just once before, but never this close up; even then, she'd never imagined that a thing could be so beautiful.

'Now dat's pretty,' he breathed. 'These belong to de ocean. Her pussnal joolry. She never give dem up without a fight. Every time mih ooman have a chile, she send me off to get one, so I kin risk mih life like her. You gotta go down, down, down, an keep goin till you don't know top from bottom. You keep goin becuz iffen you tink o de hurtin in yuh ears, iffen you tink one little second dat you can't reach it, den you never goin to get it. You ever wonder why all de good things in life so hard to get?'

She nodded.

He turned the shell to face him, awed it seemed at its beauty. Then he handed it to her. Mosan was looking at her closely when she brought it to her ear. She closed her eyes to absorb its thunder – the suck and surge, the bellow and sigh – to feel the quiet stir of fear and pleasure in her gut.

Sienna opened her eyes and nodded. What he saw on her face must have satisfied him because he showed her all his gums.

'Like I say, nice tings don't come easy.'

He gathered his tackle and placed them in his big canvas bag. With a toss of his head, he muttered, 'Watch yerself, girl! Some people don't smile to smile; some-a-dem smile to bite.'

Mosan's words did not prevent her from swimming over to the boat that evening. Her uneasiness had washed off the moment she slipped into the water, even though it was the first time she had ever swum in the lagoon.

Sookramer and the man had drawn the boat closer to the mangroves, so that if people had looked down from the houses on the hill they would not have seen her being lifted aboard by her new friends. There was something nice about the secretiveness of it all – the way everything was understood without being talked about.

There was still a lot of light left in the sky, and the beach had become a burning strip of silver. The woman turned to stare open-mouthed. 'Come,' she said, as if she were dragging herself out of a dream, 'I'll show you around.'

But it was the man who took her around, explaining the difference between cutter rigs, gaff rigs and Bermudan rigs and why their boat was a Vancouver and not a Westerly or an Armagnac. All Sienna remembered was that everything in their boat was tiny and perfect. There was a bed, a stove standing beside a shiny sink, and what looked like a small fridge and toilet.

The woman gave her something to eat called pasta, a can of Coca-Cola, two lollipops – Chupa-Chups whose wrapping she was going to keep, a big square of chocolate covered in gold paper and a packet of chewing gum.

They told her about places with pretty names like Albuquerque, Mississippi, Oklahoma and Ohio. They said they liked the way she talked, that she looked very strong for her age, that she had the clearest eyes they'd ever seen. Sookramer had even fingered her hair and marvelled at its softness. She, in turn, had been allowed to touch the woman's and – although she did not show it – was surprised that it was not as soft as it appeared.

Missa Jonko took an apple, large as a fist and red like a ripe tomato, which he began peeling with a big knife. He appeared not to be watching her, but she knew he was. In her turn, she pretended not to observe him. It was with something like mild shock that she saw him, with a flash of the wrist, drive the knife into the fruit and toss it in the water. 'Fetch it and its yours,' he grinned.

She leapt after it and surfaced a few moments later with the impaled fruit.

'Great!' He brought his palms together thunderously. 'Now you got an apple.' Turning to Miss Sookramer, he said, 'I told you she's got talent.' And to prove that he was right, he held up a silver coin and threw it a few yards beyond her.

She did not manage to retrieve it, or the others that he flung so casually overboard. When she surfaced, her face creased with disappointment, she saw that the man was smiling.

'The water flows that way,' he said, his hand sweeping in the general direction of where the lagoon opened out into the bay and then the world. 'You can't feel it but it flows. Always start a little way further up from where you want to go. Come tomorrow.'

'About this time,' the woman cut in gently, her eyes turned up at the houses on the hill.

'Yep! and I'll teach you how to dive anywhere, for anything. I'm gonna make you famous. You know why? Because Susan and I, we think you're special.'

She realised the man meant what he said as soon as she swam over the following day, because he had a can of coins on deck. Again, they'd drawn the boat closer to the mangroves.

'Y'know what's great about this game?' Missa Jonko laughed. 'I throw em, you git em, you keep em. Remember what I told you yesterday about starting further up? Here we go-oh!'

That was how, in the evenings that followed, she learnt to anticipate the dizzy spiralling of dimes, the direct plunge of large glass marbles with wondrously foliated irises, the slant of paper knives and nails, the somersault of tiny silver saucers, the twirl of metal rulers, and whatever else the man decided to throw for her.

Missa Jonko never seemed to run out of pretty things. It was as if he'd conjured these bright objects from his mind to do his bidding in the water.

The little cave she'd dug under the tuft of cus-cus grass below her cedar tree above The Silent became a bulging, glittering nest. It held three penknives with the word 'Kiwi' written in silver; a fingernail clip that was also a can-opener; a tiny brass box with engravings of naked people that looked curiously flat against the metal; a silver ring with the head of a lion on the top and, most treasured of them all, a round copper case full now with dozens of what the man called half-dollars, and which had been the most difficult to retrieve because he had ordered her to wait until he counted fifteen before she went after them.

Her days assumed the glitter of these objects. Bright days when she avoided the people who used the beach in the evenings. She developed a protective sheen around herself which guarded her from their stares, their silences, their words. She'd done this after Anna May had spoken to her. It was after her fourth visit to the boat. The woman had crooked a finger at her and Sienna had approached cautiously, since there was no mistaking the tightness in Anna May's manner, which meant that what she was about to say was going to be hurtful.

'What you doin on dem people boat? Eh? You know what you playin with? Eh? You dunno is trouble dem people does bring? I wouldn let my Preeso spend five minutes on dat boat. But little girl like you, you across deh all evenin, every day. What yuh Tanty sayin bout all o dat? Eh? Is why I never like dat ooman. She too damn careless. If is somewhere you want to come when evenin come, come to my house. You kin help me do the washin up. You kin sweep mih yard. A little girl like you have good use. I know you strong. I does watch you. But dat boat an dem people! Is warn I warnin you.' And with that she had walked off.

That was why she would no longer *see* the stares, *hear* the words or heed anybody's crooked finger anymore.

If she didn't know better, she might have believed that the man had overheard everything that Anna May told her, because from that day his smiles were replaced by a curtness that seemed more natural to him and which she did not mind, because this persistent drill, this daily bidding to slip beneath the shadowy skirts of the lagoon, to retrieve and keep those pretty things had also brought an odd sobriety in her.

Now she did the things Tan Lin asked without complaining, and Cedric's teasing no longer triggered peppery outbursts. These days, he complained that she ignored him.

If Tan Lin had heard about or noticed her evening disappearances, she was saying nothing, although one night, believing she was asleep, her aunt had brought the lamp down over her and moved it along her body, the way a fisherman would check a craft for dents or weakened seams. Then with a smack of her lips she'd straightened up and left the room.

Sienna had already rehearsed her response, just in case Tan Lin asked. She would say that Missa Jonko was teaching her to dive so that a man in America called Missa Olympics could judge her as the greatest in the world. The presents she would get for that would be made from proper gold. But it meant a lot of practise. It meant diving deeper than anyone had gone before. It meant learning to place a hook around a ring on the box that Jonko had lowered to the bottom of The Silent. It meant understanding everything the man taught her the very first time, because he did not like to repeat himself.

He had her dive until the sky drained of light and the water became too dark for her to see what lay below. It was only then that he allowed her to dry out on that part of the deck he called the coach roof, while she answered Miss Sookramer's questions.

At first, the woman's gestures and expressions had been confusing, like some new road whose twists and turns she could not anticipate. She would take in the broad things: the woman's show of teeth that meant a smile, the laugh that indicated ease, and of course the constant kindness in her voice. But there was also the hurt she sensed behind the woman's calm, whenever the man's impatience turned on her. Sookramer liked to laugh, though, and it was this that allowed Sienna to get past the odd way she sometimes said things.

A few days before, in the middle of a laugh, their eyes had met; a small silence descended upon them and they knew they had become friends.

'Are you coming tomorrow?'

It was Sookramer's way of telling her to leave. It was what she always said before lowering her voice and bringing a hand up to her mouth. 'Can you bring me something green? Some leaves or flowers – anything, please?'

Sienna would make her way to the lip of the precipice above The Silent to observe the night creep in from the sea. She would watch the muted cabin lights come on. If it was one of those evenings when the air was very still, their voices would drift up to her. She would stay there until tiredness or the night chill drove them below deck. The yellow lanterns would go out and it would be dark down there, and very, very lonely.

It was their eleventh evening in The Silent and even Anna May seemed less concerned about her visits to the boat. Something else was bothering her. No one had ever known a yacht to remain so long there.

What bothered Sienna was that Missa Jonko had ceased to comment on her diving – it was days since he'd mentioned competing for Missa Olympics.

That evening, she'd slipped into the water and, after hooking up the rope to the ring on the box he'd lowered to the floor of the lagoon, he'd raised his arm, shouted something and sent what looked like a great silver plate skidding across the water. It was no more than a disappearing dazzle by the time she responded. She moved quickly but she could not keep up with the object's ghostlike plunge. She followed it though, even when she noticed a difference in the way the water felt, even when the cold began to curl itself around her and, like a giant living muscle, the ocean began to shrug her back. It was an odd sensation and she wasn't prepared for it. Nor was she prepared for the fright that flooded her senses.

She headed upwards, surfacing explosively, choked and mysti-
fied because for some reason the lagoon had lost its bottom. The
strangeness did not stop there, for when she'd popped her head
above the water she thought she'd heard the woman shouting, but
when she blinked the water from her eyes, Sookramer was sitting
at the front of the boat as relaxed as ever.

'I didn, I couldn,' she spluttered.

'Fergeddit,' Jonko laughed. 'Just an ashtray, that's all.'

'It didn have no bottom down dere… it.'

'Aww, c'maan, kiddy. I admit it. I've been pushing you.
Everybody gits tired. Tell you what, Susie's gonna make you
some of that custard stuff you like and we'll fergeddit for the day.
Okay, Susie? Give her whatever she wants; she's earned it.'

Back on the beach, it was too early to go home. She was glad
to see Jacko struggling under the weight of a basketful of
coralfish.

'How come De Silent have bottom one minute, an next
minute it don't have none, Missa Jacko?'

The man turned his head as much as the basket would allow
him. Perhaps he had not forgiven her for keeping all his fish that last
time, or the weight of the basket had put him in a bad mood, but
his mouth twisted itself around an obscenity before he rumbled,
'Where's your manners! Where you come from! What you talkin to
me for! Go home, y'hear me? Go home an keep yuh broad-mout'
little black backside quiet. It have more tings in dat water dan
nobody round here know anything bout. GO!'

She waited the anger out. 'Tell me,' she entreated.

'Leave me, girl. Is your funeral you askin for!'

She decided to swim back to Jonko's boat. She hadn't worked
out exactly how she would ask. Maybe the same the way she had
asked Jacko, but not forgetting her manners this time.

The ladder was still down and she clambered onto the craft,
uncomfortably aware that she had never boarded without their
invitation. Sookramer's cries froze her. They must have heard her
because there came a tumbling from below, then abrupt silence.

Jonko emerged, grinning. The sea gull's eyes were narrowed

down and there was a frown above the smile. 'Forgot something?

She shook her head, licked her lips to begin the question, but he cut in pleasantly: 'Actually, I'm glad you came back. Got something for you.' He went below, but soon returned. 'This – this is for you.'

It was a pair of yellow flippers. New. And by the look of them, her size.

'Nice, huh? They're yours, but you'll have to leave them here. Of course, you'll keep them when we leave.'

'Leave?' She stared into his face, then away to the water.

'Didn't Susan tell you? Let's talk about it tomorrow. Okay?'

He pointed at the flippers. 'Tomorrow I'll show you how to use them. See yah.'

She clattered down the ladder so that they could hear her leave.

Jacko had not answered her question out of rage; Jonko for some reason she could not understand. She had no doubt that Sookramer would have told her – Sookramer whose scream she now carried in her head, whose blue-sad stare resembled those of the women of The Silent – only theirs were darker and seemed fixed on things further away. Sookramer, on whose arms and back and legs were those long, red marks she'd said the sun had burned there.

She swam fast in the sleek and noiseless sideways manner that the man had taught her. She headed for The Mouth. There, she allowed its pull to take hold of her, forcing herself to drift with it until she felt the sucking cold. Then with a violent flash of limbs, a sudden twist of rage, she pulled herself loose from its grip and headed for the beach.

From there, she stared at the little yacht, framed against the dark embrace of mangrove. Everything was quiet; even the gulls seemed to have vacated the sky. Silvery ribbons of clouds hung where the sky curved down and melted into the water. She felt like crying, but was snapped out of it when she heard the engine of Jonko's dinghy.

She watched it cut a frothing path along the edges of the lagoon. Soon it was heading out of the bay towards the grey smudge that was Krill Island, and in no time it was a small dot on the darkening heave beyond.

She heard her name then, pronounced with the by-now familiar drawl, which she used to find so pleasing. Sookramer, dripping and barefooted, was making her way over the stones which served as a jetty for boats and a place where the children caught whelks, and harassed conga eels. She walked with the daintiness of one of those speckled long-legged birds that visited the lagoon during the Easter months. Sienna did not look up. The woman lowered herself beside her. There was an odour about her – a mild freshness – which Sienna could never decide whether she liked.

'I couldn't come up to see you, Sienna. Not the state I was in. Sorry. Hedgehog's gone over to one of your little islands. Left something out there.' She stretched out her feet and examined them. They were the colour of one of Tan Lin's loaves. The toes were long and pink like earthworms.

'What's it like up there? Where you live.'

'Dunno. We live up dere. That's all.'

The woman laughed. 'You make it sound like a stroll on the beach.' Still smiling, she wriggled her toes, pulled her feet in and began picking at the nails. They were painted a silvery blue. She turned her eyes on Sienna, her forehead pleated in a tiny frown. 'I watch your shapes sometimes, moving against those fires in what I suppose is your front garden?'

Sienna, pretending to be fascinated by what the woman's hands were doing, did not respond.

Sookramer flung her hair back and released a long, hissing jet of air. 'Well, there is something terribly warm and close and unconnected about it. A bit like a dream, I suppose. Only you – you make it real. Those fires, is that what you cook on?'

'No,' she muttered. 'We just like fire.'

'How do you live? No, I don't mean that – well not like that. What makes your people laugh? How do they love?' She paused over that, seemed very worried about something, then she added, smiling, 'I've heard it said that different people love differently, although John is one of those who doesn't believe that people can love at all.' She began laughing, the way cats mew – a soft, high-pitched sound. 'What frightens you, Sienna? I mean…' The blue eyes had gone darker, the lips tighter and somehow thinner. Sookramer brought her hands to her face and stared with pleated forehead towards *Cincinnati Dreams*. 'I don't want to waste this chance.'

'You didn't tell me y'all leaving.' Sienna spoke as if it had never occurred to her before. It hadn't. Not really. Not until Jonko had said it. These people were like something she had wished for and had woken up one morning to find on the beach. Like a present. Presents did not go away. Presents were things you kept.

Sookramer pushed her hair back from her face and turned to face her. Her eyes had gone a depthless amethyst. She wasn't smiling now. 'We have to go. There's something he left back in St. Vincent. He thought he wouldn't need it, but he has to come back. He must.'

'You coming back with him?'

It seemed an eternity before she answered. 'Only if I, er, if I have to. If I have to protect you from him. He'll come back and he'll call you. He'll offer you more things and you'll come and do what he asks because, at the moment, that's what you want to do more than anything. He knows that. What he doesn't know is why. I'm not sure I know why either, but I suspect that it hasn't got a lot to do with us. Not all of it. That makes sense?'

'Lil bit,' Sienna mumbled. She fixed her eyes on the stone at the base of her throat. 'He does beat you up.'

The woman sucked in her lower lip and stared across the water. Sienna could hear her breathing, soft like the way she spoke, like the way she walked and touched and laughed. Like she had imagined Lucille, alive and whole.

'Don't you have a single idea of what this might be all about?' The woman swung round to face her. Sienna felt mildly chastised. She shifted her gaze to the red crabs that had surfaced on the sand, their yellow eyes like small revolving flames above their heads.

Sookramer was about to tell her bad things. Things she didn't want to hear. Everybody was like that. People started off by saying nice things and then as soon as a pusson began believing them, they turned around and spoilt it.

Maybe all Sookramer and Jonko had told her – how good she was at diving, how nice they thought her teeth, how quickly she'd learnt the things they'd shown her – maybe none of that had been true.

'He does beat you up,' she repeated.

'We fight – yes, more and more now – over you.'

Sienna's eyes widened.

'Look. You must not come back. You must stay away, d'you hear me?'

'Why?'

'Because it's wrong. Because we're strangers. Because you don't know us. Because it's… it's not a place for you.'

'Why?' Suddenly the hot-eyed clenching, the sudden fizz of irritation, which had never been necessary with these strangers, began to rise and clog her throat.

Sookramer's face and neck had reddened and Sienna thought she was about to cry

'Because I – I do not want you to.'

'Missa Jonko want me to!' She was halfway to her feet when the woman's hand closed on her wrist with shocking strength. 'Sit down and listen to me! I'm trying to tell you something. I'm trying to save your goddamn life! This!' Her fingers traced a large, furious circle on the sand. 'This is your lagoon. How d'you call it? Never mind. This – can you guess what this is?'

Sienna squinted at the shape. 'The boat…'

'Right.' Sookramer looked up briefly at the sea. 'Here! This is where he's had you diving.' She made a small circle near the boat. 'Have you noticed that its getting deeper all the time, that now you're almost doubling the depth you began with?'

The girl nodded.

'That's because he's shifting that boat every time.'

'I know.'

'You know!' The woman looked at her with wide, bright eyes. 'Then I shouldn't have to tell you that this is not about teaching you a better way to do anything. Right? I don't need to tell you that he's taking you closer to where he really wants you to go. Do you know where that is? Do you know what it's like down there?'

'Course – I been…'

'No you don't!' The woman's ferocity stunned her. With an urgent sweep of the hand, she cleared the drawing off the sand and began to draw again. She stopped abruptly and with a toss of her hair looked upwards.

'Look up there. That tree, the one with all the flowers; d'you see that tree?'

She could have told the woman it was her tree. It stood a little way back from the edge of the cliff that dropped abruptly down to the lagoon. She could even tell the woman the way the roots curled out of the soil like a tangle of brown eels and the secret hollow she had dug there for her things.

'Now imagine the top of that tree is the surface of the water and the foot of it is the bottom. That's where you dive to normally. Now imagine you're swimming forward from the bottom of that tree. What happens?'

The girl looked up and then across to where Sookramer indicated. She held the woman's gaze in terrified, tight-lipped wonderment.

'Dat – dat's why! It got another…'

Sookramer nodded grimly 'Yes – another bottom a little way further out. That bottom where you dive to is just the top of, well, a sort of precipice.'

'A precipice?'

The woman nodded grimly. 'A precipice – a drop deeper than you can imagine, except it's underwater. Well, put it this way: there are a couple of ledges, shelves – whatever you want to call them – on the way down. You couldn't get to the last, er, bottom. It's too deep, thank God for that. What's lost down there will stay lost. The weight of the water would kill you. There are eight boxes down there – on the first ledge – with rings on them. The sonuvabitch who dropped them there just dropped them in the wrong place.'

The girl held her breath. She remembered Mosan's words and the evening talks amongst the adults about boats that dropped

crates of gin-an-whisky along the edges of Krill island for other
boats that would haul them up at night.

In fact, Missa Jacko and his friends had gone one low-tide
night and retrieved a dozen bottles for themselves. But never in
their lagoon.

'Gin-an-whisky?'

'You're so goddamn naive, you make me want to cry. In a few
places, less than a hundred miles from here, some things are worth
a lot of money. More money than you people here will ever earn
from selling your bananas. There's a little canvas bag down there
weighted with lead. He didn't tell me it was there at first, and when
he did last night he wouldn't tell me what's in it. Money, shit, ice
– I don't know, I don't care. But he wants it more than all the rest.
Enough to think your life is worth it. It's on the second ledge. After
you place that hook around those other boxes, he'll send you down
there last. I know why he's gone this evening – the sonuvabitch.
He's gone for grease. Do I need to tell you why?'

The girl stared blankly at the blue stone.

'For the cold. At least you know that much. And then there is
the pressure. You won't feel it straight away. We'll both be gone
by then. But the cold and the weight of the water will hurt you.
That…' She waved tiredly at the sea, 'That's nothing. Down there
it's a very different ocean.'

After a while she lost track of Sookramer's words, absorbed
more by the sound of them, the way the woman wrapped her
tongue around them, the emotions that they rode on – at once soft
with rage and made harsh by a frightening indignation – as if she
were railing more against herself than Missa Jonko.

Sienna stared at the markings on the sand. By showing her what
lay beneath the surface of the lagoon – *a different ocean* – Sookramer
was telling her something about herself. There were other worlds
around them they did not know existed. And because these strangers knew more about her place than they who lived here, it felt as
if it belonged less to her and to the people of The Silent.

She felt a welling in her chest and throat. She swallowed on it
lest the woman saw or sensed her change of mood.

But why would Jonko, or any person for that matter, want to do something like that to someone else? To call them nice names, smile at them, make them feel they were important, and then, with that same smile, seek to make the sea destroy them?

She knew, as everyone on The Silent did, that each time she turned her heels up at the sky there was nothing that said she would ever see the day again. The ocean might simply embrace her and not release her. That did not frighten her. It was not the same thing. Missa Mosan told her once that no one could predict when the sea would take a life. What was certain, though, it never wasted it. It added that life to its own. With Jonko, it was like showing her a room in her own house that she had never known was there, then locking her in it to die.

A question occurred to her, and she might have asked it if the woman hadn't been still speaking.

'One thing I've learned about you, you're smarter than you're letting on. You're...' Sookramer's mouth stayed open. She reached under the nest of hair at the back of her neck and her fingers fumbled there. The silver chain cascaded like water into the palm of her hand and made an island of the blue stone. 'You like this, don't you? Take it. I – I have to go.' It slipped onto Sienna's knee, flowed onto the sand and settled at her instep. The girl picked it up, wide-eyed, speechless. She moved to hand it back. But the woman had scrambled to her feet.

'Go home,' she hissed. 'Go to your people and don't come near this place until we leave. Y'hear me! And – and for Gawd's sake don't tell him what I told you.'

Then she was running, her eyes not on the sand but on the boat approaching in the distance.

Sienna told herself that there hadn't been time to tell Sookramer that it was not Jonko's boat, because the woman was off the moment her eyes had fallen on the speck that had emerged from behind Krill Island. More truthfully, Sookramer's terror had fascinated her. Fear was something she had not thought possible with people like them.

★

Missa Mosan did not greet her. He was trying to get his hand under the tail of a hefty tuna. This was a man, they said, who never sold the fish he caught, who, by some secret agreement with the ocean, always returned with enough to feed his crowd of children, even when the sea offered nothing to others.

'Missa Mosan?'

'Yaas!'

'What is de deepest deep a pusson kin dive?'

'Deep? What deep?' He did not look at her. He was still working his hand under the fish.

'Deep, Missa Mosan! Deep-deep-deep – where a pusson kin hardly see de bottom from de top.'

The man straightened up, began working his jaw, as if he were passing the idea around his mouth.

'What kind o pusson?'

'A pusson like you. A pusson like anybody,' she replied, her eyes avoiding his.

'How deep is deep?'

'Deep,' she insisted. 'Like from de top o dat tree to halfway down de cliff.'

'Dat what dem askin you?' He was looking at her closely.

She frowned a quick denial. 'Is not dem dat askin nothin, Missa Mosan. I jus want to know'

He chewed some more. 'From dat tree up dere you say?'

She nodded.

This time his mouth clamped down on his thoughts, as if what he'd tasted was not good at all. 'Not nice, not nice,' he muttered. 'Not nice at all! A dive like dat kin kill a man. I hear you hit de bottom of de Mouth?'

She nodded again.

'Dat's what dem askin you? Dat's why dem makin you skin kuffum across dat water dere?'

'Dem teachin me to dive. Dem…'

'Don't lie for me. Next ting you goin tell me is dem tryin to make de water wet!' He turned his back on her.

She watched him haul the small boat up the sand. There was something flat and angular about him that reminded her of those one-sided fish she often spotted on the sea floor. Even his head was like that, with hair like hers, scorched a rust-brown at the fringes by sun and salt. But it was his feet that fascinated her, narrow at the heels and flared like spatulas at the front – feet that had the same compact toughness as his body. It was then she was sure – thinking of the yellow flippers that Jonko had given her – it was in the size and shape of those amazing pair of feet that lay the secret of his diving. She looked down at her own feet and decided they were like his. Not as large, but that would come with time.

'Nobody in de worl' kin dive like us. Becuz nobody *make* to dive like us.' She said this without pride or gesture and Missa Mosan took it the way she meant it. He swivelled his head around and a broad, surprised smile pleated his face.

'When dey leavin? Cos dem have to leave here soon.'

She realised that he too had been counting the days. He too had been having thoughts about Sookramer and Jonko.

'Tonight, p'raps tomorrow.' She shrugged. 'It don't matter.'

She could not tell whether it was a cough or curse that came from Mosan's mouth. He raised his head towards the tree above the lagoon. 'If it was me, if is have I have to go. I goin to tek it fast.'

He seemed taken by his idea. He chewed on it furiously, then straightened up and fixed the tree again. 'Speed, speed is what is nerecerry for dis kinda dangerousness, becuz is dangerousness I call dat. An before I go, before I decide to play rummy wid my life for nothing, I'll tell meself – I'll say, "Mosan, don ferget to tek your time comin up. Strong as de water is, cold as it is down dere, hurt as mih chest goin be hurtin, bustin as mih lungs goin be bustin, you have to come up slow, becos comin up fast kin leave a whole heap o bubble in a pusson blood… an when it reach yuh heart…" He brought his palms together with a sudden thunder-clap that shook her to the core.

'What time o day a pusson might be thinkin about?' He threw a worried glance, not at her but at the sea.

'Dunno – no time, Missa Mosan. I was only askin. I was…'

'Mornin!' he growled. 'Early as a pusson kin make it. Before de sun come up an hit de water. Ain't got no tide dat time. De water don't wake up yet. It have to be early mornin.' He looked at the sea as if seeking approval for his words, took up his crocus bag and swung the tuna off the sand.

He was half way up the hill before he checked his stride.

'Once, Miss Lady! Jus once,' he shouted without turning. 'Yooman-been not make to do dat twice. Jus once – o else.' He did not say the rest, but that clap of his hands still echoed in her head, and without realising it, she nodded.

Afterwards, Sienna never spoke about what happened. The little that The Silent learned came from the mouths of those who went out hours before the stirring of the gulls, when morning was still a faint suggestion against a sky the colour of mud-soaked canvas.

Those who boasted eyes that could spot the markings on a gull's wing in the middle of a squall said they saw the flash of yellow flippers in the lagoon near the boat. It was something their minds rejected at the time.

What was certain was the emergence of the girl, bone-soaked and shivering, from somewhere near the tree above the lagoon. The women claimed it was the chattering of her teeth that made them lift their heads from their breakfast fires. They'd turned their eyes down towards the beach and spotted the flippers arranged side by side on the sand like a pair of parrot fish.

She'd gone into the house, stripped, and pulled on every spare bit of dry clothing she could put her hands on, including Cedric's underpants. Then she'd laid down on the floor and sunk into a kind of darkness which was nearer death than sleep.

They knew it as The Chill. That was clear from the pallor of her face, and the coldness that seeped from her bones and settled on her skin in a kind of sweat.

Tan Lin's candlelight inspection of the girl's body had not

delivered any answers. If Sienna had been tampered with, she said, it was in a way that went beyond her understanding.

By then the whiteman's boat had left.

When Sienna came out of it, Cedric told her about the boat leaving, and the odd sight of a whitewoman at the prow, looking up at them, then at the yellow flippers on the beach, her blue dress fluttering in the wind, her face as pale as an early morning moon. That, he told her, was two days before a couple of big grey boats with bright disturbing lights arrived and began circling The Silent.

The flippers were no longer where she'd left them after she'd swum back to the beach, emptied the heavy little canvas bag and slipped into the sea again, this time to toss the empty sack on deck where she thought Sookramer ought to see it, since she was always first to come up from below.

Sienna imagined the white trail the boat would have made all the way out, past Krill Island. And Sookramer, sad and smiling at the prow, casting a last glass-blue stare at the houses and the beach. The sense of abandonment she had anticipated was not there.

It was as if they had never come.

LISTEN, THE SEA

Amos is watching the white girl walk the length of the headland. She is above the mouth of the channel where the ocean becomes a muscular river that flares out further down and collides with the cross tides of Kick 'em Jenny.

It is a great leap to clear the rocks below and hit the choppy water. But she does it, crouched at first, then rising and unfolding as she takes to air in a massive dolphin-leap. For an instant her naked body is a pale arc against the morning sky before the sea closes itself around her.

Amos would have thought this jump impossible had he not seen that white girl do it three mornings in a row.

His eyes follow the water down to where it comes to a boil. She is mid-channel, the pale arms rhythmic and precise in all that violence around her. She is using the force of the tide to sweep her down, while steering her body towards the shingle beach directly under his house.

Amos has a clear view of the young woman when she emerges: slight, with a thin-boned fragility that makes him think of birds.

She stands on the rock facing the water. The light from the brightening day traces the outlines of her limbs. She releases her hair from the band that bunches it behind. The stringy mass falls around her face and shoulders like a toss of bleached seaweed. With a quick deft jerk of her head she throws back her hair and slips the band in place.

When she reaches beneath the ledge of rock that overhangs the shingle beach and pulls out a bundle of clothes she must have left there the day before. Amos lifts his elbows from his window sill and walks out of his door.

Night still smudges the lower rim of the western sky. In an hour or so the sun will touch the waters and the seven little islands they call The Sisters will emerge into clearly defined shapes.

There is a heaviness in his shoulders – a reawakened tension in his gut. He goes to the drum of water, breaks his reflection with a hand and scrubs his face.

There are things he has to do today. Miss Gerty's little radio is fixed. He should take it to the old woman because it is the only company she's got, and there's an extra sachet of herb for Hillman to keep him quiet about the electricity he 'borrows' from the pole at the bottom of the hill.

Amos waters his plants; breaks from time to time to stare at the roiling waters of the channel, then at the beach. The girl has gone now. A pair of sea gulls are beaking each other on the flat grey stone on which she stood. He is lost for a while in the heavy rattling of the pebbles down below. That beach is getting louder every day. He should tell her what that means, and if she does not listen he will have to find a way to stop her.

Any other day, he would take his speargun and old tin bucket and go spear-fishing in the lagoon at the southern tip of the island. This morning, he takes the narrow limestone path to Delna's Guest House. His head is full of things he doesn't want to think about, and he blames the whitegirl for it.

He is at the cross-path that would take him uphill and across the spine of the island when he catches a flash of colour ahead. It is still early and the old sea-island cotton trees that line the road are in shadow. The girl is an animated cut-out against their dusky foliage. Hers is a long, lean-boned stride – an odd flicking of her canvas shoes at the end of every step. She keeps her head down, her eyes on her feet. Amos stays in the centre of the path. She is almost upon him when she halts and lifts her head. Large, sea-green eyes settle on his face. It is as if he's being looked at through panes of tinted glass. She smells of salt. He saw her the evening she arrived, but not this close. She's too flimsy, too magga-bone and underfed to possess the strength she displays in the water, he thinks.

He must have been standing there longer than he imagined because he doesn't realise she's stepped around him until he hears the padding of her shoes behind him. He does not look back but carries in his head a snapshot of the young woman: the mass of reddish hair bunched at the back of her head, the raised cheek-bones, the flimsy top through which he glimpsed the tattoo on her flesh, just beneath her clavicle, and the marks along her arms.

Bowman's Rise is where he climbs when he needs to clear his head. The boom of breakers against the northern precipice and the heavy winds crowd out his thoughts. From there, the entire stony coastline of the island, sequined by frothing breakers, surrounds him. The southward procession of sea-beaten rock-islands trace a receding arc all the way to Main Island. Down below, the town is a narrow patch of colour against the vast, heaving blue.

He thinks of the white girl and the way she looked at him, through him, or beyond him. It felt like a collision.

He wonders if his sister had that look and why no-one on the island noticed it. From the moment the foreigner raised her head at him, he knew his warning would be wasted, as surely as he knows that one of these mornings she will lose her timing. Whatever skill or trick she uses to defy the tide will not save her. Those killing waters will swallow her and spit her out on some dirty shore in South America – if the sharks or barracudas don't get her first.

The Osprey is a white dot against the horizon. Amos watches the boat loom larger, its twin prows already angling northwards to avoid the turbulent waters.

It is the usual way the tourists come to Kara Isle. The diving girl was a surprise. Night was already gathering around the island. The jetty and the seafront were heaving with people watching the heavy wooden inter-island schooner grumble and grind towards them, before mooring in a suffocating choke of diesel oil and dry goods.

Her bag dropped first. It hit the jetty with a thud, then folded in on itself. Amos was one of those who lifted their eyes to where it came from, saw the flash of canvas shoes as she descended the narrow ladder with her back to them, her shoulder blades rolling under her flimsy top. He looked up again to observe the impossibly muscled seamen, rough as rusted iron, who looked down from the deck on the woman's descending head. No goodbye wave from them; none of those big tropical grins reserved for tourists. Just a quick exchange of looks between the men, because they too must have noticed what he saw in those glassy, staring eyes when their ways crossed.

She looked at no one. She slung the little canvas bag over her shoulders and strode off to Delna's Guest House. The old man they called Stinkfish rolled yellow rum-shot eyes at Amos and laughed.

It is afternoon when he rises from the rock. His stomach is grumbling but he is not sure he wants to eat. He remembers that his little friend, Daphne, will come later for her lessons. She will bring her usual animated conversation and lift his mood.

He dusts himself and follows the road down to the seafront. It has its usual mix of rowdiness and sun-struck apathy. Young men sit on concrete walls with crossed arms and legs, chuckling at private jokes. Elders recline on doorsteps, staring out at nothing. The hot air hums with the burble of conversation from the houses further back.

He feels their eyes on him – the narrowed, dark-eyed gazes of the young women in particular. The group in the front of Venus' Fish-Fry raise a burst of laughter. Paula is the boldest. She rakes him with her eyes, then clears her throat. Chuckles follow him into the shop.

Venus lifts a sweating forehead. 'What for you, Missa Amos?'

'Fishcake,' he says, 'No bread.'

Another wash of giggles from outside. Venus turns her head and looks out of the window.

'Never mind them. Is jealous they jealous. All dem little woman out dere want you for theyself and dey hate you becuz you got no time for dem.'

Amos smiles at her. 'Fishcake, no bread.'

Venus wraps the food but does not hand it over. She wipes her face, speaks with a hissing, low-voiced urgency. 'Go back to America, Amos. You done punish yourself enough. Is time you leave. You not make for dis place.'

Behind him, he hears 'waster', 'grave-man', 'sketel'. He recognises Simeon's voice. Simeon's been goading him for months.

'And him,' Venus rolls her eyeballs to the left. 'That got to stop.'

'The fishcake, Miss Venus.'

'Only ole bag de fella want. This one too young for him.'

'This one' is the white girl. She is standing in the far left corner with her ankles crossed, her shoulder propped against the wall. The light from the open window settles on her hand. She is poking at a sandwich as though she finds no pleasure in the food. Again, Amos wonders how such fragility could launch itself from such a height and breach the channel tide.

He steps out the door into the sizzling afternoon. Simeon's raised voice catches him somewhere between his shoulder blades. He ambles to the jetty, throws his legs over the water, and lets the young man's laughter cut through him.

It is early evening and a skimming wind is churning the waters of the channel. From the window of his mother's house Amos watches the dolphins carouse and feed, the dark arches of their backs stitching the surface in swift arabesques. In a few days even the dolphins will avoid these waters.

Daphne is coming up the path; at the sight of her he's already smiling. He enjoys sitting with the schoolgirl, unknotting the problems of calculus and physics she brings him. She's so fast-thinking, so bright, sometimes he thinks he can see the sparks in her enormous, dark-brown eyes.

She often lingers after his lesson, wanting to know the part of himself he does not speak about. He tells her the same thing every time: it is enough that he's back in his mother's house, swapped his shoes for sandals and allowed the salt of the sea and time to locks his hair. America was a careless time and he's never going back.

Watching the young girl climb the hill, the white school ribbons bouncing on her head, Amos welcomes the spread of warmth he feels. This girlchile is whole. She knows his shame but does not judge him; does not advertise her body like other lil' girls her age. Her body is something she lives in, but all her life is in her head.

Daphne drops herself on the little wooden bench he lays out for her in the yard and scatters her books at her feet.

'No hello from you today?'

'The length of a hypotenuse – how you work that out again?'

He frowns at her abruptness. 'Forgot the formula?' He takes her exercise book and draws a right-angled triangle freehand. Her shoulders are still, her eyes following his fingers on the paper as he explains the theorem, but her hands are busy wrapping themselves around each other.

'What's happening, Half-Knee?'

Daphne does not rise to the tease. 'Tell me about America.'

He rests the book beside his feet. 'You don't want to work?'

She looks up at him through her braids. 'I don want to stay on Kara Isle no more, Missa Amos. I wan ter go. I have ter go. I wish dat touris-girl kin take me wiv her when she leave.'

'That tourist-girl not going nowhere.' He turns his head in the direction of the headland for a moment, then forces himself to focus on the girl. 'What's got into you today?'

'My mother say is only white-woman wiv wrinkle dat you like; is true?'

He grins at her. 'You sure your mammy say that?'

The girl is silent. Amos stoops and peers at her.

Daphne's made a thicker curtain of her plaits. He's never seen her like this – hugging herself, washing her hands, leaning away from him, staring at nothing in particular.

'Okay,' he says. 'So we wastin time. At least you kin tell me why we wastin time. You come here in a bad mood; I ask you what the problem is; you tell me nothing wrong. Then you start asking all kinda personal questions. I could live with the personal questions, but your sourness don't make no sense to me. So tell me…'

The child jumps to her feet and before Amos finishes, she is off.

Amos watches the white shirt of the striding girl until the high cotton trees hide her from view.

He looks around him, then at the house. It is the only thing he can think of that would upset her. Daphne tells him all the time she hates his place. She has bad dreams about it, and if she had the strength, she would send it on its way, down to the shingle beach.

His mother's house faces the wedge of land that the ocean separated from the rest of Kara Isle. Time and the waters of the channel have sheared chunks off the hill it stands on. Now the house's sea-facing wall is sheer with the cliff, looking straight down on the stones below. The old white-cedar tree barely holds it up. Most of its roots hang over the edge.

A knot has risen in his throat. He closes his eyes and for a while is lost in the drumming of the breakers on the northern shore. He rolls a spliff, is about to bring it to his lips and light it when he catches a glimpse of Daphne returning with the same fast stride. Amos hurries to the incline of the hill and waits.

When she reaches him, she is struggling for breath. Her eyes are wet and rolling. She throws herself at him and it is all he can do to keep her at arms length.

'What's happening,' he snaps. 'What's going on with you?'

'Si...Simeon.' She gasps the name, draws breath and pulls away from him.

He feels his scalp stiffening. He's looking at Daphne's twisted face and knows already what she is about to say. 'Tell me.'

The child shakes her head, the plaits bouncing wild around her face. 'He... he won't leave me alone. Keep followin me an touchin me. Touchin me all over. He won't leave me alone.' Her voice rises to a shriek. Now the girl is crouching in the dust, her books scattered about her and she's covering her face with her hands.

Amos lowers himself beside her. He touches her shoulders. She looks up at him with wet steady eyes and he's glad to see the fierceness in them, the quivering outrage. He also sees the fear and it congeals the blood in him. He pulls Daphne to her feet, walks to his door, lifts the long canvas bag he keeps against the frame and slings it across his shoulder.

He stands before the girl and speaks softly. 'I sorry. I should've seen this comin long time. Is always the lil ones like you that Simeon interfere with, and spoil. The ones who got no father to come after him, y'unnerstan? Pick up your books an follow me.'

The seafront is quiet when he gets there. He slows down for Daphne; she is out of breath when she draws up beside him.

Amos adjusts the strap of the canvas bag and walks through Venus's door.

Simeon's cackle draws his gaze to the middle of the room. He is sitting with his friends. Five cans of strong-wine are sweating on the table in front of them. Their conversation is pitched low and they are jostling each other.

Amos drops his bag. It hits the wooden floor and turns their heads.

'Yow!' He extends a stiffened a finger. 'The child tell you to leave her alone. So you do as she say, y'unnerstan?'

Simeon lifts his head. His cheeks spread out in a big white smile. He is tapping the side of his can and leaning his head sideways. 'Let 'er come and tell me that sheself.' He prods the shoulder of the young man nearest him. 'She got what woman got, not so?'

Simeon chuckles at his own joke, pushes out his legs and leans back. He looks much younger than he is; wears jeans that hug his thighs; thick-soled Nikes. His shirt is open at the front; hair cropped down to his skull. A marijuana leaf patterns the right side of his spun-round cap.

'You don't unnerstand,' Amos says. 'I not asking you; I telling you.'

Someone coughs – a deep, barrel-chested chuckle follows, and suddenly Simeon is on his feet, the back of the plastic chair striking the floor and bouncing. 'You furrin-talkin-shit-pretendin-you-belong-here. Who the fuck is you to tell me what I mus' an musn' do.' He rolls his shoulders. 'An if I don't?'

Amos has imagined this scene before, many times, with another man somewhere on Main Island, whose face he searched for and couldn't find in all the gatherings and parties there. Now it's fine by him that Simeon is about to take that fella's place. He lifts his bag, draws out his fish gun, slots in the harpoon, drags back the rubber to the furthest notch and aims it. Venus's hand is in the freezer. She withdraws it slowly, turns around and does not move.

'You didn't unnerstand me, Simeon. I sorry about that because I going to have to kill you now.'

Simeon's eyes grow still and dark and watchful. There is a glaze to his face and his hands are twitching.

'Tell me I lie, Simeon. Tell me I can't do it.' Amos tenses his finger on the trigger and he knows he's going to do it if Simeon draws a breath to speak or lifts a hand. It is clear that Simeon knows this too because the sweat has broken out on his face and neck.

Amos has no idea how long he is standing there, the spear-gun steady on Simeon's navel. Something in the man before him gives – a slow crumbling of his face and then his whole demeanour. Simeon is licking his lips and his eyes are straying everywhere but at Amos and the spear-gun.

A soft hand settles on Amos's back; then he hears his name. Daphne prods him harder and says his name again. She closes her fingers around his flesh and digs. She is repeating his name and her voice is soft and quavering. Amos shakes himself, steps back and takes her hand. It is tense and feverish in his.

'Sit down.' He brandishes the spear-gun at Simeon. The man drops into a chair, his upper body folding forward.

Amos tilts the weapon at the ceiling and releases the tension in the rubber. He backs out with the girl into the street.

'Come,' he says, dropping an arm on Daphne's shoulder. 'I walk you home.'

They stroll along the lagoon road amid the gurgling of the sea between the mangroves and the pungency of salt-soaked earth. Beneath the trees that fringe the path, red crabs crouch over their holes with pincers raised like pugilists.

Daphne makes quick, hopping movements while sidling a glance at him from time to time. She slows and Amos slows with her. 'You was going to do it, not so?' Her eyes are searching his face, and Amos finds he cannot hold her gaze.

He brings his hands up to his hair and brushes it. 'Dunno, Daphne. Maybe...'

'Becuz... becuz of me?'

He adjusts his bag. He does not want to lie to her. 'Nuh, becuz of me. I... erm...' Amos halts on the words, not sure he wants to take this girlchile so far into himself and tell her of the pleasure he got from diminishing Simeon; not sure he wants her to know how easy it would have been to kill him, and how impossible it became the moment he felt her hand on him.

'Your life belong to you,' he tells her. 'Nobody else must own it.'

Daphne pushes herself ahead, stops in the middle of the path and swings around to face him. She is struggling with something. He sees it in her tightened brows and the working of her lips.

'Which is worse, Missa Amos,' she says. 'You takin Simeon' life or Simeon ownin mine?'

'Same thing,' he says. 'Each is a kind of death.'

He watches Daphne take in his words, her eyes focused on some far point beyond his head. She chuckles and shakes her plaits. Girlchile, he thinks, throwing a sideways glance at her and smiling. Always fretting over something, always wanting clarity.

'My mother say you got so much brains, it make you crazy. That true?'

'You sure your mother say that?'

Daphne grins, rolls her eyes and flicks a foot at him.

Amos feigns a lunge at her. She swings around, trots ahead, laughing – laughing as if she can't help it. Her girl-voice is pitched high and bright and lovely. For the first time in a long time, Amos feels something like joy bubbling out of him.

In his mother's house above the stone beach, Amos sometimes feels the slow unfolding terror of loneliness. Then, the frenzy of the waters below threaten to rise up and suck him down. Segments of his life return in a sudden backwash and leave him feverish and stranded on his mother's bed. He sees himself standing on the jetty with his mother and his sister, his suitcase already loaded on the boat that will take him to the airport on Main Island, then on to Florida. It is a dazzling mid-afternoon Sunday. His mother is in her church clothes, shielding her eyes with her hands and looking up at him. The pride is there but it is quiet and his sister, Lillian, has an arm around her shoulder. Neither speaks – the understanding is there in what they do not say. He, Amos, is their investment. The future of his sister – older by a year and brighter – is the sacrifice his mother made for him. Lillian is holding onto him with the other hand, not wanting to let go. Her face is beautiful and open. She has fine dark skin and a smile he'd kill for. In the force of his sister's grip, Amos understands that she does not share their mother's faith.

A person can get lost in America. New York is light and speed and dizziness. Time is not the same there. Time is a sprinter. You either keep up or get crushed. Good intentions die quick deaths amid all that haste and brightness – which push thoughts of home so far behind, you forget you ever had one. If the past could be reconfigured and rebooted like the computers he used to work on there, he would do it now. He would give his life to change things. During his first few months back, he repeated this to anyone – even those who did not want to listen.

He leaves the house and walks to Astra's place. Astra has no interest in men, she tells him, but she gets tired of women's voices. Sometimes she needs a man to break 'the other silence', and this makes sense to him. If he meets her on the seafront, she catches his eye with a movement of the head or a finger curled against an ear.

Astra cooks for him and watches him eat. She seats him on her chair beside the window and massages his shoulders the way a second attends a boxer between rounds. He senses her flow of thoughts by the pauses of her hand and the small breaks in her breathing. Her fingers soon forget themselves and slip beneath his clothing in casual insinuating ways. He believes that she is more interested in these intimacies of touch than in having him inside her; he measures his need by how far he allows her hands to go. Tonight he does not eat her food.

'My sister, Lillian,' he says.

Astra's fingers stop. 'You sure you want to talk 'bout Lillian?' Her voice, which rarely rises above a whisper, lilts with irritation.

He turns around and looks into her face. It is a mask he cannot read. Astra is still as mysterious to him as she was that first afternoon she fell in step with him on the seafront and let slip from the side of her mouth that she wanted him.

Astra pulls the window close. Now the floor becomes a faint latticework of moonlight seeping through the board walls. A heavy breath escapes her. 'You done ask me everything I know, and I tell you everything I know. What more you want?' Her hands are rough on his nipple. 'Your sister got crazy over a man from Main Island. Got 'er belly big for 'im. He leave 'er pregnant wid the chile. He thief the lil bit ov money that she and your mother had and disappear.'

Amos leans back and closes his eyes.

'Lillian not the only woman find 'erself with child and dunno what to do. You say you never got no letter. People say you shouldn need to get no letter to help yuh fam'ly. But like I keep tellin you, Amos, you didn kill yuh sister. She de one decide to throw sheself in that bad-water over dere. Nobody didn know she carryin all dat grief. Nobody didn know she was goin to do it. That's what you want to hear? That…'

Amos leaves the chair and moves towards the door. Astra places herself in front of him.

'I don' want you to go right now, Amos. I don'. I don'. What bring this on? What happm to you so sudden? Eh? What make you go back and dig up all dem things?' Her hand tenses on his chest; he feels her breath on his face.

He lies with Astra in the tight space of her bedroom, the window open once again to the night. Her dark impassive eyes are roaming his face. In the lamplight there is a shifting lustre to them, like moonlight dappling dark-water. Close to morning she will be restless with his presence. He will creep out on soft feet and – now there is a moon – he will take the road to Bowman's Rise. He will sit in the wind up there, roll a couple of joints and allow himself the sensation of rising outside of the world and drifting un-moored from it.

Tonight though, Astra's thrown a leg across his stomach. The prickliness he is accustomed to is replaced by something else. She can't abide this new resistance of his body to her hands. She wants him to abandon the house his mother died in, return to America and make something of the life he walked away from. Her soft-voiced cajoling beats against his silence and the night outside until she exhausts herself and falls asleep against his shoulder.

She lets him go late morning. Amos follows the stony shore-line until the northern cliffs rear up in front of him. It is late October; the swollen Atlantic has already drowned the rest of the low-lying islands further east. They will surface again in June, but now the stone beaches on the windward coast are strewn with the casualties of mid-ocean disasters. On his way up, he prods the remains of a white shark, the gelatinous mass of a beached octopus, the head of a blue marlin stripped of its flesh – the sockets of its eyes like twin entrances to the cavern of its skull. He tosses back the giant reddish-brown sea worms dumped like deflated balloons onto the pebbles. Those sea-worms tell him that the disturbance is deep down on the ocean floor.

The trouble is on the surface, too. Where he comes to a halt, the limestone precipice shudders with breakers destroying them-selves against it. The westerly winds that snatch at his clothing leave his locksed hair rough with salt. He is glad he was not there this morning to watch the white girl throw herself into the channel. He wonders if she's made it; imagines her last ride down to the churning cross-tides and feels nothing.

He takes the hill to his house in long, fast strides and halts at the top to catch his breath.

He sees her sitting on the stone in front of his door with her back towards him. She's tied her head with a red bandanna. Her bale of hair is loosely held together by a multicoloured string. She's taking in his house and his shaded patch of ganja.

She hears his footsteps, turns, moves her lips as if to speak, then quickly fumbles with her bag.

'Yes?'

She holds up a cellphone. 'Can you fix this?' A soft-voiced, husky drawl.

Up close, she is not as pale as he thought. Amos is staring at the flesh of her bent elbow. The girl flashes a look at his face, then drops her arm. She tosses back her head and fixes him with a wide-eyed, limpid gaze.

'Delna at the guest house said you fix things?' She fidgets with the phone.

'What's it not doing?' Amos takes it from her hand.

'Not working.'

'Charged?'

She shrugs, scuffs the dust with her feet and tosses her head again.

Amos shades the phone with a hand and turns it on. The keys glow briefly; the screen stays blank.

'You dropped it,' he says. 'On something hard.' He points at the rubber casing. 'Not sure I kin fix it. Depends.'

'Are you from here?'

Her question takes him by surprise. He twists his lips, offers her a false smile. 'Yes, I'm a native.'

He holds out the phone to her.

'You haven't tried,' she says.

'No,' he says. 'Will take some time. Mebbe too much time.'

'I'll wait,' she says and sits back on the stone.

He goes into the house to get his tools, pauses at the window to stare out at the water. He returns and places himself on the doorstep. He is aware of her eyes on him, though she's pretending to look elsewhere.

It is the kind of job he likes – the meticulous precision of deciphering the traces on a circuit board, the pure logic of their conjunctions.

With the innards of the machine splayed out on his thigh, Amos raises his chin at the woman. 'You got a pin or something like one?'

She shakes her head.

'Got to use your finger then.' He beckons her with a cramped movement of his hand. 'That came loose.' He nudges the tiny strap that anchors the screen to the circuit board. 'You got slim fingers. Push that in.'

She crouches beside him, crabs her fingers and nudges the strap into place, then leans back, the green-gold eyes avoiding his. Amos takes his time replacing the tiny screws. He switches on the handset, scrolls the screen a while, then closes his hand around the phone.

'How you call yourself?'

She looks puzzled for a moment, then her face relaxes. 'Oh, my name? Nancy.'

'How long you plan to stay, Miss Nancy?' He rises to his feet.

She shrugs. 'Long as it takes.'

'And how long is that?'

She shoves a hand in her pocket and pulls out some folded bills. 'How much is it?'

'I don't want your money.'

He can see her tensing. Her eyes are overcast and she's angled her shoulders away from him. He's not angry. What he feels is colder – with harder, sharper edges. 'What's your name again?'

'Nancy… Can I have the phone now?'

'Which part of The States you from?'

'It's not your… Okay… Okay – LA – Los Angeles. What's with all the questions?'

'Because everything around here make sense, except you.'

Amos wags the handset. 'Expensive phone. Roaming tariff. Last call you made was six days ago. Same day you got here on a stinkin cargo boat.'

She is scuffing the dust again, her head cocked sideways.

'So! A young woman – twenty-five… thirty? She comes here to the back ov nowhere on her own – no boyfriend, no family, no friends. She look different. Big eyes – spaced wide. Lips almost like mine; big teeth – perfect white. Nice clean skin. Almost tall as me. Legs long up to her neck. High cheekbones. Hair with shine. Voice carry without no effort. A lil shoulder bag that beat up but expensive. And she swim like fish.' Amos takes a step toward her. 'We see girls like you on TV, except TV-girls ain' got no needle marks running down their arms.'

She snatches at the phone. Amos raises his arm above his head.

'We got a saying on this island: the sea got no branches to hold onto to save you, y'unnerstan? Last few mornings, I watch you jump off that cliff across there and I keep thinkin of dogs. Yuh see, when dogs catch rabies, or somebody feed them poison, they look for a place to die. Never close to home – unless they can't help it. Now I askin you, Miss Fancy: what poison bring you here?'

He lowers the phone. She grabs it from his hand. For a moment he thinks she is going to hit him. 'You're not nice,' she says. 'You're…'

'I won't kiss y'arse if that's what you mean.'

'Fuck you too.' She jabs a finger at his house and then at him. 'Look who's talking.'

Hands on his hips, Amos watches her leave – long and gracile in her rage, brightly defined by the afternoon sun one minute, then almost wraithlike in the thick shadows of the ancient cotton-tree hedge. He goes to the drum, scoops a can of water and pours it over his head. His reflection is a wavering shadow in the disturbed water, his locks a corrugated halo. 'Fuck you too,' he mutters.

The rest of the day, he's busy de-soldering capacitors and op-amps from components that would never work. Then he goes diving near the seafront until he spears enough fish to keep Daphne's mother and her children for a week.

He leaves the water when the wind picks up, walks in a slanting drizzle that buffs the rooftops and mutes the voices in the houses further back. Venus serves him quickly with a real smile. The room is full. It falls quiet.

Amos eats with an elbow on the counter, breaking the bread in small portions and popping the pieces into his mouth. Finished, he belches loudly and walks out in the rain.

Astra is standing in the doorway of Hot Head Hair Salon, a plastic bag over her head. She waves with her free hand, waves again and that surprises him. He takes his time approaching her.

Just then the white girl emerges from the side-road that leads to Delna's Guest House. Amos pretends he does not see her. Nancy does no such thing. She glares at him directly, turning her head as she passes, then lengthens her stride.

Astra has straightened her hair and is wearing silver earrings. She watches the girl walk up the street. 'You got business with she?'

'Nuh.'

'She walk past you like…' Astra fondles an earring and shakes her head.

She throws another glance up the street. 'One thing I know for sure, dat lil bitch is trouble. Delna say she bawlin every night, like she meet a thousan demon in 'er sleep. Stay 'way from her, y'unnerstan?'

'You never make no claim on me before, Astra.'

'I not makin no claim on you now.' She bares her teeth at him. 'I jus want to know.'

'Nothing to know.'

She cocks an eye at him. 'So, I see you later?'

'Got things to do.'

She blinks, pulls her brows together. 'You tellin me no?'

'I tellin you I got things to do.' He shakes the bag of fish in her face and takes the lagoon road.

Amos wants to believe that it is the drumming of the breakers that woke him this morning. The rain that started the day before hasn't stopped. The sky is a purple blanket torn in places by paler streaks of grey. He can barely see the outlines of the jetty down below. The tethered fishing boats along the shoreline are ghostly strips of colour in the day-gloom. He expects this of course – the hurricane season arriving at last, making its presence felt in water, wind and sky. It berthed yesterday, late evening, announcing itself by a change in the quality of light and the raised voice of the ocean. It is more guttural now, coming from some deeper place within itself. Everything that came before – the salt-heavy winds, the rising water, the slowly purpling sky – was a truce before the real thing strikes.

The water of the channel is no longer choppy; it rolls in undulations, the surface smoothed over by the force of its own flow.

The day before, the girl was a white smear amidst the falling rain. Amos knows her pattern now: the impossible dive, the angling outwards to the far side of the channel, the swing away from it with rapid arms, the swift downward sweep.

This morning he tells himself he wants her to die. He wants the relief of knowing she is no longer there; of not being dragged to his window to watch that leap. This is why he's willed himself to stay in bed. But the grating pebbles on the beach below transfer their restlessness to him and make him irritable.

He abandons his house, strides in the grey light down to the seafront. Main Street is empty, the houses still held in the mute arrest of sleep. Here, on his own, he remembers the silence that greeted his return – the averted gazes, the avoidance in those faces he grew up knowing. Faces as seemingly oblivious to his presence on the island as if he were a ghost; as if he left no footprint in the dust. And having no one to listen, he fell silent. In those months of emptiness he learned that it is not the loss of love that makes you want to die; it is the withholding of those small acknowledgments that give a person weight and substance in the world.

The women who came to Kara Isle were the ones who noticed him, who sensed his lack. He saw through their northern reticence to the wreckage underneath. It was there in their walk, the way they held their shoulders. Women without anchorage, cast adrift by husbands who had discarded them for younger girls or best friends; or those whose children had no more use for them. Women trying to salvage something.

Such women were alert to his presence almost from the moment they stepped off *The Osprey*. He would hang out at Venus's bar, a soft drink in his hand, not saying a word. They approached him with some obvious or senseless question. What was the weather like on the island? Why was it so tiny? Later, their conversation drifted around the ruins of their lives. They took his silence and his nods for understanding, and he measured the extent of the damage done to them by their readiness to step into his place above the precipice, because, like that Scandinavian told him once, they could fall no further. It was never about sex; it was always about being wanted.

And the girl... well, yes... he hadn't been nice to her at all; in fact he'd been brutal, his words meant to put her off; send her back to where she came from and leave his past alone. He thinks of the dive, the fierceness with which she fights the water and it comes to him that it is the life in her refusing to give in. It overrides the stubborn, bright-eyed wilfulness he saw in her when she brought her phone to him, steering her back to the shingle beach under his house every time. She wasn't wrong about him either. *Look who's talking.*

Amos is breathless when he gets to Bowman's Rise. Delna's Guest House lies half drowned in flowering bougainvilleas. Partly folded in by two sides of a wide ravine, the building looks out to the other side of the channel. One of Delna's two sons is bending over a spade at the front. The other is in the veranda stacking dishes.

Amos rolls a spliff. The wind kills the struck match. He tries again and gives up. To pass the time he traces cloud-shadows on the sea, counts the number of times Delna walks across her yard with a garment, hangs it up and re-enters for another. Frigate birds, like bits of clotted air, chase each other across the water. He stays until the sun begins leaking blades of light through the thick cloud covering, but sees no sign of the girl. He leaves the shadow of the stones and hurries down to the seafront.

Venus is outside her shop gathering empty cans and bottles. She waves at him. 'Amos, y'alright?

'Good,' he says.

She drops the bag of litter and straightens up. She's fiddling with her headwrap and squinting at him. 'I been worryin 'bout you, Amos. I worry 'bout you all de time.'

'You saw that erm – that girl?'

Venus frowns at him. 'Girl – which girl? Ah, you mean de touris' girl? The one in my place?'

'Your place?'

'The magga one from overseas?'

'Uh-huh, the magga one from overseas.'

Venus smiles at him. 'She change over to my place. She didn' tell you? She ask me for a room coupla days ago.' Venus lowers her voice. 'One of Delna boys start botherin her. Dem all want to be like Amos. But dem not Amos. Dem don't got what Amos got.' Venus's whole body is quaking with the chuckles. 'I watch de way she been watching you when you hold-up Simeon in my place. An even if you nearly make me wet meself from frighten, I was glad for it. I say to meself, Lord-God, Amos know how to catch dem wiv or wivout fish-gun!' A laugh bursts out of her.

'She there now – in your place?'

Venus nods and smiles. 'She went walkin this mornin. Come back so damn tired, she gone straight to bed.'

It is late evening. Amos returns from wandering around the island. The town is clattering with rain. Amos wades through the milky light and re-enters Venus's bar.

Nancy is at the far end of the room. Her hands are on the table, her palms laid flat, the slim fingers splayed wide. Her eyes are trained on them. He ignores the turning heads and weaves his way towards the table.

The girl lifts her head abruptly and her hands go still. Amos pulls up a chair and sits in front of her. He's conscious of the clink of glass, the scuff of bottles on plastic tables, the shuffling of feet around him.

'I kin offer you a drink,' he says, 'but you going to refuse.' He passes his hand over his soaked hair, releasing a sprinkling of water.

Nancy looks at the droplets on her arms, then at his face. She places the heels of her hands under her jaw. He wonders what she is thinking. Someone in the room chuckles and he suddenly feels exposed.

'I come to say I was a lil rough on you. I come to talk to you.'

He pushes back the chair, lifts a hand and drops it. 'I come to say…' The words dry up in his mouth.

'Say then.' She is speaking quietly. Amos senses no hostility in the words.

'I here to tell you that tomorrow you won't make it.'

She creases her brow and smiles. 'What makes you so sure?'

He sees the challenge in her stare.

Amos rests his elbows on the table and leans forward. He is conscious of the damp clothes clinging to his skin. 'I know,' he says. 'We…' He gestures at the room. 'Everybody here know. You see, from childhood we learn the weather the way you learn the alphabet.

June – too soon
July – stand by
August – you must
September – remember
October – all over…

Is a rhyme full ov warning, y'unnerstan? You learn to read the light out there, the things the ocean throw up on the beach. You listen to the sea like how you listen to a person' voice and unnerstand their mood. You watch the way the water move and know what that mean. This morning you must've felt the change, not so?'

Nancy makes a movement with her head. He doesn't know whether it is in confirmation or denial. He feels exhausted, and a fool. Amos pushes himself off the chair, holds himself still for a while, because he feels unsteady on his feet. He's embarrassed at the pleading in his voice. 'Dunno what else to say,' he mumbles and walks towards the door.

Outside, the rain is replaced by a fine feathering on his skin. The moon is a smudge of brilliance behind the clouds, but there is a glint on everything. He descends the steps to the narrow strip of sand beside the jetty and lowers himself under the sheltering sea-grape trees.

The scuffing of footsteps reaches him and without looking up, Amos draws the blade he carries since his clash with Simeon, and lays it beside his leg.

She comes to a stop above him, her arms folded around herself, then sits on the sand a little way from him.

'You didn't finish,' she says. 'October all over – what happens in November?'

'That's it. No more need for rhyming.'

She is silent for a while, staring out at the nothingness beyond. 'They talked about you when you left. Said you drowned your sister?' She leans away way from him. 'That really pissed Venus. She shut them up. Said you weren't on the island. She told me that's probably what made you stand up for the child. Were you really going to kill that guy?'

'Yes,' he says, and turns to look at her. He thinks he hears her breathing, despite the coughing of the waves on sand.

'Thought so,' she says. She is quiet for a while. When she speaks again, her voice is small and strained. 'And what do I do next morning? I skip my dip and bring my phone to you. That's me. That's Nancy for you. That's…' She is scooping sand with her hands and making little mounds around herself.

Amos dips into his shirt pocket, takes out his plastic sachet and builds a spliff. He lights it, draws, then holds it out to her.

She shakes her head, raises the scarred arm in front of her. 'The day I left, I promised myself never to let anything or anyone inside me again.'

'I grow it myself,' he says still holding out the joint. 'Won't cook your head. It calm the sea inside you.'

She plucks the spliff from his hand, seems to be squinting at the lit tip; then draws on it. Amos gives her a while, watches her body loosen until she drops her elbows on the sand and looks across at him. 'Some questions want answers… like you and that guy. That's heavy, you know… It… it wasn't about the phone. And you weren't nice at all.'

'Well, I wasn sure I was going to shoot 'im; y'unnerstan? I…'

'Don't!' she snaps. 'Don't change it now. Don't polish it!'

A breeze comes off the sea and ruffles the leaves. They glitter like a shoal of netted fish above the girl. Amos builds another spliff, strikes a match, then changes his mind. He drops the flame and watches it die a quick death on the wet sand.

She angles her chin at him. 'They say that you're a prostitute.'

'I don't do nothing for no money,' he says.

'It's not the only way to sell yourself.'

A spurt of irritation prickles his scalp. He eases up on his elbows and glares at her. 'What fella done this to you?'

'Fella?' she breathes. She stubs out the joint and lies back, her head propped up by a crooked arm. 'I've given a lot of thought to that.'

Nancy rises from the sand – a rapid fluid movement that catches him unawares. She stands above him now, her head tilted towards the sea. 'Which is worse you think? A mother who never touched you since you were a kid, or the man she replaced your father with, who touched too much? Which one leaves you more fucked-up?'

He is measuring out the words in his head, assessing the weight of each one before he answers, because he thinks that whatever he says right now will make all the difference in the world. He is drawing breath to speak when she swings her head abruptly, her whole body following up the movement and Amos knows it is too late.

'Gotta go,' she says, 'I need my sleep.'

He follows her to the doorway at the back of Venus's place. Her cheeks and eyes are hollows under the bulb that lights the yard. She is hanging on the threshold and he hopes she's feeling the same reluctance that resides in him.

'Can I,' she says in a voice so soft it seems to slip beneath his hearing and settle in his chest. 'Can I feel your hair – before I go?' Her hand alights on his head. Her touch is light and querying. His head is full of the sea-scent of the girl. He can hear her breathing – the slow rise and fall of her life-tide.

He takes her hand and lowers it. 'Stay,' he says. He swallows on his fluttering voice and blinks at her. 'That's… that's all I came to say this evening.'

A small smile twitches her mouth. 'And then?'

'That's all I came to ask.'

'The sea has no branches, you said. And now you're offering me one?'

'Mebbe I offering meself one too.' Amos lifts his head and holds her gaze. Her eyes are seamless bits of glass in the yellow light.

'Uh-huh,' she says, 'Makes a lot of sense now. I realise… I'm… I'm stronger than you. You see, I prefer…'

She stares past his head for a long time, sighs, hunches and hugs herself. 'Maybe. Maybe I come first thing tomorrow. Maybe I come tonight. Maybe I stay in that dinky little house of yours until we fall together. But right now – it's Amos, isn't it? Right now, Amos, I need my sleep.'

Amos swings his head in the direction of the hills. 'I'll wait,' he says.

Nancy nods, flutters her wrist at him and turns away. He listens to her footsteps as she climbs the stairs. A door creaks, then slams.

Amos walks the sand-road home. The air is agitated with the sound of gulls fishing in the shallows. The channel glints darkly under the watery light of the moon.

Beyond it, the black Atlantic breathes.

4: FLIGHT

IS EASY

His head is in the air, and he seems unaware of the gesturing calling women hunched over the stalls that line the street on either side. Busy walkers swirl around him on the sidewalk, and she on the other side, considers the man from under lowered lashes.

A black leather bag hangs from a long strap on his shoulder. The cloth bag in his right hand says CARICOM. The other words, in red, are hidden by its cotton folds.

He's neither tall nor short. The skin of his arms and face are the colour and sheen of nutmeg shells. His hair looks freshly cut. This is a fella that she could press a nice shirt for, hang his trousers on a line to dry, watch him step out of their doorway every morning and walk down the steps of a perfect little concrete house with baskets of flowers hanging off the veranda.

He would come home every night, tired from work but satisfied, and if he's worried or pressed down by the day, there would be food for him, a soft chair to rest his back against. She would not fuss around him when he rests, but move quietly until he stirs and talks to her about his day. And when they've had enough of talking, they will retire to a clean bed.

She's so forgotten herself that, for a moment, she does not realise that the man's materialised beside her.

He wants to know how to get to the house they call The Rectory.

Before she answers, she dares a quick glance at his face and just as she imagined him from across the street, his face is smooth and shaved and cared-for.

'Is easy,' she says, raising a finger at the sharply climbing road behind him. 'Up Market Hill. De steps on Lucas Street make de climbin shorter, but if you take it, de sweat break outta you. So, easiest is hardest.

'Top of de hill, turn lef, Anglican Church goin be right behin you. Cyahn miss it – it big an ugly like it got no right mongst dem pretty lil pink house up dere.

'In front ov you, de court house. Look like a weddin cake dat some wicked man kick down an mash-up. Used to be pretty befo. Used to be really nice – yunno?

'Walk a little, till you come to a road. It nice an smooth an well-take-care-of. Right at de end of dat little road, you see a pretty concrete house, not big, not small. It got a yellow veranda wit' a few basket ov flowers hangin down. An you reach.'

He's pulled his brows together and she is worried that she did not make herself clear. But then he mutters thanks, smiles and turns to look at the climbing road. He smells of faraway, foreign things. He takes a step, then turns abruptly, his brows still pulled together.

'You always talk like that?'

A flush of embarrassment heats her skin. She does not know how to take his question, feels herself retreating. 'Is how every-body round here talk,' she says; and then she's riled, but it is just a feeble stirring in her stomach that she knows will never reach her voice. 'How I talk?' She looks away.

'Nice,' he says. 'Real nice.' And then he's gone.

She sees that he is following her words exactly as she offered them. Once or twice he looks up, checks for the signposts that she gave, and keeps on climbing.

At the top of the hill he turns. Her eyes follow his rising hand. She does not lift hers in return, but gathers her skirt around her knees and sits before her tray of fruits and spices.

FLIGHT

Most mornings, the ambulance has already been and gone. A couple of *aide-soignante*s sit on the courtyard benches, their heads bunched together while *gendarmes*, dressed like robocops, walk the grass and patrol the squares of tape.

Always, these women choose the fifteenth floor, two days after their exam results. They would pack their bags, their books and scarves and leave a tidy room. What are they thinking when they leap?

Adara is not with her today, standing breast to shoulder, looking out across the campus, past Grenoble to the Swiss Alps.

Adara of the soft hands who smelled of argan oil and sleep, who filled her mind with photographs of minarets, hot bazaars and the veiled curves of the women.

The last two winters made them warm together, disdainful of the glaciers of air sliding down the Alps and the *Frenchness* of the French who'd replaced their names with *étrangère*.

They survived the loneliness – she and Adara – and the language that rebelled against their tongues.

In bed, a couple of days ago, a snowstorm stirred from the heights of the Jura Mountains rattled the high walls of her room. Adara spoke of home, family-honour, the contentment of religion; of watching falcons hunt, and what grace there was in killing. The memory of her betrothed fluttered her lashes and softened her nervous mouth. And she, Teresa, distracted by an impulse, listened with half a mind, until – startled and appalled – Adara lifted her hand and brought it up before her, fingering the red trace there. The amber of her eyes had darkened. Bedouin eyes, Teresa thought, gone pale from staring at hot distances.

'Look at what you done, Teresa! Now I can't go home.'

Leaving France is always easier. L'immigration wishes you *bon voyage*, hurries you into the air.

And as the thrusting engine lifts, she sees, far ahead, the white smile of the Alps.

She turns a downward eye at the strutted roof of Aeroport Isère, awkward from this height and angle.

Like the wings of a mangled bird.

RAISING TYRONE

Me like that girl ever since me meet her on me doorstep in the rain and bring her inna me house. Me decide me really like she fi Tyrone.

She talk to me nice an respeckful; seh her madder from Wales and her fadder from one of them small island, though she never tell me which one. Perhaps me never ask.

She waiting outside of me door two hours fi Tyrone. Inna the cold! You nuh call that love?

Me tell her, seh, never mind sweetheart, me warm you up with a nice cuppa cocoa.

Nice girl yuh see? Pretty nuh rarse. She got long eyelash – no false ting dat – and she eye dem big an lovely like cat eye. The way she look at me: nice smile, nice teet – I see she likkle shy.

Me really like that girl fi me son.

Me see all them other gyals dem come round after im; them hang round me house till big argument start about im other woman dem. When me find it get too much fi Tyrone, me march upstairs to im bedroom and tell dem straight, dem haffe leave me place. Sometimes dem lef in tears. Few times, one or two come back and 'tan-up 'cross the street facin me door; dem stay deh till bad weather drive them off.

But me no care; like my madder use to seh, that's life. Long as me know is not Tyrone fault. Every young girl out there want a piece of my Tyrone. Dem never satisfy. Im give them likkle sinting, them want more. Is so woman stay; we never satisfy.

But this one – she nice. She fit Tyrone perfect. She light-skin like im, yunno. Dem goin mek nice pickney; pickney hair won't break no comb. Dem pickney going ave clare skin-colour that help them get on better in the world, specially in this yah England.

See im picture deh? Filim star pose! Good lookin, nuh rarse. See how im lean back boasy on im car? Is so im stay. Im 'mind me of im fadder, Munro. Strict, yuh see? Munro never mek no joke. Yunno how much time me used to have fi call police fi Munro? But im had good-looks; is why me did fall fi im so hard.

Me tell Tyrone, doan tek no back chat from no woman, cos me never give im fadder no back chat. Me tell im ee'z a man and man haffe stanup fi imself. Im don' ave no problem cos he nice-lookin and ooman tick on the ground. He doan haffe tek no shit from dem. And yunno, im lissen to me, cos anyone of dem get fiesty with im. Two bax! Just like im fadder. Heh!

Same temper like Munro too, an same bad-man walk. Like me seh, is so im stay.

What about me? What about me! Well me'z im madder and Tyrone gots to ave respek fi me. Me tell im from im small, a good son never disrespek im madder. Im tek it in. Caar yuh see how good im is to me?

Me not sayin he don't get likkle upset sometimes. But im save most of dat fi outside, and them likkle woman who won't leave im alone. Nuff times im get vex, break up a coupla tings – mostly me dishes, yunno. Dunno what im got 'gainst plate-an-saucer. But the vexness never last fi long. Afterwards im tell me sorry. Last time was the window. Me mek im find the money an fix it. And yunno im fix it? Better than dem dutty thief dat call demself carpenter in this ya Englan.

Me never blame im becos me know im tek the hothead from im fadder, Munro – that daag. Besides, like me seh, im temper never last fi long.

But that girl me tek in from the rain. Is she me want fi im. What she name again? Mavis or Marva or Marble. Anyway, me know er name start with 'M'. Me tell she seh, whenever Tyrone get likkle rough with 'er she mus come an lemme know. Me goin talk to 'im, because is she me prefer fi Tyrone.

See im deh! See how im pretty in dat picture? Is good breeding and good feeding dat! Is so me raise im. Proper. Strict, yunno. Strict like my madder used to be with me. Yuh think I could a gwaan like all them likkle woman I see im bring up regular to im room? Naah sah! Me wouldn ha been here today. Me would ha been dead.

So! Mek im gimme likkle pickney granchile with that gyal, who goin look like my Tyrone, walk like my Tyrone –an pretty same way.

With manners an good prospects like my Tyrone.
Cho!

GIVING UP ON TREVOR

The roof lights went off and on a couple of times; the driver banged the glass of the cubicle. 'Road finish. End ov jorney. Bus stopping heyah!' A flustered voice at the back mumbled something about ignorant Nigerians.

Ennis sucked her teeth, glared at the rain-streaked windows, then at the impassive face at the wheel.

She had to walk the part of Harlesden High Street she hated most. Once past the library, she would get a cab to Wembley Mews.

More mist than rain outside. Not the kind she would bother to shelter from, but a fine persistent drizzle that would soak her if she stayed in it too long.

She dipped into her handbag, fished out her scarf and tied it on her head. As she walked, she registered her progress along the pavement by the noises and smells on either side of her: the crack of dominoes in the pub on her left followed by the deep-throated uproar of old West Indian laughter, then the slinging match of slack-chat. Across the street, the soft assault of male voices under the awning of the Indian takeaway where young men, the peaks of their caps pulled down over their noses, leaned against the shopfront with hands stuffed in their pockets.

She adjusted her bag on her shoulder and hurried through the smells of twice-fried Chinese food, overripe plantains and something-or-other the Turkish man in the shop across the road was shaving into the pursed mouths of a row of pitta bread.

Just before the library, the noises and the smells cleared up. The road ahead empty; there was even a breeze.

She heard a soft whinnying to the left of her just as she reached the music shop. Three young men – cowled, chins pressed down on their sternums, raised feet planted against the wall of the shop, hands making bulges of their pockets. They were at the mouth of the alleyway that led to the posher houses further back. The whinnying came again, though now she no longer thought that it was the young men taking the piss at her expense.

She would have walked on had she not heard the cry, pitched higher, then abruptly cut short. The protestations of a woman. No mistaking it, and the tremorous underlay of fear.

She turned to face the alley. The seepage of misted light from the streetlamp overhead revealed nothing. One of the men pushed himself off the wall. She eased her handbag to her front, raising her chin at him, holding his gaze until he shrugged and dropped his back against the wall.

She could just about make out the shape of a man and the slighter one of a woman close up against him, their profiles defined by the brightness at the other end of the alley. Then came his voice – edgy and upbraiding.

She would have turned away, made herself believe she was mistaken, but the man raised his voice again and although the rage in it was foreign, she would have recognised it anywhere. Her son had the girl pulled up against his chest, his left hand stiff under her jaw.

She was about to speak when the hand dropped and the woman disengaged herself. Then she was half-running, half-limping up the street, the sound of her high heels clattering on the dirty flagstones.

The three young men had moved off up the street with long, side-shifting strides.

Her mouth had gone dry; she felt a pulsing at her temples. She remained where she was, no longer mindful of the rain, her eyes on the back of the boy until he disappeared at the other end of the alleyway.

She was soaked when she got home. The numbness that had slowed her pace hadn't left her limbs.

She dropped her bag on the kitchen table, went into the

bedroom and changed into a pair of slacks and a pullover. In the darkened room she sat on the edge of her bed, swallowing on the congestion in her throat.

It was past midnight when she stirred – not knowing where the time had gone. She should have been in bed by now, or finishing off her work at the computer. There was a letter to write to the hospital, an email to the mechanic about picking up her car sometime during the weekend, and a notice to Selfridges to cancel the sofa she'd ordered the week before. The one-to-one talk she wanted to arrange with Mr. Wallace was important, but that and the other things could wait.

Instead, she climbed the stairs, unlocked Trevor's door and stood looking about his room as if she might uncover something about her son that had escaped her.

His toiletries and array of grooming products were laid out on top the chest of teak drawers in which he kept his socks and underclothing. On a matching table to the side of it, a bright array of trophies won in his earlier years when the school in Harrow wanted to make an athlete of him – until she visited the principal and changed all that. Above them, framed copies of his degree and school certificates.

On the little bedside cabinet was a full-length photograph of him she preferred not to look at. Tonight she stared at it. It brought back an old sensation – one so sharply defined, so present, it felt as if she was nineteen again, arriving at the bus stop and encountering his father, Spooner, for the first time. Spooner with his back against the signpost, appraising her, then locking her in a gaze that told her what he wanted before he said a word.

She would have turned the picture away had she not felt a draught and realised that Trevor had arrived, although she had not heard the door or the jingle of his keys. She moved only when she felt the vibration of his footsteps on the stairs.

If Trevor was surprised to see her on the landing he did not show it. He muttered a greeting, brushed past her and walked over to his bed. He dropped a couple of music CDs on the duvet and busied himself with the table on which his trophies sat.

'Could we have a word?'

'Not now, Mam.'

'I wasn't asking,' she said. 'Come downstairs.'

He would take his time. To pass the wait she emptied the dishwasher, dried the plates and stacked them on the shelves above the cooker. She was hungry but did not want to eat. She was about to raise her voice and call up to ask if she should prepare something for him, but suppressed the urge and turned to tidying up the kitchen counter.

She sensed his presence before she saw him at the kitchen door. That silent way of his – from the time he was a child – no longer startled her, although she'd never got used to it.

She rinsed cups she'd already washed and dried, reluctant to turn to face him. Instead, she focused on his blurred reflection in the window above the sink. 'Tell me it wasn't you,' she said.

She thought he was going to lie; found herself half-hoping that he would. But he knew that she would see through any bullshit straightaway. That was his father's greatest frustration with her.

She dumped the sponge in the sink and turned around to face him. 'Who's the girl?'

Trevor passed a hand across his forehead. Shrugged.

'It wasn't Lena. I'm sure of that. Sit down.'

'I'm alright here.' He crossed his legs and bumped a shoulder against the door frame.

Suddenly she did not know what to say. Under the bright ceiling lights of their kitchen, her son looked as she had always known him – a clean-skinned, soft-spoken young man, dressed with the tastefulness she'd taught him. He'd angled his head downwards to avoid meeting her eyes.

She replayed the resentments of the evening – the driver who'd dumped her off on a street she'd avoided as soon as she could afford to; the youths whose presence had unnerved her. It was as if it was all intended to confuse and disorient her.

The shift in Trevor's tone pulled her thoughts back to the present.

'That was not…'

He was watching her with a steady, sidewise slant of his eyes. The rest of him was very still. This coolness, the feeling that her son was pushing her away, raised the heat in her.

'Don't look at me like that,' she snapped.

'What you did was dangerous, Mam. I'm telling you.'

She took a breath and pressed her weight against the hard edge of the granite counter.

'You mean stopping on the street to call out to my son because he had his hands around a woman's throat?'

'I'm just saying, it was…'

'I heard you first time – dangerous. Why?'

He shifted his stance, his hands pushed down the pocket of his coat which he hadn't bothered to take off.

'Since when you come like that?' She twisted her lips, making a show of it as her eyes travelled along his face, then down the length of him. 'What you been hiding from me, Trevor? All this time? Because, come to think of it, I doubt this is the first time. And as for *dangerous*…' She dragged her bag across the table, slipped a hand down a side pocket, took out the sheathed surgeon's scalpel and dropped it on the counter. 'Not for me, Sonny. No man or boy will ever lay his hands on me. Not again. I want you to understand that.'

'Again?' he grunted.

She let that pass.

'This is the result of my twenty years busting my arse for you: good school, decent education…'

Trevor flicked his wrist, made a low-throated dismissive sound.

That straightened her back and froze her. 'You telling me that don't count for anything?' She could not hold back the hurt in her voice.

'Not much.' He shrugged.

She brought her hands up to her face and kept them there until her breathing quietened.

'Okay,' she said reaching for her bag. She pushed past him, went into her bedroom and pulled the door behind her.

★

She tossed in and out of sweaty dreams in which faceless men with wide-rimmed hats stood on rain-soaked streets brandishing blades and calling out her name.

She got out of bed close to morning and parted her blinds. Outside, winter had returned; the grass along the edges of her driveway was frosted white, the metal rails bordering the road below glowed like molten iron in the yellow spill from the lampposts above them. Somewhere in the distance, the rattle of an early train overlaid the low snore of traffic on the North Circular.

Straight ahead, rose the three leviathan tower blocks, one of which used to be her home in Harlesden, their darkness made more pronounced by the scattered squares of light pockmarking their facades.

She closed the curtains and switched on the light. In her underwear, she stood for a while staring at the closed wing-doors of her wardrobe. She took a breath and opened it, pulling jumpers, cardigans and trouser-suits off their rails and dumping them at her feet. And when the way was clear, she drew out a narrow full-length mirror and stood it against the doorframe of the wardrobe.

She was breathing heavily when she finished. She hadn't done this in a long while. Not in years. She avoided showers, preferring the soapy concealment of a brimming bathtub; went nowhere with friends if it meant staying over at their place. During the couple of short holidays back home in Grenada, she stated her preference for moonlight swims. When it came to changing into scrubs, her fierceness about her privacy was known throughout the hospital.

In Grenada – where she came from as a child – they called it 'sweet blood'. Here she'd learned the name: keloidosis – where the skin remembered everything, every angry contusion, each stinging assault against itself and in protest, threw up a dark ridgework of scars. Spoilt skin, the bitterness and shame of it. After Spooner, she'd never taken another man to bed. Skin was the part of her that Spooner loved the most, the part, when he realised that she was leaving him, he'd made sure no other man could have the pleasure of.

The only person who'd ever seen her like this was a stranger. One midsummer afternoon when she'd retired to a quiet room to change, she forgot to lock the door. She was about to slip on her uniform when it opened, and she turned to see a woman standing in the doorway with a bucket and mop in her hands. The eyes that travelled along her body were set in a face as unrevealing as a stone. Those eyes had taken her in with an understanding that froze her where she stood. It was as if in this small room, with the ticking of machinery next door, the subdued sighs and sobs of barely articulated pain in the wards beyond, she and this woman were secret sharers. The woman lowered her eyes, backed out of the door and became a cleaner once again.

The next day a small tub sat on a shallow nest of newspapers in the furthest corner of the office: a yellow paste with bits of leaves, an indecipherable medley of odours, amongst which she detected the whiff of sulphur and teatree oil. Beside it, was a strip of absorbent tissue on which was scrawled: *please rub thank you.*

Occasionally she saw the woman bent over something dropped or spilt in the corridor. The cleaner would never look at her. Ennis preferred it this way, that the woman and she remained within the boundaries of their uniforms.

At eight o'clock she phoned the hospital and said she wouldn't be in. Could Doctor Ashton cover for her since she'd done the same for him a couple of weeks ago? She left a message for Mr. Wallace asking for a meeting at any time that suited him, made herself a cup of coffee and sat waiting at the kitchen table for Trevor to come down. It was quiet up there. She'd never known him to sleep past nine. At ten she climbed the stairs, knocked on his door. She heard no answer, knocked again then let herself in.

His bed had not been slept in. She puzzled for a while over the fact that she hadn't heard him leave. At some point close to morning she thought she'd heard the rise and fall of Trevor's voice – first the boyish bantering tone he reserved for his girlfriend, Lena, then a deeper, more throaty register. She liked Lena – a slim, fiery, brown-eyed, red-haired girl who gave as good as she got, whom Trevor had several times returned to after long silences and breaks that sometimes lasted months. She hadn't heard from Lena in a while.

She was only aware of having fallen asleep at the kitchen table when the bell woke her with a sustained ringing that suggested the person outside knew she was in.

She stood behind the window blinds facing the driveway. There was the shuffle of something through the letterbox, then retreating footsteps. She made out the man as soon as his back appeared – David Marne, whom liaised with from time to time on the ward about some of the patients the ambulance brought in.

She rushed to the door, swung it open and called.

He swivelled around on his heels.

'Ennis,' he said. 'Oh! That's good, you're in. I phoned the hospital.'

Inside, he slipped off his jacket and hung it on the rack behind the door.

She led him into the kitchen. 'Coffee?'

'Tea, if you don't mind. No milk, no sugar.'

She quickly retrieved a cup and made the tea. 'How've you been, David?'

'The usual. You?'

'Same old… It's been a while.'

She placed the cup in front of him. He blew on the liquid, his eyes roving around the kitchen. 'Nice!'

She dropped the dripping tea bag in the bin. 'What brings you, David? And so early?'

He looked up and frowned.

'Ennis, I'm here because you and I go back a long way.'

'Tell me, David.'

'Is your boy in?' He rested the cup on the table. 'I'd rather…'

'Trevor left this morning. Usual time.'

'What's he been like lately? I mean…'

She shrugged. 'Can't complain. Fine.'

'What time did he get home last night?'

'Why the questions, David?'

He shook his head at her.

'I thought you'd come here as a friend,' she said. 'Those are police questions.'

He sucked in air and leaned back against the chair. 'Okay, Ennis. It's habit, sorry. There's a woman recovering in your hospital. We took her there because it was the nearest. Swollen neck, blocked trachea from internal bleeding. Can't breathe.'

Ennis lowered herself on the other chair. David's eyes were fixed on some point above her head.

'Somebody helped her off the pavement and brought her into McDonald's, High Street, Harlesden. They left her there. Shop staff called us, asked for an ambulance. Lucky we came with one. He shifted in his seat and eased the cup away from him. 'Without the oxygen she would have died.'

'And what's that got to do with…'

David made a sweeping motion with his hand across the table. 'She won't tell when she recovers. I've been doing this job long enough to know fear, Ennis. A few minutes later someone called. A woman. Same thing: bloody terrified. What kind of man puts that kind of fear in a young woman?'

Ennis shook her head and blinked at him. 'What's that got to…'

'The caller gave us your son's name: Trevor Bates. That's all she said before she rang off. The number registered but it was one of those SIM cards you buy off the street for a fiver, then throw away. Call came in around 8.30. That's why I asked what time he got home.'

Ennis shook her head and swallowed. Found herself speaking with the accent of her childhood. 'Roun' six o'clock. Trevor was upstairs.'

She was conscious of David's steady grey eyes. He brought his hands together, steepled his fingers, then rose to his feet. 'That's alright, then.'

She rose after him. Saw that he hadn't drunk the tea.

'You've met my Trevor,' she said. 'You saw what he's like.'

David smiled 'That was – how long – five years ago?'

He reached for his jacket, settled the garment on his shoulders, and hung about on the threshold, looking straight out at the triple towers.

'I'll tell you something, Ennis. In my department we classify them. I know you folks don't like that, but in a job like ours it helps. Over the past couple of years we're seeing a new kind: educated – even talented – well-dressed. Charming to a fault. They know the bits of law they need to know. But, my God, the things they get up to…'

'You've just described every decent young man I know. I'm sorry I can't help you more.'

David lifted his shoulders and dropped them. He was looking at her, still smiling. 'Not at all,' he said. 'Body language tells you everything.' He glanced at his watch. 'Got to go, Doc. By the way, I left my card. Letterbox.'

She watched him retreating down the driveway. Stood there following the white car along the narrow feeder road until it sidled onto Harrow Road and shot off.

When the cold began to seep into her bones she went inside. She phoned Lena, listened to her chirpy greeting, then left a message.

'Gimme a call, girlchile. Been thinking lots about you. I haven't heard from you in a while.'

She messaged Trevor. *Come home. Need to see you as soon as.*

She hadn't picked up her clothes from the night before. She shoved them aside with a slippered foot, reached down the far right corner of the wardrobe and lifted out a Russell and Bromley shoebox. She brought it to the living room and laid on the table. She was still sitting with the box in front of her when Trevor arrived.

'In here,' she said.

The room was almost unbearably bright with the afternoon light streaming through the windows. Trevor coughed a greeting, soft-footed across the room and drew the curtains shut. She could see what girls liked about him: lean and brown as a loaf; ectomorph like his father, with a smile that promised much.

'I have something to show you,' she said.

'What?'

She sensed a new cautiousness in his tone.

'David Marne came this morning. Remember David Marne?'

His eyes were on her face, his lashes thick and lovely as a girl's. He nodded slowly.

'Today I lied for you. I've never had to lie for you before,' she said. 'David told me what happened to that girl – that girl you – the girl who was with you in the alleyway. She's in hospital.'

Ennis leaned back against the chair and closed her eyes. 'A woman phoned and gave your name.'

She pushed herself forward, drew the shoe-box towards her and opened it. From the stack of folded papers there, she retrieved one with a red ribbon tied around the middle.

'I want you to go to Grenada. You know about the little house I built there. Your uncle Winston's been looking after it for me. I'll send you money every month. I'll call Winston tonight and tell him to expect you. These…' she pushed the paper towards him. 'They're deeds for the house and piece of land around it. I can book you a ticket tomorrow.'

The right side of his mouth was pulled up in a half-smile. Her son was observing her with such amusement that she felt chastised. He pulled back his head, stretched out his feet and crossed them. She wondered, as she had been doing these past two days, how a man could be so perfectly replicated in his offspring.

'Not for me,' he said. 'What you want me to do over there – climb banana trees?'

Ennis dropped the document on the table and lowered her head. She sucked in hard, bit down on her lips, but could not hold it in. The sobs took hold of her.

He was silent while she fought to calm herself.

'The girl who gave my name,' he said. 'Did, erm, David tell you what she sounds like?'

The question brought her to her feet. 'What? What you just said?' She saw him pull back, not so much with his body as with the sudden blunting of his gaze.

'Watch yourself,' she grated. 'Just watch yourself.'

With an abrupt movement of his body, he pushed himself back against the chair, and for a moment it seemed to her that he was that other self – the one she hadn't known existed. Then Trevor was on his feet – a fast fluid movement that caught her unawares.

'Nobody got nothing on me,' he said. 'I'm out of here.'

Ennis woke up to the far-off sounds of sirens and looked out to see that the drizzle had eased up, replaced by a spring mist. The world outside looked smudged although the sounds were clear and sharp as glass.

She checked the time. Six forty-six. She heard the soft padding of footsteps upstairs, the dull shudder of the bed and wondered if he'd brought Lena back with him.

She toyed with the temptation to take another day off. There were two procedures she was booked for with Mr. Wallace this afternoon. Minor stuff – a child with a pebble down her ear canal, a teenager with a badly infected tonsil. Nothing he couldn't handle without her.

The doorbell rang. She sat back at the kitchen table with a cup of coffee at her elbow and let it ring. It kept on ringing.

A swift rush of footsteps down the stairs and Trevor was standing over her.

'Mam,' he said, 'I've been here all night.'

'Is Lena up there with you?'

He shook his head.

'What's happened?' she said.

'Nothing, Mam. Just…'

'Then why're you asking me to lie for you?'

Trevor raised open palms at the ceiling. 'It's no big deal, Mam.'

The doorbell rang again. A voice loud-whispered her son's name.

'Hang on,' he said.

The door opened. A rush of words followed, cut short by Trevor's overriding voice.

Her son sprinted up the stairs. A small storm of rattling and shuffling overhead, then he was down again and out of the door.

She stared at him hurrying down the driveway with a short, quick-stepping figure beside him.

Ennis dressed for work. First, salve for her skin. After that the undershirt – still warm from the dryer – and carefully pulled on.

Sometimes she itched, the rawness always there just beneath the surface, her skin remembering. Dragging her back. Returning her always to the memory of that evening by the bus-stop on the high street in Harlesden, heavy with Spooner's child when she told him she'd rather die than spend the rest of her life in fear of him. By then, she'd been long enough in A&E to learn something from the women they rushed in on stretchers and wheelchairs at any time of night or day. There was a kind of man out there in the world who would knock a woman senseless if he could not beat the sense out of her; who, because he could not crush her with his will, fell back on his strength. It had nothing to do with upbringing – that she was now sure of. It had nothing to do with anything that she could find words for.

There, in broad daylight, on the open high street, with a switchblade in his hand, Spooner tried to kill her. Later, when she thought about it, it was always there, even in the early days of courtship. She just couldn't see it – Spooner's sweetly-coated hatred which she mistook for love.

Once again in Trevor's room, Ennis looked around. He'd stuffed his dirty clothing in the basket. Normally he brought it down and left it against the washing machine. She lifted out the canvas bag that lined the basket and rested it against the door. She opened Trevor's wardrobe, felt along the rails where his jackets and his good shirts hung, touching their shoulders until her hand rested on a silken softness. She retrieved the coat, held it up and cast an eye down its soft grey length. The tails were damp; a greenish suggestion of moss stains along the back. She carried the bundle downstairs and dumped it in the airing cupboard, thinking, as she dropped the latch, that Trevor should have had the sense to throw away that coat.

The heaviness that had been with her all morning lifted when she stepped outside her door. Bright, crisp air, a dormant lawn prettified by snowdrops, early crocuses and winter aconites.

She called a cab and was told to expect a thirty minute wait. She didn't mind, she would still get in an hour or so before her shift began.

At the bottom of the driveway, her phone buzzed.

'Where are you, Doctor?' The voice of Nyla, the ward clerk.

'Just leaving.'

'Can you hold on please? I've been trying you for an hour.'

'You were?'

'Hold on.' In the background, the calm tones of Mr. Wallace. Nyla spoke again. 'We're sending a car. Stay where you are.'

Ennis called back the cab station and cancelled. Already her mind was taking her into a state of taut awareness, of pared down movements, and a focus that blanked out everything outside the shadowless ring of light, and latexed hands that parted skin and tissue.

When the car arrived she climbed in beside the driver.

'Two in two days,' he said, his heavy arms curved around the steering. He swung his head in the general direction of Harlesden. 'Girl again, I heard. Not good, y'know.'

Girl again. When she was heavy with child, she remembered not wanting a daughter – not only because Spooner did not either, but because of the girlhood she had lived before she left the island. They told her it was better here. She'd learned that it was not better – just different.

Mr. Wallace was standing over Nyla's desk. She was busy clipping papers together.

Mr. Wallace reached out and wrapped long restraining fingers around Ennis's elbow.

'It's done,' he said. 'Couldn't wait. Chest x-ray showed a whiteout.' He lowered his shoulders and looked into her face. 'You alright?'

She nodded. Nyla handed her a sheaf of papers. 'Casenotes. Recovery.'

Ennis scanned the notes, her eyes pausing over the words that mattered: trauma… interstitial… haemotoma. She passed them back.

With his hand still under her elbow, Mr. Wallace urged her away from the desk. 'Patient will survive. You wanted to see me? I got your message.'

'Yes, I…'

'You sure you're alright?'

She looked up into his face. If there was a man in the world she felt she knew it was this surgeon. She had stood beside him for the best part of her working life, first as a scrub nurse, now as his assistant.

The cafe was quiet. They sat in the far corner, by the window beyond which the huddle of old brick buildings backed into high glass structures that receded into a grey West London skyline.

'Sorry I rushed you in,' he said. 'But you know how these things can go.'

'That's fine,' she said. 'I wanted to tell you first; I'm taking the redundancy.'

He rubbed his eyes, was silent for a long time. She sat studying his face.

'What will you do?' he said finally.

'I'll go back home to Grenada. I've been thinking about it for some time. There's a hospital there. Besides, I have enough to live on.'

'What's enough to live on?' He sounded irritated.

It seemed to Ennis that they were talking about something else, even if she wasn't sure exactly what that other thing was.

'I'm sorry,' she said.

'It's your life. Who can stop you?'

She waited for him to say it first – the thing that she could never bring herself to put in words to him.

He eased aside the half-drunk cup of coffee, rested both elbows on the table, placing his chin on his turned-down hands.

'You're a lovely woman, Ennis. I can't say I haven't been, well,

distracted by that. For a long time. But it's not·about that; we've
handled it well, haven't we?'

She nodded and looked away.

'Remember when you were our scrub nurse? I think "scalpel"
and you're already passing it to me; forceps, curette – whatever;
the right shape, size, number…' He moistened his lips and fixed
his gaze above her head. 'I'm always surer when you're there. At
least I can be honest for once; I'll call it by its name, Ennis. It's
intimacy. I used to think marriage was supposed to be like that. In
my mind, with this job, there's more at stake. We're trying to
make a stopped heart beat; to hand back life, and when it works,
it's like a delivery.'

He dropped a hand on hers, then quickly lifted it. 'I've said too
much, haven't I?'

'No,' she said, rising from the table. 'I feel the same way too.
I – I have to see the girl.'

She went to her room and dressed in her scrubs, then took the
lift to the fourth floor. It was always busy up here in ICU: a muted
world of junior doctors, nurses and consultants rushing about in
soft-soled shoes. The gurgles and ticks and beeps of electrocar-
diograms, ventilators, IV lines and pumps; of feeding tubes and
catheters – all patrolling the thin, smudged line between life and
death.

As she entered the ward, she saw the girl – her hair a splash of
red against the grey sheets. Lena. She halted. She had not wanted
to like this girl. She'd always kept the necessary distance from
these young women her son brought home, saw for a couple of
weeks before he sloughed them off.

But Lena had wished for conversation; she'd asked her questions about herself; would beg her to speak her 'island-talk' –
which cracked up both of them with laughter.

There was that night Lena ran into her room and would not
leave till morning. She hadn't asked her what the problem was
and Lena never said. Ennis told herself that she must have known
all along, but she just didn't want to accept.

Now there comes the memory of Trevor's quick sharp words

last night, the distinct contours of an argument. Perhaps Lena had told him she was leaving him.

Ennis did not take the elevator back down to the third floor, she wanted to avoid people. She felt exposed. She stopped above the car park, pressed her shoulder against the wide glass walls and let its cold intrusion seep into her skin.

In the courtyard below a child in a red hat, a doll swinging in one hand, was hopping around her mother's legs. Directly under, in the parking bay, an ambulance had just pulled in, and by the urgency with which the paramedics were wheeling out the trolley, she knew that Mr. Wallace would be wanting her soon. Saving a life, he said, was just as good as bringing one into the world.

What about this, then? This giving up on one? This tearing of yourself away from the awful weight of love?

Ennis took out her phone and dialled in the numbers. She waited until they answered, then asked for David Marne.

A QUIET TIME

Kisha returns to the little farmhouse tired and light-headed with the things she discovered from her walk, especially the small, tree-covered hill at the bottom of the road which stands out, ragged like a Rasta's head, against the sky. She spotted it the first evening she arrived with Muriel and the boy. An hour ago she climbed its slope and gazed down on the cows, the farms, the small flower-covered cottages just beyond, and the road that loops around it like a noose.

When she enters, they are lying on the large beech-wood table in the kitchen. Her sister has her dress rolled up over her gleaming thighs; the waist of the young man's trousers forms a bracket beneath the tensed muscles of his buttocks. The boy could have been asleep except for the slow, random shifting of his hips.

Kisha backs into the late Normandy afternoon. Her feet take her past brown, shaven fields, dead bracken and limp, sun-struck flowers. She sits at the side of the road and sucks in air. A diffuse headache is throbbing at the back of her eyes.

She hasn't eaten anything since morning, but she might as well climb the hill again, sit on the large round stone up there and try to clear her mind. Who knows how long those two are going to be on that table.

With a small eddy of outrage, she rises and brings down her Doc Martens on a snail. She watches the creature squirm and die at the end of its semen-like trail. If she'd known that this 'holiday' was going to mean witnessing her sister's goings-on with that *kid*, she would have stayed in London.

She resents the quiet turbulence in her guts, the deep-down flaring of her nerves which, even here on this footpath, turns her mind to the butterflies copulating on the edge of stalks, the man-smell of dried grass, the rank of bulls in the fields that roll away from her towards that little postcard village.

This is not what her elder sister told her back in London. A quiet time, she promised. Ten restful days in Normandy. It was a present for the favour she had done for her.

It was Muriel's thirteenth call in two weeks. Before that, Kisha hadn't heard from her in three years.

She pretended she didn't recognise her sister's voice – filed down, buffed and polished until there was no evidence of the real Muriel behind it.

She wanted to say, 'Hello Muriel Martin. What the fuck you want from me this time?'

Instead she queried quietly, 'Y'awright, Sis?'

Her sister sounded conspiratorial, as if they'd been girl-talking every day. 'Girrrrl, I found a man.'

'Found?'

'Yep, and I'm going to keep this one.' Muriel laughed – short, musical, throaty. 'Want to say hello?' Her voice hollowed and faded into a string of background chirpings.

'No,' she said. 'He there?'

'Mmm…Mmm!'

'Serious?'

'Mmmm-hmm!'

'How old?'

The briefest of silences. 'Does it matter?'

'How old, Muriel?' Kisha smiled into the phone.

'Well, you know the saying, Keesh: wimmen stay stronger, longer.'

Kisha could hear the metal creeping into her sister's voice. 'Uh-huh?'

'He's twenty in ten month's time. Somming wrong with that?'

'No, not at all.'

'Okay. Friday then. Just the three of us. The Angel? They've got a decent café above the cinema. Eight alright with you?'

'Hang on, Muriel.'

'Whatsimatter, Sunshine. Don't you want to see me?'

'Did I say that? And don't call me 'Sunshine'. You…'

'It's important, Kisha. Besides, don't forget you owe me. Eight o'clock then!'

Muriel hung up.

She was there an hour or so before them; spent longer than usual in front of the mirror. She ironed her best top and the Ted Baker jeans she'd spotted in an Oxfam shop. And though partial to silver, she passed half a morning rummaging for the gold chain Toni had bought her for their Valentine. She even swapped her big silver hoops for a borrowed pair of emerald studs.

From her perch on the stool above the square her eyes fell on the youth first. He looked like any other lean-limbed young man on the street, with loose, army-green trousers, and trainers designed to draw attention to his feet. Clean-cropped, as if he'd just come from the barber's.

Maybe it was the crisp white shirt at a time when creases and hoods were all the rage that drew her eyes to him. Perhaps that easy, loose-limbed stride – his head and shoulders following through with every step he took, almost as if he were drifting. It was all that pulled together that made it clear to her that he was foreign. A West Indian just arrived.

Her sister walked beside him, like someone taking a child to the funfair for the first time. She looked like money: a charcoal-grey, loose-fitting suit that yielded with every swing of her jangling brown arms. She'd swept her hair back from her forehead like a cobra's cowl and was sashaying across the cobbles with black Gucci shoes so highly polished they appeared silver in the daylight.

Kisha felt her breathing quicken.

'Hello, girrrl.' Muriel gurgled, eyes bright, smile tight.

They exchanged frank, assessing gazes. Her sister was at that stage when the struggle with the body really began. Kisha saw it all the time: women who spent half their salaries on oils and creams and gels to smooth out the slackening flesh at the base of their throat; who fought the gradual surrender of their faces to the shape of the bones beneath, and the way the hair at the temples went slightly lighter than the rest. You picked up these things from working for six years in a hairdressing salon on Stoke Newington High Street.

'Looking good,' Muriel told her, smiling.

'You too,' she nodded. And Kisha meant it. Muriel was still lovely to look at. A person would have to search real hard to see the things she'd just observed. Her sister always made much of her light-brown colour, her long and not-so-very-black hair and eyes, and that nose which, she said, on the authority of her research on the Internet, she traced all the way back to ancient Syria.

It turned out that Muriel had not so much met the youth as saved him.

'I spent my hols in Jamaica this year. Had to sort out some things over there for Mother.' Muriel glanced down at her nails and threw a vacant look across the cafeteria. 'Mother talks about you a lot more these days, y'know.

'Talk is cheap. To hell with her.'

'Kisha! She's our mother.'

'More yours than mine. Gwone, Muriel, I'm listening.'

'Anyhow, I saw Rikky from my window. He was up against this hotel fence near the beach, you know, and four big guys were kicking the shite out of him. One of them was trying to slash his face or something. God, those people – they're so violent!' Muriel widened disbelieving eyes at her.

'He gave as good as he got though. I've never seen anything like it, Keesh. I made the hotel call the police. He came over to thank me afterwards. That's how…' Muriel swivelled her head at Rikky and threw him a girlish grin. The young man smiled back.

Before they sat down, Muriel said, her lashes fluttering like moth-wings, 'That's mah maaaaen, Keesh. Say hello, Rikky!'

The young man took her hand and said hello in a voice that caught Kisha by surprise. It was too deep to belong to him, too rich and ripe for a youth as baby-faced as he. It was as if he'd borrowed an older man's throat.

Muriel dropped her voice almost to a whisper, 'Rikky's here on holiday and he's not going back.'

Kisha nodded neutrally.

Now her sister was leaning into her face 'I, I'm asking you a favour, Keesh.'

'Go on, den.'

Muriel sat back, tried to hold her eyes, gave up and focused on her chin.

'Well – I'm asking you to marry him. For me.'

Muriel had dropped the Loans Manager intonations. She was now Muriel of the loose, uncertain mouth and the nervous hand that wandered to her throat and stayed there.

'Sorry?'

'I'll, I'll uhm – pay you, if that's…'

Kisha placed the cup of coffee down so gently she scarcely heard it touch the table. 'That's what you asked me here for? Uh? Three years – and you haven't even bothered to find out if I'm dead or living in shit. Then you call me outta the blue to meet you here. To ask me this?'

'I'm offering to…'

'Hold it right there! Don't go no further.' She'd levelled a finger at Muriel's face.

A thin film of sweat had forced its way through Muriel's makeup. 'You haven't changed, Kisha. That temper of yours still sooo nasty. I thought time might've, well – made things a bit better, y'know. Look, you're thinking it's because of my job. It's not. It's… it's a couple of other things…'

'Like?'

'It's not a favour I'm asking, y'know. I'm offering to…'

'Like what, Muriel?'

Muriel would not look at her. She threw a quick, furtive glance over at the youth. Now she looked slightly afraid. 'Shane,' she muttered, 'Remember Shane?'

Kisha did remember him – too much chat, too much curly-perm and so much gold around his wrists and neck; he was like a walking pawnshop. 'Flash Pants?'

'You never liked him. After you, well… left home.'

'I didn't leave; Mother threw me out.'

'Well, you weren't around anymore. A few things happened. Me and Shane, we sort of decided to, y'know…'

Kisha narrowed her eyes and leaned forwards. 'You married that, that bloke? Christ! How long did it last – coupla weeks? Did it? And now you're in a twist coz…'

'It wasn't like that. Jeezus, Kisha, you make it sound so crude!'

Kisha laughed. The boy lifted his head and stared at them.

'Sort it out yourself, Muriel.'

'I can't. I really wish… It's only for a year, you know. He'll stay with me. I'll sort myself out, you divorce him and then…'

'No.'

'For God's sake! We're supposed to be sisters.' Muriel dragged her handbag off the table onto her lap. Her fingers hovered above the clasp. 'How much is it worth to you, Kisha? Tell me. A coupla grand? Three? Just tell me.' Muriel's stare was hard and accusing.

'No way!'

Muriel got up, creating a small eddy of perfumed air around her. 'You got a short memory,' she breathed. 'That's all I can say.'

'Quite the opposite, actually. Reminding me again of the time you saved my arse?'

'I'll phone,' Muriel muttered, barely turning to glance at Kisha. 'You still owe me, y'know. Come on, Rikky.'

She gave them half an hour, got to her feet, pulled out some coins and walked out onto the High Street. She stared at the entrance to the busy shopping centre and decided to do some window-gazing.

You still owe me… Muriel kept saying that. A time had to come when she would set her sister straight.

Over the years, she'd managed to stuff that night before the Carnival in the back drawer of her mind. Now here was Muriel dragging it out and shaking it in her face.

An all-night rave in Camden. They'd decided to burn out the hours in the party there and carry the mood with them to Notting

Hill – she, Muriel and her friends. Muriel was misbehaving like a drunk on steroids, although she never drank.

She, Kisha, had spliffed out long before entering the black-walled building, drifting in her own little purple haze and shifting on the rhythm whenever she felt like it.

She was sharing the mood with a youth-man who floated across to her side. He didn't say hello. Just looked her in the face, smiled as if answering something she was thinking and picked up her rhythm. He was clearly on a similar kind of high.

A couple of hours later – she couldn't remember if they even spoke – they stepped outside together. Nothing heavy. Just taking in the chill out there because, with that kinda high, she knew it would feel like mint on her skin.

The trouble came from behind her – a thickset, pink-haired young woman in red jeans that clung to her ham-sized calves like lycra. Girlchile grabbed herself a fistful of her hair, spun her round and started to diss her. Kisha could still see that face: thick and tight with hatred because her man had decided to step outside with another woman to take some flippin fresh air. Make matters worse, the girl was brandishing a knitting pin. With intent!

Without pausing to draw breath, Kisha reached out, smashed her knuckles in the girl's eyes and, before red jeans could steady herself, she followed up with a knee in her gut. It was later, after the police came, that Muriel told her the girl was pregnant.

Kisha had left the scene by then. Was four hours out there in the cold on a bridge above the Thames before heading home. When she got to her flat, Muriel was parked outside. She'd stayed behind to check out the drama, she said, and when the police asked, she told them she'd never seen the 'assailant' before.

But one of the girl's friends, she said, had described her in detail. Especially the way she had her hair.

'Got it down to a T, Kisha – the way you sew them silver threads through it.'

Throughout that night and the days that followed, it felt as if London was spilling over with police sirens. Muriel helped her pull out the silver threads and she, afraid to step out of her doorway, sat in her flat for a month while Muriel brought her the things she needed.

It was Muriel's idea to cut her hair – hair that was thick and strong and raven black. It never moulted. It never thinned or dried or cracked – the kind of hair that bounced back from the assault of hot combs, creams and gels and perms used to curl it, twist it, clip it, snip it, tress it and distress it.

In the times when things were really bad with her, she neglected it completely, sometimes for months. It was the first thing her girlfriends touched when they examined her. They always knew how she was doing by the way she had her hair.

Muriel did the job herself. At the end of it, her sister stood back, the scissors in her fist, staring at her baldness in the mirror. A half-smile had softened Muriel's mouth.

There'd been a look of wonder in Muriel's eyes – that and something else, which after all these years she could not put a name to – as they both stared at the hair in a thick nightfall on the floor.

This, above all else, was the memory that stayed with her: the eagerness of her sister's fingers and the ease with which they'd moved around her scalp that night.

She'd never grown it back.

She'd even learned to like her semi-baldness. People look at her, check themselves and look again. If it's a man, he never holds her gaze for long.

The headache has taken over completely by the time she gets back. Muriel is sunning herself on the sloping bit of grass that passes for a back garden, her loose flowered skirt pulled up to her knees.

The young man is stretched out on a long plastic chair beside her sister, his eyes covered with one arm. They've brought out a bottle of Calvados and a small basket stuffed with baguettes, cheeses, slices of veal, and the foie gras he's taken a liking to.

'Want something?' Muriel queries sweetly.

'Sorry?'

'You hungry?' Muriel gestures at the basket.

'Nuh.'

Kisha sits slightly behind her. From here she can see the houses that these sprawling fields support. A sunset like a bale of kente cloth is spread above their heads. She watches waves of quarrelling birds drift across it, their wings scribbling darkly against that glow and shine.

These little houses are a far cry from the tall, indifferent boxes that stand above Hackney's streets. In fact, from here, after just three days, London feels like an unreal and distant Legoland.

'Whyd'ju bring me here, Muriel?'

'You mean, why did you accept my invitation?'

Muriel fingers her dark glasses up to the top of her forehead and rolls her eyes.

'Well – perhaps I'm being silly. But I didn't expect it to be so, sort of, well… y'know – so…'

'So?'

'Well, tight – I mean, closed. We been here three days and it's not as if it's just the two of you. We don't talk. We don't eat togever; we don't check out the place togever. Just this… this… Dunno, man! A little bit of…' She wants to say *respect* or perhaps *consideration*, but somehow the words sound more appropriate in her head than if she were to say them.

Muriel levels steady brown eyes at her. 'What you getting at, Sunshine? You didn't have to come, you know.'

It is the Loans Manager voice. Kisha hunches her shoulders against it. 'You asked me, didn't you?'

'And I didn't have to, Keesh. Because I already paid you.'

Muriel replaces her Ray Bans, her mouth tensing in a half-smile. 'Better learn to live with it.'

Kisha surprises herself by smiling. This, she thinks, is the real Muriel. The one who ties you up so tight you don't even have a free finger to scratch yourself.

Apart from what Muriel told her, she has only a sketchy idea of where they are. France was Paris, not endless fields of half-dead poppies and cows wherever you rest your eyes. They are in a converted barn between some place called Forges-les-Eaux, and

Neufchatel, and a good few miles from Dieppe. That's all she's bothered to register.

She stares at her sister for a long time, then at the boy who's fallen asleep in the deckchair. Something shifts abruptly in her mind. It lifts the headache nibbling behind her forehead and makes her look about her. It suddenly feels as if she's just arrived.

'Going to catch a nap,' she says, and leaves them there.

She's in a coffin of a space with a single mattress thrown over a palette made from rough board. Muriel and the youth have the bigger room on the other side of the partition.

From here, their tossings fill her nights – the growling of the youth like the bulls in the fields that hoof the grass and stare at her; Muriel's sighs and pleasure-sobs that slip so easily into giggles. Eventually, Kisha drifts off to sleep, but when she wakes in the morning, her body feels as if it has been soaked and spun and tumble-dried.

Another woman, she thinks, would keep her well away. She would do all the little, nasty things that wimmen do to prevent someone from 'distractin' her man. Not Muriel. Her sister has to bring her here, grab her by the neck and bury her face so deeply in her shit, she can barely breathe.

For some reason, these two are dragging her back to her time with her mother, who never said a word to her without a sneer, whose eyes stung her with a million awful statements, until she – skinny, dark and gangly-limbed – felt herself being reduced to nothing.

For the first three mornings here, she's been walking the track that leads to the little mound in the middle of the fields she now calls Rasta Hill. She spends an hour there, or sometimes longer. When she returns, Muriel is out on her own 'personal time', which is a joy-ride through the sleeping country lanes that lead out of the village. Kisha often glimpses the top of the yellow Mercedes gliding like a bright metallic insect between the tall hedgerows.

Now, she doesn't much feel like taking a walk. She eats a light breakfast – or rather, picks at the grapes and bits of cheese and bread, and places finger-daubs of raspberry jam on her tongue, along with dollops of fiery mustard that feel like small explosions in her mouth and nostrils. She enjoys the sensations more than the food.

With Muriel gone, the youth takes up no space. He sits at the table, his legs hidden in its shadow, his hands on the wooden surface. His head is always slightly down, as if he's studying his fingers, so that all she sees are the lids of his eyes. It's as if he's put all the life within him on hold. Doesn't even look like he's awaiting Muriel's return.

This is a bloke who moves only when he's got to, she decides, who keeps his real self hidden behind those half-shut lids. A boy who's mastered the trick of biding his time.

Toni said the same thing about her too.

And yet Muriel said he was a 'street bwoy' – one of those youths who learned to use a knife before he could walk. His hands, she realises, are like his voice. They don't belong to him. They are older than his face – older than his age. She sees that Muriel hasn't started on his nails yet. She wouldn't be able to do much about the scarred thumb, or those high-ridged tendons at the back of his hands, which give those spidery fingers a life of their own.

Kisha doesn't know why, but she begins to make him do things. First, it is to fetch a cup for her which he rinses before he hands it over. Then it is to put the kettle on, which requires him to fetch the matches, light the stove, fill it and place it on the hob. Requests that demand of him a whole series of movements.

To pull the window shut he needs to unwind his legs, straighten himself out of the chair, cross the floor and stretch his full length up to reach the catch. It is the same to drag the heavy, beech-wood table a little further from the wall.

His strength is almost casual; like his voice and hands, it seems to have no connection with his body. He simply does what she orders without a single utterance.

Maybe she wants to catch a glimpse of the life he is so careful to conceal from her and Muriel – or to see something of the intent and the danger she thinks she notices in those 'knifeman's' hands. Maybe she just wants to break through that carapace of reticence.

When it happens, it does so with a laugh and a drawl that catches her off-guard and sends a shiver down the skin of her arms.

'Why you doan come out with it,' he says.

'Sorry?'

'You waant me. But you doan know how fe say it.'

'Pardon?'

'Yuh hear me firs time.'

With a jerk of her hand, she knocks the cup off the wooden table. It hits the stone floor and fragments like a small grenade. She feels the hot liquid on her feet and winces. His trouser ends are soaked but he does not move.

'How dare you? You…'

'Me not wrong. Me never wrong 'bout dese tings.'

'My God! What kind of person are you?'

'Me do what me haffe do.' Now the voice belongs entirely to him.

His eyes are directly on hers; his gaze is not threatening, just quiet and assessing. 'Wha mek yuh sister hate you so, den?'

'She told you that?'

He laughs. 'It doan have no love between you two.'

She finds she cannot look at him.

The throbbing of Muriel's engine reaches them. The youth lowers his shoulder. A limpness comes over him.

Kisha steps out for a walk.

With Muriel out there mid-mornings, burning rubber on the road, the youth makes two cups of coffee and hands her one. Sometimes he places a bowl of grapes before her, still dripping with tap water. He says nothing; nor does she. And even if Muriel's arrival cuts short their earlier confrontation, somehow it feels as if their conversation is complete.

She's imagined it happening differently – him following her out there, the awkward talk, the ugly slug of words between them that – despite their challenge and abuse – would make it easier for her. But he is there before her, on her stone, in one of those sleeveless T-shirts.

He's drawn his knees up to his chin, arms straight down beside him so that he looks like an oversized 'N' perched on the massive 'O' of the stone. With a start, Kisha realises that he must have followed her to this place before.

His presence makes the hill feel different. She notices for the first time the hints of rust in the purple moss that covers the sloping earth, the patch of darkness just beyond them where the lower branches of the trees tie themselves together in a sort of cave. She can smell the sweaty dryness of the fields below and hear the hollow humming of the land beyond. She knows that she will never want to set foot on this hill again.

He smells of the meat he's been feeding on every day, and of the fierceness with which she lets him take her. He is too confident, too sure of his effect on her for it to be any good. There is neither ugliness nor pleasure in it for her. Just fact.

Near the end, when his body begins to tense and shudder, she arches herself high and hard and throws him off.

He is still gasping when she straightens up. She's heard it said that men, brought to that point and abruptly let down, become violent or docile. He is none of these. There is something both chastened and defiant in the way he looks – not at her, but at the grass between his feet.

They descend the hill. She leads the way. Half way down, they meet the conspiratorial eyes of a short, wide man, his face brown and rugged as bark. He barely pauses from swinging the small scythe at the roots of the grass that he is gathering.

She wants to say, to the man – or to the youth – that she's never done this sort of thing before. She isn't the kind. Never knew she had it in her.

As soon as their feet hit the path, she feels his hand on her arm. 'You nice,' he says.

With a surge of irritation, she swings her head to face him. 'Can't say the same about you.'

His jaw hardens. The danger she sensed in him, which a short while ago had in some way been confirmed, washes over her like a mustard bath.

'Me leave 'er fuh you.' he says softly. The urgency is in his grip.
'Why?'

'Is how me feel. Here.' He touches his stomach where his navel would be beneath the shirt.

'Kinda quick, innit?'

'Me do what me have ter do.'

She wonders what he means by that, decides she knows and smiles.

'Well... we're married. So, technically...' She runs a hand across the prickles on her head, thinking that she would have to cut them back as soon as she gets to London. 'Fact is, though, I don't want you. Never did. But you wouldn't understand that.'

He mutters something, the tail end of which is, 'crazy...' It brings a small smile to her mouth.

Her sister's car is parked almost in the doorway when they walk into the yard. Muriel is sitting at the table. The heels of her hands are propping up her face. Kisha has a quick impression of the bulk of her sister, her dark solidity against the bright backlight from the window above her head. Kisha steps into a silence so thick, she feels as if she is wading.

Her eyes quickly scan the space: the small basket of wild black berries and pears; the four loaves of bread that Muriel invariably brings back with her; the heavy bread knife – the handle of which is touching Muriel's elbow; her sister's heavy breathing.

'You! Get in here.' Muriel's voice erupts from her stomach. Kisha feels the young man brush past her. His hands are stuffed down his pockets. He places his back against the wall.

Muriel swings her head towards her, her lower lip pulled inward, her eyes bright with hatred.

'I thought you weren't into men. I thought you were a bloody...'

'Say it, Muriel! Say it: Lez? Dyke? Say it!' Kisha feels an old and deadly anger stirring in her blood.

'That's why, that's why Mother threw your black arse out.
Frickin' African.'

Kisha leans a shoulder against the doorway. 'Senegalese, actually,'
she says, her eyes fixed on the spot where Muriel's elbow meets the
table. 'Wolof. He didn't know she had me. She told him she wasn't
going to; then she kicked him out; yes, like she kicked me out. She
told you who your father was, didn't she? She never told me mine.
I found out though. Like I found out that girl – all them years back
– wasn't carrying no child. And no fuckin police came.'

With quivering lips Kisha turns her gaze fully on the boy.
'Funny, Muriel, innit? The only thing we got in common – me
'n you. We're not into *men*.'

Muriel moves like a small eruption. She grabs the knife. Kisha
stoops almost at the same time and straightens up with the brick
they used as a doorjamb. But the youth is already between them.
She notices with a quiver of disbelief that the knife is in his hand.
She's never seen a person move so quickly.

'Done it, Muriel,' he says. 'Me say, done it!'

Muriel tries to fight her way past him, but wherever she turns,
she finds him in front of her. She strikes out at him, sobbing. The
only time he dodges her swing is when she lashes out at his face.
The rest he takes unflinching. Then, as if her whole body has
deflated, Muriel slumps back in the chair.

Kisha drops the brick. 'He saved your life, Muriel Martin.
Now you're both even. I'm getting outta this… this cowshed.'

She is in the room and back out in an instant with the bag she
packed the night before. Muriel follows her movements, as if her
eyes are attached to her by a string.

Kisha strides through the doorway, eases herself around the
car and pauses to contemplate a clutch of starlings skidding over
the clean-shaven fields, and the brown crosshatch of farm roads.

The main road is ten miles or so away, perhaps further. But
someone will stop for her. There will always be people – a farmer
on his tractor, or some driver passing through who will be struck
by her strangeness in this landscape and want to get a closer look.

She is counting on that to get her home.

TELL NO-ONE ABOUT THIS

Ara is smiling on the ride down the escalator from the seventh floor. She wants to get home quickly, lock her door, throw herself on her bed with her phone pressed against her ear and listen to Rasheed.

Ahead of her the hi-gloss marble floor is a clatter of hurrying heels as her workmates slap their passes against the sensors, flash their IDs at Security and flounce through the sliding doors.

She steps off the escalator, tosses the tail ends of her scarf over her shoulders and strides towards the exit.

She feels a tap on her shoulder, shrugs and swings her handbag and her pass towards the woman who's touched her.

'Step aside, please!'

Two men place themselves between her and the sliding doors. She hears hot intakes of breath behind, hisses of impatience. Ara steps aside.

The woman who is looking into her face is the shortest of the crew. Her chest and chin are pushed forward. She shifts her shoulders like a man. The name on her badge is Claris.

Claris jabs a finger at her bag, then swings her arm in the direction of the small white table to the left of the busy glass doors. Ara slips the strap from around her neck and drops the bag on the table.

'Open it,' the woman says.

Ara twitches at her tone, looks back briefly, catches curious glances from the faces streaming past. She registers the quick avoidance in their eyes.

Steadying her hand, she opens her handbag and stands back to watch the woman probe the inner pockets. There isn't much in there: her red leather purse with her Visa and Oyster cards, a small bottle of hand-sanitising gel, the square of linen she kneels on at the back of her office twice a day, the packet of Lil-Lets she bought during her lunch break and the white, freshly ironed handkerchief her mother gives her every morning before she leaves for work.

The woman's cropped head is millimetres above the mouth of her bag. She runs her fingers around the lining, lifts it to her ear and shakes it. The Lil-Lets and the handkerchief fall onto the surface of the table. She scoops them up and drops them in.

Ara locks eyes with her. 'Looking for something?'

She takes in the young woman's low cut hair, the row of stud holes on the right side of her upper lip, the glassy blue-green eyes.

'Doing my job.'

'Job?'

'Yes, job. J-O-B.' The young woman narrows her eyes and twists her lips. 'Like what I get paid for? Know what I mean?'

Ara feels her mouth go dry, the hairs prickling the back of her neck. She glances at the men, then back at the woman in front of her. She shapes a word with her lips and follows it up with a slow sweep of her eyes from Claris's booted feet up to her narrow face.

The woman flushes, though she couldn't have heard her, and if she did she wouldn't understand – the word mouthed in her parent's language. A small convulsion shakes the woman's shoulders. Now her voice is low and conversational. 'Nice scarf. Always wanted to know what it feels like with one of them other ones on.'

Ara lifts her brows.

'Know what I mean? Them whatchumacallit – them black ones with the little window in front your eyes.' She snaps the bag shut, exposes a row of little tight-packed teeth and hands it over. 'You're free to go now. Cheers.'

The doors sigh open and let her out. It is a sunny evening, leeched of its midsummer warmth by a chilly wind that lifts itself off the river and frets at her dress and scarf. There is a yellow glaze on everything. The high construction cranes fingering the London skyline glister in the sun like giant candles. She can see the great white belly of the Dome beyond them and imagines a pregnant spider thrown onto its back, its legs rigid in the air.

For a moment she stands breathing heavily on the wide pedestrian walkway that will take her to the Underground.

You're free to go… The woman's words are slinking down her spine. They settle heavy at its base. She wishes to find words for what she feels. But they are lodged in a bitter little knot in her throat. It isn't just the words. It is all the things that *khwajiah* was telling her with her ratty little eyes and compact sneering body.

Now Ara is thinking what she should have said – *almost* said: Why me; why none of the others; what do you take me for? And, at the risk of losing her job and displeasing her parents, she should have told her to fuck off.

But then she would have had to face her mother's soft-spoken condemnation – the hand raised just under her nose, her fingers splayed and rigid through the chattering prayer beads, reminding her of what happens to high-tempered daughters who bring shame on their family.

She started the day with her mother on her mind – how she corrupts her acts of giving with insults. How readily a put-down comes to her. Like this morning. She's standing before the hallway mirror settling her hair. She hears her name, looks up the stairs to see her mother on the landing. She follows the beckoning hand to her parent's bedroom. Her mother sits her on the duvet and opens the ancient rawhide case which, thirty years ago, she said, crossed the Nile with them on their way to the airport in Khartoum.

From the stacks of folded fabric and yeasty fragrances of *bakhoor*, her mother lifts a shimmery square of blue cloth, white-patterned at the edges. The headscarf looks weightless in her hand, like a weave of cloud and sky. She hands it to her and dips into the case again, coming up this time with a wooden box that she tips onto the bed. Three beautiful gold bracelets settle on the sheet, and a chain, so fine and polished, sits in Ara's palm like amber liquid. Its pendant is a Hamsa hand with a pale blue opal in the middle.

Ara takes the gifts with both hands, nods her thanks before

handing it back for safekeeping – that is until Rasheed takes her to their new home in six weeks.

Her mother rises to her feet. 'And this,' she says, holding out a dress. It is a pale olive green with cream trimmings along the hems. There is a soft gloss to the fabric. Ara knows it's worth much more than her father's monthly wage. Her mother asks her to put it on.

She stands in the dress, feeling light and somehow cossetted by its embrace. She imagines herself at her henna party, smiling at the lovely things her friends will say when they see her walking in it.

Her mother's movement breaks her musing. She's gathering the fabric from around Ara's ankles. Now she is holding up a handful of the cloth to Ara's face. Slow words issue from her barely parted lips. They have the sibilance of a secret. 'Let no man lift this above your head, Ara, except the husband you will sit beside next month.' Her mother drops the hem of the dress and turns her back on her.

The rest of what she says comes over her shoulders. 'We couldn't choose the country you grew up in, but you don't have to learn their ways.'

Ara does not know how long she's been standing on the walkway looking across the city at nothing. She thinks back to the searching of her bag and suddenly feels observed.

She glances at the cameras overhead. They are everywhere, on the top of every other lamppost that lines the walkway. They hang hooded over doorways. She spots them on the supporting poles of wire fences and against the side of every rising edifice. The city's compound eyes.

She imagines little rat-faced women with men's shoulders concealed in windowless rooms inside these towering hives of concrete, steel and glass, peering at their screens and noting every flutter of her headscarf. She wants to hide her face.

She suddenly remembers Sirah. Her friend will be waiting for her at the barrier beside the station entrance, where the fat tobacconist narrows his eyes at them and mutters under his breath. Sirah works in her brother's jewellery store a short walk from the Underground and always waits for her.

The station is a hurried ten-minute walk away. When Ara arrives, Sirah is not there and a prick of betrayal runs through her. She allows the human tide to suck her down the gaping maw to the trains, barely registering the slap of Oyster cards against the yellow sensors, the staccato slam of the automatic gates as she breaches her barrier and descends with the crowd for the westbound.

The platform is packed. There is a shifting wall of dark suits spread almost to the lip of the platform, just above the tracks. She hears the whine and stutter of the rails, feels the tepid, muggy rush of air the arriving train pushes ahead of itself, and decides to take the next one. But then, between several shoulder-gaps further up the platform, she glimpses a flare of yellow and knows that it is Sirah's headscarf.

The crowd is rearranging itself, preparing for the push on board once the doors slide open. Ara gets a fuller view of her friend's profile and guesses, by the clenched activity of Sirah's mouth, that her husband has summoned her home, or something is up with her child.

Perhaps little Asfa's condition has worsened. Sirah has shown her photographs of the boy – a grey-faced six-year-old with eyes so hollow and dark-rimmed it's as if their sockets are smeared with kohl. Sirah won't say exactly what is wrong with him, but Ara knows it is an illness he could die from without warning. Sirah says he's already outlived the time the doctors gave him.

If they are lucky they will find two empty seats together. They are almost always lucky.

She is looking forward to the familiar sinking into conversation with her friend that becomes less inhibited as the train eases itself out of the city, worming its way deeper into Harrow Weald.

She ignores the flat Nigerian accent telling them to 'Mind da doze, pliz' and squeezes her way inside.

Sirah is already in and seated. Ara's eyes are on the vacant seat directly facing her. She heads for it, gets there quickly and turns to lower herself. She is aware of the heavy abrupt press against her left shoulder, the smell of sweat and something faintly industrial, but she is there first; is gathering her dress and turning to lower herself when she feels the body under her.

She pulls up sharply, stumbles. An anonymous hand steadies her from behind. The broad red face of a very large man is looking down at her, smiling. The woman on her right is absorbed in her Kindle reader.

The man who's stolen her seat is adjusting an old canvas bag between his feet. His boots are imitation Timberlands. He's rolled up the sleeves of his dark blue overalls to his elbows. The black, lopsided woolly hat on his head matches the colour of his arms exactly.

A throb of rage surges through her.

'Ibn kalb!' she snaps. The curse has left her lips before she's formed it in her mind.

Sirah gawps at her, then at the man, before she looks down and begins fiddling with her ring.

Ara might have left it at that, knowing that by the time they leave the city and emerge into the Edgware suburbs, the train will be almost empty. But not only has the man almost knocked her over in his rush to take her place, the powdery stuff that covers his overalls has rubbed off on her dress.

She unzips her handbag and retrieves her handkerchief. 'Fi ginitaak!' she hisses. She keeps her eyes on his face as she dabs at the side of her dress.

If he understands the insult, he does not show it. His eyes are flat and uninterested. They are focused on the placards above her head advertising holidays and health cures.

Ara wipes her dress more carefully as her mind conjures her mother's admonishing hand.

She nudges Sirah's leg, hears herself speaking in her father's irritated tone.

'Abid! No wonder they kill off each other and run to people's countries.'

'Not here, Ara... not...' Sirah's Arabic is as soft as it is appalled. A film of sweat has broken out on her face.

'It is the truth,' Ara says. 'There is no dishonour in the truth.' She realises that she's raised her voice.

Sirah rests a soft hand on hers. 'A little soap and water, inshallah. That's all. Let's talk about Rasheed, or your posh translating job…'

The rest of Sirah's words are chewed up by the clatter of the train switching tracks. The intercom crackles – a metallic voice announces the next station. Bodies rouse and rustle, followed by the scuff of hastily gathered suitcases.

Ara's armpits are damp from the heat and the strain of holding herself upright. She throws a contemptuous sidelong glance at the seated man, but his eyes are closed, his chin pressed into his chest. She can barely distinguish his lashes from his skin. The powdery stuff that stained her dress is all over his boots. Building site, she thinks. Then she revises it. Warehouse – one of those windowless tin boxes hugging the highway or hidden under some dirty railway bridge. That, she thinks, would explain the dust.

'Ibn kalb!' she mutters, then turns to look down at her friend. 'Couldn't wait for me, Sirah?'

Sirah widens honey-coloured eyes at her. 'Asfa,' she says, and brings her palms together. Her friend's answer is mild and apologetic with a lilt of the Bedouin inflection that Ara envies. Sirah raises her voice as the train rattles over the tracks. Sirah's eyes are wet, her gestures animated. The clatter of the carriage mangles the rest of her words and all Ara hears is 'serious… very… this time.'

The young man sitting on the other side of Sirah rises to his feet. He smiles at Ara and nods at the empty seat. He is very handsome. Ara watches him squeeze himself and his bag through the packed aisle. Moments later, she feels the rush of air as he opens the adjoining door and crosses to the next carriage.

The young man makes her think of Rasheed and the wonderful accretion of secrets between them from the moment her parents accepted him. She would not wait out the months in

silence, for a man she did not know, to come to her and take her
to his house. From the time her parents said his name and asked
her to trust their choice, she went out of her way to find his
number, phone him from the secrecy of her bedroom and insist
that he speak to her, so that she could begin to feel something for
this stranger to whom she's meant to submit her life. When at last
she asked to see his face up close, just him and her alone, he came
and waited where she told him.

She is there again with him in the tree-shadowed space behind
her father's garage. He is bolder than she expects, more demanding. There is one thing, he tells her, that he wants before they sit
together in the presence of their families and make their marriage
vows. He's taken her hand in his and is drawing her to him. He
looks into her eyes and asks permission to uncover her head.

She sees the desire in his gaze as he edges back her scarf, eases
his fingers beneath the fabric and slips it past her ear. His breath
is like a soft brush on her face. And even as something inside her
rears up and drags her back, she finds her body leaning towards
his. She lifts quick fingers to her lips, looks up through the
branches of the blossoming mayflower at her parents' bedroom
window.

'Tell no-one about this,' she whispers, her own voice quivering and urgent in her ears. 'Not ever in your life, Rasheed.'

Rasheed places a hand against his heart and swears.

Ara settles herself in the seat the young man has just vacated. A
drawn-out snore returns her attention to the low-life in front of
her. His own snort wakes him up. He plants his hands on the
armrests as if about to launch himself to his feet. He looks around
him blinking – a sweeping dark-eyed gaze – then eases himself
back down.

'Khenzeer!' she mutters in Sirah's ear. 'See that look? I bet my
salary he's illegal.'

'A little soap and water,' Sirah says. This time her friend's wet
eyes are looking directly into hers and her brows are pulled
together.

★

There's a muffled effervescence of shuffling feet and adjusting postures as the wheels of the train begin a juddering, jittering dance along the tracks. Ara knows this bit of the journey well and likes it.

The jittering doesn't stop, or if it does it becomes something else. A roar, then a thundering so bone-deep it feels as if it has its roots inside her guts.

The thundering is above her and beneath her. She is aware of her seat convulsing, her body lifting, then the head-darkening jolt as something strikes her on the shoulders and darkness falls around her.

And then the screaming. Her own screaming followed by a space of silence – brief, yet so protracted it seems to have no end.

She does not know where her feet are. Something sharp is pressing against her rib cage. She is dimly aware of the grinding wail of metal, the caustic choke of burning rubber, the snap and grate of things.

When Ara lifts her head, a greenish phosphorescence sur- rounds her. She is looking up the incline of what used to be the flooring of the carriage. A slow dark creep of fluid fans down the sloping metal towards her face. She watches it come and cannot move.

She is groping for an anchorage in her mind, something recognizable in this topsy-turvy, buckled gloom; some concrete point from which she can navigate her way back into a sense of where she is and what is happening.

She realises that her face is pressing against glass, and in slow adjustment to this greenish twilight, her eyes rest on shapes piled at the lower end of the tilted carriage. The large man who stood above her is a folded sack in the far corner. A burbling sound comes from him. At her end, bodies lie against each other in a tangled heap. A bare foot – pale as paper in the old light – sticks out in the air.

Beyond them, from the narrow doorway that leads into the

adjoining carriage, comes the crash of falling things. She thinks she sees movement, but she is not sure.

Ara turns her head, sees that she is on the fractured edge of the reared-up carriage. Down below the rails are grey metallic scars against the darker bed of oil-soaked wood and gravel.

She cannot find her feet. She slips her hand along her body and realises that she is still attached to them. A tear runs up the length of her dress to the stitching at the waist. She raises a hand to her head, feels for her scarf. It is not there.

Ara sits up slowly. The carriage rocks, then settles abruptly. She imagines it balanced like a seesaw on something precarious. She begins edging her body backwards.

There are sounds around her – human sounds of pain so muffled it is as if they are buried underwater. Ara hears herself cry out.

Now she looks about her and tries to make herself believe that this is not as she is seeing it. Is it a nightmare punishment – some out-of-the-blue rebuke for her transgressions with Rasheed? She's broken every prescript of her mother's from the moment they accepted him for her.

It is a thought that nails a wedge of terror in her heart. It comes to her as a rush of regret – that Rasheed's promise of himself, of his warm breath on her face, will never be fulfilled. She has no doubt that she is going to die, or that she is dead and does not know it yet.

Ara lifts her head and a scream unravels from her throat. She cannot stop herself.

She is still screaming when she sees, at the edge of her vision, the hands reaching up to her, the fingers dark and beckoning as if they belong to the gloom.

He's lost the woolly hat and one sleeve of his shirt is hanging off an arm. His hair is not as she imagined. It is cut close to his skull and curly; and his face is long and slim, the cheekbones high and prominent. He is standing on the edge of the platform, inches above the deep drain of the tracks. He's beckoning her with his hands.

She draws back, conscious of the torn dress, her exposed flesh. Little throaty sounds escape her. The hands hang in the air a while, then they withdraw. When they re-emerge they're gloved.

And still she hesitates, feeling disconnected and half-drowned in this dislodged world of hums and moans and shifting metal.

He shakes his head, still urging her with gestures to the brink of the broken carriage. She pushes a hand at him. Ignoring it, he reaches up and curves an arm around her hip. She feels the roughness of the glove against her skin as he strains to lift her down.

On stable ground, she realises that the terrible jolt that tore through everything has jackknifed most of the carriage off the rails onto the platform. Through the darkness in which the rest of the train is buried, she hears sounds – hollowed-out shouts, preternatural sobs.

Directly underneath, a soft voice calls. It draws her eyes downwards past the twisted metal and cables. Sirah's yellow scarf is a lazy toss of colour against a rail, and just beyond it, a woman-shape – a mess of hair, pale bare shoulders – the rest melding with the darkness. The part of her friend that Ara sees looks broken and malformed. Ara presses her palms against her eyes, feels herself sinking. The stranger's hands are under her armpits, holding her up and steadying her.

The man leans over and is motionless, as if he is listening for something beyond the sounds that reach them. Then he straightens up.

'No use,' he says. His voice is low. She senses no feeling in it.

They are standing in a narrow gap on the pale tiles of the platform. His raised arm draws her attention to the steady yellow glow of the Way Out sign beyond the broken carriage. It is still lit up. With another movement of his hand he tells her that to get to it, they have to scale the carriage that lies across the platform.

He turns his back on her and begins to climb. A gasp escapes him. Now she sees the torn trouser leg, the seeping gash just above his left knee. He is stuck for a while, his shoulders heaving.

He mutters something vicious and begins the struggle upwards. His hands and his right leg are doing all the work.

Once on top he looks down at her. Things groan and shift above them. He raises his head at the domed roof from which cables hang like entrails. 'Fall soon,' he says. 'You come now or I leave you here.'

He lays himself flat and lowers an arm to her.

She reaches for the hand and she is clumsy. She doesn't want to be. There is a hollowness in her gut and a confused wariness of this stranger whom she was wishing dead a while ago.

She's terrified of him leaving here without her, but feels the resistance of her will at what he is requesting: that she lift her face and arms to him. That he closes his fingers around her and draw her up to him.

He says something impatient. She thinks it is a curse. She rises to the balls of her feet and tries again. He catches her wrists. Half of him is over the edge. He grimaces with the effort to drag her up. Animal sounds break out of him – grunts and hisses and gasps.

Now that she is up beside him, he slides down to the floor on the other side and stands below with open arms. She aims for the spot to his left and lets herself go. He catches her and steadies her. She pulls herself loose and steps away.

His shape is a dark outline against the glow of the emergency lights behind. He's drawn himself upright and is glaring down at her. 'There is no honour in a stupid death, just a stupid death,' he says. 'You are not naked. Your friend over there is naked.' He jerks his chin at the upended carriage. 'She cannot think of honour now.'

He pulls off his dirty gloves and dumps them at her feet.

For a moment, Ara cannot absorb his words though the sounds and their rhythms are familiar. She blinks at him, feels her skin go cold when it comes to her that he is speaking Arabic. It is measured and modulated. Formal but beautiful – the way she gets paid to talk to clients at the bank. She knows that by this manner of speaking, he is placing her at a distance, pushing her away. There is nothing in his accent or his choice of words to betray his provenance.

'Stay here then, and die. Allah knows I did my best.' He turns to leave.

She hears herself cry out.

He does not look back.

She follows the shifting back as best she can through the cold fluorescence of emergency lights, sidestepping piles of shattered concrete, squeezing past tangles of wire-work.

Once or twice she catches up, especially when they are picking their way through darkness. She stumbles often in those moments, colliding with the injured leg, which draws from him a grunt.

When there are no more exit signs, he navigates by looking at the roof. She knows now that he will not abandon her. He lingers at the top of stairs and limps on when she is a couple of steps behind him. At times her legs give way. He stops, steps back, hauls her up by an arm and releases her abruptly. There is something punitive and wilful in his action. He never looks at her.

She's lost her sense of time; has no idea of destination either. Ara does not know exactly where this stranger might be leading her. There are moments when she believes there will be no end to the climbing, the lifting, the squeezing through, the fearful avoidance of sputtering cables; that in this anchorless hollow beneath the city, all there is and will ever be is this limping man-shape in front of her that she's attached to with her eyes.

They are on level, undamaged flooring. She senses a change in him. His limp is slower, more cautious. He looks back and points. She draws up and stands beside him. The tiled tunnel curves ahead. At the end of it there is a bloom of luminance, a colder, neutral light. The glow becomes stronger, more broadly spread as they walk forward.

Ara looks up at the striated ascent of twin escalators, dead but still intact, past the silhouettes of the swing-gates, to bluish light spilling in from the street. She thinks she hears hammering above, sirens and the far-off drone of voices.

He says something. When she looks at him his eyes are closed and he's resting a shoulder against the wall. She can view his face more clearly – the skin so smooth and fine, she cannot see the pores. He's much younger than she thought and this surprises her.

She stands a little ahead of him, studying his face. His eyes are lidded, his head turned slightly downwards.

'Jazak…' She moistens her lips, tries to say the rest but wants him to look at her, to acknowledge her gratitude while looking her in the face. But he's somewhere inside his head, his chin angled in the direction of the stairwell.

'Jazak – Jazak Allah Khairan,' she mutters.

His big dark eyes are boring into hers. He answers her in English. 'No need for thanks. It is not for you I do this. You understand?'

His words sink in and they confuse her. She focuses on his rage. It is dismissive, low-voiced, intimate.

'I am more than this, you understand?' He swipes a finger at his clothes. 'No slave; no dog; no asshole. Where I come from, many hundred people work for me.'

Ara raises her head and it is all she can do to hold his gaze.

'You say the same god speaks to us? Then I ask you this, Mundukuru: why do we hear his words so differently? Why not your friend here with me? Why you?'

That fast flash of distaste that draws his brows together and quivers his lips is like the brief opening of a doorway into himself. Mundukuru. She absorbs the insulting word. Feels relieved by it, even grateful. Mundukuru – a Juba curse; a Southerner, she decides, from the country her parents fled.

Ara looks down at the wounded leg, then at his face. He's in pain. He's clamping down on it, lifting himself above the hurting, but it is there in the tensed brows, the stiffness around his mouth.

The pounding overhead is louder. Urgent voices descend on them. Ara feels the stranger's hand on her shoulder and steps nearer.

'Go,' he says. His voice is low and urgent.

She shakes her head, 'And… and… you?'

'Go now!'

She shakes her head again.

'You don't go right now, I strike you!'

She winces at his words. Does not know how to take them.

'Maa jazeel al-shukr,' she says. This time he does not reject her thanks, but he does not answer her.

She wants to ask him how he'll manage the stairs; wishes to offer him her shoulder.

She can make out the words of shouting men above, the hydraulic hiss of heavy machinery.

'Go! Emshi alaan! Leave me alone. Emshi yellah.' Now his voice is raised.

Ara nods. He will speak to her no more; she sees this in his face.

Before she turns, she dips into the pocket of her dress, points at his leg and holds out her handkerchief with both hands. She feels stupid. The gesture is ridiculous and his expression tells her that, but his face softens as he takes it.

A press of men and women in overalls and uniforms receive her at the top. She feels herself enfolded in a blanket, being spoken to, then lifted and tilted up the steps to the public road. Her head becomes an echo chamber with all the questions and exclamations crashing in on her until a woman's voice cuts through the din and there is calm.

A pair of gloved hands sit her on the sidewalk and feed her something warm. The pavement is packed with blanketed people. She hardly sees them. She sips and rocks and stares at the mouth of the Underground.

She almost misses him. He's surfaced on the other side of the road. She's staring at the unsteady back progressing along the sidewalk.

The street is boundaried off by yellow tape. It is void of life apart from the pulsing blue of police cars and ambulances. He is exposed. She feels her heartbeat rising.

Ara is startled to see the woman, who is still kneeling beside her, following her gaze. Her eyes are grey and steady.

'Was that man with you?' The peak of her cap is like the pricked ear of a dog.

Ara shifts her gaze. She holds the woman's stare a while. Says nothing.

The woman drops the cup on the pavement and rises to her feet. She brings her radio to her mouth.

'DC, Lisa here. IC3 male, proceeding east along Regents Road. He's limping. Do you have a visual, Tim – over?'

A fast voice answers her.

'He's right near you, Tim. Less than six yards past vehicle A77. On your right. Blue overalls – navy blue that is. Torn right sleeve – almost off his arm. Can't miss him – he's limping. Over?'

Another fast reply.

'Yes, that's him. Will you stop him, Mate. Over?'

The woman shoves off in a fast stride, then launches into a run. Ara watches her churning heels and her heart increases pace.

Before the woman gets there, the door of a van slides open. Men approach him from all directions. Their hands reach out and drop onto his shoulders.

They urge him backwards until he's flat against the vehicle. Their hands are busy on his body. He's turned his face upwards as if his mind is somewhere else. The largest of the eight spins him round to face the van. They spread his arms and feet. He looks pinned up against the white vehicle. One shoves a hand into his pockets and turns them out. A flake of white emerges. It hesitates at the edge of his pocket, then flutters to the pavement.

Ara watches them walk him towards a pulsing row of blue lights further down the street. As she stares, she is remembering the warm indifference of his palms; the breath of his effort on her face; the press of his fingers on her back and thighs as he eased her through impossible gaps and urged her body into shapes that allowed her to pass through them.

A BETTER MAN

She'd been looking forward to the two-bar electric fire in the living room to warm herself. She'd just walked out of a drizzle that had misted the world outside from the time she got up this morning – as if the night before had bled into the whole day.

Shehu had his elbows on the little dining table when she entered the flat, his face turned up towards the ceiling. Her bulging laundry bag sat on the floor behind him.

He did not return her greeting and a familiar heaviness came over her. She crossed her feet, swallowed on the creeping dryness in her throat, leaned a shoulder against the wall of the narrow corridor, and waited.

She sensed another presence in the room before she noticed the woman seated sideways on the old sofa, one leg over the other, a silver-strapped sandal dangling from her foot. Her purple nails were busy on the keypad of her phone. The woman kept her head down, a pile of tinted braids making a curtain around her face – the Congolese girl who'd just taken up residence with six other women in the flat above.

'I need you to leave. Right now.' Shehu swung a long arm at the bag.

She said nothing for a while, her eyes shifting from the young woman's down-turned head, to him. She felt brave enough to ask him why. The woman made a clucking sound, sucked her teeth and carried on with her finger-tapping.

'You're not contributing anything,' he said.

She knew that Shehu was not talking about money. He'd stared at her face, then along the rest of her, and everything he did not say was in that glazed look: two months in his bed with him and she still would not let him to touch her.

'I have nowhere to go.'

'What's new? It's Friday, you have the whole weekend to find a place.'

He swung himself to his feet, threw a withering sideways look at her. Without the frown, Shehu was good-looking and laid-back. Half-Fulani, he'd told her. And proud of it. The other half he never mentioned.

He was happy, he'd said, to give her time.

'Shehu…'

He grumbled something under his breath and strode toward the kitchen. The last word she caught was, '…useless'.

It was this that hurt her most.

Her feet took her through the drizzle to the 349 bus stop. She thought of phoning Gabriela, the laughing, older Saint Lucian woman who shared her shift, and lived on Stamford Hill. She imagined Gabriela offering sympathetic words, then advising her to call 'one of her people'.

She pressed her back against the dripping railings of the playing field that ran parallel to the main road, the yellow laundry bag against her feet. The 349 arrived, hissed to a halt, then moved off. More came and as each one left she raised her head at the misted windows, reached for her phone, then changed her mind.

She watched the lights of the grocery store and small post office across the road go off. Shortly after, the Indian man came out, locked the door and pulled down the shutters, his wife a couple of feet behind him, hands held palms down over her head to keep off the rain. She disliked this smiling, sari-clad woman who made a point of not touching her hand when she dropped the change in it. 'You Idi Amin people,' she'd said.

The traffic grew heavier; the heavy rush of air of passing trucks dragged at her clothing. In the thickening evening, the streetlamps had turned the pavement a simmering yellow.

She was brushing the water from her hair when she became

aware of the man at the edge of her vision. Same height as Shehu, the same bony muscularity. In the glow of the bus stop advertisement, she saw that he was blue-dark, like the men at home. Neat in his white shirt, black tie and dark jumper – a painted crest with white print across the front: LPS Security. He held a Tesco bag of shopping tautly in his hand. It was as if he were listening to the very air around her with his body. She felt the stirrings of an old defiance in her blood.

'Are you alright?' His English was slow and careful; his voice soft and resonant – the kind that made you turn your head towards it in a crowd.

She pretended she didn't hear him. The plastic bag rustled, and she '*Habari gani? Nini tatizo?*' He'd switched to Swahili. There was a new certainty in his tone.

She did not return his greeting; and she certainly wouldn't tell him what the trouble was. She was aware of her own breathing now, and the dampness of her clothes. She couldn't tell how long he stood there, his free hand rubbing the drizzle into his close-cropped hair, the long, blue-black face quiet as dark-water. She saw that he was quite young.

'Maybe I help? I am not a bad man. Maybe I help?'

Another bus rolled up, the headlamps making of him a flat black manshape. A woman stepped out of the vehicle, a tumble of children behind her. The bus heaved and wheezed and trundled off, lifting a wave of dirty water onto the pavement. The man looked down at his shoes, raised his head at the retreating vehicle, shook his head and began walking on.

She heard him sigh; the bag of shopping rustled as he turned to face her.

'Alans Road. After Farm Foods.' He pointed at the store ahead. 'Number five. Blue door. *Kwa heri.*'

He hoisted the plastic bag onto his shoulder and left her there.

She counted six more buses, then the traffic subsided. Now, there was just the occasional car racing to beat the lights at the junction ahead, and men's laughter in the cab station next door. A group of women from the Turkish hairdressers across the road stepped onto the pavement, a hum of words between them, their scarved heads turning every now and then in her direction. The fat-bellied man in the shop next door had left his kebab counter and now stood facing her, his shoulders filling up the doorway. Outside the cab station on her left, a huddle of smoking taxi drivers. She felt their frank assessing eyes.

She took up the yellow laundry bag. During all her time in London, she'd been living by the words of a woman who saved her, when the rest of her village left her for dead: *If the river can't climb a rock, it will makes its way around it.* She headed up the street, the picture of a blue door in her head.

The ground floor flat was no different from Shehu's or any other she'd passed through: a small electric heater on the floor of the living room near the fireplace, a bare plastic table in the middle of it. At the back, the tiny kitchen with a row of MDF cupboards above a three-hob stove.

She dropped her bag by the door.

He handed her a towel. Light blue. Clean. She thanked him in Swahili. 'Only for tonight,' she said. Then she thought again. 'Maybe tomorrow too… I… I…'

His cheeks lifted in a quick smile. 'Ah – she can talk! You from Acholiland, no?'

She nodded.

'From The Camp, no?'

She nodded again.

'Family back there?'

She said nothing.

'I understand,' he said. 'We are like Christians when they die – no-one knows if they went to heaven or hell because they don't return to tell anyone.'

'Only for tonight…'

'Up to you,' he said, flicking a quick wrist at the sofa. Again the careful English. 'You hungry? Spaghetti? With cheese?'

He strode into the kitchen and began busying himself over the stove.

She dried her hair, rested the limp towel on the back of a chair and scanned the room. 'You live on your own?'

Her question halted his hand over the pot. 'Better for me,' he replied, without turning.

He brought the plates to the table and pulled out a chair. Long dark fingers, confident hands, a deeply scarred thumb.

He asked her to sit. She told him, no. Ate standing while taking in the long head, the neatly barbered hair, the jawline that made her think of the delicacy of bird-wings.

'Tell me your story; I tell you mine.' He'd leaned back against the chair, the food barely touched. Charcoal eyes – a pinprick of light in each one.

She told him of her home in Pamin Yai in the north – a place of cattle, rocks and maize; her months in The Camp near Gulu Town, then here.

She could hardly offer more than that. Here in London, she'd let its strangeness suffocate her memories – the welcome racket of this new world, the cold which, even in summer, still found its way into her bones, the daily wordless gathering of litter from between stiff indifferent feet at Liverpool Street train station.

Her treks from flat to flat had also helped with *not* remembering: the shared rooms in Northolt, Harlesden, Peckham, Elephant & Castle… the bickering of her housemates when the electricity ran out, or when the rent was raised and they either paid and starved or packed their things and left.

She swayed on her legs and listened to him speak in that beautiful voice of his, always in Swahili. Coal-dark lips moving around words that left her with images of a boy running from a disembowelled place named Kivu, picking up the languages of the people in the places he passed through. And though she would never let him know this, she found herself liking the way he talked – this oddly familiar stranger, his calming voice turned inwards, sometimes hesitating, often over the awful things he said he'd seen and preferred not to speak of.

At the end of it, he'd rolled up the left leg of his trousers and shown her the hole gouged into his calf; then made a gesture which took in the living room, the dripping streets out there, the world.

'This Africa – they tell us it is cursed. They help us kill each other off, and when we're all dead, they'll have it for themselves. They will never leave us alone.' He held out a hand to her. 'I'm Kiki Kinkela.'

It came as a shock to her that, until then, they hadn't exchanged names.

'Miya,' she said, and withheld her other names.

She woke to an empty flat, a faint memory of warring voices in her head; of things being broken and turned over. She rummaged in her bag, went to the shower, then dressed, avoiding her reflection in the mirror over the sink. She pushed a head into his bedroom. His bed was neat. A green blanket rolled up like a carpet across the light-blue sheet; a small lamp on the bedside table without a shade; the light socket in the ceiling empty.

She dialled Gabriela, counted to the fourteenth ring, then cut off, reminding herself that the woman had said that she hardly used 'the thing' and only carried it because her eldest daughter insisted.

When he returned from work, she'd cooked. She'd gone to the vegetable stall on Ponder's End Road, bought green plantains and chicken and made her own version of *matoke*.

He'd knocked on his own door and she let him in; he'd eaten the food and thanked her and when he went to shower and change, she allowed her eyes to rove around the flat again, as she had done all day. She did not know what she was looking for. There was nothing on the walls to halt her eyes. Everyone she knew who came from somewhere else – all the people she'd shared rooms and mattresses with – brought something from home with them. Or if they didn't, they recreated it. Sometimes it was a picture, or the colours of the clothing they were drawn to; or, like her, the food they chose to cook, or simply the ingredients they brought to it. There was nothing in this flat to place this man who'd been living there for five years. Yet he'd told her who she was so quickly and with such ease that she felt exposed.

'Maybe you can stay, I mean, after the weekend? I'm not chasing you.' He'd come out and seated himself at the table.

She picked up the plates and cutlery and brought them to the sink.

'I'm not chasing you,' he said again.

She did not turn around or answer him, aware now of his eyes on her and the dreadful leadenness that had crept up her back and settled under her shoulder blades.

She didn't realise he'd left the chair until she felt his breath on her neck, his hands reaching down to untie the knot of her lesu. She closed her hand around the cloth, raising the fabric up to her throat. She turned to face him, her eyes on the curved neck of his tee shirt. *Nedda*, she muttered, *Hapana!* and slid her body sideways, her back against the counter.

She looked him in the eyes, because that had always worked, and said the same thing she'd told Shehu the first time he placed his hands on her that way: 'I can lay with you if you want; but I can't, I can't take… have…'

His reaction was not like Shehu's – the slow retreat in the eyes, the firming of the lips, the slight turning of the head away from her, the gradual easing back.

He followed her gaze to the laundry bag, still leaning against the wall beside the front door. He drew breath and swallowed, and she noticed for the first time, the very fine scars on the skin of his throat.

'It's fine,' he said, lifting the plates from the sink and holding them under the running tap. 'I promised myself to be a better man. You still stay, I won't…'

'I won't stay,' she said.

He shifted his head towards the window, staring through the flimsy curtains that misted the streetlights outside. 'The damage is here?' He pointed a finger at his head, 'or…'

'Does it matter?'

'Sorry,' he said and headed for his bedroom.

On the sofa, she drifted between wake and sleep. The spill of light from the street lamp outside, softened by the curtains, filled the room with a twilight glow. It reminded her of the time of day her mother called *lak nyango* – when the sun had just risen and had not begun to sting, casting long cool shadows across her father's fields.

The cotton plants and maize were shivering with rain. A time for trapping the sweet white flying *ngwen* that emerged from the anthills after a heavy downpour.

She was running after her elder sister, Payaa, through the dripping cassava and tobacco, the air above them shimmering with silver-winged insects. All she was thinking of was the *odii ngwen*, the delicious ant-paste that their mother mixed with honey and gave them, along with roasted cassava.

Then, to the left of them, the maize shuddered and came alive. Eight men stepped into their path. She saw again Payaa turning back towards her, a scream twisting her sister's mouth; then the fast flash of silver before her sister's body hit the red earth.

They ordered her to sit down. She remembered the glint of their blades as the men threw them on the grass and began walking towards her; saw again their approaching shapes against the great Pamin Yai rock that stood above their homes. Remembered Payaa's last amputated cry and the roar of Ayago river in the distance.

Nothing else.

She must have fallen asleep because the howling woke her up. She sprang off the sofa and stood in the gloom, her body leaning toward the noise of the thrashing bed. It could have been another woman, but the sound came only from him, guttural and gasping. She heard no pleasure in those sounds, just the thumping and the awful, gasping noise.

And words.

She pushed open the door, entered the room and switched on the bedside light. It did not wake him. He seemed to be in the grip of something awful. Whatever disturbance he was living through made a flailing, throbbing thing of him. Spittle and words torn from his mouth like bloodied cloth, and those two words: 'Sit down…'

He was an Acholi man. The language of his nightmare was the same as hers.

If he'd really crossed Rwanda on foot from south Sudan, drunk the piss of others to survive the desert, escaped the AK47s and machetes of the children and men who burnt and killed so easily, his was an escape far different from hers.

A better man, she thought.

She lowered herself on the bed, felt his sweat-sheened body quieten under her hand, his eyelids fluttering like trapped moths. As he emerged from his dream, his face grew still, the lips settled once again over his bared teeth, until he became the watching, dark-eyed man who'd met her at the gate by the bus stop.

She watched him from under lidded eyes, asked, 'What is your name? Your real name.'

He blinked at her, said nothing.

'Nyingi anga?' she insisted.

He was still heaving from the dream. She eased back, her hand still on his chest.

'I don't need to know your name. I know what you are: *olum* – one of those who left the bush. Mama Auma,' she said. She felt his body stiffen under her hand. 'You are worse when you call her name. Who was she?'

She didn't need to ask; she already knew.

A small change had come over him. She felt it in the swelling of his chest.

'I am not afraid of you,' she said. 'I died once; I have no more fear of dying.'

She pushed her weight off the bed and stood. 'Mama Auma – you killed your mother too. Her *cen* is strong in you. All those people… they have followed you here. They are alive in you.'

She left him in the room, went to her bag, dragged out some clothes, stood in the living room and dressed.

She heard the rumble of the first trains at Ponders End; the bang and trundle of the bin trucks down the street. And birds.

Her hand was on the handle of the door when he came out – a shadow in the gloom of the living room. That voice of his – so lovely to listen to – reached across the room to her.

'I was a child,' he said. 'Wan dano mere calo dano adana ni ya.'

He was reaching out to her now in the language of their nightmares. *We are humans too*. Maybe if he hadn't camouflaged himself with lies at first – maybe…

'I saw what a Joseph Kony child could do with a machete and a gun,' she said.

She lifted the bag, stepped out the flat and pulled the door behind her.

BIRD

She went rigid with grief when the old man died. That was late last year – the rainy season, Mam said – although she couldn't remember the rain. What she remembered was the last thing Sago said to her.

A pusson could be gone and still be here…

Some nights she thought she heard him tapping against the bedroom window. She'd rush outside, raise her head to the wind for the seawater smell of the old man, the drag of his naked feet on the dust.

Day time, she walked the narrow limestone roads of the island, not really searching – not after all these months – but to ease the heaviness in her stomach, the numbness in her limbs.

The last time she saw Sago was the foreday morning he came to her mother's house, knuckling the wooden walls exactly where her head lay. She was out the door before he finished tapping, into a twilight so quiet, she could hear the breakers on the northern shore. There was still a moon – too bright to look up at without squinting.

'You got your voice with you?' he'd said.

She'd dipped into her pocket and held up the little lambi shell, pearly pink by day, now pale under the moon. The old man took it from her hand, made a show of inspecting it, then handed it back. He said the same thing every time. 'Is de flute ov warriors. I talkin 'bout Makandal and Nanny and that other woman who born right here.'

He'd brought the shell to her mother's house the year before; narrowed his yellow-black eyes at the bandage around her head, then sat at her mother's doormouth. He'd chipped away at the upper end of the shell until he'd made a hole. Then he pressed it against his lips, filled his cheeks, and made a sound that bounced around her head, filled up the world and scattered the sea gulls on the headland beyond the beach.

'You got a voice now,' he said, holding it out to her. 'When school-chilren hit you with stone and tell you that you dumb-an-chupid, blow dis in their face and deafen deir arse.'

The old Rastaman had taken her past the beach front, beyond the far edge of the mangroves and the heap of boulders, then along the limestone track to the Bay of Caves. Every now and then he stopped, lifted his face at the moon, drew a few quick deep breaths, then lowered his head and moved on.

He'd sat her on a stone above the black-sand beach and eased his body down beside her. He unrolled his locks and she followed his gaze, taking in the glint and roar of the ocean straight ahead, the water gnashing against the rocks below, the toss and hiss of the tall mint grass behind. Then she'd pulled her brows together and flicked two questioning wrists at him.

'You want to know what we doing here?' he grumbled. 'Hold on, nuh! Impatient is yuh name?'

She made a plosive with her lips, jabbed a finger at his thick locks-fall of hair, then pointed at the tangle of mangrove on their right.

'Haul your tail,' he chuckled. A fit of coughing seized him and she watched his quaking shoulders as he struggled to steady himself.

He pushed out his arm towards the beach below. It was silver-black in the moonlight. 'Keep watching,' he said. 'Give it a coupla minutes or mebbe longer.' He folded his arms and sat back.

She kept watching, saw that gradually the sand was coming alive. Like it was breaking off little bits of itself, becoming a wave of scurrying darkness heading for the water.

She turned puzzled eyes to him.

'Turtles,' he said. 'They bornin tonight.'

It seemed to her that the ocean itself had hushed as the

creatures emerged, and the little waves scooped them up in quick rhythmic surges, bearing them away.

The sky was brightening when the sand became itself once more. Like all the times before, when Sago took her from her mother's house, the magic of the new thing that he showed her swelled her throat and left her with a fluttering heart.

'I ask you this, Miss Dee,' he said. 'How come they know that moonlight splittin ground up here and is time to born and go? Eh? How come they know is de ocean they got to head for and not all that darkness back there?' He nudged a thumb at the land behind them. 'Jah great. Not so?'

He'd pushed his body forward, gathered his hair and made a hive of it around his head. She could barely see his face.

'How long since you make me your grandaddy?'

She straightened an arm and flicked three fingers at him.

'Three years. Add a coupla months to that,' he said. 'And I been doin awright, not so?'

She fluttered the air with rapid hands, nodding as she did so.

'I feel so too,' he said.

They'd fallen silent, she peering at the dark patches in the face of the cliff at the far end of the beach, the old man swaying quietly beside her. Another fit of coughing gripped him. He sighed and nudged her with an elbow.

'Miss Dee,' he said, 'I been tryin to hold on long as I could for you. I can't no more. Mih spirit beggin for release.' He took her hand and rested it on the swelling under his ear. 'Nine months gone, it was a lil button. Now it turn a cricket ball. Didn want to tell you before, but it cross my mind you have to know. It been spreadin all over me. I ain got long to go.'

She began making rapid shapes in the air with her hands.

'You not makin no sense,' he mumbled. 'I don't catch one word you say.'

He eased his back against the stony bank.

She was rocking back and forth, arms hugged around herself.

He nudged her again.

'Yunno, Miss Dee. Is like them likkle turtle; when time reach they got to go. Can't do nothing about it. Difference is, a pusson could be gone, but they kin still be here.' He'd placed a finger on her forehead. 'Right here. Y'unnerstan?'

She kept her hands in her lap, her eyes on the spreading smear of daylight on the horizon.

Next day, jusso, Sago gone...

Jusso...

'The girlchile have to cry,' Miss Tiny said. 'To get Sago off she chest, you have to make she cry.'

'She never cry,' her mother said.

'Not even dry-cry?'

'Nuh.'

'I bet if yuh cut she arse she cry. If was me! I do anything to get dat rusty school-teacher-turn-mad-rastaman outta she head.'

'Nuh!'

'So! You goin let she run round dis dry-arse islan till she dead?'

'Tiny, haul y'arse.'

A sizzling evening, with the whole of Kara Isle sheltering from the heat. Even the ground-lizards had raised their bellies off the earth.

The distressed bleating of her mother's goats descended on them from the sandstone ridge above the bay. She was busy polishing her shell with one end of her dress.

'Go bring down dem goat, Dee. They sufferin up there.'

Her feet took her past the Bay of Caves, around the spine of the island, through the wilting manchineel until she came upon the tree that Sago told her was as old as the beginning of the world. Time and sun had charred its bark a deep black. Its trunk lay parallel to the chalky earth, its branches plaited around each other. 'See how it twis'-up? Is all the pain ov this lil island that it carry. From time.'

The goats were on the other side of the ridge. She ignored the safer route and clawed her way up the sandy hillface.

Once on top, she dusted her hands, adjusted her skirt and

hopped along the hilltop. The three animals were gasping in the heat. Her mother had tethered them to the only tree up there. She let them loose, watched them leaping down the slope, an avalanche of dirt racing after them.

She did not want to follow them home, but stood squinting across the waters, making plosives with her mouth, appraising the grey procession of islands that Sago had named for her: Mayreau, Canouan, Mustique, Bequia…

Something in the air disturbed her daydreaming – a sound, like a loose sail in the wind. Only there were no boats on the water down there.

The flapping came again and she swivelled her eyes to where she thought she heard it. Saw nothing but the barely visible dust track that broke off at the edge of the ridge.

Another flutter pulled her gaze up to the branches of the tree, to what looked like the torn-off portion of a sail. Except the cloth was agitating and there was no wind.

A bird. Bigger than her.

A great ruffle of white feathers ran along its underbelly to its tail. The yellow beak was broad as a fisherman's knife, curved downward at the tip like a giant hook. Through the weave of branches, past the pale webbed feet, she saw its eyes: night black, white-ringed. Shiny. She felt a shiver run through her.

Her mind dragged her back to an early morning with Sago on the jetty, facing the sea. She'd followed his pointing arm to a drifting shape beneath a bank of clouds.

'Dreamflyer,' he said. 'Soul-carrier.' He was smiling at the sky.

She'd shaken her head, lifted a hand and sketched the shape of a bird.

Sago shook his head. 'Nuh! It might *look* like a bird, but is not a bird. Is a Dreamflyer that you watchin there. Is the wind take on de shape ov a bird fuh de pleasure ov riding on itself.'

She fluttered her fingers in his face.

'Is evidence you askin for? What happen, you turn lawyer now? Okay! Which bird you know does walk on water, eh? Or sleep on wind for months, never touchin land. Dem fly ahead ov storm, move between all de oceans ov de world like you step over to yuh neighbour yard. You know any bird could do dat? Eh?'

He sucked his teeth and glared at her. 'An *s'pose* I tell you that dem is the eyes of Jah. Dem see everything. Dem carry the soul ov all Jah children back to Africa and rest dem at the feet of Selassie I. You don' believe me? Well, *proof-o-de-fact*,' he shot a finger at the sky, 'Dreamflyer can't leave Jah earth without it mother, de wind, to lift it up.'

The thrashing of the bird brought her back. She looked down the hill at the wilting corn and peas, the sagging cotton trees, the rows of rusting galvanized roofs against the yellow shoreline, the dazzle of the sea and sky beyond.

She rearranged her skirt and began to climb the tree.

The branches bent under her weight. She would not look down, knowing that if she slipped it meant a straight drop onto the rocks below.

She levered her body upward until she was under the creature; saw that the left wing of the bird was jammed between a tight netting of leaves.

She edged herself away from it and tried to climb above it. The big grey head jerked sideways. A single, night-black eye rested on her and stayed there.

She passed a tentative hand along the heavy feathers of the trapped wing. The bird erupted. She wrapped her arms around a branch and held on tight until it quietened. Began to strip away the leaves, the smaller branches; then strained against the larger ones until they snapped. The bird remained at rest while she eased the massive feathers through the tangle. Then with an abrupt shudder it was free. It brought its great wings forward, folded them against its sides and remained where it was.

She uttered a plosive, drew closer, examined the three black claws held together by a white translucent web; the proud curve of the neck; the quick shutter of the membrane that flicked over its eyes.

She laid a hand on it again, just under its shoulder and was amazed at the rate of its hammering heart and the oiliness of its feathers.

She looked down at the overheated land, then out to sea. No wind. There hadn't been for days. Already the water was turning glittery gold with touches of pink on the swells. A yellow haze hung over the chain of islands in the distance. She sat with the bird, her hand on its shoulder and watched Bequia, Mustique, Canouan and Mayreau fade into the oncoming night.

Soon her mother would be pushing her head out of the window and shouting her name. With Sago not there anymore, she did this all the time now.

But she would not leave this creature stranded. She would sit with it and wait for wind all night if she had to.

But the longer she rested against this Dreamflyer, the more certain she was that if people found this bird with her, they would kill it becuz on Kara Isle, anything they did not like or understand they destroyed. Like the strange creatures they sometimes pulled out of the ocean; in all the sea-stories she'd ever heard them tell, at the end of every one, something always died.

The day was cooling and with it she felt a shift in the air. The bird must have felt it too, because it had edged itself around to face the sea. A small wind fingered the hem of her skirt and stirred the fine feathers at its throat. But she knew that it was not strong enough to lift it.

She thought she heard her name, but wasn't sure. More voices, pitched faintly in the air, then her mother's, clearer than the rest.

Another gust fluttered her skirt. She wondered if it was enough to lift the bird. She tapped its feet. It edged further forward, a murmuring rising from its chest.

Now, with the voices drawing nearer, she sensed the tension in the creature. It had raised its head, was shifting it with rapid, jerky movements.

She wedged herself between the upper branches, urged it forward with an outstretched leg, ignoring the drop below her, her eyes on the darkening sky.

When she heard the swelling hum of voices down the hill, saw the glow of torches, she kicked out at the creature. It lunged, not in a clatter of wings, but in a silent plummet towards the water. A solid shadow falling.

Just before it struck the sea, its body quaked, seemed for a moment to be struck by something invisible which lifted its wings and arced the creature upwards. Then it dipped, the great wings fully stretched out. It lifted and dipped again, rising higher every time, and faster, until she had to tilt her head to watch it climb the air.

Way up there it rested on the wind, making easeful circles above her. She thought she heard its cry – something between a rattle and a bray. Then it leaned a dark wing upward, became a shadow drifting towards the last of the light at the far reaches of the sky.

When she could no longer see it, she looked down at the fluttering hem of her skirt, then at the wound its claws had left along her leg.

Her mother called again.

She picked her way down the tree, sat on the stone beneath it, and made shapes in the air with her hands.

ABOUT THE AUTHOR

Jacob Ross is a novelist, short story writer, editor and creative writing tutor. His latest book, *The Bone Readers*, marks a new departure into crime fiction, and won the inaugural Jhalak Prize in 2017. His literary novel *Pynter Bender* was published to much critical literary acclaim and was shortlisted for the 2009 Commonwealth Writers Regional Prize and chosen as one of the British Authors Club's top three Best First Novels. Jacob is also the author of two short story collections, *Song for Simone* and *A Way to Catch the Dust*, and the editor of *Closure, Contemporary Black British short stories*. He is a Fellow of the Royal Society of Literature and has been a judge of the V.S. Pritchett Memorial Prize, the Olive Cook, Scott Moncrieff, Tom-Gallon Literary Awards and The Commonwealth Writers' Short Story Prize.

ALSO AVAILABLE BY JACOB ROSS

The Bone Readers
ISBN: 9781845233358; pp. 270; pub. 2016; price £7.99

Secrets can be buried, but bones can speak...

When Michael (Digger) Digson is recruited into DS Chilman's new plain clothes squad in the small Caribbean island of Camaho he brings his own mission to discover who amongst a renegade police squad killed his mother in a political demonstration. Sent to London to train in forensics, Digger becomes enmeshed in Chilman's obsession with a cold case – the disappearance of a young man whose mother is sure he has been murdered. But along with his new skill in forensics, Digger makes rich use of the cultural knowledge he has gained from the Fire Baptist grandmother who brought him up, another kind of reader of bones. And when the enigmatic Miss K. Stanislaus, another of Chilman's recruits, joins him on the case, Digger finds that his science is more than outmatched by her observational skills. Together, they find themselves dragged into a world of secrets, disappearances and danger that de-mands every ounce of their brains, persistence and courage to survive.

Jacob Ross brings the best traditions of crime fiction to the Carib-bean novel with a fast-moving narrative, richly observed characters, a powerful evocation of place and a denouement that will leave readers breathless. With its compelling sense of place and cast of characters with real emotional depth, *The Bone Readers* artfully delivers for the Carib-bean what Ian Rankin does for Scotland.

The Bone Readers is the first in Ross's Camaho Quartet.

Winner of the inaugural Jhalak Prize, judge, poet Musa Okwonga said of *The Bone Readers*, "by turns thrilling, visceral and meditative, and always cinematic", while author Catherine Johnson added that it "effortlessly draws together the past and the present, gender, politics and the legacy of colonialism in a top quality Caribbean set crime thriller".

Bernardine Evaristo in *The Guardian* wrote: "Ross's characters are always powerfully delineated through brilliant visual descriptions, dialogue that trips off the tongue, and keenly observed behaviour."